Can't Hold a Candle

L. J. Hutton

Dog Rose Press

ISBN: 978-1-7396943-8-8

Published by Dog Rose Press 2025

Chapter 1

Holly made the last curl on the bow as the little girl watched on, her eyes as big as an owl's with wonder at the pretty box.

"Would you like a bag for that?" Holly asked, knowing that the answer would be yes even before she got the child's enthusiastic nod.

She slipped the present into one of their pink paper carriers and handed it over. As the little girl took possession of it, as though it was filled with the crown jewels instead of an assortment of soaps, bath-bombs, and candles, Holly looked up and caught the grateful look of the girl's father.

"That looks amazing," he said. "If I'd tried to wrap it for her, it would have come out with more sellotape on it than paper."

Holly laughed with him, adding, "I've had plenty of practice. I hope your wife likes her birthday present."

As he ushered his daughter out of the shop before she could find any more goodies to buy, he said, "I think my present's going to come as a disappointment after she gets this. I should have come to you for mine as well. Thank you so much."

Dropping the catch on the door behind them, Holly thought that this was a nice end to what had been a pretty grim day, even if she would have to get the vacuum out and clear up the dried mud he'd brought in on his workman's boots. That little girl had been as full of wonder as if she'd walked into an enchanted forest, but then with the ancient oak beams everywhere, it probably did look as though she had walked back to another time. Holly sighed. It had been lovely to do something for the cash-strapped dad and his daughter – that wasn't the problem at all.

It was rather that the shop had been open for not quite three weeks, and already she was near exhausted. It wasn't helped by her being here on her own for the whole time. Even just going to the loo was like a military campaign, with her having to judge when she could drop the latch on the door and scurry through to the back. And she'd learned after the first couple of days that nipping around the corner to the nice cafe that did fresh sandwiches wasn't going to be an option, either. They were always busy, and queuing wasn't something she had time for if she wasn't to miss customers in this critical opening phase of the shop.

Heaving a sigh, she went through into the back room and pulled the vacuum out of the cupboard. At least she'd been able to override her business partner Angie's decision to have a pink carpet put down.

"Just think of the winter!" she remembered herself saying to Angie, as she now plugged the vacuum in and started cleaning. "One week of slush and it'll look like mud! Please, Ange, let's go for a practical brown or grey."

Well they'd got a tweed-like brown, and even so there was no getting around vacuuming it daily. Wiping their feet on the proper mat in the doorway seemed to be beyond most customers, and though Holly had had years of retail experience, it still never failed to amaze her how mucky some people were. Then as she got to the back room where there was the big rack of bath-bombs, she felt the tears welling up. Somebody had dropped one on the floor and it was now nothing more than a pile of chunks and powder. One of the expensive ones too.

She knew who it was – that group of three teenagers who'd come in last thing while she was with the dad and his daughter. Two boys and a girl, who she'd heard giggling in the back, and who she now suspected had thought it funny to play football with the bomb, because there was no way it had come off the rack and skittered across to another stand to end up where it was now, and in that state. If she'd not stayed open for the dad and daughter, she'd have been closing as the kids came in and could have turned them away since they were obviously just bored, looking for mischief, and never going to buy anything.

Finishing the vacuuming with a tissue in one hand, she put the cleaner away and then went and slumped at the desk in the little office they had made in the part of the building's cellars that were attached to the shop. The pub next door, which occupied the rest of the building's ground floor, had their own section of cellars, and sometimes when she was down here, Holly could hear them rolling the barrels around. The first time she'd heard one of their deliveries, it had nearly frightened the life out of her, hearing the bumping and clunking on the other side of what was a very slim, modern partition wall. She'd never thought herself a fanciful person, but in that moment she'd been quite willing to believe in ghosts and ghouls, and things that went bump in the night. Of course afterwards she'd felt a real fool, but the worst after-effect of it was that it brought it home to her how isolated she was here.

"Why did you do this to yourself?" she sniffled aloud, as she cashed up the till, and put the takings into the smart new safe that Angie had had installed down here. "You left a secure job for this!"

It didn't help that she was feeling singularly abandoned right now. When this project had first been mooted between her and her best friend Angie, it had been many years ago when they had been working together in a department store in Worcester, now long gone. Wouldn't it be great, they had daydreamed, if we could have our own shop selling pretty gifts like soaps and candles and other stuff. Back then that's all it had been – a daydream. But then Angie had married Christopher – a man Holly had never quite managed to take to, in part because unlike all the boys they'd grown up with, he refused to answer to his name being shortened to the normal 'Chris' or even 'Kit', and instead insisted on everyone calling him 'Topher'. And he'd got really nasty with her when she'd honestly misheard the first time and thought he'd said 'Tofu'. Angie had collapsed in giggles, but he'd held that one genuine mistake against Holly ever since, even refusing to let her be one of the bridesmaids at their wedding as Angie wanted.

On the other hand, Holly had had to swallow her pride where he was concerned, because hardly a year on from them getting married, Topher had won the big prize on the Euro Lottery, and he was the one who had bought this glorious old half-timbered building in Ledbury, and who had financed Angie's dream. Holly had no illusions that Topher thought the shop was Angie's and Holly just her employee, even if Angie had insisted that the dream just wouldn't work without Holly on board. That hadn't been helped by Holly having to insist that right from the start she would get a monthly salary out of the shop.

"I'm so sorry, Ange," she'd said, "but I've got to have *something* to pay my rent with."

Angie's response had immediately been, "Well give up your scummy little Housing Association flat and come and live in the top floor flat."

At the time, Holly had almost been tempted to do that, but Louise, another of her old schooldays friends, had said aloud what she'd been trying to ignore, "And what happens when Topher doesn't want you traipsing through his flat all the time? You won't be able to just walk out and get another flat with no secure job behind you. Look how long it took for you to get this one. Don't risk it, Holly! Keep something of your own."

Because the trouble with the top floor flat wasn't in the flat itself, it was the fact that it shared its access through main flat on the two floors below. When this amazing building had originally been built in the fifteenth century, there had only been three floors and the cellars – even so, an incredibly luxurious house by the standards of the day, and owned by one of the most important men in the area. So the stunning hanging staircase in ancient oak, which still served the floors of the original building, hadn't gone up any further than the current second floor. When the top floor had been added nearly two hundred years later, a new staircase had had to be put in too, and this went up from part of the main landing, not the old staircase, necessitating walking along the main flat's upper landing to get to it.

Yes, she would have had her own front door at the bottom of that later staircase, but she would have to walk past the bedroom doors of what was intended to be Angie and Topher's amazing new home, and she really couldn't face those potential confrontations. Regarding that, she would have thought Topher at least partly justified in any future complaint of invaded privacy, because if she rolled in late one night, anything they might be doing in the master bedroom would be fully audible to her, let alone if they were caught up in the passion of the moment and hadn't closed the door! No, that had never truly been an option.

And yet tonight, worn out as she was, Holly would have given a lot to be able to lock up and just go outside to the external door to the flats, and let herself in. Not that there was a stick of furniture upstairs yet, anyway. Instead, she was faced with the prospect of a wretched drive back to Worcester in the rain, and in a car she didn't wholly trust to get her there in one piece. When she'd pointed out that she didn't have a car to Angie, and that it was virtually impossible to get from Worcester to Ledbury by bus which didn't take ages to do the thirty miles, Angie had immediately said they would buy her a car. Holly was going to share in her good fortune come what may, she declared, and if that meant getting her a car so that she could drive to their dream shop, so be it.

Yet what Holly had been given the keys to only qualified as a car in that it had four wheels and an engine. Quite where its last MOT had been done, she shuddered to think, because the last time she'd tried to stop in a hurry, she'd found out the hard way just how bad the brakes were. The clapped out Ford Fiesta had been another of Topher's triumphs over her. He hadn't even tried to disguise the sly, smug grin he'd given her when he'd brought it to her flat, one of his friends driving it while he followed in his brand new, top of the range Mercedes. And even his friend had seemed glad to get out of it, and had looked askance at Topher when he'd made his pompous speech about having lived up to his promise to give her a 'company car'. She'd half overheard his friend protesting over giving her such a 'dangerous heap of junk', but Topher had just laughed as they drove away, and when Holly had come to insure it, she discovered that he, and not she, owned it. Meaning she couldn't even get rid of the damned thing, and try to scrape enough together with what she got for it to get something safer, if not much better in appearance.

So tonight she had to walk over to the town's main car park, and then negotiate the country roads to get home, by which time she knew she would be too tired to cook herself a proper meal. That was something else which was starting to tell on her. When she'd worked in the centre of Worcester, it had been easy to pop out during her lunch break a few times a week and get proper food to take home with her. At least she'd had microwavable packs of fresh vegetables every day back then, even if sometimes they were only with pasta or rice if her budget was tight. Yet after getting through the previous week, by the time she got to Sunday as her only day off, she was so worn out that the prospect of going shopping had been appalling, and going shopping on the way home had soon proven too wearing.

Of course it wasn't meant to be like this at all.

"We'll split everything equally," Angie had said. "You do one weekend, and I'll do the other," because Angie had been determined that they would open on a Sunday to take advantage of people coming into town to soak up the medieval atmosphere.

However, going by the first Sunday, nobody else in this sleepy market town bothered opening on a Sunday apart from the pubs. Even the cafes were shut.

Much worse, though, was the absence of Angie in every respect.

She had been so enthusiastic in the beginning; more so than Holly, if she was being honest with herself. For Holly, the lure was more about getting away from a store manager whom she loathed, and who treated concession managers like herself as sub-humans, while letting the company's own managers get away with little short of murder. Hard work she had expected, because unlike Angie, who could afford to throw in the towel whenever a job got too tedious – given that she had well-off parents who would finance her until she got something else – Holly had got used to gritting her teeth and getting on with things. In that respect she had always had realistic expectations of just how much she would be putting in.

And in the beginning, after Topher had surprised Angie with the purchase of this, one of the most prestigious buildings in town, Angie had been all enthusiasm. They had planned the shop and stock layouts, with Holly being the one to have to put the brakes on Angie's wilder ideas. There had been some minor disagreements over what to stock, and again it had been Holly who had insisted that they have some higher value items for sale.

"We're going to have to sell an awful lot of bath-bombs to make end meet otherwise," she remembered herself saying, and Angie's response of,

"Why? It's not like we have to pay rent for the shop. Topher's not charging us for the space, and that would be our biggest outgoing."

"Maybe not," Holly had reasoned with her, "but we'll still need to pay Council Tax and pay for the lighting and heating. We have to be making a sensible amount, Ange, otherwise even Topher will have to find a paying business to rent this place out to."

Angie had finally conceded that point after Topher had backed Holly for the one and only time. But a week away from opening, Angie had come bouncing into the shop, eyes shining and declared, "Topher's booked us a Caribbean holiday!"

Holly had been stunned, but not half as much as after she asked, "Oh… That's nice. When are you going?"

She'd expected something along the lines of 'next summer' or at least the spring. When Angie declared,

"Wednesday!" Holly thought she'd misheard.

"What? Which Wednesday?"

"*This* Wednesday, silly!"

"But Ange, we open *this* Friday! That means you won't be here for the opening! Anyway, surely you have to apply for visas and things? That takes time. Are you sure he meant in two days' time?"

Angie did an excited little dance on the spot. "He surprised me! He's had it all planned for ages! Oh isn't this amazing, Holly! Crystal clear seas. Miles of white sand. Cocktails on the beach! I can't wait!"

Instead, Holly had just felt sick. So Topher had had this planned for some time, had he? Probably the moment that they'd told him when they planned to open, if she knew him. It was another of his petty revenges on her for something she'd never quite worked out, beyond that one silly slip with his name.

"How long are you going for?" she remembered asking in a voice choked with tears, and which Angie had never picked up on.

"Two weeks!"

"*Two*! Angie, that means I can't have a day off in all that time!"

"Oh don't be daft! Why will you need a day off? It isn't like your old job. You can just sit here and take the money. Bring a book in and read. There's no Mr Duckworth breathing over your shoulder now. Get used to it, Holly, you're free now!"

And there it was. That side of Angie that her friends Louise and Sam had warned her about – the inability to stick with anything for long. They'd all been friends at school, but Louise and Sam had been giving Angie some distance even by the time they'd all left. Now they had a very poor opinion of her.

"She's selfish," Louise had said to Holly over and over. "I don't know why you stand for her. She uses you."

But Holly had refused to see that. To her, Angie was the friend who had always been there for her during the terrible days of her dad leaving her mum, her sister, and herself for the third time, after promising that this time he would stay. Holly couldn't have got through those weeks and then months without Angie.

Yet as she pulled the shop door shut behind her and tested it to make sure it was all secure, she could hear in her mind Louise's words, "Your loyalty is both one of your best traits, and your worst weakness, Holly. One of these days you're finally going to wake up and see how Angie walks all over you. I just hope it isn't disastrous when you do."

Well the disaster was here, because Angie hadn't answered a single one of many calls to her since she'd left that Monday, and now here Holly was, left holding their 'baby' all alone.

Chapter 2

As she turned to go, Holly looked in through the glass door of the pub next-door. People were in there enjoying themselves. A group of young men and women were at the nearest table, obviously having come straight from work, and celebrating someone's birthday, going by the gift bags tucked out of the way on the floor. It looked so warm and inviting. Dare she go in and have just one small glass of wine? Would it matter that much? And then she thought of the wreck of a car, and what would happen if this time it took her into a ditch, and the police turned up and breathalysed her. No, not worth the risk.

Regretfully she turned and hefty her large bag over her shoulder, starting the wretched trudge back to the car park. Right now she felt like some character out of a Dickens novel, walking the medieval streets and down on her luck. When she got to it, the car coughed and spluttered itself into life, and she drove home through the drizzle mechanically, only focusing on the cars on the road rather than where she actually was. So she pulled up outside her flat almost surprised that she was here already.

"Oh God, this won't do," she groaned. The more tired she got, the more danger there was that she would lose concentration.

As if in sympathy, her stomach growled loudly, and on an impulse Holly got back in the car and drove the short way to the local fish and chip shop. Returning home with the comforting smell wafting out of the paper bag, she hurried inside and then devoured them. It was hardly the healthy option, but tonight she couldn't summon the will to care. The chips were so hot that the first few nearly burned her mouth, but it felt like a feast, especially when washed down with a glass of wine. Normally she didn't drink during the week, both because of having to be up early in the morning, but also because a bottle a week was all she could afford on her wages. Then she laughed bitterly.

"Wages? What bloody wages?" she growled as she went and washed her hands, and suddenly she desperately needed someone to talk to.

Louise didn't answer her call, but then Lou had a husband and kids, so at this time on a Friday they might have taken the kids out somewhere. However Sam picked up the phone, and as soon as Holly started speaking she interrupted with, "What's wrong? I can hear it in your voice, Holly. Something's happened."

"Angie's dropped me in it," she told Sam with a sigh of despair.

"Dropped you in it? Oh my God, how? What's she done?"

With the tears starting to flow, Holly explained how Angie had vanished right at the critical time. "It was one thing to do the opening by myself. But after that first Sunday when there was just nobody about, I realised that I'd have to shut at least the Sunday afterwards or I'd never make it through the week."

"I should jolly well think so!" Sam was aghast. "Does she have no idea how much hard work it is dealing with customers all day? ...Oh! Silly me! Of course she doesn't, because this is Angie we're talking about. The one who chucks in jobs when she's had enough, or gets tired, or because her parents are paying for some trip to somewhere exotic."

Holly snuffled into the next tissue before adding it to the growing heap in the waste bin. "Except that it's Topher who's paid for the trip this time. I don't know why that man hates me so much, Sam. I've never done a thing to him."

"Oh, Holly, you just don't get it, do you? You're competition for Angie's affection in his eyes. He's one of those men who needs to have the adoration of everyone around him, and you just don't fit into the mould. If you fawned all over him, and were 'properly' subservient, or at least admiring towards him, then he might overlook you taking Angie's attention away from him. But you don't play the game according to his rules."

"Play the game? Sam, he has her every evening, and he's out doing his own thing during the day. Stuff he doesn't include Angie in anyway – like his taking up golf to start building his 'network' of business contacts, though God alone knows what sort of business he's thinking of. How can I be taking her away from him?"

"It's not what you actually *do*," Sam said gently. "It's the principle of the thing – if you can dignify his control-freaky attitudes as a principle, which I don't. Just the fact that he comes home and Angie tells him all of the stuff she's done, no matter how insignificant or trivial, highlights it to him that this was all stuff *he* didn't get to do with her."

Holly was stunned, but as Sam's words sunk in, she could see that she was right.

"Holly? …Are you still there? You've gone awfully quiet."

"Yes, I'm still here. I guess I'm just starting to see things in a different light."

"About time, too!"

"Oh Sam, not you as well. Louise is always telling me that these days I go through life blind to people."

"Honey, you're not blind to people," Sam said, softening her voice. "You're one of the most caring people I know. If anything you're too empathic, and it's that that blinds you to the conniving buggers in this world. And Lou and I do understand. After your bloody awful childhood you were going to go one of two ways – either never trusting anyone, or overcompensating for them and trying to keep them close. That's not your fault.

"Good grief, your dad left three times and came back twice, and then just as you were getting over him going your poor mum died. And if that wasn't enough, her sister was then happy to take your little sister on, because she was only six, but refused to have you because you were a teenager. That's a lot of abandonment for anyone to have to process, and we know that if Angie hadn't talked her mum and dad into letting you take over the attic above their garage, you would have been out on the streets or in care – and I'm not sure which would be the worse of those two.

"But you were so knocked about by everything then that you just didn't see how Angie bragged about saving you, like she'd just bought a stray puppy home from the pound. She wanted the praise and kudos, it wasn't just about helping you. Angie needs to be in the spotlight, and yet for all his promises before they married, I don't think she's going to get that off Topher."

She took a deep breath, crossed her fingers knowing that Holly couldn't see down the phone line, and went on, "Do you remember what you said when you first met Topher? You said that there was something off about him, even then. I remember you coming to have a coffee with Lou and me in our lunch hours, and telling us that you couldn't see what Angie saw in him."

"I remember. I thought he was so arrogant. At first I wondered whether he came from an even wealthier family than Angie's because of the way he looked down his nose at everyone."

"But he isn't, is he?"

"No. He's more my class. The only difference is that his mum and dad stayed together, but their house was a rented terraced one, just like ours. And his dad was forever being cautioned by the police for either being drunk and disorderly, or because they'd been called out by the neighbours to a domestic incident at their house. Topher's not remotely posh. That's why I don't get his attitude."

She could hear Sam's sniff of disgust. "What he's frightened of is everyone *knowing* that that's the kind of family he's come from. But look at how he's starting to act around Angie. We all tried to warn her after we found out about his crazy mum – even Louise and me, and Angie hardly ever sees us these days. 'He's going to try to control you,' we warned her, but would she listen?

"Well *you* listen now, Holly! Open your eyes, because he's starting to control *you*! You're already financially dependent on him to pay you a wage out of the shop. That's not good. It's not good at all. He's not a registered company like you've worked for before. There's no safety net for you if he takes his millions, and clears off to some exotic place where they don't extradite people from."

"Sam! He's not a criminal! You're making him sound like one of the Great Train Robbers."

"Okay, he hasn't done anything *yet*, but he doesn't have to hold up a bank or pull off a jewellery heist to be a bloody scammer. And he *is* scamming you in a way. He's got you working for damned near free on his wife's fun project, and if it all goes base up, it's not going to touch him, is it? Not with millions in the bank! He can just clear your stock out of the shop and rent it out to someone else. But you? You'll be hunting for jobs, and right now the chances of you getting back into even something like a charity shop manager's role are very slim. There are too many retail people out of work. God, I wish you'd never agreed to do this bloody shop with Angie."

"Me too."

There was a pause, and then Sam said tentatively,

"Do you take much cash? I mean as opposed to card payments?"

"Err, yes, surprisingly we do."

"Then take a bit of advice – don't bank it!"

"Don't bank it? Why?"

"Look, I'm sorry if this sounds harsh, but what if Topher hasn't set up that direct payment for your wages?"

"Oh Christ!" Holly felt the fish and chips turn a somersault in her stomach. She hadn't thought of Topher messing with her like that. She'd always believed that when Angie said it was sorted, that Angie herself had set things up. But could she trust to that now? Gadfly Angie was far more likely to have told Topher to do it, and then never bothered to check up on him.

"I'd hang on to every scrap of cash you get, if I were you," Sam continued sagely. "If you get worried about too much of it on the premises, then put it into your own bank – somewhere *you* can get hold of it in an emergency!"

"Heaven's, I've not taken anything like that much," Holly protested. "I'd be bloody delighted if we had."

"Then all the more reason to hang on to what you have. How long have you got before the payment to you is due in your bank?"

"We agreed that it would be on the fifteenth of the month, though I wasn't happy about that because having had my last pay-check from my old job at the end of the month before, it's meant I'm having to go six weeks before getting paid."

"So you'll be really in the lurch if you don't get that money?"

"Well and truly!"

"Then start setting what he owes you on one side. And if you've any sense, still don't bank anything, because if suppliers come knocking, you might need something to at least pacify them and get them out of the shop."

"But all the stock we've got at the moment is paid for!"

"Is it? Have you seen evidence of that? Or did you just see the invoices come in, and hand then them on to Angie as the one with the money?"

By now Holly could feel the cold sweat of panic starting to run down her spine. Sam was uncannily right on all counts.

"I trusted her," she said weakly. "I trusted her because she's my friend."

There was another of Sam's heavy sighs down the phone. "And I repeat – we love you dearly because of that trust. Just think of it this way, if I'm wrong and Angie has set everything up properly, and all the payments go through, then you've lost nothing. The money will still be in the safe waiting for her when she gets back. You haven't stolen it!

"Even if Topher gets one on him, and tries to threaten you over taking your wages, any solicitor would soon tell him that he'd be hard pressed to cause trouble for you when you've only taken what you and he agreed upon. And the same goes for you paying any suppliers. You'll only be doing what you're supposed to be doing – running the business for them."

"Thanks, Sam. You've made me see that I'm going to have to do something about all of this, even if I don't want to."

They chatted briefly about other things, but soon ended the call. For the rest of that evening Holly fretted and was sure she'd never get any sleep, but when her head went onto the pillow simple exhaustion took over, and the next thing she knew, her alarm clock was going off. It took her no time to shower and get ready, and she was in the shop by quarter to nine. The opening time was another thing that she and Angie had disagreed upon. Angie was all for opening at nine and closing at six, or even later, but Holly had argued that when most of the other non-essential shops didn't open until ten o'clock, there wasn't much incentive for shoppers to come earlier. In that she's already been proven right. Nobody came shopping for non-essentials before ten and the High Street was deserted.

So now she let herself in, but didn't put the shop lights on or leave the door unlocked. Instead she went through and down to the basement office and opened the safe. This week she'd been worrying that she'd not yet banked even last week's cash, but that had been down to her not being able to get to their bank within their opening hours, especially since there wasn't a branch of their bank in the town, and she would have to get into Worcester city centre to access it. That made her feel better about what she was going to do now, though.

Counting out the notes, she carefully put the amount she would need for her rent into an envelope and sealed it. Talking to Sam last night had nudged her into thinking more clearly about this mess, and she reckoned that when it came to things like the Council Tax for this building, everything would be in Topher's name, given that he'd bragged about living in the stunning flat upstairs. With him being the way he was, she'd be amazed if he'd even got Angie's name on the deeds.

Therefore such costs relating to the building itself she could afford to ignore – if anyone was going to get prosecuted it wouldn't be her, however callous she felt about making that decision. However, her own Council Tax on her flat, and the money for a couple of bills, went into another envelope. For now she'd hold off on taking money for food, because even she had enough to scrape by on in terms of savings as long as she was sensible, but next month would be a different matter.

Oddly enough, once she'd done that she felt a lot better, and it dawned on her that subconsciously she'd been worrying about her personal bills even more than the shop's, despite her consciously telling herself that Angie wouldn't let her down like that. It also helped that she could think of it in terms of Topher letting her down, not Angie. What was more, Angie had made great play over Topher having done a business degree at Worcester University, and if he wasn't the marvellous business guru that she built him up to be, even so Holly was pretty sure that things like cash flow must have been mentioned somewhere on that course. So there was no excuse for him not to have organised the finances properly.

Feeling a good deal lighter in spirit, she went and opened up at ten, and managed to get through the day without becoming overly stressed, taking the executive decision to shut the doors at five o'clock so that she would get home at a sensible time. In the gaps between customers, she had started thinking back to life before this, and that one of the joys of having a day or two off in the week to compensate for working Saturdays and alternate Sundays, had been that she could go out on that weekday. Being reliant on buses or trains had meant that she rarely went further than the local supermarket on the Sundays she didn't work, because public transport was scant on that day. But on a Wednesday or Thursday, she had enjoyed catching a bus up to the Malvern Hills and going for a walk. Well the weather forecast for tomorrow was good, and if she didn't dare risk the car's brakes on the steep inclines of the Malverns themselves, she was pretty sure that it would cope with a shorter run out to the area known as the Old Hills.

A walk in the fresh air and then a decent meal will do you the world of good, she told herself firmly. *You've not been at home for long enough to mess it up this week, and the washing can wait as well. A bit of personal TLC is what you need.* And with that in mind, she made sure that a couple of the lovely bath-bombs came home with her as a treat, along with a packet of the scented tea-lights.

She forced herself to make a brief detour to the supermarket on the outskirts of Ledbury, and picked up a pizza for tonight and a roast dinner ready-meal for Sunday. It was a bit extravagant when she was on such a tight budget at the moment, and making something from raw ingredients would have been cheaper, but she'd promised herself that for this weekend – or what was left of it – she would give herself a much needed break. The pizza made for a quick, easy, and filling meal, and then she sank up to her chin in bubbles for a while, with just a few tea-lights lit and placed wherever she could safely put them.

All of which meant that by the time nine o'clock rolled around, she was feeling more human and like her old self than she had in weeks. With that also came some of her old fire, which meant that she was moving from being upset to angry.

"Damn you, Topher!" she growled as she flicked through the TV channels, hoping that there would be something on worth watching; something that would provide a relaxing distraction from her worries. "It's *me* who ought to be in a snit with *you* for robbing me of my friend, not the other way around."

Disgusted at the mindless pap on offer, she went and dug out the video of Angie and Topher's wedding last year. It wasn't masochism, tormenting herself with the sight of the person who was well on the way to wrecking a long-standing friendship. She wanted to watch it now with a clear head and a sharp eye. Had she missed something vital back then? Was there something in his behaviour, some hint of why he would pull a stunt like this, that she'd wilfully ignored because she couldn't bear to think of her friend being miserable married to this man? Because there was a small but growing worry in her mind that he must have done something to Angie to gain this much control over her.

Before she switched the video on, Holly checked her Facebook, Instagram and TikTok accounts. Anyone looking at hers would think her the most boring woman in the world, because she hardly ever put anything on any of them. But it was one way to stay connected with a bunch of friends she had limited time to see in person, and of all of them, Angie was the one who posted something almost daily on every one of the sites. Now, though, there was a worrying absence.

Facebook. Nothing.

Instagram. Nothing.

TikTok. Nothing!

It just wasn't like her to disconnect from her social media accounts for even one week, let alone more than two. Therefore Holly was now getting worried in a whole new way, because if Angie was having a ball on some tropical island, there was no way that she wouldn't be splashing it all over her different feeds. There were earlier photos of the lovely old building they'd bought on Instagram and Facebook. And TikTok videos by the dozen, of snatches of tours around the half-timbered interior, all of which had had scores of responses. But on that fateful Wednesday when Angie had gone down to the airport, all posts stopped.

"Oh God, Angie! What has he done to you?" Holly fretted as she hit 'play'.

Chapter 3

The video lurched its way into life, and Holly was taken back to the ceremony in the lovely old church of St John in Bedwardine. Angie's mum was there, dolled up to the nines, and her dad looking uncomfortable in a morning suit whose coat tails were clearly irritating the life out of him. There was Angie's kid brother, looking no more comfortable in his own grey morning suit, her sister trying to hitch up the plunging neckline that the other bridesmaid – Topher's sister – had insisted on, and Topher's kid sister looking bored, and swishing her bouquet around in a way that threatened to have it shedding flowers even before the ceremony had begun.

The scene moved on from those waiting inside the church to Angie arriving with her dad, and then a rear view of her walking up the aisle on his arm. That was the first time that Topher came properly into shot, and now Holly couldn't help thinking that he was hardly the nervous but thrilled groom-to-be.

"Woah! What was that!" she exclaimed, sitting bolt upright and hitting rewind. The video camera had been too far away to pick up the voices up at the altar when nobody was speaking up, given that the ceremony hadn't actually started. But Holly rewound the shot scene three times, and by the end she was sure she had lip-read what Topher had said from the zoomed in shot.

'She's mine now', she was sure he was saying there, and his expression wasn't nice. If ever there was a man staking his claim it was him, and he was saying it to Angie's dad, not to Angie herself, who was looking over her shoulder the other way and grinning at her mum.

Fully alert now, Holly watched the rest of the video, and though there were no other obvious hints as to Topher's state of mind, she saw with fresh eyes how he was hardly a man thrilled to be embarking on this new life with the woman he adored. There were glances he shot Angie's way when he thought nobody was looking. Only brief snippets of him to be sure, and if you weren't watching for them you would miss them, but once on the lookout, you couldn't mistake those looks of disdain. This was what Lou and Sam had seen and she had refused to acknowledge.

"Oh, Ange! What have you got us into?" Holly groaned, knowing that she herself had blindly trusted her friend in the belief that Angie really knew this man whom she'd married. Granted it had been something of a whirlwind romance. Angie had only met Topher for the first time little more than a year before the wedding, indeed had started dating him only six months before he proposed – or as Holly found out later, Angie proposed to him. Then inevitably the next year had been spent organising the wedding of the year – or at least as far as Angie and her mum had been concerned it was going to be. Angie's dad had probably been less enthusiastic about the amount it was all costing, but then as a well-known local businessman, he'd used the wedding as much as an exercise in corporate entertaining as celebrating his oldest daughter's nuptials. It had been a huge event, with the reception held out at Bransford at the local golf club and huge conference centre, at which Angie's dad was a regular attender.

Angie had been desperate to have Holly as one of her bridesmaids, but Topher had put his foot down over that.

"They should be family," he'd said to Angie, who'd relayed his words in tears to Holly. At the time Angie had been so stressed and emotional, having been trapped in the vicious blender of her mum's aspirations, her dad's need to be networking, and Topher's demands, that Holly hadn't had the heart to press it.

"Don't worry," she'd said. "I understand. It's okay, Ange. You and I are still mates first and foremost. If this makes your life easier, then I'm fine with it."

She hadn't been, in truth. She'd come home and sobbed her heart out, because they'd sworn as teenagers that they would each be each other's main bridesmaid, and that nothing would come between them on that. Yet to everyone else, Holly had put on the brave face and smiled, and said that family pressures meant that she wouldn't be wearing the glamorous dress. Not that she would have been seen dead in her version of the dress which Topher's mum and sister eventually chose for them – and it was *them* who chose, Holly now recalled, and not Angie, despite it being Angie's wedding. It looked more fit for a sexy nightclub hostess to wear than to a wedding, and she'd had a moment of glee when she noticed how Topher's sister was dithering in her skimpy bustier, with her shoulders bare in the chill of the old church, on a not very warm day to start with.

It certainly wouldn't have done herself any favours, being on the short side and stockily built, even if she was quite trim. It did even less for Angie's sister, who was some years younger and had never shed her teenage plumpness. Even Topher's sister hardly looked glamorous, because being rail-thin, she had no bust to properly fill out the hugging top with, and looked more like a lurid pink satin clad skeleton than a lovely bridesmaid.

All this Holly now saw with fresh eyes. On that fateful day she'd seen the dresses for the first time, yet had been too caught up in the moment to think beyond, 'thank God I didn't have to wear that!' Now it was very different. And as she watched she became increasingly surer of something. So much so that at the end she rewound and watched it again, although with the sound off and something more pleasing on her stereo at the same time.

Every time Topher caught Angie's dad's eye he was all smiles. It was Angie's dad he was buttering up, not Angie! Her mum he ignored unless he had no choice but to speak to her, such as at the wedding 'breakfast', where he was seated next to her. On those occasions, or at least where the video showed him, he was being polite but hardly engaging, going by the way Angie's mum was breaking eye contact with him to wave to some relative or friend on a regular basis.

"You bloody scheming bastard!" Holly breathed as she finally switched the video off. "It took me far too long, but I see you now, Indiana Christopher

Sykes! And by-the-by, what the heck was your mother thinking of when she saddled you with that first name? No wonder you chose to go with Christopher, even if with the less usual shortening! Did she think you were some junior adventure hero who was going to rescue his mum from her god-awful marriage? Good grief, but that would warp a better person than you, because you've too much of her own selfishness in you to have ever done that for her, in spite of the damned name.

"But now I see your bloody game and I'm wise to it! You married Angie not for herself, but for the contacts her dad could bring you. What have you done with her? Where is she?"

Those questions plagued her for the rest of the night. However, come the morning she resolutely got up and got ready, then drove over to the Old Hills and enjoyed a gentle stroll along the more gradual slopes than the main hills. If less strenuous than a walk on the Hills themselves, it also didn't tax her limited energy as much, and she returned home feeling a good deal better.

There was little she could do about the whole Angie-Topher situation, she realised, especially with them being so very far away. Only when they deigned to come back could she do or say anything, but she did spend the late afternoon looking at the job vacancies and working out what her options were. Therefore she got to the shop at around nine-thirty on Monday feeling a little more in control of the situation, since there were jobs out there which she could at least survive on, even if they were hardly her heart's desire.

That didn't last.

Around eleven o'clock the door opened and a man whom she recognised as being the main barman from next door came in. She'd noticed him because she would've had to be blind and lacking a single hormone not to. Tall, dark, and well on the way to being handsome if not too picture perfect, he had the healthy glow of someone who spent a lot of time out of doors, probably playing every sport known to man and a few others besides. What she hadn't expected was the distinct Australian accent as he said,

"Hi there! I'm Jesse, from the pub," and gave her the kind of white-toothed smile that spoke of very good dental care when he was younger.

"Hi, I'm Holly," she replied, smiling back, but wondering what on earth he was doing in here. He didn't seem the kind of man to want to luxuriate in a bath full of coloured bubbles. "Can I help you with something?"

"Well it's about this coming weekend."

"Oh?"

He looked at her slightly worriedly now. "You do realise that it's the Mop Fair this weekend, don't you?"

His words hit her hard, and without realising it she groaned, "Oh God!"

"Not a fan of funfairs?" he asked, clearly perplexed.

Realising that she would have to explain, Holly sighed. "I'm not that much of a killjoy," she began, "but the friend who was supposed to be a partner in this venture," and she waved an exasperated hand at the shop, "has cleared off on an exotic holiday and left me holding the baby, so to speak. When we talked about the Mop, it was always with me being able to get my car out of the town and drive home without getting hit by the road closures, and her being the one to man the shop for as late as she wanted. She's going to be living upstairs, you see."

He frowned. "I thought this place was run by the new owners of the building?"

"*Hmph.* I suppose you could say that. But in truth, while it's Angie's husband who has the money and bought the place, this shop was supposed to hers and mine. It's something we'd talked of doing for donkey's years, and then all of a sudden this was the chance to do it."

"Oh, I see." Only clearly he didn't.

"Topher whisked Angie away on this supposedly 'romantic' holiday only days before we opened, and I haven't heard anything from either of them since. I've been holding the fort on my own ever since."

"Oh!" Now she saw him totally revising his opinions, even if he was too polite to say anything. "Hmmm...only I was going to ask how late you intended to stay open. We're anticipating being pretty busy, and I didn't want any of our more 'enthusiastic' customers causing you any trouble. But I have to admit that I thought that the bloke I spoke to when he came about the rent would be here with you, not just a lady being here on her own."

Holly could feel her heart sinking to an all-time low. The chances of them getting much custom had always been slim in her opinion. People who were coming out for a fun night at the fair weren't likely to be spending cash on beauty products or fancy candles. She looked around at the more expensive Yankee Candle jars, and the pretty glass shades and plates that went with them, and had a horrible vision of tipsy customers from next door blundering in, thinking it was another seating area, and so much glass-wear going flying.

"I think I'll be closing early," she said with a grimace. "But thank you for coming and talking to me, because I've been so focused on making it through each day I'd totally lost track of where we are in the calendar. …I'm still not sure what I'm going to do, mind you. Parking will be hell, and I'll probably have to abandon my old wreck halfway back to Worcester and walk the rest of the way in."

He looked shocked. "Does it get that bad?"

Now it was Holly's turn to wonder how he didn't know. "Did you not realise that the main car parks are shut for three days? They set the fair up there as well as in the streets, so they need it clear the day before to set up ready for the first evening, then the days of the fair itself, and it's taken down overnight and gone by the morning after, but without all of those spaces there's just not enough places for even everyone who works here to park, much less the visitors. I came to the Mop a couple of times in the past, and thought then that it must be hell for the people who live close to the centre."

Jesse looked glum. "Oh heck. I'm in a shared flat further across the way, but my car is mostly on the main car park. But I need it to be able to do things like runs to the wholesalers for snacks and stuff. Damn! I thought I'd be able to just nip out first thing in the morning if we needed to resupply. I'd better do an extra big shop tomorrow when Julie can be left in the bar for a few hours."

"Sorry to be the bearer of bad news. I thought you'd know since you were the one to remind me that it's this weekend."

He shook his head. "Nope. All I knew was that some of our customers were excited about it happening because of the boost in trade. I wasn't here this time last year, and neither were any of the current staff, so nobody told me."

Holly felt quite sorry for him. "Sounds like you've been dropped in it almost as much as me."

He smiled. "Well maybe not quite as badly. At least we've been budgeted extra staff at the weekends, although I'll admit that I've been rushed off my feet when we've unexpectedly got busy on the odd Monday, or a Tuesday night when I'm on my own."

He looked down at her. Not hard when he had to be easily six-foot-two and Holly could just about scrape up to five-four on a good day.

"If you get worried during the day… you know, if any roughs come in… don't hesitate to come and yell help." He saw her immediately look around at the stock. "Look, your stock should be covered by your insurance. If you've taken every sensible precaution, the insurance will pay for damage. But don't put yourself in harm's way to save it, okay?"

Holly smiled gratefully at him. "Thank you. That's really kind of you, and I feel a lot safer knowing that." She hadn't thought things out that far, and now she hoped that Topher had been organised with the insurance too, because she herself had sorted that all out and then just passed the final bill on to him to pay.

As Jesse gave a cheerful, "No worries," and vanished back through to next door, Holly thought what a refreshing change it was to have a man around who was actually more concerned about her as a person. She had no illusions that he'd even been flirting with her. Men didn't flirt with her, it just didn't happen. Every date she'd ever been on had been set up by someone else. He was just a genuinely nice bloke with a proper sense of priorities.

But it did make her halt in her tracks when it dawned on her that once upon a time she'd been quite envious of Angie having Topher, who had sworn he was going to treat her like a princess. Given that, even back then, Holly hadn't had anything beyond a one night date in far too long, she had watched Topher fussing over Angie in the early days and prayed that one day somebody would look at her like that. However, right now she would swap all of Topher's false promises for the sincere care in the friendly conversation she'd just had with Jesse.

"At least he seems like someone you could make a friend of," she sighed to herself, going back to her seat behind the counter. The town was incredibly quiet today, possibly because all of the locals were intending to come in at the end of the week, and she knew that this shop wasn't established enough yet for anyone to be coming back in to buy more of what they'd already tried. There was a part of her that had always been less than happy at trying to make their dream happen in this particular location off the High Street, and on a narrow, one-way street at that. As soon as Angie had come to her, full of enthusiasm and grand ideas, Holly had wondered whether Ledbury would be a big enough town to support them. Sinking into the chair, she recalled her own words,

"Ange, it's a lovely town and you've got a fabulous house, but is ours the right business to go in there? Wouldn't it be better for Topher to have another paying tenant in the shop, and us look for somewhere busier? If you don't want to be in Worcester, what about Cheltenham? Let's start small, and then if we make a go of it – and if this shop becomes vacant again – then we could set up a second branch here."

But Angie had been horrified. No, absolutely not, had been her response. The dream was to have a *beautiful* shop, and you couldn't get more beautiful than this glorious old building. Yet trade this far seemed to be bearing out Holly's assessment, and they were going to struggle badly unless they could have a really cracking Christmas where they established a regular clientele.

Holly was so lost in her recollections and worries that the phone ringing startled her.

"Hello, *Heaven Scent* of Ledbury, how may I help you?" she managed to splutter out. In three weeks the damned thing had never rung once, and she was astonished that anyone was calling now.

"Holly? Is that you?" the familiar voice of Angie's mum came in her ear.

"Oh! Hello, Meryl." Knowing who it was was almost a let-down after that moment of anticipation.

Before she had chance to ask how Meryl was, though, Angie's mum was demanding,

"Do you know where our Angela is?"

"No, Meryl. In fact I was hoping that you would be able to tell me."

"What? You've not heard from her?"

"Not a thing since she left for that holiday."

"Oh!" There was a stunned silence on the other end for a moment. "I thought she was just avoiding us after the row we had."

"Row? What row?" Then Holly winced, realising that she had no right to ask. It was just that it was so out of the blue. Angie hadn't said a thing about any row with her mum. Her rows with her dad were almost legendary, but her mum, never. "Sorry, Meryl, that didn't come out right. It's just that she never said a word about any disagreement with you."

There was a sniff down the phone line. "*Hmph*! ...Well I might as well tell you. She was having second thoughts about being married to Topher."

"*What*?"

"Hmm, I see. She never said anything about that to you, then?"

"No! Not as much as a hint. I thought it was still love and roses all the way."

"Well it wasn't. Weeks ago, she rang us up in floods of tears. Said that she'd found something out about Topher that was enough to have her thinking about a divorce, and she wanted her dad to fund her a good lawyer."

"Bloody hell! I know nothing of this! ...And would he?"

Meryl's voice became angry. "No he wouldn't! And I backed him this time! We'd warned her over and over again that there was something very wrong with Topher. But would she listen? No she wouldn't!" Suddenly Meryl's voice cracked. "We sent her away, telling her that she'd made her bed and she'd have to lie on it. Oh Holly, what have I done? Where's my baby girl?"

Holly had the sick, churning feeling in her guts again, but right now Meryl needed to hear that she wasn't to blame – which in Holly's eyes she wasn't.

"Meryl, you didn't do anything to cause this," she said soothingly, beyond glad that the woman couldn't see how white she'd gone - seeing herself in the mirror they'd placed so that they could see at least part of the back room – and how much she was obviously faking this calmness. This was too close to her own thoughts of last night. "For heaven's sake, they'd not been married a year. It was understandable that you'd be less than happy that she'd be talking about a divorce already."

Meryl sniffled, and Holly could envisage her with a pile of soggy tissues already. "She's never stuck at anything, you see. I saw it so clearly right then. We'd always let her do what she wanted, but we made such a mess of things. We thought that she'd just grow up, but she didn't. After she broke it off with Tom," Angie's previous fiancé, "who was such a lovely chap, we sat her down and had a firm talk with her. We told her that marriage is a compromise. That she wouldn't find anyone who would let her have things all her own way, all of the time. In fact we said that

that wasn't love, because it wasn't showing him, whoever he was, any consideration."

There was a heart-wrenching sob. "She told us that she wouldn't accept anything less, and said what did we know what a good marriage was when we rowed so much."

"Oh Meryl, I'm so sorry. Could she not see that every couple have arguments? If you don't, then you aren't talking much, or one of you is allowing themselves to become a total doormat for the other – the way my mum did for my dad."

Meryl gave a hiccup of a sob. "You saw that first-hand, didn't you. When Angie came home and said that your aunt had sold the house and taken your sister but not you, I said straightaway, 'Angie, bring her back here! We haven't got a bedroom to spare – not with three of you – but she can have the attic over the garage.' I told her then that she didn't know how lucky she was."

That almost undid Holly. So it had been Meryl, not Angie, who had come to her rescue! The knowledge was like having the rug ripped out from under her. Everything she had stood for from Angie down the years had been based on that one, life-saving act of kindness, and now it turned out that she'd not been the one she should have been thanking at all.

"No, Angie never did grasp how lucky she was," Holly said, hoping she didn't sound as bitter and shaky as she felt.

"But you can understand that we were far from happy when, just a few months after that talk, she came home and declared that she'd met the love of her life – Topher!"

"Oh I can, especially as we were all so shocked too. We thought that she'd be grieving over losing Tom, given that he'd finally had enough and broken it off with her. I think that was the first time anyone beat Angie to making the break-up call, and she took it really hard. If it's any consolation, Meryl, a couple of other friends both said that they hoped it would be a wake-up call for Angie. You know, not getting any younger, and that playing the demanding princess wasn't attractive when you're over thirty."

"We wondered whether she might have gone begging to Tom, you know," Meryl told her after a noisy snuffle into a tissue. "I still had his parents' number and gave them a call when I didn't hear from her after the row. I thought she might have tried to wheedle him into playing the knight in shining armour to her maiden in distress. But they said no, he hadn't heard from her in over a year, and anyway, she'd have had trouble catching up with him, because he works away a lot now. Apparently they don't get to see as much of him now, but his mum said he's happier, especially as the place he works for now isn't linked to ours – so he doesn't even hear Angie's name cropping up." She had to stop and blow her nose. "I get why they weren't exactly pleased to hear from me, but it's so sad that we don't see Tom anymore. I liked him far more than I ever have Topher.

Holly was confused. "If she didn't speak to you after the row, how do you know about the holiday?"

"Oh, she sent us a letter. Very brusque. Very 'I told you so', and that they were going to live the dream now. Except I didn't believe that six weeks ago, and I don't believe it now." Meryl's voice cracked again. "What's he done to her? What's Topher done to my baby girl, Holly? Where is she? What's happened to her? What's he done?"

Chapter 4

It took Holly several more minutes to calm Meryl down a little and ring off, but in truth she could understand her panic. Something was clearly very wrong, and she couldn't just put Angie's silence down to her having a ball on some tropical paradise. She'd watched too many episodes of the BBC's *Death in Paradise*, she realised, because right now she was having visions of Angie's lifeless corpse lying under a palm tree just off a beach, and a group of Caribbean detectives scrutinising the body.

Then something else in what Meryl had said hit her. As far as she'd known, Angie had been surprised by the holiday as a last minute thing dropped on her by Topher, and that announcement to Holly had come four weeks ago. But Meryl had said the letter to her came way more than a month ago, and which, allowing for the slowness of the postal service sometimes, could hardly mean it was sent that same day. Was Meryl so distraught that she simply thought it was over a month ago, or was there something more sinister in all of this? Had that joy and surprise on Angie's part when she'd broken the news to Holly been just a damned good act, and the holiday far more planned?

Until this phone call, Holly would have just brushed it off as Meryl being a worried mum, but that innocent revelation that she had been the one to save Holly nearly twenty years ago, now wouldn't leave her alone. At what stage in all of those years had it not been possible for Angie to tell the truth? They were adults now, both having passed thirty some years ago. It wasn't that hard to look back on their teenage years and laugh at some of the other things they'd done, so why could Angie not say, 'of course it was Mum really, but I wanted you to stay friends with me,' or something like that? It would hardly have led to any rows, because Holly was still grateful, and they'd been friends for long enough for the details to matter less than the fact that it had happened. It was the continued lie which bugged her now, more than what she'd lied over, given that it had been over such a major event in Holly's life, and something which had coloured how she behave for the whole of her twenties.

Why didn't you tell me the truth? Holly fretted. *What's going on here*?

After she'd sat there for another three hours without a single customer coming in, worrying herself silly over Angie, but also the Mop Fair and what she was going to do about it, and with it raining heavily outside as a discouragement to casual browsers, she got up and dropped the catch on the door. She wrote a note asking for people to ring the bell if they wanted to come in, and that she was counting stock in the back. But really she wanted to go down into the office and start checking up on things.

Her first phone call was to the insurance people, and to her relief that was paid up and all was fine. What wasn't so good was that it became clear that as far as they were aware, someone connected to the shop was living on the premises – not a problem during normal trading hours, but where would things stand if someone broke in and did damage in the evening? More disturbing was that when she rang the bank, they wouldn't answer any of her questions because apparently she wasn't one of the people on the shop's account, despite her being sure that Angie had given her the bank's form to sign as proof of her signature, and had then taken it away again. That really wasn't good, and immediately Holly resolved to hide the card machine away and ask for cash wherever possible.

She then rang around their suppliers and checked that the stock had been paid for. The main companies had, but a couple of the smaller ones who provided the handcrafted items were still waiting. Apologising profusely, Holly dug out her own cheque book and wrote them all payments. She could put the letters in the post tonight, and if she went and paid cash into her bank first thing tomorrow morning, it should have cleared by the time the people got the cheques and then had chance to pay them into their own banks. It left a nasty taste in her mouth, though, hinting that Topher thought that the 'little men' didn't matter. Yet to Holly, their products were the ones which made this shop stand out from any of the other places in the wider area (like Worcester and Cheltenham) which sold the bigger companies' products. These were the ones who would keep customers coming back here rather than anywhere else.

She was so absorbed in what she was doing that she didn't take much notice of the faint whistling, presuming that it was someone working down in the pub cellar. Only when she got a whiff of tobacco smoke did she look up, thinking that it surely ought to be against health and safety regulations for someone to be smoking down in the cellar with all that alcohol around.

What she saw made her give a little shriek. There, seemingly working away on the old cellar wall opposite her, was a workman. A shortish man dressed in overalls, but with a battered jacket over them, and a cloth cap on his head. Clamped in his teeth was a pipe, and that was where the scent of tobacco was coming from, yet a foot or so out from the pipe the smoke just vanished. He seemed to be working away with a trowel, and yet Holly couldn't see what he was putting on the wall.

"Oh God, we're haunted!" she gasped, too shaken to move.

She looked down at his boots and realised that they were nothing any modern workman from the last fifty years or so would wear. And the more she looked at him, the more she was convinced that he must be Victorian, or at the very latest somewhere pre-First World War. As her pulse relaxed from practically leaping out of her body, she could see that he was quite happily working away. At one point he put the pipe down on something out of the vision, and began actions which she guessed were smoothing something out, and while he did this he was whistling that merry little tune again.

Then suddenly he was gone. No workman, no whistling, no tobacco scent.

In that moment Holly realised that where he had been had temporarily looked darker than the office did now, with its modern fluorescent strip light. He'd been working in a place much more poorly lit. Of course if this house had been built many centuries ago, then the cellars had to be old too, and would certainly have been here in Victorian times. Yet however friendly he had seemed, that settled one option Holly had been considering, which was to stay overnight down here. Nothing on God's green earth would persuade her to spend the night down here alone now. She might not be the most highly educated woman in the world, but she knew enough to know that over a century ago men had very different attitudes to women. What might his response be to seeing a woman who looked like a ghost to him if that opening in time went both ways?

Hurriedly putting everything away, she went back up to the shop and stared out of the door. There wasn't a soul about. Granted, the rain was torrential now, and nobody would be out in that if they didn't have to be. Even the pub had closed up between the lunchtime trade and the early evening post-work customers, making Holly suspect that Jesse had gone off to do some of that vital restocking he'd talked about while he could.

That didn't make her feel any better either, because it made her aware that once the pub closed on the Fair days, she would be here very much alone.

Yet who could she ask to come and stay with her? She knew that much as Louise and Sam would be worried for her, their solution would be to let the shop take its chances, and for her to go home as normal.

But looking around, and having just been through all of the invoices, Holly knew just how much money was still tied up in this shop. If the worst came to the worst, and it got broken into, where would she stand if Topher decided to play nasty and say that she should have watched over it? Common sense said it was ridiculous to expect her to stay the night, but the other part of her kept saying, 'he's a multi-millionaire now, he can afford to hire sharp lawyers who could tie you in knots.' She couldn't afford to fight him back under those circumstances, and if something had happened to Angie, there'd be nobody who could vouch for her conscientiousness and diligence over security, or anything of much else.

It would have to be the flat, she decided reluctantly. She had a key to the downstairs door so that she could go and pick up any post for them. That had definitely been Angie. She couldn't imagine Topher wanting to know that she'd been into what he probably considered his private space. But now she had very little choice.

Shutting up early, she got all of her things together, then went out into the street, locked up the shop and went to the other side of its window to the street door to what was above. It was a magnificent piece of old oak, very fitting for the building and almost certainly an original, aside from the modern high-security lock, there was a big old iron key to fit in the equally old lock. Luckily it was well oiled and the key turned easily, and scooping up the pile of junk mail, she let herself in and locked the door behind her.

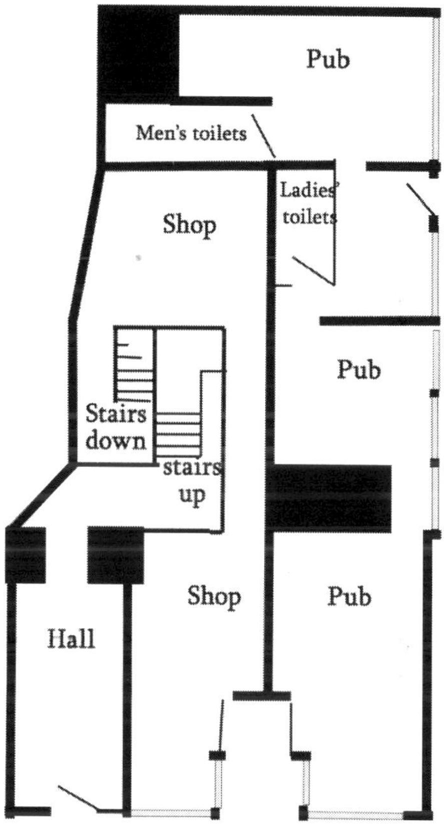

Ground floor plan

The hallway was magnificent all by itself. Huge beams running across the ceiling were the same ones that continued on through her shop and on into the pub, and they effectively divided this hallway into bays by the uprights which supported them. Each of the bays still had the original oak wainscoting, carved in a linen-fold pattern, and all were nearly as black with age as the beams. In an attempt to reflect what little light came in through the two tiny windows on either side of the door, all of the plasterwork had been painted white, though much of it was peeling and less than pristine. The poor old place definitely needed a spot of love and care, Holly thought.

There was nothing beyond the original old hallway at this level, and she walked to its end and began climbing the staircase having switched the lights on. At first floor level the stairwell had no natural light, but up on the second were two huge mullioned windows, very good for getting more light in on the stairs, but even before she got to them, Holly could feel the chill they let in. Angie and Topher were going to need some very clever secondary double-glazing on this listed building if they were going to live here during the winter. But then, Holly thought bitterly, going on the current showing, they were just as likely to clear off to somewhere hot and sunny for the dank days after Christmas. There'd be no fighting the chill of this place for them, and in an odd way that made her angry, because this building was a jewel which ought to be treasured for all that it was, not just some investment counted in pounds or dollars.

And yet there was something about this place that made her feel sad in a wholly different way. This hadn't been a happy home in a very long time, she thought, and she wasn't sure what it would take to make it one again. Every time she came up here, which admittedly hadn't been a lot, she thought of another and altogether older friend, Sally, who was a psychic and someone she knew totally separately from Angie. Sally would have a field day with this place, and now that Holly had thought of her, it occurred to her to ring her up and ask her advice about the ghost. She would feel a lot happier about spending the night here if Sally could reassure her that while she might see the ghost, that the ghost wouldn't see her.

She paused at the top of the first flight of stairs and looked up into the gloom of the next floor. Had she imagined it, or did it sound like there was something up in the top flat?

"Oh for God's sake, woman, stop jumping at shadows," she reproved herself crossly. "It's probably the bloody roof leaking in this downpour! Something Topher can shell out the money for. It's not your problem. Ignore it!"

Glad to move out of the void of the stairwell she gratefully moved into the big front room, which looked out over the street. It was a cavernous space despite the low ceiling, and always felt more like a function room than a space you would make into a lounge. Mind you, that wasn't helped by the unsympathetic strip lights someone had put in during its days as an office, which gave off a harsh white light that only highlighted how long it had been since the ceiling had been painted. The walls were all wood panelled in the same old oak, which sucked up the light like a sponge, and there and then Holly decided that this would not be the room she stayed in.

Not least, that was because there were no curtains up at the windows, and since the buildings across the street were all rather close because of the narrowness of the lane, anyone in those flats would be able to see straight into here once the lights were on. If Jesse had said he lived directly opposite, she might have considered it, because she could imagine him keeping an eye on her in the nicest way, not spying creepily on her. But the thought of some random bloke gawping in, and realising that there was a woman up here on her own, wasn't a nice one.

The same went for the other front room, although that was fractionally smaller and only had front windows (not side ones as well, which the main room had because the overall building took up part of the corner plot on that side), and therefore also faced onto the lane. Instead she went into the room behind the main one, and which lay alongside the stairs and landing. Once upon a time this must have been two individual rooms, because there were two separate doors into it from the landing, but quite early on the rooms had been joined, and the panelling flowed smoothly through a wide arch between them. This was a much cosier space despite being no smaller than the second front room. It also looked down onto what was now the narrow alleyway which the pub used as outside seating, though in the house's heyday might have been part of its own garden before it got built on, and the thought of hearing normal human activity appealed to Holly. She might even go down and have a fortifying drink or two if she didn't need to drive that night.

Back at her own flat she had an inflatable mattress and a decent sleeping bag from the days when she had first moved in, and hadn't been able to afford a bed straightaway. If she dug them out tonight and brought them in tomorrow, she could set up in here without anyone wondering what she was doing. By the end of the week there would be too many people working to set up the Fair for anybody to see her carrying a sleeping bag in, and the fewer clues she gave anyone that she was alone in this vast space the better.

I can put the shop kettle and the stuff for a hot drink into an anonymous bag, and bring those up on the night, she thought. *There are bound to be loads of food vans about that I can get something hot from, so it won't be too bad.*

She had already discounted the second floor as a place to sleepover, because up there she wouldn't hear a thing if anything did kick off in the shop. All those solid oak floorboards would muffle sounds very effectively. But she also had the creeps even more up on that floor, even back when Angie had shown it her and been laughing alongside her, and Holly knew that after a night up there on her own that she'd be jumping at the slightest sound. That was emphasised by the way the rain was audibly hammering at the big staircase windows, and if that dripping kept up too, she'd be a nervous wreck by the morning. Unable to face those claustrophobic, gloomy upper rooms, with their even lower ceilings and smaller windows, Holly went back downstairs and let herself out.

After a trip to her bank on the following morning, she lugged the mattress and sleeping bag up into the flat, and then went into the shop. She'd only gone downstairs to get the float for the till when she smelt it again, tobacco. Glancing around, there was no sign of the old workman, but the scent of his pipe was getting stronger, and Holly fled upstairs.

Luckily, with the heavy rain having passed over, she had a busy morning, and even the afternoon was better than she'd had in several days. She stuck to her resolve and made a point of asking for cash in preference to cards, so that by the end of the day she'd only done a handful of electronic transactions, and there was a decent amount to tuck away in the safe. If she could keep this up, she might manage to keep enough actual money to both pay herself, and to reorder stock when she needed to. What wasn't so nice was realising that she was already thinking of being on her own here long-term, and Angie only ever flitting in and out now and then – that was if Angie was okay and ever came back from the Caribbean in one piece, which was something else which bothered her.

It meant that once she was back at home she decided to call Sally. It would be refreshing to talk to someone who didn't know Angie personally, and who therefore would have an impartial take on the situation. At first they did the normal catch-up chat, but as soon as Holly got into the details of what was going on with Angie, she could hear Sally's sharp intakes of breath.

"I don't like the sound of this," Sally said frankly. "I know I don't know Louise and Sam, but I'm with them on this one. I think Sam's advice to hang onto all the cash you can is sound. In fact if she hadn't already told you to do that, I would have."

"I'm worried about Angie herself," Holly added.

"Oh, I think that one is going to have to dig herself out of whatever hole she's got herself into," Sally declared sternly.

"You've got one of your feelings about this? A message?"

"Nothing as definite as that," Sally admitted, "but a strong sensation that someone is covering something up, and that there have been lies on both sides. I don't think either of those two is actually an innocent party."

"Wow! That's interesting."

"And you're not immediately protesting Angie's innocence," Sally observed dryly. "That's a change, and a good one."

"It's hard to do that after what Meryl said."

"Indeed it is. And I agree with what you've said. ...Surely at *some* point, Angie could have been honest with you? That's what I mean about this sense of deceit lingering around her. I can't give you a more accurate reading than that – not without something of hers to focus on, anyway – but I fear you'll find that isn't the only lie you've been fed."

"What about my Victorian ghost? Should I be worried about him too?"

Sally's laugh was genuine. "No, he sounds quite a cheerfully chappie to me. He's probably just reliving what he enjoyed doing when he was here in the flesh.

And if you've not seen him up until now, I would think it's likely that around now is a significant anniversary, maybe of his passing, or of something that meant a lot to him in life. He might linger for a week or two, and then you might not see him again for another year."

"Thank heavens for that!"

"Now if you'd said you'd seen a man in almost medieval dress, it might be a different thing."

"Why?" Holly didn't like the sound of that.

"The Civil War, of course! Ledbury didn't escape the conflict, even if it didn't have a major battle there. I got a bit curious over this, you know, because I always wondered why the Sealed Knot had Scottish soldiers in their re-enactments of what wasn't much more than a skirmish at Ledbury. But it seems that after the famous Battle of Naseby, Earl Leslie and his Scots headed west to retake Hereford for the Parliamentary side – though in truth, I don't think the Scots were that enamoured with Cromwell. I think they thought he was just better than the king! Well that old place you're in was standing back then."

"Oh crap. When was this battle?"

"Err...1645 if it was the same as Naseby, if I recall, though this was more of a skirmish than a great battle. Yes, it was 1645, because it was the three-hundred-and-seventy-fifth anniversary a few years ago when there was some sort of 'do' due, and it had to be cancelled because of Covid. You said that the building is *fifteenth* century, so that's a couple of centuries before then, depending on how late in the fifteenth it was built. But still well over a century before. You never know, it might've had to be repaired after the soldiers had rampaged through the town."

"Oh thanks, Sal ...*not*! That's really going to give me the heebie-jeebies stopping there overnight! I don't want some bloody, hacked about Civil War soldier walking through the walls to disturb my night. I've got enough problems as it is!"

Sally laughed. "Don't be so gloomy. And it's hardly as though anything in that house is going to be drawing a ghost out right *now*."

"I do hope you're right, Sal, I really do, because I think seeing some headless horseman galloping through the shop might be the last straw for my nerves right now."

Chapter 5

Sally's words about ghosts haunted Holly's dreams that night, which meant that she got up with only one more day to go before the Fair feeling distinctly ragged around the edges.

You're too gullible by far, she lectured herself sternly, as she stared at the dark circles under her eyes in the bathroom mirror. *Why ever didn't you stop to question things a bit more? Then you wouldn't be in this mess in the first place, worrying yourself sick over a shop you don't even own, and what other people will think of you if you walk away.*

She knew the answer, of course. Something bedded deep in her psyche had a longstanding dread of people abandoning her. She'd learned that when she'd eventually summoned up the courage to go and ask for some help from a therapist. The woman she'd been sent to had been lovely, helping her to understand that her dad walking out on her and her mum when she was only five had been bad enough, but for him to come crawling back a year later, only to leave again when she was eight, had done some damage.

By the time he'd come back again when she was nearly ten, and for him and her mum to have had her sister Sophie as a 'marriage patch' baby, only for him to leave for the final time the year after, had done deep-seated harm. With her mum then getting breast cancer three years later and then dying when she was sixteen, and with no member of the family, not even her dad, willing to take on the child who had 'forced' her mum and dad to get married in the first place – even though she had hardly made the choice herself – had all built up into a determination to hang onto people long after it was healthy to do so.

The therapy had also explained why she'd had so much trouble developing any kind of meaningful relationship with a man. On the one hand, she was terrified that they'd walk out for no apparent reason, which was how her father's disappearances had seemed to her as a child; and on the other, had left her with such a void in her self-confidence that anyone would find her worthy of their interest, that she never expected anyone to find her attractive. But that great gaping hole in her confidence had been the reason why she'd been so easily sucked into Angie's schemes. And schemes she now feared they were, rather than the mutual longing for a dream which might never happen, which was what the shop had been for her. If Angie had needed a sucker to do all the donkey work in the shop, while she merely enjoyed the having of it, it now pounded in on Holly that she had been the obvious choice by a mile, the perfect patsy.

Well you're well and truly stuffed now, she thought miserably as she opened up the shop again. *What the hell can you do? Shut the place up after less than a month, and then refuse to speak to Angie if she ever appears again? That's just childish,* even though she knew that if the shoe was on the other foot, that that was exactly what Angie would probably do, now that she was looking at her friend without the rose-tinted glasses on. But in truth she knew that it would take couple of months at least for her to find another job, and if nothing else, here she had some control over where the money went to. Far from ideal it might be, but until either Angie or Topher, or both, returned to demand their investment back, sticking it out was her best option while she looked for a proper, paying, job once more. Moreover, as long as there were some direct debits to Topher's bank for the Council Tax and utilities for the building – and she thought that when it came to anything he thought was *his*, Topher would have been more conscientious – then she was hardly in danger of the someone evicting the business and her along with it.

Mercifully it was another decent day trade-wise, and between that and the previous day, she managed to claw back the money she had used to pay the suppliers. However, today was Saturday, and as the afternoon wore on, the road closure signs started to go up in readiness for Sunday, Monday and Tuesday – the main days of the Mop fair. By four o'clock, trade had dried up completely, and with something like relief she shut up shop. Tonight she could afford to go back home, because the only people out on the streets would be the workmen getting everything ready, but it was as she was getting the money in the safe that she banged her shin yet again on Angie's desk.

For some reason Holly had never quite worked out, Angie had insisted on them having a separate desk each. It had seemed such an extravagance to her, and she had happily found a good solid wood one in a second-hand store which worked perfectly well for what she needed. Angie, however, had insisted on a brand new, top-of-the-range desk from IKEA, complete with locking drawers. And it was those drawers that Holly found herself looking at with growing suspicion. What on earth had Angie got here in the shop that warranted such caution? In the old flat, maybe, because that would be where she stored personal things like bank statements until they could furnish the flat upstairs, but not here.

Turning the spindle lock on the safe to shut it, Holly sat back on her heels and looked at the desk. Typically of Angie, she had assumed that it would come ready assembled, and had then thrown a hissy fit when confronted with a pack of parts. So it had been Holly who had got down on her hands and knees and put the damned thing together, but that meant that she knew only too well what an illusion of security those locks were. More to the point, she still had the spanners and allen-keys in her own desk, and a few carefully undone joints would give her access to the desk's secrets.

"Sod it," she growled, "if you didn't want me to pry, you shouldn't have dumped me in the shit!" One way or another she was going to get to the bottom of what was going on.

A few turns of the allen-keys and the casing of the desk sprang apart enough that she could get the 'locked' drawers open. Inside she found a strange assortment of items. One was the details of a self-storage unit in Worcester, which didn't make any sense until she found the sale of Angie's flat – the one she'd had before she married Topher, and the one that Holly thought she still owned. Yet this sale implied that Angie had hung onto the money from that flat, because it had gone into a building society account that was in her name only, and her maiden name at that. That was proven by the building society statements that were hidden there.

What the hell are you up to, Ange? she thought fretfully. Because it was clear that any contents of her flat with any sentimental meaning to her had gone into the storage unit, not to the place which she had shared with Topher while they were sorting out where they would live. She knew that must be the case, because things she knew Angie would never get rid of hadn't been at the shared flat on the odd times she'd gone over there, which was why she'd also thought that Angie had kept her old flat. That had been before Topher's big win, of course, and in those early days Topher had wanted them to rent a place closer to where he worked than Angie's flat to save on commuting costs, and which at the time had sounded all so normal. But then had Topher never questioned where the money was coming from to keep her old flat going? Because Holly knew she'd been adamant that she wasn't going to rent it out. Or did he simply assume that 'daddy' was paying for it in the way he handed money out to Angie on a regular basis?

"We'll buy in a year or two when Topher's career is more established," Angie had told everyone back then, "but my flat's only appreciating in value, so we're hanging on to that to act as a deposit on something bigger."

It had sounded so rational, yet now, looking at what she'd found in the desk, Holly was full of doubts. There were only bits and pieces, but they all built into a picture of Angie trying to separate her life out from Topher's, and that just didn't gel with the excited Angie who had been so enthralled with the idea of heading off to the Caribbean with him. It worried Holly terribly, because the only thing which made sense of any of this was that Angie was starting to suffer from some sort of schizophrenia, being on the one hand the woman who was still very much in love with Topher, and on the other, someone who didn't trust him further than she could throw him. And if Angie had become that mentally fragile, how much easier would it be for Topher to trick her?

Oddest of all was a DVD with the words 'wedding video' scrawled on it in Angie's bold, looping script. It wasn't the official DVD, that was for sure, because that had come in a nice case with a picture of the happy couple on the cover. So where had this come from? Perplexed, Holly tucked it into her handbag to watch later, and having pushed the desk back together, tightened the casing back up again, confident now that she could get into it whenever she wanted. And with a growing horror she realised that she might have to prove that Topher had discovered that Angie was going to leave him, thereby giving him a motive to assault her which had then proved fatal.

Once back home, and having eaten a proper meal, albeit a microwaved one, she sat down and put the

DVD on to play. The opening scenes were very much like the official video, and Holly realised that this was the video shot by another friend of Angie's called Mark. She'd seen Mark wandering around with his camera on the day, and knew that he had a business making videos for companies, so hadn't thought anything of it at the time, beyond the fact that it was nice that he was focusing on the people the official photographer wasn't bothering with. And indeed, he hadn't been seated that far behind Holly herself in the church, given that she wasn't included in the main party.

So she found the first watch-through saddening, because it reminded her just how much she had been cut out of the proceedings, even at the evening function. But why on earth had Angie had that locked away? There had to be something on this film that meant more than just happy memories.

Giving herself a mental shake and a telling off for letting herself be dragged into maudlin thoughts, Holly went back to the start. This time she took her time over it, pausing it to look more carefully at the faces outside the church and those coming in. But it was only as they got into the main ceremony that she realised that Mark had suddenly stopped moving the camera and was looking straight ahead. Yet it wasn't that he no longer had a view of the altar. Taking it back a bit there it was, a definite clear view of the altar between a tall skinny bald man, and a little lady in a fussy fascinator of a hat. So why had Mark suddenly stuck in that other spot?

She watched it until he moved the camera again, and another time, only then realising that there was something on the audio beyond the ceremony. Right in front of him was a slim blonde woman, nicely dressed, but hardly done up as if coming to the wedding breakfast afterwards. That hadn't struck Holly as odd, because a lot of family friends and neighbours had come to the church who couldn't be fitted in for the sit-down meal later – or more likely, she now thought, who just hadn't fitted the right profile to be invited to it. But now she realised that the woman was speaking.

Under her breath Holly heard her saying, "Don't do it, my love! ...No! ...No, please don't say you will. ...Think of the kids! What will I tell Bobby and Callum? Chris, you're their *dad*, you can't do this to them!"

What? Holly stopped the playback, stunned.

For a second she thought that the woman must have been mistaken. Had she wandered into the wrong wedding? There had been another wedding after Angie and Topher's on that day, so perhaps the woman had come early, but not early enough to see the bride and groom? No, that was ridiculous. Mark had panned past her several times, and she'd been there as long as he had.

Then it dawned on her that 'Chris' really *did* mean Topher. But why did this woman call him by the name he refused to answer to to anyone else, and so affectionately as well? Almost as bad was the thought that if this was the woman whom he really loved, was that the reason why he wouldn't let anyone *but* her call him Chris?

By far the worst, though, was the burning question of Bobby and Callum, and how old they were? Grim though it might be, if they were nearly teenagers, then with Topher being in his early thirties, they could be the product of a teenage fling that hadn't survived into adulthood. Was this woman hanging on to the memory of something that had died long ago?

Holly herself was a painful example of what that could do to the child involved, because her parents had not quite been out of their teens when she had been conceived, and she knew all too well what could happen if both sets of parents insisted on the young couple sticking it out. Yet in Topher's case there had never been any inhibitor to him getting married in church, such as a previous marriage. He and Angie had had a full marriage in the church, not just a blessing. That implied that whoever this woman was, he had never actually married her.

For the woman, Holly had only sympathy, having watched her mum's distress at her dad being lured away by the promises of someone 'better' as they had matured, which in real terms meant someone more compatible with the man he had become. As far as she knew, her dad was still with the woman he had left her mum for the second time, briefly broken up with because of his guilty conscience (or more likely hers), and then returned to, unable to live without her, and in his case with two children being no compensation for the lack of her. No, in that scenario Holly didn't blame this woman at all, not least because if the children were older, she had already had her relationship with Topher long before Angie had appeared on the scene.

More worrying, however, was if these boys were only little – which in Holly's mind meant still under somewhere around seven to ten years old. Allowing for a normal gap of two or three years between children, that could mean that Topher had still been seeing this woman even as he had been courting Angie, and that didn't sit comfortably with her at all. Even if this unknown woman had tried to entrap him into marriage by getting pregnant, it still didn't excuse Topher not facing up to his responsibilities as a dad – and again, that was something Holly knew far too much about from firsthand experience.

What she liked even less were the worrying thoughts on what had made him take up with Angie, in that case? Because from where she was sitting, it was quite one thing to have a relationship in which you'd had kids, but which subsequently failed over time; and quite another to rush into a new relationship before the old one was even over. And she'd have accepted Topher falling madly, wildly, and passionately in love with Angie once upon a time, but not after watching those videos again with a sharper eye.

"Who the hell are you?" she asked the paused screen, frozen on the woman at the one point where her face was turned just enough towards the camera to at least get a hint of what she was like. She wore little or no make-up, it seemed, and if hardly a stunning beauty, from the little Holly could see, she was a normally attractive person. Certainly she was someone who would stand comparing to Angie.

"At least you aren't so shallow, Topher, that you went for the looker," Holly conceded.

Nor could it be that he had never wanted kids, and so had gone with Angie because she was adamant that she didn't want them either. In fact Angie had begun to feel the tick of time even worse than Holly, and on several occasions had said that she wanted her and Topher to have a larger place than her previous flat from the start, precisely because she wanted to have a family as soon as possible. So Topher wasn't running from fatherhood to Angie. That couldn't have been the lure for him to leave his kids. Angie had been quite vocal in her intentions even when Holly had been around them, so she knew that there could never have been any confusion there.

Thoroughly worried now, Holly went through the video again. The first part was all in the church, but then Mark had moved on and taken a lot of footage during the reception and the evening party. Up until discovering the audio of the church, Holly had had the sound down out of courtesy to her neighbours – the walls here were paper-thin and the young mum next door had little ones who would already be in bed by now. Now she plugged in her headphones and turned the volume up enough to hear the background noise.

Various snatches of conversations filtered through, most completely meaningless or just the normal sort of stuff people chatted about at such functions. So when she suddenly heard Topher's voice, it came as a shock. He wasn't in the shot at all, and must have been stood behind Mark.

Indeed he probably hadn't been talking to Mark, or even aware that he was standing so close that the mic' on the camera would pick him up, because he was speaking quite unguardedly.

"Are you sure you've no regrets over this," someone was asking Topher when Holly skipped back a few seconds.

"Nah," Topher said quite cheerfully, "she'll never know."

"Are you sure about that?"

"Look, Wesley, she's a spoilt brat who thinks of nobody but herself. She wouldn't dream that I'm not madly in love with her. The bloody woman thinks that everyone is just falling over themselves to be near her."

Holly had to pause the playback just to get her breath. Christ, that was callous! And no wonder the other voice seemed vaguely familiar, because if Topher could be said to have a best friend then Anthony 'Wesley' DePaoli was it. Angie hated him, perhaps because he had never made much effort to flatter her, but Holly had thought Wesley okay if hardly someone she would make a friend of.

Wesley's attitude to all of this was thrown into a whole other light now, though. If he was fully aware of the double life his so-called friend was about to start living, then was it more that he was scared stiff that he'd say the wrong thing to Angie and give the whole game away? That became more of a reality as Holly listened on, with Wesley saying,

"Fuck me, mate, that's bloody callous! I know she's self-obsessed, but you knew that right from the start. Why the hell have you let it get this far?"

"Because I need her money!" came Topher's angry hiss.

"But I thought you said it was her old man who held the purse strings?"

"He does, but for all that he tries to put his foot down, the mother always takes Angie's side, and in the end he pays up."

"Shit!" Holly heard Wesley say in awed tones. "I never had you down as that money grabbing, mate."

"It's not for me, you nob! Laura's MS is getting worse. If she ends up in a wheelchair in a couple of years, or even worse, *somebody's* going to have to take care of Bobby and Callum! Jeez, you know that Callum's only four now, and Bobby's only two years older. They'll need someone around to collect them from school and do stuff for them for years yet.

"Well I can't do that if I'm working all the hours that God sends at that bloody awful job I've got, can I? I can't be in two places at once. I've tried doing it the right way. I've tried taking on a second job to try and put something aside against the time when we'll need it. And what happened? I ended up collapsing from exhaustion and in A&E myself! Bugger all good I am as a dad like that!

"I tell you, at that point I damned near took out extra life insurance for a couple of years and then chucked myself off Worcester Bridge, because at least that way Laura and the lads would be taken care of. But then along comes Miss-full-of-herself Angela Wright, throwing herself at me, making all those silly bloody statements about me rising to the top of my profession, and how I'd soon be looking her father in the eye as an equal. It only took me one visit to her parents' house to see how much money got wasted there! Laura could feed the kids for a week on what got thrown out after a Sunday lunch at that place! …I'm not kidding, Wesley. What her mother pays for the Sunday joint is Laura's budget for food for everyone for more than half the week, and that's after I've paid the rent and the bills. It's obscene."

Holly had to pause the video and snuffle into a tissue. Not because she was so angry at Topher, but because her heart was breaking for the woman she had never met. How many times had she seen Meryl going to the supermarket and coming back with a huge joint of beef that, even with six of them sitting down to Sunday lunch, there was enough that her mum would have made something to go around for all of them for the Monday as well?

Too many times, was the honest answer. She herself had been just as appalled as Topher, but because she was dependent upon the Wrights' charity, she had bitten her lip and stayed silent when the residue had just gone into the kitchen bin. Oh, Holly could understand Topher's disgust only too well, because it had been her own. And now she was having some very confused feelings about him too. If he'd married Angie so that he could get a bite of the family money, that was plain wrong. But by the same token, if the woman he loved had that crippling and killing disease, and he had tried everything else to provide for his kids, that made him a very desperate man, but not necessarily a callous one. His solution to his problems was wrong in all sorts of ways, but Holly suddenly had sympathy for Topher in a way she had never expected to.

The video continued with Wesley saying, "But

her old man's not going to write you a blank cheque, so how does it help?"

"Look, I've told her that my income is far less than what it really is, okay? I'm in line for a promotion if old Terry finally buggers off and retires, and when that happens, I shall make sure that the increase in pay is only a few quid as far as she's concerned. I'll feed her some bullshit about me needing to prove myself to the company, and she'll buy it as long as *somebody* funds her endless bloody shopping trips for clothes she only ever wears once. I've got it all worked out. The last time she had a clear-out of her wardrobe, I offered to drop the stuff off to the charity bank on my way to work. But she's close enough in size to Laura that I was able to take it all around to her. Some of it still had the bloody labels on! How wasteful is that? But Laura cried she was so happy to have some new clothes for herself instead of shoving all of our money into clothes and food for the kids."

"Shit," Wesley breathed, but still loud enough for the camera to pick up. "So even her clothes go to help Laura? I think you're wrong to do this, pal, but…well, fuck me, I hope I never have to make choices like yours!"

Oh Mark, what have you done? Holly thought as she had to pause the video to recover herself. *Did you give this to Angie almost straightaway, or did she do something to infuriate you – like she does with everyone sooner or later – and you sent her this more recently as an 'up yours' gesture? Because whatever the reason you sent her the unedited version to the one she got along with the pro video, you may have unleashed the bitch from hell on Topher. What he's done is morally wrong, but what Angie might do on discovering it makes me feel sick with worry.*

Chapter 6

Holly went to bed that night feeling dreadful. Her guilty feelings of sympathy for Topher weighed around her neck like her personal albatross, even as she continued to worry over what had become of Angie. Because for all of her new-found perspective on Angie, it wasn't that easy to step out of the years of friendship and stop fretting over her. Not least was the nagging thought that, having come up on the big one on the lottery, Topher had suddenly ceased to have a use for Angie.

All of a sudden, Topher had found himself with many times Angie's father's money and with some to spare. There was no need to go begging, or to secretively filter money away to the family he truly loved. Which led to the question of whether Angie had been such a burden, such an unutterable pain in the arse to live with, that when given the easy way out, Topher had grabbed it with both hands and done away with her far away from England? That really bothered Holly. Just how wretched had Angie made his life in his eyes? Because with her new-found perspective on Angie, Holly had to admit that Tom had had awfully good causes to end his engagement with her, given that Angie had become the jealous fiancée from hell.

So had she been as bad, if not worse with Topher? Had he come to wonder whether he'd sold his soul to a very devil incarnate to protect those he loved? Had he come to dread spending even an evening with demanding Angie when, having seen how stable the woman he loved had come across as on the video, what he'd really wanted was someone far more normal? And that was even before you got to the kids, because Angie as a step-mum would have been something evil on a scale even Disney couldn't have whipped up. For all of her professing that her biological clock was ticking like mad, Angie would only ever want her own little prince or princess, not share someone else's child-caring duties.

Worse, what could Holly do about it? She could hardly go to the police and tell them, because what proof did she have, other than that one conversation which implied that Topher had married Angie under false pretences? They could hardly arrest him on that alone, however much of a motive it might seem. Not without a body, anyway. Nor was there any bigamy involved as far as Holly could tell, so nothing illegal at all.

In truth, he now had enough money to both pay Angie alimony, and to keep those whom Holly was increasingly thinking of as his 'real' family in a manner they had hitherto only dreamed of. Even if Angie stripped him of half of his winnings, he was still a wealthy man by anyone's measure – certainly enough that he would seem greedy to be depriving her of her share. Indeed, had he ever told Angie the full extent of his winnings? Had it, perhaps, been an even larger sum? Because Holly knew that the details beyond the word 'millionaire' would have drifted past Angie without sinking in. She would already have been planning her new wardrobe full of designer clothes without pausing for a moment to do the actual sums. So right at the start, Topher could have already siphoned off a couple of million, or more, to the woman and kids he'd rather have been with, and Angie wouldn't have noticed a thing.

What on earth do I do? Holly fretted as she dragged herself out to her car in the morning, already dreading the fact that she wouldn't be home for another two nights.

It didn't help that the weather had turned drizzly again. It wasn't actually pouring with rain, but a grey dampness already looked set to hang on for the whole day. If the day had been bright and sunny, she might have had her mood lifted, but in the dank, dull light it was hard to be optimistic. Instead it was hard to summon any enthusiasm for a day when the trade barely trickled in – normal Sundays were worse than useless for sales, and the fair wasn't making a scrap of difference in terms of extra custom. So much so that it was quite a relief to find that five o'clock had finally come around, and she could shut the door.

She took her time cashing up, then carried the kettle and other stuff around to the flat's door. For the time being she simply put them down in the hall, and then decided to treat herself to a drink in the pub, since for once she didn't have to drive. Her car was way back up the town, tucked away on a small side street, and hopefully where it wouldn't get vandalised. So bracing herself for the unaccustomed experience, she shouldered her handbag and went into the pub.

What she wasn't expecting was for Jesse to be clearing tables, and for him to spot her instantly and come over to speak.

"Great to see you!" he enthused, and actually seemed to mean it.

"Well I don't have to drive tonight," Holly confessed with a wry smile, "so I can risk having a couple of drinks."

"Then the first one is on the house," he said cheerfully. "After all, you're our neighbour here. What would you like? ...Wine, gin, or maybe a beer?"

Slightly taken aback, Holly struggled to decide. Normally her choices were governed by price, which meant that she usually went for a beer on the basis of getting a long drink for less money than with wine or spirits. As if reading her mind, Jesse asked, "Do you like gin? Only we've got a lovely smooth Scottish one behind the bar. Goes great with a Mediterranean tonic. Would you like to try it?"

"That sounds wonderful," Holly admitted. "I'm not a gin expert, but if you say it's good I'll give it a try."

He ushered her to a vacant bar stool at the far end of the bar, as if knowing that she would feel uncomfortable sitting at a table alone, not that there were many empty tables even this early in the evening. When the gin came, it was in a fancy glass with all the trimmings – a far cry from the G&Ts she'd had in Angie's flat on a girl's night in. And the taste was way better than the cheap supermarket gin she'd had at Angie's as well. Yet that brought up another thought, because Angie had never held back from talking knowledgably about the different boutique gins that were still coming on the market in the boom in gin popularity. So why had she never produced a bottle of one of those to share with a group of her supposed closest friends?

Granted, Holly hadn't been the only one at those evenings, but equally there had only been half a dozen of them at most, and the way Angie splashed cash around, it now struck Holly as telling that she would rather drink cheap stuff than share anything good.

"Don't you like it?" Jesse's slightly worried voice broke her thoughts.

"Oh God, no! It's lovely! It's just that it's triggered another thought about my missing friend, and how I don't think I know her as well as I always thought I did."

He came and leaned companionably on the bar by her side, watching all the time that the barmaids were keeping the customers served, but not such a control freak that he needed to keep on at them all the time. Holly liked that. He clearly didn't feel the need to keep on asserting his position.

"So are you thinking that you've been used?" he asked gently. "Forgive me for asking if you feel you can't answer, but after I came and talked to you the other day, I went away and thought about what you said. And the more I thought, the more I felt that you'd been well and truly put upon."

"You're dead right there," Holly sighed, and took another sip of the delicious gin. It didn't matter how much it cost, she was having another one of these.

"Two of our other friends – well *my* friends now, really – keep telling me that I close my eyes to what Angie does." She took another sip and realised that the glass was already nearly empty. "I thought that they were being unfair to her, but in the end we agreed to disagree over Angie, because we're good friends in every other way. Now though..." she shrugged. "Now, I'm not sure what to think. I never, ever thought Angie would treat me like this. Just goes to show how wrong you can be, and what a crap judge of character I am."

Jesse went behind the bar and came back with another of the gins, then waved her hand away as she tried to pay for it. "No, no, I think you need this – and I don't just mean the gin. I mean the night out too. And please, don't be so hard on yourself. You sound like you've been a good friend to her. But you know, people change, and if you're with them all the time, sometimes it's hard to see that change going on, because it's all just little things. Something dramatic everyone's going to notice. But the normal shifts over time are things that people who've been away for years spot instantly, but others hardly realise have happened."

Holly was shocked, but also knew in her heart that he was spot on. Angie had changed a bit, but it was Holly who was different now. It was so many years since they'd been at school together. Years in which Angie had been able to carry on being the flighty teenager in almost every respect, but ones in which Holly had had to grow up fast and take responsibility for herself.

"I think in some ways I've changed more than she has," she confessed to Jesse.

His comfortable, relaxed smile with a question in it did more to ease her into confessions than any badgering by her longer-standing friends. "I think I've grown up but she hasn't," she was finally able to admit. "For me, there have always been consequences. I didn't have the best of childhoods," and hopefully that didn't sound too 'poor me', "whereas Angie had a doting mum and dad, as did most of my school friends. But whereas they've all grown up, got married, had families, and generally turned into fully functioning adults, I'm starting to see that Angie didn't. Hasn't.

"She still sees herself as 'daddy's little princess', and why *shouldn't* she have everything that she wants? Because, in truth, there's never been a time when her mum and dad *haven't* stepped in to give her whatever that was, especially when her boyfriend or whoever didn't. ...Oh God, I sound such a cow trashing my mate like that!"

Jesse leaned in a little further and squeezed her hand comfortingly. "No, you're not! You sound like a friend who's been sticking up for someone for far too long, someone who sounds to me like a very spoiled young woman. My mum and dad moved heaven and earth to give me the best chances possible, but they never held back from making me aware that not everyone had the same advantages. Not that I got everything I asked for by a long way! I was made to appreciate the value of what I was given, even if it was given willingly."

Holly smiled back at him, feeling her pulse flutter a bit at being this close to such a gorgeous man who wasn't an out and out arse from the very start. *Hold it together Holly*, she begged her psyche, *don't start burbling and going all gooey eyed at first contact!* Recovering with, "Then good for your mum and dad. It's only been with Angie going AWOL that her mum, at least, has woken up to the fact that Angie might just have cleared off with no word to anyone just to spite them."

"Wow! That's harsh! And no way to treat your parents, either."

"I know." She took a deep breath and wondered whether she could tell Jesse about Meryl rescuing her, because right now she was desperate to talk to someone. As if reading her like an open book, Jesse went and grabbed a spare barstool and came and sat by her.

"You know that the bar is the modern confessional," he said with a grin. "What gets told to the bar staff stays with the bar staff."

It made Holly laugh, but also made her give a gulp of relief she couldn't have held back for anything. "Oh thank you," she babbled, and frantically hauling a tissue out of her bag, because she had tears already prickling at the back of her eyes. She had to take another swig of the gin to settle herself, but then told Jesse about how it now turned out that it had been Angie's mum all along who had saved her all those years ago. It wasn't until she'd spluttered it all out, most in long and barely coherent sentences, that she realised that Jesse had reached out and covered her hand with his, and was holding it tightly. And looking up into his face, saw nothing but genuine sympathy there.

"That's bloody awful," he said. "Christ, what an awful thing to find out, and even worse right now, when your 'friend' has doubly done the dirty on you."

"Who's done the dirty on her?" one of the barmaids asked, coming over to join them during a temporary lull in customers. The fact that this girl was tall, athletic, and had the lingering tan of Australia along with her accent made Holly think that this might be Jesse's girlfriend. Sure enough, he introduced her as,

"This is Shea-Lea, my fiancée." Then told her much more briefly what had happened to Holly.

"The absolute bitch!" Shea-Lea whistled. "What a way to treat your mate! And poor you, too. That's not the kind of thing you want coming to light just when you've been left holding everything together on your own. Look..." and she pointed out of the side window up to the first floor of the building across the little side alley, "that's our flat up there. So tonight, we'll come and give you a wave to make sure you're okay. And Jesse will give you our mobile numbers. If you're at all worried, just call us, okay?"

"Oh God! That's so kind of you," Holly said with relief, though with an undercoat of envy that they had each other and both were so nice. "I'm just so worried about leaving the place with nobody around when the insurance thinks the owners are just upstairs. I've never had to deal with anything like this in the past. All the other shops I've worked in, I might have had times when I worked alone, but my bosses were always totally separate businesses to whoever owned the building, so of course the insurance covered that and there was no expectation of anyone being there after hours."

Shea-Lea gave a knowing nod, "And I bet never when the boss was a nob of a bloke who might blame you for any damage just out of spite." At that point she hurried back along the bar to serve a group of young men who'd just come in, but her words brought it home to Holly that even though she was having second thoughts about Topher, he was unlikely to be thinking any different about her.

If in truth Topher thought that little of Angie, then it was also no surprise that he'd been so antagonistic towards her. But it also dawned on her, as a third gin miraculously appeared in front of her and continued to dissolve her stress, that it might have a lot to do with why Topher had never wanted her close to Angie. It wasn't jealousy – it was fear! Fear that the pal who had had to do far more standing on her own feet would see through him, and might tell Angie.

In the first instance, losing Angie's money would have been catastrophic for Topher's plans to prop up his other family. Then in the second, he must have been scared stiff that if Holly spotted what Angie was too self-absorbed to notice, that he could become entangled in a dreadful divorce proceedings which his family would also get dragged through. Therefore the avoidance of both disasters had partly hinged on keeping Holly off-balance and at a distance. Was that even behind the dreadful car? Had he hoped that she would refuse outright to use it, thereby making it impossible for her to be with Angie every day?

God, Holly thought, as she valiantly tried not to drink the third gin as fast as she had the others, *he must have been praying that if he made himself as obnoxious to me as possible, that I'd just clear off and leave them be. Angie offering me the top flat must have had him near shitting himself in fright! No wonder the car is such a wreck. He must have been praying for me to say, 'I'm not having that!' and storming off. Not just accepting it and gritting my teeth. Did he think I was already suspicious and hanging on in case Angie needed me?*

That was a worrying thought, because it made sense of why Topher had seemed to deliberately mess things up with regard to setting up the shop. He needed herself out of the picture so she couldn't wreck his plans! Yet right now there was nothing either of them could do about any of it. He didn't know that, as of now, Holly was less likely to rat on him to Angie than he thought, and she had no way of telling him.

She looked up to see one of the young men in the group eyeing her up, and prayed that he wouldn't come over and start chatting her up – which was pretty cockeyed, even for her. Normally she thought she must have some secret disfigurement that only men could see, because in any all-girls outing, she could guarantee that she'd be the one who wouldn't get chatted up, and had prayed that just once that might change. Yet right now, the worst thing she could think of was having to make small talk with a stranger. However, with great tact and skill, Jesse slid past her to the man, said a couple of words she couldn't hear, and the man just went 'oh!', smiled sympathetically at her, and then turned back to his friends.

Jesse, you're a hero, she thought, *and Shea-Lea, I hope you know what a diamond you've got there*. But she was pretty sure that Shea-Lea did.

Outside, the funfair that had appeared all along the High Street, in the car parks, and down one of the side roads, was by now in full swing. Reflections of technicoloured lights flashed brilliantly through the pub windows, and the music blared from the different rides despite there being buildings in between, all blending into a barrage of noise when combining with the squeals of excitement and fear from the faster rides. There was no way she was going to be able to go up to the flat and just have an early night, she realised with a mental groan. And an early night would have been really welcome, whereas she had the feeling that she'd be dragging herself through the next couple of days, but with very little to show for them.

Duncan McAllister 1

Ledbury, July 1645

Duncan McAllister swore at the rabbit that had laid him low. Or rather at the memory of the rabbit, because the beast itself had been caught by his nephew Sorley, and ended up in Goodwife Joan's cooking pot some days ago. Part of his ire was wounded pride. That he, Duncan McAllister, the finest poacher this side of Argyll, who had crept up on many a deer and caught it, whisking it away from under the nose of the laird on whose land it had been before the laird knew a thing, should be brought down by a bloody rabbit hole was downright embarrassing.

Part of it, he knew, was that besides being exhausted, he hadn't expected a rabbit hole in such a well-tended vegetable patch as this house possessed. Normally, one of the men or lads in the household would have seen the cheeky bugger off in short order. But as he now knew, the master of this fine half-timbered house was off fighting with the king, and had taken his men with him, and the mistress had vanished off to the safety of her cousin's house out in the countryside the moment the word 'soldiers' had been mentioned at the Market House. That didn't impress him, because it meant that Goodwife Joan and the kitchen girl Mary had been left alone in the huge house, and potentially prey for any marauding soldiers.

Duncan had no problem fighting any man, but he took a dim view of soldiers going in and beating up and raping women and girls. Stealing food if you had no other choice was one thing – and God himself knew, he and the men he'd marched the length and breadth of England with, had been forced into doing that as their supplies had dwindled and then run out. But helping yourself to the women was not. That was something he'd instilled into young Sorley already, even though the lad was only twelve years old.

That was something else Duncan was berating himself for. Although by Highland standards, Sorley was plenty old enough to have been accompanying him on things like cattle raids, this bloody war with the English was a different matter. Not that he'd had much choice in the matter, not once Lord Elcho had decided to round up all the men he could summon to go and join Earl Leven's army. No, the rub was that he hadn't needed to take Sorley all the way to the tower at Glencarse in the first place. He'd only been going to deliver coin and messages to the McAllister steward there, from the steward at Menstrie Castle. He could easily have gone alone and left the lad behind, which would have meant he'd never have become caught up in this mess at all.

Menstrie Castle in Perthshire was one of the homes of William Alexander, Earl of Stirling, this branch of the McAllister lairds having anglicised their surname some time ago. The laird himself had long been down in London at the court of King

Charles or in Edinburgh, acting as the king's Secretary of State for Scotland for many years now. But the earl's two youngest sons, James and Anthony, were at Menstrie with their tutor, and so there was a full household there.

Not that Duncan was himself a native of Perthshire to know that without being told. No, he was a Highlander born and bred, and his family lived in Argyll on lands owned by the Earl of Argyll, the great Archibald Campbell – a man who had already proven himself a great fighter for the Covenanter cause. Had the Campbell's man at Menstrie not sent him to Glencarse, things would have turned out very differently, so in Duncan's mind this was all that factor's fault.

Once it had all gone so wrong, it hadn't even been as if he could have told Sorley to run for it, while he distracted those who'd come for men. They'd been trapped in the stables, grooming the horses, when Lord Elcho's men had turned up, and though Duncan was a bonny fighter, tackling the twelve hard men all by himself whom Elcho had sent, had been beyond even his capabilities. So they'd shouldered their packs and joined the wretched march to meet with the main force, with nary a chance for the lad to make a run for it. It didn't help that while Duncan had every faith in Sorley's ability to fend for himself and live off the land, the fact that they soon passed beyond anywhere that Duncan knew, let alone Sorley, meant that he couldn't even give the lad directions on how to get home. How on earth they were going to get out of this mess currently defeated Duncan, because by now they were many months' march further south, plus he was sure that they'd at one point been marching in a more easterly direction, only to then turn and come west.

The mess began in September last year when Lord Elcho – the most politically important laird whose lands lay closest to Menstrie – had suffered a crushing defeat at the Battle of Tippermuir. Even under the present circumstances, Duncan could muster a snort of derision for that encounter. Vastly outnumbered, Highlanders led by the legendary General Montrose, and with support coming from the equally renowned Highland warrior Alasdair MacColla, had launched one good Highland charge and put the fear of God and all his archangels into Elcho's local Perthshire militiamen, who had collapsed like so many wet paper bags. It wasn't so much a defeat as a total rout. As a born and bred Highlander, Duncan couldn't help but approve of that. Lowlanders weren't fighters and therefore not worthy opponents. Highlanders were legendary warriors, so no wonder they'd won.

Subsequently short of men, and yet still compelled to fulfil his obligation to provide men to help with the ongoing fight with King Charles, Lord Elcho had then sent some truly hardened ruffians to round up anyone they could find to fill the ranks. Therefore it had been Duncan and Sorley's misfortune to be in the wrong place at the wrong time when they turned up at Menstrie. What Duncan hadn't remotely expected was that rather than heading up to Aberdeen, where last he'd heard of fighting, instead they found themselves subsumed into the ranks of the men marching under the command of the Earl of Callander, and heading south over the border into England to join those under the Earl of Leven at Newcastle.

As far as Duncan was concerned, Newcastle was foreign parts enough, but at least Leven knew his stuff, and they breached the walls and took the city with remarkably few losses, so even then he'd remained optimistic. Surely the fighting would not last if victories came this easily? Given that Leven had played no small part in the great victory at Marston Moor, near York, last year in the July of 1644, that was no surprise. Indeed, it had been following that great battle that Leven had moved his Scottish army back north to Newcastle, which was when Duncan and Sorley had joined his army.

For his part, at that stage Duncan had continued to hope that their time there would be blessedly brief, given that they'd scarcely had time to get used to the camp before Newcastle fell to Leven on the twenty-fifth of October. Instead, while Leven himself cleared off home to Scotland for Christmas as winter truly arrived, the unfortunates like Duncan and Sorley were stuck in Newcastle for the season. He wasn't even amongst those who got sent to fortify Morpeth or Hexham – smaller places he might have engineered their escape from. But then those left in charge at Newcastle were smart enough to keep recent conscripts like Duncan close, only sending the die-hard believers out to the less guarded places.

As March came around, and the weather began to improve, albeit not by much, a nasty rumour began spreading through the camp: Cromwell, ever distrustful of the Scots, was pressing for Leven's army to utilised further south so that they couldn't cause trouble on the Border. Duncan didn't like the sound of that one bit, and the only consolation was that seemingly, neither did Earl Leven. The laird managed to hold off moving in any direction until April had moved into May, but then they were on the march, and it was southwards. They were already at Ripon in Yorkshire when word reached them of Montrose's royalist victory in the far north of Scotland at Auldearn, east of Inverness.

Word again crept out into the camp that Leven didn't want to move too far from the Scottish border in case he was needed back at home to prevent the royalists from taking control of Scotland. For an all too brief few weeks, Duncan dared to hope for a return home, as the army turned northwards once more, then ground to a halt outside of Appleby in Westmoreland. At least from there the border was within striking distance – if only he could get Sorley out, because the lad was now trapped working in the officers' kitchen tent.

When it really went to hell in a handcart was as the month of June rolled around. Suddenly they were on the march for real, and in totally the wrong direction. In his despair, Duncan wondered whether he had offended some heavenly person, despite his heartfelt prayers. Because while a force was left to keep a watch on Carlisle to make sure that the king didn't sneak across the border to join with Montrose, Duncan and Sorley were amongst those who found themselves in a place called Doncaster by the middle of the month. They were told it was still in Yorkshire.

For all the good it did them, it could have been on the far side of the moon.

Across the county border in Leicestershire, a great battle got fought at Naseby on the fourteenth of June, but the Scots weren't part of that. Given that Leven had played his part in the previous large-scale battle the previous year at Marston Moor, Duncan wondered how it was that they weren't involved, but nobody bothered to inform him. Yet when Naseby was reported to be a catastrophic defeat for the king, once again Duncan dared to hope that this might be the end of it all, but it wasn't to be. It seemed that Parliament was determined to crush every bit of Royalist resistance, and since the king's position in the south-west had been weakened, for reasons Duncan couldn't fathom, south and west was the direction they now marched in.

They got to somewhere called Mansfield by the twentieth, and then Nottingham on the twenty-second, and by now Duncan was well and truly lost. What he liked even less was hearing that finally they were likely to come into direct conflict with the forces led by the king himself. They were to march on Worcester – a city, he was told, which was known for its loyalty to the king – and so the start of July found them marching onwards, crossing into the county of Staffordshire at a place called Tamworth. It certainly had a useful looking castle, and somebody said that it had been a great fortification even back in the days when the Vikings had raided the land.

Onwards they went down into Warwickshire through a small place called Birmingham, and then to another market town known as Alcester. Duncan thought it pleasant countryside, and it was clearly fertile, going by the number of prosperous-looking farms, but it lacked the awe-inspiring grandeur of his native Highlands for him. Indeed he was positively homesick by now, though he dared not say so to Sorley, who was also pining for the north.

Quite why they never actually got to Worcester was forever a mystery to Duncan. Instead, they seemed to turn slightly northwards but still westwards, being told that they had to cross a mighty river called the Severn. Duncan didn't give a damn about that. He was more worried by the way they were already having to live off the land, and these lands had already seen armies marching across them the previous year. He pitied the poor folk who lived here, because however good the land was, that didn't help when the crops got trampled, and when you'd barely harvested something, and the next week a horde of famished soldiers swarmed in and took it all off you.

"This is bad, lad," he said to Sorley, because now that they were on the march, Duncan had at least managed to get Sorley back by his side. "We're going to be fighting these folk for every loaf of bread. This isn't food for fighting men. We'll all be as weak as kittens unless we start getting some proper food in our bellies. I haven't seen a decent sized hare in days, and even the bluidy rabbits are looking thin on the ground! If the locals are out trapping them for food, not just keeping them off the crops, we're in serious trouble."

Chapter 7

Holly did at least make a quick dash to one of the food stalls and got herself something hot to eat, then made sure the bottom door was securely locked and went upstairs. For a while, she moved her camp chair to the big window in the first of the side-facing rooms on the first floor where she was camped out, and sat people-watching. The location of this once splendid merchant's house was on the cobbled lane leading up to the ancient minster church in Ledbury. The building Jesse and Shea-Lea's flat was at the rear of, was a Georgian building at ninety degrees to this one at its rear, and with the others in its terrace of the same era facing the ancient Market House at the front, which dominated the High Street. The little alleyway, where *The Renegade* had some benches outside, only led to the backs of a couple of what were now High Street shops on the ground floor, and went nowhere else.

It was good to see folk out having a good time out there. Jesse obviously ran a good bar, because there was no hint of trouble down there. But beyond their building, there was nothing to bring people up the lane apart from the church and another real-ale pub further up, which tended to attract a slightly older and calmer clientele. Yet that very quiet was also what bothered Holly. The rest of the houses on their side were lovely, and many were half-timbered like their building, but people didn't tend to use the front rooms much, if the lack of lights on in them later on was any indicator. Should one of her neighbours hear screams, tonight they were as likely to think they came from the fair rides out in the High Street.

Back when she'd introduced Holly to the shop, all Angie had noticed was the picturesque cobbled lane to the minster.

"Just imagine how many tourists will pass the door!" had been her take on it.

However, Holly had realised far in advance of tonight that for the locals, there was little reason to come and shop up here when they were the only actual shop. A couple of cafes and a local museum, yes, but not retail outlets of any kind.

"It's going to be very quiet and lonely up here between Christmas and Easter," she'd tried to get Angie to see, but Angie wouldn't hear a word of objection.

Now it was Holly sitting up on the cold first floor, wishing like mad that they'd been in a smaller place on the main thoroughfare, where there'd at least be a policeman or two patrolling tonight. She'd brought a couple of fan heaters from home to fend off the night chill, and was glad she'd done so. The room she'd decided to camp in had a lovely old fireplace, but it was blocked by a gas fire which looked like it had seen better days, and Holly had no wish to die of asphyxia tonight if the damned thing leaked. But tucked up the corner and with the door closed, she was out of draughts, and once the funfair closed down, she began to hope that she was going to be able to have a quiet night. True to their word, after the pub closed, she saw Jesse and Shea-Lea in the window opposite and they gave her a cheery wave before drawing their curtains. It was reassuring, though, that they didn't go straight to bed, going by the fact that their living room light stayed on for an hour or two, and by the time it did go out, all was quiet down on the streets.

It was then, when all the noise had gone, and Ledbury settled down to its usual quiet night, that she became aware of the dripping sound from up above again. It wasn't as bad as before, but just when she'd think she'd imagined it, there it would be again, that solitary *plop* of something wet hitting the floorboard. *At least it's not a pipe leak,* she thought, as she rolled herself into the sleeping bag. *That wouldn't just be an occasional drip! And if it was worse the other night when it was bucketing it down, it's probably something just drying out up in the roof space. But that's not my problem, it's Topher's!*

Then it suddenly hit her that maybe Topher wouldn't be around to sort anything at all! *Oh bugger! I'd better go up there before it rains heavily again and stick a few plastic buckets around the place. But not tonight. I'm too tired tonight.*

She must have gone to sleep soon after that, because it was deep into the small hours when she woke up to what she was sure was someone singing. It was very distant, as if out on the main High Street, or further up the lane towards the church. But whoever they were, they weren't a happy drunk. In fact, she would have called it something closer to a mournful lament.

To her relief, there wasn't a soul about when she looked out of the window, just the sign for *The Renegade* swinging slightly in a breeze that wasn't even enough to whistle through the old windows. The 1980's/90's style rock guitar player on the sign was just about visible, with his black jeans, and black hat dipped over one eye, with his bright red guitar slung across his back the most visible thing in the shadows. The only thing she could see moving at all was a cat wrestling with a burger wrapping to get at the discarded contents. Not that she could see far when her view was only across the lane. But after standing there for a few minutes, she couldn't hear the singing anymore, and decided she could safely go back to bed.

Yet as soon as she got back into the room next door, she could hear it again.

"Bloody hell!" she swore aloud. "Have a bit of consideration for the workers, you maudlin sod!"

Grabbing her big torch she marched through to the back room, and squinted as best she could sideways out of the window towards the far end of the alley. But again, there wasn't a soul about, and the singing had vanished. Growling under her breath, she headed back to her bed only to hear the singing again, and this time it froze her to the spot. It was coming from upstairs!

For an instant she thought her heart would stop.

How the hell had anyone got into here? The bottom door was, and had always been, well and truly locked, and it wasn't the kind of flimsy door to jemmy the lock on with ease. Yet upstairs, echoing down the beautiful hanging staircase, was where the song sounded as if it was coming from.

Feeling a sudden and desperate need to pee, she finally managed to move, and scampered into the little loo, situated off the landing. Nothing on God's green earth would get her up to the next floor and the proper bathroom at the back, which she would have to use tomorrow or risk going to work smelly, but not tonight.

But once she came out, a couple of more rational explanations came to her. One of them being that until tonight and seeing the town lit up by the fair, she hadn't realised that this building was taller than the ones on the High Street. Not by much, but it was, and the lane had a slight uphill lie to it, all of which meant that she'd seen the lights on the tops of the huge rides quite clearly even from the first floor, let alone the second. So why wouldn't sound carry as easily? What a twit!

On the other side of the building, it fully butted up to its also slightly shorter neighbour. You couldn't even have passed a piece of paper between them, and she knew that the other building was fully converted into three apartments. But its top flat would only be through the wall from the staircase here, so no wonder she might be hearing stuff from there. Was it even live, or just a rather too loud recording? Especially as the neighbours probably assumed that this place was still empty upstairs, so why would they be considerate?

"You bloody fool, Holly," she chastised herself, as she burrowed into the warmth of her sleeping bag. "It's whoever it is up in *that* top flat, not here. Or it's some drunk howling at the moon in the Market House. Get a grip and go to sleep!"

But the unknown singer lamented on, and all Holly could make out as she drifted in and out of sleep was that he had a strong Scottish accent.

Come the morning she was surprised that her alarm woke her, having expected to be barely asleep at all. So she bundled herself out of bed and then stopped and swore. Damn! No hot water!

Bracing herself to have to have the chilliest of wash-downs in the rather basic bathroom which Angie had briefly shown her, Holly grabbed her clean clothes and towel, and made her way reluctantly up the main stairs to the second floor. She'd simply flipped the switch on the main fused board downstairs when she'd come for the kettle yesterday evening, thinking only of the need for some light on the stairs to avoid breaking her neck, and to be able to run her fan heaters. So it was a bit of a shock to hear some gurgling and spluttering from the pipes as she turned the tap on the bathroom basin on, and then have piping hot water coming out.

"Oh you daft sod," she chastised herself. "You put everything back on, not just the lights, so the immersion heater must have cut in too, even if it was on a timer and the wrong time for now."

With that thought, she tugged the pull-cord on the old-fashioned bathroom heater, and was thrilled to see its solitary electric bar start to glow red. Dear God, in this tiny bathroom she might even be warm when she stripped off! The bathtub had seen better days, but it was passably clean, and so Holly dared to run herself a bath, even happier to discover that she had a bath-bomb in her wash-bag too. Plus it said everything for how thrown off kilter she'd been last night, that she'd set her alarm for the same time as at home, but of course, that factored in an hour's journey to get in, which today she didn't need.

So all in all, she returned to her makeshift bedroom warm and clean, and feeling a good deal more optimistic than she had yesterday. Grabbing her coat, she was even happier to recall that the local *Greggs* was literally just around the corner, because all she'd been able to face last night had been a hotdog and a few fries. With that being pretty much all she'd had since the previous breakfast, she was now ready to gnaw on her own leg she was that hungry. With *Greggs* being the kind of place that catered for takeaway breakfasts, they opened long before the smarter cafes were and would be open now.

Coming back clutching an omelette breakfast roll, a bacon baguette, and a bacon and cheese wrap, she knew she had enough to replenish her energy and have some left over for lunch. It wasn't the healthiest of diets to have every day, but for this next couple of mornings it was hardly going to do much damage. Indeed, with the sun shining, and the fun fair still up and poised for the coming day, she felt more as if she was on holiday. *An evening in a pub, a night camping out, and then bacon for breakfast!* she thought joyfully, as she relished another bite of the roll. *You haven't had time out like that in ages!*

Indeed, that realisation was something of a wake-up call, especially coming back clutching the hot rolls and seeing Jesse opening up the pub for the cleaners, and him giving her a cheerful wave through the glass door. Unshaven and tousled, he was even sexier than he'd looked spruced up, and Holly felt deeply envious of Shea-Lea. But she also recognised that here were neighbours who she'd actually spoken to more in these few days than she had the people who lived around her flat in Worcester. All she ever saw of those was them scurrying out to work and back in, much as she did, all of them in too much of a hurry to pass pleasantries, like commenting on the nice weather, let alone anything more meaningful. Here, she was beginning to realise, there was a community. Somewhere very different to her cluster of social housing flats, which had been tacked on to a posh new-build estate as part of the builder's obligation to provide affordable housing, but which wasn't wanted by the rest of the householders.

God, you needed a change, she told herself, as armed with the trusty kettle, she went back down to the shop. *Angie might have done this in all of the wrong ways, but she was right about that.* Well she didn't want to become Angie's tenant for her home as well as her job, not after all of this, but maybe seeing if she could move her own flat to somewhere around here might be a good idea. Somewhere where she could walk to *The Renegade* where she felt safe as a woman on her own, and could at least get out once in a while. Moreover, if Jesse himself was spoken for, he certainly seemed to be attracting more of a younger age group to the pub than the family-filled eating houses she had nearer to her flat. Might there even be a chance of a date? Because that had been a rarity for far too long.

Filled with her new-found determination, once again she didn't open up straightaway, going downstairs to the office and opening the safe, but this time she didn't just put her basic bills to one side out of the takings – she sorted all of it out into what she could reasonably spend. Fear of being cheated by Topher had overnight turned into fear of being hung out to dry by Angie, and that was a very different matter. Nor was that helped by the re-orientated and disconcerting belief, which refused to go away, that Topher and not Angie was the one lying dead and undiscovered in the Caribbean. So if that was the case, and Angie had got her hands on his bank account details, how much of his money was left to do things like pay for this shop? Because Angie would spend first and think later – that was wholly in character even before this.

Holly wouldn't cheat any of their suppliers, but Angie had been the one who wanted this building and no other for their business, and so if anyone came chasing for bills for the whole place, Holly was prepared to put her hands in the air and say, "it's nothing to do with me. You'd better find her, because I don't know where she is," which was nothing less than the truth.

You've played the wrong woman for a fool, Angie, Holly thought angrily. *You've never given a thought how I've managed to survive all these years on so little. But it's from making sure I set every penny I earn aside, even if I don't need it there and then, because I've learned the hard way that rainy days can be just around the corner. Well you've become my rainy day, and I'm damned if I'm going to let you drag me down with you. Your mum and dad will come around and pick you up and sort you out eventually. I'm on my own. I should have learned by now, you can't count on other people – not even the ones closest to you.*

Indeed, having realised that she had electricity in the flat, at least for the time being, Holly was rethinking staying there, because whoever was paying the electricity bill for upstairs, what little she'd use would be something she could pay if pressed, but was also the least Angie could pay in compensation for the mess she was dragging her through. *Why am I opening up on Mondays when they're dead?* she pondered as she refilled the racks of bath-bombs and candles. *If I come in on Tuesday morning, then stop here overnight until the weekend, that'll save me a mint on travel.*

Heaven alone knew what was wrong with the wreck of a car, but she'd swiftly discovered that it guzzled petrol like a teenager on cheap cider. So cutting down her journeys from fourteen a week to just two was going to save her a fortune. And it might even be possible to catch the train in from Worcester on the Tuesday and go back on it on the Friday, just bringing the car in on Saturday if public transport wasn't viable on a non-weekday.

She'd not considered the train before, because Angie had rushed the opening date forwards to the extent that Holly had literally finished working at her old job on the Saturday, and started setting up with Angie on the Monday, with Angie vanishing on the Wednesday. Plus, Holly had been so used to catching buses to and from work it had never occurred to her that this time she might be able to do it by train. Yet with the station only a brisk walk away, as one of the locals had since told her, and without Angie here demanding that they be open at nine and never, ever closing before five-thirty at the earliest, Holly was realising that with luck, she might not need to risk life and limb driving the dreadful car, as well as saving money.

Doing a quick online search, she realised that a nine o'clock train from Worcester would get her in in time to open up by ten, and as long as she shut at five, she was likely to catch the six o'clock train back, with most times the journey only taking about twenty-five minutes. Granted, she would have a decent walk to and from the train station at her home end too, but if she'd been able to switch off and rest for the journey, that wasn't as bad as it might be.

I'm taking control. I'm taking control, she kept saying to herself as her mantra for the day, and felt much better for it. After her erratic childhood, nothing scared her rigid like feeling that everything was flying away from her, so this sense of getting a grip on the reins of this runaway horse she'd been riding for the last few weeks was a balm to her shattered soul. What made her sad, though, was realising that once again she'd been able to rely on nobody.

It's the story of my life, she thought with a sigh as she put the cash float in the till and went to open up. *When push comes to shove, even the people I sometimes think will help me let me down in ways I didn't expect.*

How do other people get through life? Who do they rely on? Parents? Partners? And why does that not work for me? What on earth have I done wrong to deserve this?

Duncan McAllister 2

The one bright spot in their lives was that it rapidly became clear that while the king might be calling upon the local militiamen to support him, no sooner had they been levied than they deserted. It was the reverse side of the problem the Scots had – they needed the food, and the militiamen were more motivated to defend their own farms and crops than the king's honour. Therefore there was no major force in their path that they might need to fight when already struggling, only small groups of local men. On the other, the further west they got through Worcestershire, the worse the roads got. One thing that had really stuck out to Duncan, as they'd traipsed their weary way southwards through Yorkshire and the Midlands, was how much better the road were than in most of Scotland. Now, though, they were on the kind of roads that became thick with mud in wet weather, and were full of potholes and stones, very much like they knew at home. The difference there was that Duncan had never tried to march along one after several thousand men and horses had already churned it up in front of him.

Filthy dirty and sore of foot, they limped through the market town of Bromyard, though knowing its name did little to inform Duncan. Their arrival was deeply unpopular with the townsfolk, who barricaded their doors and did everything they could to ensure that the Scots didn't rob them of their food, for with it being well into July, many had decided to harvest what grain they could already and hide it as best they were able. It meant that Leven, or rather his captains, had little choice but to let their men scavenge as they went. It did nothing to help the pace of the march, nor in keeping track of men, but the only alternative was to let the men get weaker and weaker from hunger. Cavalry played an important part in how this war was fought, yet finding fodder for the horses was another problem.

The army ploughed valiantly onwards over the increasingly hilly ground until two days later they arrived in Ledbury to no warmer reception. The final straw for Duncan was that it had become increasingly clear that there was no means of taking the wounded with them. All the horses were needed for those fighting on them, and they'd long since found that it was pointless liberating spare horses when they could barely scrounge enough to feed the ones they had. So the moment the rabbit had struck, and Duncan had collapsed on the ground with his leg at a strange angle, he and Sorley had known that nobody would be coming to help them out – indeed might not even notice they were missing for a few days. The only thing that might happen would be that one of the men would come and get Sorley, and take him onwards without Duncan – and Duncan had no intention of letting that happen! Come hell or high water, he was getting Sorley back home, not leaving him to die in this alien place.

"Are you a Covenanter yourself, Master McAllister?" Goodwife Joan had asked him, when she and Sorley had helped Duncan hop into the house on his remaining useful leg. Sensing that this was a loaded question, Duncan had answered carefully,

"I had nay choice but to follow a Covenanter laird."

Joan had pursed her lips at this, and given him a weighing stare while he took in her very plain dark skirts and bodice, and the simple, unadorned cap on her head. Even a servant might trim her cap a little more than that if she wished, and so Duncan guessed that if not an actual Covenanter – because such a thing only existed in Scotland – she might belong to one of the English Presbyterian churches which leaned that way.

"My parents signed the Covenant in thirty-eight, as did everyone in our family, including me," Duncan confessed. "But it was more because we didn'a want the king telling us how to pray. We didn'a want to *fight* the king over it. For myself, I was happy enough with the way things were the next year, when there was a lot o' sword rattling at the border, and then the king promised to leave us in peace – or at least that's how the word filtered down to the likes o' us." He shook his head in disgust. "I didn'a think the king would go back on his word like that. The man has nay honour."

"What did he do?" Mary asked, wide-eyed at this news they hadn't heard.

Duncan sniffed. "The man said he'd call a general assembly right away to discuss what our leaders wanted, and a full parliament in Scotland only a few weeks later. On our side, our leaders promised to disband the army. But when the call went out for the assembly, it included those very bishops the Covenant wanted to do away with." He waved a hand in the general direction of the outside world. "Down here ye have a cathedral and a bishop in every shire, wi' lots of wee towns in between, so you ken your bishops. Up in Argyll where I was born, I hadn'a a clue where the bishop might be, let alone who he was, tucked away as we were in a glen in Argyll, miles away from anywhere."

He saw their astonished faces. "Oh, I ken what a cathedral is, and I ken the abbey down at Saddell, where the great Somerled, Lord of the Isles lies. We're no' heathens wi'out kirks."

"Who?" Mary asked. "Lord of *where*?"

The two women saw the horror at their ignorance on the faces of Duncan and his young nephew.

"Ye no' ken who *Somerled* is?" the lad said, astonished at such ignorance.

Mary and Joan shook their heads, Joan at least, a bit worried that this might be such an offence as to have this fierce fighter of a man turn nasty, even with a broken leg.

"Steady, Sorley," Duncan cautioned, "they probably dinna ken a single place north o' the border beyond Edinburgh." He thought for a moment, wondering how to explain this. "How far west are we here?" he began with. "Are we near Wales yet?"

"Oh yes," Joan said with certainty. "We're on the east side of Herefordshire here, but the west side is the border with Wales," though the way she spoke of it, to her it must be the most heathen outpost of civilisation.

Trying to ignore her antipathy to Celts, Duncan continued, "Ah! Well imagine following the sea from Wales all the way north, past places in England, and on up to Scotland." Not that he'd ever seen Wales in person, he was just remembering a map he'd seen years ago in the big castle at Inveraray. "That far north, it's no' a smooth coast, but one wi' lots o' islands off it. Some are big, like Islay, Jura, Mull, and Skye. But many are just wee islands wi' just few folk on them. You'll have heard o' Mull on account of wee Iona being just a whisker off its coast." He saw blank incomprehension on the women's faces. "Iona. Home and resting place o' St Columba?"

"If you say so," Joan said weakly, but clearly not having a clue who St Columba was.

"*Ach*, we're amongst heathens, Uncle!" young Sorley groaned, appalled.

"We are most certainly not heathens, boy!" snapped Joan. "We are good, God-fearing Christians!"

"Then how come ye dinna know of the saint who brought the Christian faith to Scotland?" demanded the lad. "He was gied Iona by the King o' Dál Riata himself, who invited him over to convert his folk. I haven'a schooling, but even I know *that*."

"Where's Dál Riata, then?" demanded Mary, clearly spoiling for a fight with this lad who was even younger than her, and who she thought had no right to come into their home and start making a fool of her.

"Dál Riata," Duncan cut in to explain, "was an ancient kingdom that covered all o' the western seaboard o' Scotland. What is now Argyll and a bit more, but that's what it was hundreds of years ago." He was doing his best to hang on to his patience, because he recognise what Sorley was too young to see, which was that they were at the mercy of these two women. Upset them, and one or both of them might go running to the nearest militiamen, or clubmen as he'd been told some of the groups around here were called, and betray their presence here.

Duncan was under no illusions as to what might happen to two isolated Scots whom nobody knew were here. That was the trouble with this bloody awful fight they'd been dragged into. Their friends were already marching onwards, of that he was sure, because the army had already passed a second night at Ledbury so that Earl Leven could send out letters in response to ones he'd received on getting here. He surely wouldn't linger longer.

A couple of men who served in the tents of the main men said that there was disagreement between Leven and Cromwell going on in those letters, but none of them knew what that might means for themselves. Therefore Duncan feared that it might be a while before they came back this way again, if ever – for there was no guarantee that they would march back the way they had come – and Duncan had no idea where he was, in truth, not even in terms of where their next camp was intended. Were they someplace he had even a vague familiarity with, he might manage to find a way to hide himself and Sorley, but not here. He might limp off with the help of a crutch, only to run straight into a garrison in some place he'd never heard of, let alone knew it was in his path.

So he began again, "On his mother's side, Somerled was grandson to King Alexander of Scotland. Now Alexander had no male heirs, and the crown went to his younger brother, David. Already there had been some question of who was rightful king, because the heirs of King Malcolm II were a bit doubtful in that all were via female lines, if ye ken what I mean?"

"A son should inherit," Joan said firmly, on surer ground on this at least, even if she'd never heard of these kings.

"Aye, he should, but if no sons are available it gets a wee bit fraught, ye ken? So Somerled held the west for King David – even tried to unseat him at one point, but that failed. Well King David was no' such a good king, so it's probably no bad thing that ye had two fighting for the throne down here in England at the time, because had it been King Henry – who followed them and spawned Richard the Lionheart – Somerled might ha' been fighting *him*!"

"And your Somerled would have lost!" young Mary said with some glee.

"He wouldn'a!" Sorley bit back. "He was a grand warrior. He only died because he was betrayed by men who saw a way to become more powerful themselves by controlling the young new king. *And* he was having to fight on two fronts on account o' the Vikings causin' trouble again."

Quickly intervening to prevent a full spat ensuing, Duncan said, "I was telling you this no' just fer the history lesson."

Yet Mary wasn't going to give up. "How do you remember all this?" she challenged him.

"Because our heritage is in our names," Duncan said simply. "Where I live, it's much harder to have all your family written down aside from baptisms, marriages, and burials in the kirk. For the rest o' us, we ken our lineage by being taught it at our ma and pa's knees. It matters for us. It matters because o' who we owe allegiance to. Lairds who we have nay choice but to fight for."

"*Oh,*" was Joan's gasp of understanding. "So this Somerled you were talking about before? He's important because of that?"

Duncan nodded. "Somerled remains a great man in the eyes of those o' us from his auld kingdom because he was the last truly Celtic contender for the Scottish throne. Ye see, when King David's grandson, Malcolm, inherited the throne, he was too quick to bend his knee to the English king. That was the King Henry I just mentioned, ye ken. But that line had no' exactly been *English* kings fer that long, so it was thought a bit o' a cheek to be claiming the Scottish one as well. Well Malcolm didn'a live verra long either, and it was another grandson o' David's, William, who inherited.

"But what I was coming to is that it wasn'a until *that* William that we even *had* a bishop o' Argyll. Aye we had kirks and abbeys, but no' a bishop. *That's* why I know the abbey where Somerled's remains lie, and that's why the lad here is called Sorley. That was Somerled's family name, ye ken? He's named after a great Celtic warrior."

Young Sorley stood a bit prouder at that, and was gratified that the two women looked at him with rather more awe than they had before.

"But that's why the great Norman abbeys didn'a get their hands on so many kirks and monasteries in the west as they did in the east," Duncan carried on. "We're more spread out, and more remembering of the auld ways. We've kenned the word o' God and the Bible fer a long, long time, but parts o' Scotland have only had bishops foisted onto them in the last few hundred years. And that came about because o' Scottish lairds marrying wi' yer Norman English ones, and them wantin' their fancy bishops from the big abbeys in Normandy. Our Celtic kirk didn'a fleece the poor folk fer enough coin fer their liking! Plus, some bloated kirkman who spends more time in Edinburgh polishing his career in politics than in listening to God is no' going to get much respect our way. And many o' our folk are still Catholic."

He saw the distaste on Joan and Mary's faces and hurriedly added, "I'm no talkin' about the ways o' Spain and France here, ye ken, but the auld Catholic faith. That's why I was blathering on about St Columba. A man o' great faith. A man o' simplicity. Someone who brought the word o' God to Scotland from Ireland, wi'out all the trappings and the incense, and the grovelling to gold-encrusted icons.

"I went on pilgrimage to Iona wi' my pa and his older brother – that's young Sorley's grandpa, by the way – and St Columba lived a life o' poverty, contemplation, and prayer. It's a bleak wee place, is Iona in the winter. Nay surfeit o' luxuries there! Even growing vegetables would be a challenge out there, wi' the salt wind tearing in off the sea. And it would be fish or sheep to eat, if ye could catch the fish or when a sheep died – 'cause the sheep were a lot more valuable for their wool than their meat."

"Not like Archbishop Laud, then?" Joan said, referring to King Charles' man who'd caused so much upset and with the beginnings of understanding.

"No. Nothing like him." Duncan agreed. "So even the Catholics amongst us might ha' been for the king – because they believe in the divine right o' kings to rule – but that doesn'a mean that they're all for every change King Charles wanted to make. It's way more subtle up north as to who is on which side."

Joan exhaled heavily, her own doubts coming to the fore "I think down here, what nobody wants is a return to the persecutions of Protestants that happened under the late Queen Bess' sister, Bloody Mary. We were all relieved – or rather my parent's generations were – when her heir was your King James, who was proving himself to be a proper Protestant ruler with a Protestant queen. ...And that was all peace and prosperity up until his son took over. I don't know where King Charles gets his ideas from, but they weren't what we saw from King James."

"Spain is the short answer," Duncan told her, and saw her surprise that he would know that much. To him it was just as astonishing that someone who lived not a hundred and fifty miles from London should know less than he, who had lived closer to five hundred away. But then the political stakes had been so much higher for men like himself in Scotland for much longer.

"When he was but a prince," he told them wearily, "he was sent to court a Spanish princess. The wedding didn'a take place, but the young prince was aye impressed wi' the absolute control yon Spanish king had o'er his people. Really took his fancy, it did. And he resolved that when his time came, he wouldn'a pussyfoot around his courtiers like his father had done."

"How on earth do you know this?" wondered Joan.

"*Huh*!" Duncan huffed. "Because when I was younger, I had to serve our laird, Archibald Campbell, Earl of Argyll, that's why. I was a mere man-at-arms in the big hall when other lairds came a'calling. There to provide security from anyone who might want to come and cause a ruckus and disrupt things. But it meant I was there when the politics were debated, and I remember all too well how they all were feeling they were caught in a cleft stick!"

He realised he needed to make things a bit clearer. "I'm young Sorley here's cousin, ye see? His pa is the one who got the family croft and the allegiance to Earl Campbell. But places like ours can only support one family. I was always going to have to find my own way in the world, and serving Earl Campbell was an easy one. It gave him our family's due service and proved our loyalty – so securing his family's place, and because o' that, my own family's place wi' their wee cottage on the croft. It also meant my sisters were safe while they were at home. And I was no' my father's favourite by a long way, that's my older brother."

He gave a wicked grin. "I was too much the young rogue, though once I'd left, our father soon learned who had been the teaser of our sisters, and it wasn'a me! ...Which is verra much the position young Sorley found himself in. He too has an older brother who is the spitting image o' their father in looks and behaviour. My cousin Archie begged me to take the wee troublemaker off his hands and foster him for him, me being often a long way fra' home, ye understand? But Sorley's been a good lad and biddable too, while his older brother's been revealed as the troublemaker." Duncan gave a wry grin. "I dinna think that young Sorley is any too keen to return home anymore after his time wi' me, are ye lad?"

Sorley's face split into a wide grin as he shook his head.

"The lad has a talent fer soldiering," Duncan confirmed. "And Archie might beg all he likes fer Sorley to come back, but he's shit his nest wi' Sorley, shoving him off like that fer no reason o' the lad himself's." He leaned in confidentially. "From what I saw, the croft will go to wrack and ruin wi' Sorley's brother Sandy in charge, and I dinna see young Sandy sticking around fer long when it does happen. So young Sorley going back wi' some spoils o' war in his pocket will allow him to put the croft to rights, and gi' him a nice place to rest when his fighting is done."

"But why bring him all the way into England?" Joan asked, beginning to realise just how young Sorley was.

"Aye. Well I didn'a ken quite how that was going to turn out," Duncan confessed. "To be frank I thought we'd stop at the border as we did before, no' come *into* England...let alone come *this* far! ...But once we were in the army and marching, it was no' that easy to get out o' it, if ye get my drift? Past Berwick I kenned north and south by the sun and the stars, but *where* we were in relation to the border, well, that was a different matter. And once we were a way away, at least wi' the army we were no' as vulnerable as two Scots on our own. I had no wish fer us to be lynched by a mob!"

"No, I can see that that wouldn't have been wise," Joan admitted, feeling rather more sympathy for the two now. "Well you are welcome to stay here until you are fit to move on," she dared to say, hoping that this act of charity would not come back to haunt her, especially with the breadth of Duncan's shoulders and the obvious muscles in those arms.

"Greatly appreciated, madam," Duncan said politely, and with a smile that did all sorts of things to Joan's equilibrium.

No man had the right to set her pulse all a flutter with his smile the way he did. And how blue were those eyes? She'd not seen a man with eyes the colour of a clear, bright, summer sky before, and certainly not along with hair the colour of burnished copper. Duncan McAllister was an exotic arrival in her quiet, widow's life, and she had the feeling that it would never be quite the same again.

Chapter 8

Understandably, with the two car parks closest to the town centre still shut off for the second day of the fair, it was a very quiet day trade-wise, but Holly refused to fret over that. Hopefully the following weekend would be brisk once the locals returned, so as long as she had some good days then, there really wasn't any cause for concern. And as the afternoon drew on and the fair began to wake up, this time Holly had no qualms about shutting up early and going up to the flat. Later on, she'd promised herself, she'd go down to the pub and have a couple of those lovely gins Jesse had made her, but for now, she wanted to explore the upstairs properly.

All she'd had to date was a couple of whirlwind tours with Angie, when she'd not really had chance to truly look, Angie being in full flow about what changes she was going to make, and how her interior designer was soon going to sort it out. It meant that looking back with clearer eyes, Holly could now see what she'd missed. This hadn't been Angie in normal high-spend shopping mode, wondering which of two indulgences she should take, or both, with neither being essential or that considered a purchase. This had been Angie presenting her with a done deal.

Something Holly was kicking herself for not having spotted sooner.

Since when had Angie been that decisive about a whimsical purchase? The short answer was never! The only times Holly could ever recall her being like that was when it was something she'd been planning for a long time. What had thrown Holly this time was that in the past, those decisive moments had always been obvious total disasters once Angie had come clean and told her the full scenario. The kind of things which Angie had known – even with someone who was as on her side as Holly – would instantly be meet with a chorus of horrified groans, and begging her to take it/them back, get a refund, or whatever other options was open to her. So the fact that this had seemed to be positively reasonable for Angie, had thrown all of Holly's warning systems off. In fact, all she could really remember was Angie saying something about getting someone to rip all, 'that gloomy wood panelling off and put some luxurious wall paper up,' to which Holly had replied,

"Ange! You can't do that! This is a Grade II listed building! You can't do what you like with it!"

And Angie's reply of, "I've bought it, and if I want it ripped out, out it comes! What can they do, anyway, once it's gone?"

The fact that, at the same time and in a grim repeat of several previous nightmares, Holly herself had been going through hell with one of the store's junior managers, determined to get her out for no other reason than he didn't like women, had somewhat dulled her ability to care about Angie's decorating dilemmas right then. Moreover, she'd thought at the time that the purchase would take far longer than it had, and that she'd have to stick her own bloody awful job out at least until she could find something else – which meant not rocking the boat with the said manager. And of course, it was also before Angie had dropped the additional bomb of them opening the long-dreamed-of shop downstairs in a scant few weeks' time, thus giving Holly a way out, all of which meant that she now found herself viewing the old building with totally fresh eyes.

Coming up the lovely old oak staircase, there were no windows facing onto it on the first floor, the only natural light coming from the tall windows a full floor up again. Even so, Holly thought it was crying out for someone to hang a beautiful chandelier from that second floor ceiling, because even by the dreadful, stark strip-light, the staircase was a stunning piece of craftsmanship. So much so, that Holly felt herself being draw to go up another floor, which was hard to resist. But she'd promised herself that she'd look around each floor in turn so that she got a proper sense of what was where up here, and so she resisted the urge.

Turning onto the landing, she headed to the two big front rooms, which once upon a time must have been where the medieval merchant and his family had entertained their peers. Yet walking into the first room she came to, Holly thought it a rather unpleasant room. The low ceiling brought the supporting dark beams down close enough to feel claustrophobic despite being a large floor space, and while it had windows onto the street and the side, the heavy oak panelling made it a gloomy place. There was something deeply unsettling about this room, and Holly couldn't imagine what it would take to make it into a pleasant lounge where she would want to linger.

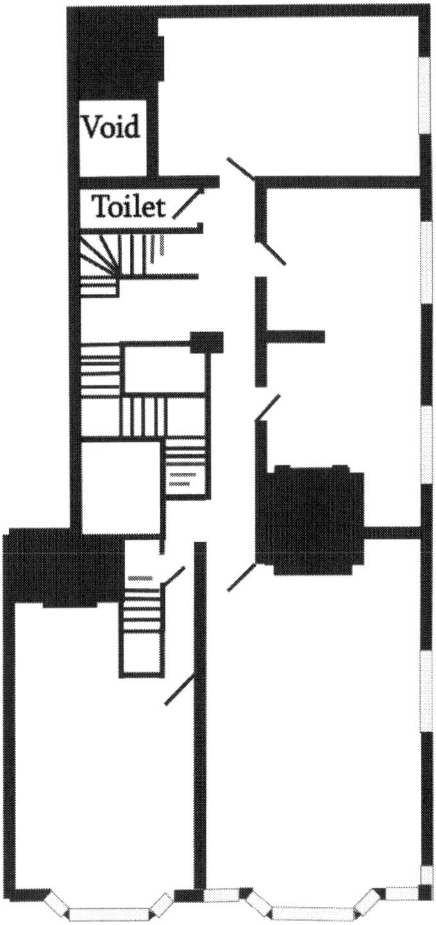

First floor plan

Nor was the other, slightly smaller front room any more charming on second visiting. It too had a grim atmosphere about it, and was equally dark. Both rooms had been used as offices in the recent past, which made the homely atmosphere of the next room back along the landing, where she'd overnighted, all the more curious upon reflection, now that she wasn't just running in and out to set stuff up. Set back along the length of the building parallel to the landing, a huge chimneystack divided it from the front rooms, with fireplaces here and in the main front room. Dividing the room in half lengthwise was a bulk of wall, wood panelled like the rest of the room, which partially protruded across the room's width, hinting that they might have been intended as two separate rooms once upon a time, even if by the time of the panelling they'd been made into one.

There was no door between the two halves, only a wide arch taking up the other half of the divide, and Holly wondered whether this might have been the actual family's space. The front rooms could have been where they entertained, but this might have been an altogether more private space. Certainly the oak panelling flowed consistently from the front half around the partial divide and into the rear half. A second door led out of the rear room onto the landing again, and the solitary loo on this floor was across the landing from it.

The only other room on this floor was the far back one. A room wider than it was deep, it ran behind the double room she'd slept in, the landing, and the loo, and with only the one window in the short end which looked onto the alleyway, it let in very little light. Yet for all of its stygian gloom, this back room wasn't cold and almost hostile, as the front ones were.

"What the heck went on in the front to make it feel like that?" Holly wondered aloud, as she closed the back room's door, and made her way back past the loo to the staircase, and went up a floor.

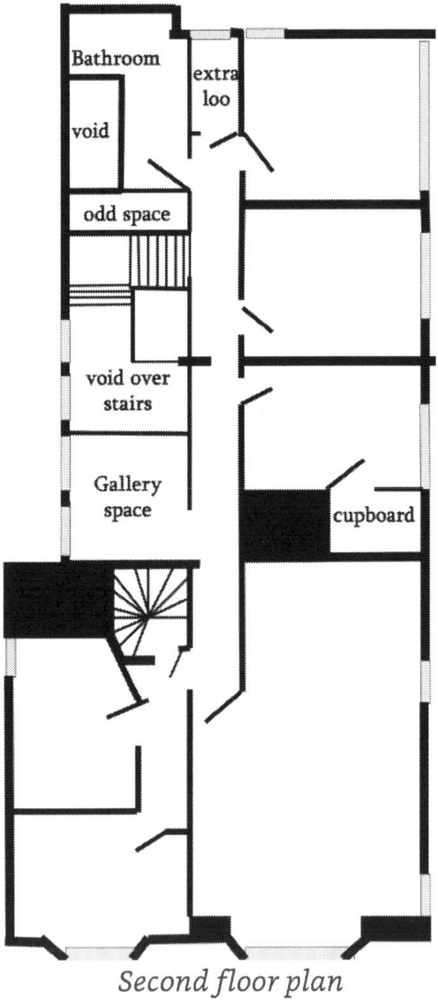

Second floor plan

Looking down the stairwell was an unsettling experience. An unexpected wash of fear came over her, and a desire to run from something dangerous. On top of that was something which might have been simply vertigo, but which felt suddenly as though she was about to topple over. ...No, not topple ...be *pushed* over!

"What the heck?" she gulped, pulling back from the heavy oak railing. There was no way anyone would accidentally fall over that thing, it was too high, let alone it giving way. Five hundred odd years later and it was still as solid as the day it had been put up, so why would she feel like that? Yet something was sending shivers of fear up and down her spine that had nothing to do with the here and now.

It was enough to have her moving swiftly away from the balustrade and down the corridor towards the front of the building again. And here was the lesser staircase which led up to the top floor where Angie had tried to push Holly into taking as her own flat. That now rang false with her, especially as it had come on quite late in the proceedings. Angie hadn't mentioned it the first time she'd shown Holly the house, only once the shop was mentioned. *What was that all about, Ange?* she wondered. *Why were you pushing me so hard? Because it surely wasn't out of consideration for me or I wouldn't be here like this now!*

What surprised her rather more was the way that there was now a lock on the door and no sign of the key. Had she imagined it in her previously stressed state, or had that very modern and high-tech lock not been there before? And if not, why had Angie felt the need to have it put on now? Because it wasn't that she didn't trust Holly – not with so much money tied up in the shop and Holly cheerfully being dumped upon to deal with it.

Sighing in frustration at the peculiarities of Angie's mind in those last weeks, at least it settled one thing for Holly: if there was a leak up there in the roof, she had no way of getting to it, so it couldn't be blamed on her if it got worse. *You'll have to get your own buckets and do your own mopping up,* she mentally sighed, already past caring what magnum tantrums that would generate from Angie at having to do her own clearing up. But without Angie's endless chattering on at her, Holly was also now able to notice that that sense of being hunted and frightened was even strong at this stair's door, yet faded as she went into the biggest room at the front on this floor.

"Ooh! That's odd," she found herself gasping, because although this room was freezing cold, there was none of the oppressive atmosphere of the room below it. It was no lighter, having a smaller main window looking down onto the cobbled lane, although with the side window further back than it was in its downstairs version, it gave the back of the room a better distribution of the gloom, so why did it feel so much less oppressive up here? Again, heavy wood panelling sucked up the light like a sponge, and the ceiling was so low that any man of six-feet-four or more would be in danger of cracking his head on the supporting beams and strip lights. But with a bit of care, this time she thought that the room felt as if it could be a nice lounge – especially with yet another of the grotty gas fires gone, and the lovely old fireplace opened up, and a roaring fire in it.

Above the lesser of the oppressive first floor rooms, on this floor there were two smaller individual rooms, which Holly guessed might have been family bedrooms once upon a time. And it was now that she thought she might have an answer to her late-night singer. The front one of the two bedrooms had a front-facing window, but the back one had a window to the side, making it blindingly clear that this was now on a level with the adjoining house's roof. It meant Holly found herself looking out across the tiles towards what was clearly a little window into a room up in the attic space next-door. Not that it was a mean space by any means. It wasn't some cramped loft conversion, but looked like one of two or more full attic rooms, created under the eaves when the Georgian house itself was built – probably to house the original family's servants.

When Holly went back out onto the landing and back to the main staircase where there were now the tall windows, she could see through the leaded panes that whereas this house was deeper than it was wide, next-door was the opposite. Double-fronted, but only two rooms deep, the building itself had ended and didn't block the light to the stairs. Had she been able to get closer to the windows to be able to look out of them, she felt she would probably be looking out onto her neighbours' garden.

Well that's your answer, she told herself sternly. *It was probably someone a bit pissed who stumbled through that archway they have through to where they park their cars. There's no gate on that, so it could easily be done*. If they were heavy sleepers next-door, or in the case of the downstairs flat had even decamped to a friend's house, knowing that the fair would be noisy, no wonder they didn't noticed the trespasser. *I bet they won't be happy if he's been ill on their drive*, she thought sagely, feeling even more comfortable about spending more time here now that she had a logical explanation for what she'd heard.

To the side of the second floor above where she'd slept last night and again looking down to *The Renegade's* outside benches and tables, there were two properly separated rooms, and once more Holly thought these might have been family bedrooms, or guest rooms, because they were nicely panelled – too nice to have been servants' rooms. A final back bedroom, and the bathroom plus an extra separate loo completed this floor, making Holly wonder whether she should think about moving her bed up to the room above where she'd been, if she was going to make a habit of this. It was all very well being able to wave at Jesse and Shea-Lea, she realised, but unless she was going to put curtains up, she was the one who was going to have no privacy.

Whereas all she looked out onto on their side up here was once again merely the roof tiles. Plus it was a much smaller room, having what looked like some sort of storage room or potentially a walk-in wardrobe cut out of part of it in the huge chimneybreast alcove, created out of the massive chimney stack which had its foundations down in the cellars, and cut the pub's front and back almost in half with its bulk. When she tried the door, though, it had swollen with the damp and wouldn't open but the light bulb had gone in this room, meaning she couldn't even see how it was stuck. So that would remain a mystery space for now, but at least up here the fireplace was both exposed and of a more modest size. If it should turn bitterly cold, there was a chance she could light a proper fire in it,.

On the other hand, if there are old birds' nests up there, you don't want to set the chimney on fire, she warned herself. There was certainly a strong whiff of something deeply unpleasant, she now noticed on the second investigation of the room. No, maybe she wouldn't stay here, because that didn't smell like just a pigeon rotting up the chimney but something much bigger. Possibly some poor cat that had explored a bit too far into the chimney stack and come to grief – and both the thought of it dying trapped and frightened, and the truly grim smell, were enough to convince her to stay where she was for now. The little corner where she had her camp bed was private enough, and it was hardly as though Jesses was going to spy on her when he had the lovely Shea-Lea right there with him.

"Let's get through these next few nights," she told herself sternly as she went back downstairs, making sure that she'd turned all of the lights out. Her one alteration this far had been to find the immersion heater in the cupboard of the bathroom, and make sure that its clock was right so that she'd have hot water tonight and in the morning. *Don't plan too far ahead,* she cautioned herself as she decided to go in search of something a little healthier for dinner tonight from the fair's food trucks. *For all you know, the police could arrive within days and the whole place be shut up by lawyers as they try to sort this mess out. Put your energy into finding another job! Because I think I'm going to need it!*

Having found a rather nice vegetarian option at a stand down the side street by the car parks, which she hoped would counterbalance the surfeit of bacon at breakfast, Holly took her time wandering around the fair tonight. There wasn't much she could do in the flat beside sitting and reading, and the day had been so slow she was well on the way to finishing her current book already. At this rate she'd be scouring the charity shops for cheap replacements tomorrow, so it was actually nice to get up and walk about for a while. She dreamed of owning a kindle so that she could borrow books and read to her heart's content, but the cost of the device itself meant it was still something she was saving for, whereas charity shop books could regularly be picked up for under a pound. She did have an old laptop, but she'd need to get it here first and it was a heavy old thing – not something to have on your lap while you read, though she did do that sometimes at home when she could prop it up on the arm of the sofa.

For the first time she had chance to look around the town at her own pace. The Market House was a beautiful black-and-white building, the ground floor of which was an open space that anyone could walk around, with stairs going up to an upper floor that was closed to the public. But it was far from the only lovely building in this central area. Not quite a square but more of a tapering rectangular space, on a normal day it was busy with traffic, so standing out in the road to look up at buildings was taking your life in your hands. However, today she could see that behind the Market House, the row of shops were on the ground floors of a line of very handsome Georgian buildings. Facing them across the road was a building that Holly thought were almshouses, and then closer to the crossroads at the narrow end of the space was another fabulous old timbered building that was a very prestigious hotel – somewhere Holly could only dream of staying in.

Something else she noticed was that she felt perfectly safe walking around the town on a darkening evening. Possibly that was to do with the fact that the town was full of families, and though the fair filled the street with cheerful coloured lights, there was also something about the place that reassured Holly in a way she'd not felt before. It emboldened her to walk down the side streets to look at the stalls there, and if the buildings here were more what she thought of as normal, there was still that well-loved feel about the place. In what was normally the main car park in the centre of town, she wandered around, taking the time to look at the back of the lovely almshouses and by the time she'd done a loop of the car park, she'd also found another old timbered building. Only when she started to get cold did she make her way back past the Market House, up the lane, and into the pub.

Once again it was heaving, and so she was able to pay for her own gin with one of the barmaids without Jesse offering her another free one. That had been incredibly kind of him when she'd been falling apart, but she didn't want to seem like she was presuming upon that kindness. However, having gone in later, it was that much later when she finished her second drink, by which time the pub had calmed down more, and Jesse and Shea-Lea spotted her. So she was able to have more of a normal conversation with them, at which point she remembered to ask them if they or their staff had seen the ghost of the Victorian workman in the cellars.

"A ghost? Wow! Cool!" was Shea-Lea's gleeful response, which made it fairly clearly that they hadn't and weren't taking it that seriously. But another of the bar staff, whose name turned out to be Steph, said,

"I've heard someone singing. Always late at night and outside, and long after we'd closed after a bar extension, so beyond midnight."

"I heard someone last night!" Holly admitted, trying to brush it off with a laugh.

"My Aunty Megan's a bit of a psychic, and she reckons it must be the ghost of a Civil War soldier," Steph carried on, making Shea-Lea say,

"Jeez, Steph! Give it up! Poor Holly's got to spend the next two nights in the place alone! We're trying to cheer her up. Don't scare her to death with all this crap about real ghosts!"

"She's already seen one," Steph protested, "so I don't see how my saying what I know should scare her any more than she is already," but she took the hint from Shea-Lea's steely glare and grabbed a cloth and the spray, and went off to clear tables.

"Not our best asset," Jesse said softly and with a cheeky grin once Steph was beyond hearing, which at least made Holly giggle in response.

Shea-Lea rolled her eyes, adding, "Aimee works at half her speed, but is so cheerful and happy with the customers she gets them buying more just to sit and chat to her. But when it's just Steph at the bar, you can watch customers grabbing their drinks and retreating to a table to get away from her."

The conversation moved on, and so it wasn't until Holly was back in the flat on her own that her thoughts turned once more to what Steph had said. Like a lot of people, she had a vague knowledge of the English Civil War, but the names of the main battles at places like Edgehill and Marston Moor were about the extent of her knowledge. So she'd never thought much about there being local connections, yet now Sally's words came back to her, and she started to wonder what had gone on around Ledbury. She piggybacked onto the pub's free wifi with the little tablet from the shop that Angie had left behind, but an online search didn't reveal much beyond the fact that there'd been a Sealed Knot re-enactment of the skirmish at Ledbury during the summer of 2019. However, the real fight had taken place in April 1645, and that had been before the Scots had marched south, so she didn't think it could be this. However, later that year the Scots had come through in July, and then marched back in September – or rather, they left after hearing that the king had entered Worcester on the second of that month

Oh golly! thought Holly, recalling Sally's words about significant dates for the ghosts when talking about the Victorian workman. *The second of September? That's scarcely a month ago! I wonder if my singing man builds up to a full haunting around then*

and is still lingering? That was a bit worrying, because the chances were she'd still be holding the fort here, and in truth, her best chance of coming out of this whole messy situation with her own reputation intact, would be to trade as best she could up to Christmas, even if she had to close down after that. At least then she would have managed to sell a lot of the stock, even if she couldn't order in more, and at that point, she'd have a couple of full months' sales records to prove that she hadn't jumped the gun if she did close the shop down. That might make all the difference to her getting another managerial job in retail, especially if whichever solicitors were involved by then gave her some credit, by way of a reference, for having made as much as anyone could be expected to do out of such a situation. *Forget the ghosts, look after the shop*, she told herself firmly.

Duncan McAllister 3

For the first week or so, Duncan could do little but lie on the servant's pallet bed up in the attic, as his ankle swelled spectacularly. Sorley had bravely followed his instructions and pulled the ankle straight again before binding it up, but the pain had caused Duncan to pass out and for days he had to resort to the willow bark tea Goodwife Joan brought up for him. He was grateful that it helped to prevent him from crying out in pain every time he inadvertently shifted, but he was also sure that she was slipping poppy juice into him somehow, because he was shockingly drowsy.

He got his explanation at the end of the first week when he woke up to find Goodwife Joan sitting on the stool by his bed. "I'm sorry I had to dose you, Master McAllister," she explained, "but who should turn up demanding a bed for the night but Mistress' cousin, Sir Simon."

The way she said Sir Simon's name made Duncan think that she held a dim view of him. "Ye dinna like him?"

Goodwife Joan gave a sniff of disgust. "I never did *like* him. Always too full of his own importance, and he's got worse since his father died and he inherited the title, such as it is. You'd think him a great lord instead of a local squire, the way he carries on. But he came here on his way to join the king's men, or at least to tell us that's what he's doing. If the king is depending on men like him to fight for him, then he's in a pretty bad way...but then maybe that's not a bad thing. At least then this dreadful fighting would stop."

"Sorley?" Duncan asked, almost dreading what her answer would be. If this was a Royalist household, at least in terms of the owners' loyalties, then this cousin might feel entitled to round up a useful looking lad to join his own men.

"Oh, don't worry," Joan said, immediately all smiles. "He hid in here with you, and he dragged a heavy chest across the door so that nobody could get in. He slipped out of the window and across the roof to fetch bowls of stew I brought up to our room. My, but he's a nimble lad! I told Sir Simon's men that there was nothing in here besides old furniture, and that something must have fallen down behind the door. They weren't going to argue when I put them up in the second best bedrooms instead of up here – it's better than they normally have."

Duncan looked around him. "Where's Sorley now?"

"Out tending the garden. He's already caught and skinned that rabbit that brought you down, and its fellows who'd moved into the burrow. He hung them up to tenderise and you'll be having them in the stew tonight. That lad's a worker, though. He's already got the weeds out, and he's harvested what he can and stored it for us – hidden as much as he could away behind some loose boards in the stable, too. Right now he's digging over the beds and working compost in. When old Eric comes back with the mistress, he'll be right pleased. He begged her to let him stay, but she said she needed him to make sure the kitchen garden where they've gone can feed them for as long as they're there. Now he'll come back to the compost heaps turned, the oldest stuff used, and a new one begun. Mary and I couldn't have hoped to do that much, even if we have less to do of our own jobs while the family is away."

Duncan silently offered up a prayer of thanks for Sorley. Had it been the lad's brother, Sandy, it would have been a different story, because Sandy had never liked getting his hands dirty, and without someone chivvying him on all the time, Sandy would have hidden away up here, eating the food but doing nothing to replenish it. Instead, it sounded very much as if the old gardener had been gone a while, and Sorley would be leaving the household better off when the time came for them to move on. That in turn would hopefully mean that Goodwife Joan and Mary wouldn't tell anyone who their unexpected guests had been, or at least not until the family got back, by which time Duncan hoped they'd be far away.

How that was to be accomplished, however, was another matter. The Scots were still in the area – or at least some of them were. Sorley had gone scouting and reported back that General David Leslie had torn through the town again, hardly a week after they'd arrived, heading for the border. However, Earl Leven was still besieging the city of Hereford, which was holding out better than expected. Also, with the loss of virtually all of his mounted men, who had gone north with Leslie, the men still with Leven were struggling to forage too far afield from Hereford, and Sorley had missed the few who had come anywhere near to Ledbury to be able to summon help.

The ferocious swelling in Duncan's leg and ankle gradually abated, but it was clear that it was going to take several more weeks before he could hope to put weight on it, let alone march any distance. So the two Scots were grateful for Goodwife Joan's continued hospitality.

"She fancies you," Sorley teased Duncan one night when bringing him up his bowl of stew.

"I dinna wish to lead her to think there's something more to come," Duncan confessed, "but if smiling at her and having our wee chats keeps her thinking kindly o' us, then that's what I'll do."

Sorley nodded, then gave a disgusted sniff. "There's nay chance o' me doing that wi' Mary."

Duncan gave his young cousin a stern look. "I ken she's no' the best favoured lassie, but…"

"Nay!" Sorley interrupted him and with a vigorous shake of his head. "I dinna mean her looks. I'm no' like Sandy, who looks away from any lass who's homely. Aye but Mary's a cross-patch. I canna do right fer wrong wi' her. It's nay wonder that she doesn'a have a lad she's waiting fer to come back. If she's the same wi' the local lads as she's been wi' me, I bet they ran a mile to get away from her. There are poor lassies wi' less in looks than her who still have someone who loves them, because they're kind o' heart and sweet o' temper. This one ye'd be waiting every day to find out if ye were going to eat yer dinner or wear it!"

Duncan saw what the problem was, but also the implications beyond what Sorley had seen. Mary might not be quite out of her teens, but she'd have to be a fool not to work out that fewer young men would be returning than left. That meant that Ledbury and the villages around it would have more spinsters than normal amongst the younger generations of women, as and when this war ended. So a young lass who had been singularly unsuccessful this far might very well be feeling her prospects were bleak, especially if she was already of a gloomy turn of mind.

"Are ye sure she's no' just missing her lad?" Duncan asked, though with little hope.

Sorley rolled his eyes. "Oh, I'm sure! I'd just dodged the tin mug she threw at me before storming out, and I said to Mistress Joan that her lad must be an aye brave soul." He gave a wicked grin. "Mistress Joan said that none o' the local lads had that much fire in their bellies. That after the last time one o' them had dared to sneak a wee kiss, and she walloped him wi' the kettle she'd taken to the well to fill, she's been shunned by all o' them."

"Jesu preserve us," Duncan swore with feeling. "Listen, Sorley, fer the love o' God, be careful around her. I've come across men and women like her before, and they're bluidy dangerous. One wrong word to her and she'll be telling the town we're here wi' not a care fer what happens to us…or to Joan, because I doubt any militiamen will look kindly on her fer taking us in. If I have to, I'll say I forced my way in here and threatened them."

"Ye'd never do that!" Sorley protested.

"No, I wouldn'a, but we're no' back home where folk ken me and you. It's what I've been tellin' ye' lad, we're no' just the strangers in town, we're the bluidy enemy just because we're Scots. Never mind whether any men that get brought down on us support the king, and therefore are against us, or are fer Cromwell and Parliament and should be on our side, 'cause neither side really want us here, no' even those who but months ago were begging us to come and fight. They dinna trust us, ye ken? Especially Highlanders like you and me. We're wild savages to them. Useful to fling at their enemies to die instead o' them, but they'll no' welcome us into their homes fer a wee bite o' something to eat, let alone gi' us a bed fer the night. Aye, but we've been lucky wi' Goodwife Joan. If she'd ha' sent Mary screaming fer help the moment I went flat on my face, we'd both ha' been swinging from a beam in the Market House's undercroft."

Sorley sighed. "Well I'll do ma best, but knowing what will please Mary and what won't would take a saint to work out, and I'm no' that good."

Duncan didn't want to say more because he didn't trust himself not to be honest with the lad. Aye, Goodwife Joan had been more than kind and generous, all things considered. But Duncan wasn't a fool, and he saw full well how her eyes got a sparkle in them whenever she was with him. The trouble with that was that he felt nothing for her beyond normal gratitude. Used to the women he'd encountered in the households of the lairds he'd visited, Duncan knew how to have a laugh and a joke with them without ever crossing the line of what was right and proper.

Where Goodwife Joan's sense of humour had gone to, Duncan had the feeling that it was a long time ago, if she'd ever had one. Despite his best efforts, he'd never raised as much as a titter out of her. Indeed some of his attempts to tell her the daft stories that had had women in other kitchens roaring with laughter had been met with a slightly startled look of incomprehension, which wasn't just to do with her not understanding his Scottish accent. How on earth her husband had coped he couldn't imagine, because life for ordinary folk like them was tough at the best of times. You had to find some joy where you could.

Indeed he'd never managed to get her to speak of her husband beyond the fact that he was dead, so maybe that was where the problem lay? Had he been a wife beater? Duncan didn't know, and for all that he'd had nothing but sympathy for a woman who went through that, letting it sour the rest of your life after the wretch was six feet under was something he struggled to understand.

Yet there was also a block on Duncan's part. Isobel Gunn, the lass who'd stolen Duncan's heart, but had been married off against her will to another. Isobel with her winning smile and kind heart, who he couldn't even wait for anymore, because she'd preceded her fool of a husband into the grave along with her third child. Try as he might, Duncan had never met another woman who could dispel Isobel's ghost, none who could hold a candle to her memory. He'd met many a bonny lass in his time, but every time his head thought he was getting close to committing to her, his rebellious heart kept saying *no, she's no' Isobel.* Not that these days he had much to offer any future wife. At his age, most men had come into whatever wee croft they were going to, or at least a home on the farm of some better off relative. Instead, where was he? Stuck here, hundreds of miles from home.

Duncan had missed his home before, had missed seeing the mountains of the west and the fingers of lochs cutting deep into the land with their wooded slopes, but he'd never really been homesick before. Now he was struck with a terrible longing, and also a fear that he might never see home again. And so in the depths of the night, while Joan and Mary slept soundly in their beds in the room across the way, Duncan began singing the songs from home, the ones that just by giving voice to them brought a little bit of the Highlands into this dark attic for a while.

Chapter 9

Holly was much more relaxed than the previous night when she turned in on her camp bed, helped by the room being less frosty thanks to the heaters having been on for longer with the doors shut. So she was deeply asleep when she was brought around by the sound of that singing again. A quick glance at her watch told her that it was three in the morning, so way too late for anyone to be rolling out of any pubs, not even with a late licence running for the fair. Remembering this time that she had the lights, she had no hesitation in going and flipping the light switch on. The stark spotlights which had been put in in these rooms left no shadows in which anything could lurk, meaning she knew beyond doubt that she was alone in here. That was a relief, but what wasn't so good was realising that this time the voice sounded so much closer.

With a shiver, she pulled on her heavy fleece and her trainers, then wondered whether it was sensible to be thinking about going out onto the landing.

Oh for God's sake, Hol' pull yourself together! she reprimanded herself sternly. *There's no bloody back door anyone could have crept in by, and you don't even have any ground-floor windows on the house that someone could break in through down in the hall –*

they're all on the shop and the pub, and even you have to go outside and back in through that massive old oak door. There's nobody in here with you!

On the other hand, if she got up and started putting lights on, it might make the inconsiderate sod outside wake up and realise that the big house was now occupied, and they needed to be a bit more thoughtful about getting wasted and rowdy in the early hours. So she took a deep breath, stepped out onto the dark landing, and flipped the landing light switch. Then gave a shaky laugh at the surge of relief she felt at seeing nothing. Good grief, she really was becoming a jittery snowflake if she could spook this easily! Because common sense said that of course there wasn't going to be anyone, or even anything like a stray cat, there.

However, if she was going to see anything of what was going on, then having ruled out the alley on *The Renegade's* side, she had no choice but to go up to the second floor where she could look out onto the other side. Wishing that the Dutch courage of the couple of gins earlier in the evening hadn't worn off already, she grasped her heavy torch, more as a weapon than from needing its light now, and went to the stairwell. Just to be sure, she looked downwards, but of course there was nothing down there. So with a deep breath, she switched on the upper lights and made her way upstairs.

The sensation of vertigo wasn't much better, but this time she was prepared for it and stayed well away from the balustrades, hugging the solid walls. So feeling less disorientated, this time she risked walking from the landing out onto the little upper gallery which overhung the stairs, and which gave a wonderful bird's eye view of the beautifully turned wood spindles and handrails. Even so, she still couldn't see directly out of the stairs' leaded windows, and she wondered, as she'd done before, how on earth the servants had got up to clean these windows in an age when the whole house would have been lit by dusty coal fires. Mops with very long handles, was her thought, because even standing as near to the balustrade as she dared, there was no way she could reach across even to the first panes. But what it did confirm to her, looking through the currently clean windows, was that there was no sign of anyone outside.

There was nobody sitting out in next door's garden with a lantern or even a torch. On her way out tonight, she'd had a quick peep through the archway from the street, and had spotted a rather expensive looking fire pit in the garden, but tonight there wasn't so much as a glimmer of lit coals down there. Even standing and peering hard into the darkness until she absolutely had to blink, she couldn't see a thing moving down there – and tonight was a clear night with a bright crescent moon shining down, so it wasn't total blackness out there.

Then it came again!

The voice.

Singing.

Upstairs!

And as she whipped around to look over her shoulder to where the locked door to the third floor was, she saw a blur moving fast long the landing.

That's all it was. A transparent blur. But with it came a strange scent.

Wool. Damp wool – like back when she was a kid and her mum had left one of the heavy old charity shop blankets out too long on the washing line, and it had got drenched in a sudden summer thunderstorm. The blur was gone in an instant, vanishing and not returning, but the scent of damp wool lingered. Then she realised that the singing had stopped. But another sound came, and this time it was from below.

Almost paralysed with fear, Holly wedged herself back into the corner of the walls on the gallery, watching the lit stairs with eyes like saucers. The sound of several heavy men's treads came on the stairs, but they got to the quarter turn before the landing she was on and stopped. Yet there was nothing at all visible. For a second Holly thought she might wet herself in fright, but when the footsteps turned and started going back down, she forced herself to risk peering over the balustrade. No, there wasn't a soul down there.

She waited, frozen stiff both with the cold and fear, but knew that this was ridiculous; she needed to get back downstairs and go to bed. *I'm not having that damned mushroom pasty again!* she mentally swore. *Must've been bloody magic mushrooms in that to have me seeing and hearing things! The burgers would have been safer!* And yet as she went down the stairs, she could have sworn she heard someone saying in a deep, male, Scottish voice,

"*Shhh*, lad. Be still. They've no' gone yet."

Again, to her surprise, she got back to sleep, being woken by her alarm going off. Yet after she'd got ready and been out for another takeaway breakfast, she decided that she needed to speak to someone a bit more clued up about this sort of thing. In the cold and rational light of morning, she knew that if there'd been anything off about the pasty, that it would have been more likely to give her an upset stomach than make her see things.

Sally, it would have to be Sal she talked to, because she was the only person she knew who wouldn't laugh their socks off at her. So hoping that Sally would be at home, and not out teaching at one of her art therapy classes, Holly took her hot coffee down to the office and made the call.

"Hey, Sal, do you have time to talk?" she started with, but instantly there was no fooling Sally.

"What's wrong, my love, that you're ringing me this early in the day?"

With great relief, Holly unburdened herself to Sally, ending with, "I'm not going barmy am I? Not coming unravelled with all of the stress?"

Sally's warm Worcestershire voice instantly responded with, "No, of course you aren't. It'd be understandable for you to feel more than a bit on edge, sleeping alone as you are in what's little short of a deserted building. But I've done many a therapy session with people for stress, and I've yet to have any of them seeing things from that far in the past, let alone smelling them."

"Oh, thank God!"

Sally laughed. "Maybe thank the *Goddess*, but yes. ...However, you do have something really intriguing going on over there. You say you *smelled* damp wool, and then heard a Scottish voice?"

"Yes. I mean, what the heck is that about? We're in Herefordshire not Scotland! Of all the weird and wonderful things for me to hear, why would it be a Scotsman not a local soldier?"

"It's less strange than you think," was Sally's calm response. "There were two times when a Scottish army made it down into these western shires. Neither is as well known as they should be, but at least the Scottish army who fought the very last battle in the English Civil War in 1651 got a memorial put up to them on Powick Bridge. But earlier in the Civil War a Scottish army on the other side..."

"Cromwell's?"

"...Parliament's – because Cromwell wasn't fully in charge at that point. ...Forgive me if I'm telling you what you already know, but to put it simply, just because the Parliamentarians were against the almost-Catholic changes that Charles I was trying to make, it didn't mean that they were all of the same mind. Up in Scotland, they'd already had what are often now called the Bishops' Wars, which were essentially about whether the Scottish Kirk ought to be overseen by bishops or not. It got very bloody, and many men who started off on one side then changed over to the other."

"Wow! That must have made things pretty tense!"

"It did, and it might surprise you to hear that one of the other people who wasn't happy about Parliament having to lean on the Scots in order to defeat King Charles was Cromwell himself. He led a group of non-conformist Protestants called the Independents, and they were none too pleased that, as the price of the Scots helping the English Parliament against the king, they demanded that their Covenant be adopted for *all* Protestant worship in England. Nowadays we'd wonder what the fuss was about, but then we're a very secular society these days. Back then it really matter to almost everyone.

"The time you need to know about is 1645. The civil war had broken out three years before in 1642, and the first proper battle of the Civil War happened in Worcestershire at Powick Bridge in September of 1642, where Prince Rupert of the Rhine won against the Parliamentarian Earl of Essex. It means that for all that we're talking about somewhere on the far side of England to London, our western shires were hugely significant."

"Oh yes, I remember reading somewhere that the first and last battles of the Civil War were fought near Powick. Fancy a little village just outside of Worcester being that important!"

Sally laughed. "Yes, it's hard to imagine why it was so vital, but of course you have the rivers Severn and Teme meeting there, so an important river-crossing point to give armies access to all sorts of places, including routes into Wales. Yet not a lot happens around here for quite a while after 1642. Then in early July 1644, Leven and his Scots were at the Battle of Marston Moor, helping to inflict a heavy defeat on the Royalists under Prince Rupert, so you can see that the Scots were involved in English politics up to their ears, and on both sides too. It wasn't a given that every Scot was for Parliament at this stage, nor at any other point, in truth.

"But here's where it gets interesting for you, because in the April of 1645 – and remember that there wasn't a lot of actual fighting going on over the winter because of the problems of moving supplies around on what we'd think of as pretty awful roads – Prince Rupert chased Massey and the Roundheads out of Ledbury, where you are. Now the conflict between Massey and Rupert was all about cavalry – and Rupert was very much the dashing Royalist cavalier and a superb officer for them. Indeed, at Marston Moor, Leven's Scots are counted amongst the cavalry, so I think it's reasonable to think of them as being pretty mobile, and that being why they moved west so swiftly. Yet your ghosts don't sound like cavalrymen but foot-soldiers, which I find intriguing."

"Wow! So actual fighting here around Ledbury?"

"Yes."

"And a Scottish army was really involved?"

Sally sighed. "*Hmm*, this is where it gets a bit harder to be one hundred percent sure about times and places. You see, we know that a year on from Marston Moor in the July of 1645, Covenanters – and they are called 'Covenanters' in the surviving records rather than just 'Scots' – stormed Castle Frome in Herefordshire, and that's not far from you, either, is it? Neither of us are exactly military people, but I'm sure you'll agree that common sense says that, even if the main force was cavalry, that the cooks, washer-women, and all the other folk who traipsed in the wake of an army, would hardly have had time to venture far away in the scant time between late April and July. Therefore they must have been lurking in the vicinity, or at least Hereford*shire*, even if we don't have exactly a day-by-day account of what they *were* doing."

Holly was now curious. "How come you know so much about this era, Sal? I didn't have you down as someone who'd want to know about battles and things."

She heard her friend sigh. "You're right in one way. The battles themselves don't interest me at all. It's the Scots, you see? This comes right in the middle of a century of the most horrendous witch trials in Scotland."

"*Witch* trials? Okay, now I get why you might be interested." Holly knew that Sally considered herself to be a modern-day witch, with a compulsion to help and protect people where she could, especially when conventional methods had failed against things which weren't so easily pinned down as purely physical. "…'Trials' sound nasty?"

"Oh, they were. And the punishments for those who went to trial were barbaric. But more worrying was the way that ordinary women were harassed and 'questioned', often violently, without ever getting the dubious justice of a trial. Honestly, Holly, some poor souls seem to have been held prisoner in the local manses – that's vicarages to Sassenachs like you and me – on no other grounds than the local minister not liking them!"

"That's awful!"

"It was. And the more I dig into it, the more I've become convinced that the worst places for witch trials were the places where the Covenanters had the strongest hold. They were very, 'thou shalt not', you see. That led me to getting interested in the times during that same century when the Scots came south of the border. I wondered whether there was any hint of the same attitude to women down here, you see?"

"And was there?"

"Not that I've found any solid records of yet, but then again, we are in the time of an Englishman, Witch Finder General Matthew Hopkins. He was downright notorious over in the east! And he *was* a full-on witch hunter, starting in 1644, and going on until 1647. There were some horrible trials over in East Anglia back then."

Holly gulped. "He got going in 1644? Oh no, that's a bit too close for comfort when you were talking about Leven and his Scottish Covenanters being at Marston Moor in the same year. Isn't that somewhere up towards York? So not exactly a hard march down into Norfolk, and then on to Suffolk for them, or at least for men influenced by them."

"Exactly. So in 1645, when the king's supporters took a beating down in the south-west, the Parliamentary committee begged Leven and his Scots to take advantage of this. Leven marched them through to Bewdley, where they crossed the River Severn, and as soon as they were across, he sent men ahead with David Leslie and two other leaders called Callander and Middleton. They were the ones who assaulted the castle at Castle Frome, garrisoned it for their side, and then went on to attack Ross-on-Wye."

Sally took a deep breath. "But it's Leven himself who you ought to know about. I had to dig back to an old biography of him written back in Victorian times to find this after you jogged my memory, but he took the rest of his troops over awful roads through Bromyard and *Ledbury* to get to Hereford by the very end of July in 1645."

"So an actual Scottish army marched west through here in July of 1645? Did they fight any battles here?"

"I don't think so, not actual battles, but you can't imagine that they got this far without a scuffle or two. Not every local would have been on the same side. And rather more to the point, all of those men needed feeding, as did any horses. This far from Scotland, by then they weren't using their own food and fodder, brought south with them. That must have run out long before this. So they'd be raiding and pillaging as they went just to survive."

"You do realise that my ghostly soldier being a woman-hating raider does nothing for me feeling safe in here?" Holly joked, but only in her voice. Inside she was quaking more than a little!

Sally was quick to reassure Holly, "Oh, I don't think you need to worry about some ghostly Covenanter taking exception to you."

"That's a relief!"

"It's more that I'm trying to figure out who was where and when. And whether you've got some significant event coming up – aside from Halloween, or should I say Samhain, in a couple of weeks."

"Halloween!" squeaked Holly, suddenly looking at the calendar on the wall and seeing just how close that was. "Oh, blimey, Sal, I don't think I want to be here alone on that night!"

However, Sally was soothing. "You don't have to stay there on that night, my lovely. If it gives you the heebie-jeebies, then go home to your flat. Nobody's expecting you to take on calming all of that old house's ghosts."

Holly took a deep breath. "No, Sal, you're right. Not my circus, not my monkeys."

"However it's that sense of someone hiding upstairs in your house that's got me intrigued, you see. If it's the Covenanters going through in the summer of 1645, then why would a Scotsman be hiding when they were on the winning side at that point? And that brings me to the other time that the Scots went through Ledbury, which was only months later when Leven's men followed Leslie's to go back north, and that's when there's another skirmish in Ledbury. That anniversary is coming up in November, and that's got me thinking about anniversaries explaining why your ghosts are more active right now.

"Colonel Scudamore, who was the royalist governor of Hereford, had a regiment of horse – which basically means dragoons – and they were chased through Ledbury by a Roundhead leader called Major Hopton, who almost certainly had a high percentage of Scots with him, if not all Scots. I've not been able to find out if Hopton himself was Scottish, but then the lowland Scots wouldn't have all been Mac-*somebody*, so you can't tell by a name. As best I can tell, both sides had been looking for provisions, and there weren't a huge number of men involved, but given that the men from Hereford had just gone through six weeks of being besieged by the Scots, there must have been a lot of bad feeling towards them."

"*Hmph,*" Holly sniffed. "But the same thing applies as to the earlier incident, doesn't it? Why would a Scotsman be hiding when they were on the winning side? And are my ghosts loitering around because their time of death has passed its anniversary, or is it coming up?"

"That's it," Sally agreed. "And I'm still curious as to where my ladies from up north went to if there's a chance that they came down here."

"You'd better come and ask my ghosts," Holly joked, and then gulped as Sally said,

"I was going to suggest I come and see if I can make contact."

Mercifully a customer came in at that point, meaning Holly could hurriedly ring off. But as the day wore on she kept coming back to Sally's last words, none too sure of how she felt about the idea. Part of her was just as curious as Sally, but the other part couldn't help but be a bit worried about what might happen if they riled the ghosts up too much. Sally could go home to her nice little cottage out at Bransford, but Holly had little choice but to work on here, even if she didn't spend her nights in the flat.

How far afield might the ghosts roam once woken up? Those men hunting them had sounded as if they'd come in through the old front door, which these days only serviced the upper floors. But once upon a time it had probably had doors through from that hall into the shop where she was now, and Holly wasn't looking forward to nights around Halloween if she was going to have bloodied Scots ghosts lurking around her! Not so very long ago, she would have laughed at someone being worried about such things, but the last couple of nights had seriously revised her views on the matter of ghosts.

That night she repeated her evening by going and getting hot food, but then the weather turned drizzly, and it wasn't conducive to wandering aimlessly around the fair, especially as with this being the last night of the fair, some of the stalls had already packed up and gone once the afternoon trade had passed. That meant that she had little choice but to go upstairs for a bit. Her budget only ran to a couple of drinks per night, and already she was thinking that tonight she would forego the pricier gin with all the trimmings, and settle for one of the nice draft beers instead. *Hops to help you sleep*, she told herself as well. *Then maybe you won't hear the singing.*

Duncan McAllister 4

Unable to do much, and certainly not daring to even go outside to the vegetable plot – because if danger came, he wouldn't be able to run back inside – Duncan was bored stiff. Used to being an active man all of his life, this sitting around with his leg propped up nearly drove him mad. Luckily, Sorley found two good stout lengths of wood of the right size to be made into crutches, and so he took those and shorter pieces to make arm rests out of to Duncan. For a day, there was frantic whittling with his dirk, and then Duncan had the means to get about a little. He still had to scoot down the stairs on his bum, as the fastest and safest way, but he was no longer confined to one room.

Remembering how much they were dependent on their lady hosts, on the first day Duncan waited until he could hear Joan and Mary thumping away at the washtub in the wash-house out by the well before he made his move. He knew he'd be making lots of thumps and bumps until he got the hang of the crutches, and didn't want them thinking he was spying on them. On the other hand, he was desperate to find out just how strongly Royalist this household was, because that might determine how fast he and Sorley might need to leave.

He managed to get down the servants' stairs from the attic to the top floor without falling, and took a moment to stand leaning on the rail of the main staircase. It was a piece of workmanship the like of which Duncan had never seen before. His sole experience of places that had more than one floor and needing a staircase had been castles. Everyone he knew in a personal sense lived in the same single storey longhouses. For anything hung up on the rafters, they used a ladder. There was no need for anything permanent. So he stared in wonder at the beautifully turned spindles and the way the staircase hung from a few stout uprights.

It made him appreciate that this was a far wealthier family than he'd appreciated when he'd been brought in half blind with tears of pain.

"Oh Sorley, lad," he breathed. "What have I got you into?"

Motivated to move and find out more, Duncan hobbled his way around this topmost floor, quickly realising that these were the family bedrooms. Not that he'd ever seen a bedroom before, either. At home, everyone bedded down in communal spaces – there simply wasn't room in the longhouses for anyone to have a room to themselves. The most privacy his parents had ever had was an old wool blanket draped across a rope at the end of the house. Nor had he ever been upstairs in the castles he'd visited. It was public rooms only for the likes of him, and at the big castle at Inveraray and elsewhere, he'd billeted with the other soldiers in the out buildings, or occasionally on benches or the floor in the great hall. Beds with carved wood frames and feather mattresses weren't for the likes of him.

What he swiftly realised was that it would be deeply frowned upon if he was found in any of these rooms, and the big front one in particular. Goodwife Joan struck him as being the kind of woman who would be scandalised if she thought he'd been going through her mistresses small clothes, for instance, and the front room was definitely the mistress'. He was also worn out far faster than he liked by just this first foray, and so by the time he'd wriggled his way back up the stairs to his pallet, he actually fell asleep on it for a while.

Oh God, he thought upon waking, *this is no good. I have to be able to move! I can't expect Sorley to defend me.*

It was enough to get him up the following morning, and shuffle his way all the way down the stairs to the ground floor and the kitchen. If Mary cast him black looks for taking a seat on a stool in there, at least Joan seemed delighted that he was up and about.

"I'm no' a man to be lazing in bed," he said by way of explanation. "Is there anything I can do for you while I'm sitting here?"

"Not unless you can darn socks," Mary snapped with withering sarcasm, then was shocked into silence when Duncan replied,

"I'm a soldier, lass, o' course I can darn socks."

So for that afternoon, Duncan was set up by a window looking onto the vegetable garden, and set to work on the family's socks and stockings that had been left behind. He shocked the two women by the neat job he made of it, though Mary managed to take offence at Sorley's innocent question of, "Can the men here no' do their own? Old Eric I ken might no' have the nimble fingers and the sight to do his, but surely the lad could help him?"

"It's not a *proper* man's job," she retorted, and flounced out, leaving Duncan and Sorley looking at her retreat in bemusement.

Joan simply shook her head. "Mary's been listening to too many sermons about equality," she sighed. "The trouble is, she's taken being equal in the sight of God to mean equal here on earth, and she fancies that she's as much right to live as mistress of a house like this as any." She gave a rueful smile to Duncan. "It grates with her that you've made a far better job of the darning than she does. I have to do all the main family's, so she gets left with ours because she can't or won't do a good enough job to work on the best fabrics and woollens. Before the war, Mistress had a maid who helped, but she ran back to her family at the first sign of fighting."

It brought it home to Duncan what a danger Mary was. This young lass who took offence at anything and everything, without stopping to think, was the worst person to have around them right now. With that in mind, the next day he refrained from going down to the kitchen. The less reason he gave Mary to hate the sight of him the better, and he encourage Sorley to come upstairs to eat his midday meal under the pretext of keeping him company.

"Let's keep ourselves to ourselves as much as possible," he warned the lad.

However, when Joan took some of the rugs from the main parlours down to give them a good beating in the yard, Sorley and Duncan offered to sweep and mop the floorboards. Duncan couldn't do much beyond holding the pan for Sorley to sweep into, and so he spent a lot of time looking around him. The big first-floor front room was hung with family portraits, and the wood panelling gleamed, proof of Joan's industry with the beeswax polish. Heavy tapestry curtains hung at the windows, meaning that Duncan could shuffle close to the leaded panes of glass and look out without being seen.

It was the first time that he appreciated that they weren't on the main street itself – something he'd been dreading because it would be so conspicuous to leave – but that there was a troublingly steady if limited flow of people going past.

Sorley joined him at the window, openly staring out, far more anonymous as just another serving boy. "There's an aye big kirk up the lane," he told Duncan. "Come through to the next room. Ye can see the tower through the side window."

Sure enough, when Duncan had hobbled through, he could see across the width of their burgage plot to where a similar house to this lay in its own burgage plot of the same size. He couldn't have known it then, but this was a view Holly would never have, because by then the neighbouring house had been built in the 1800s. But in this time, he could see beyond the other house to a fine stone church tower. Somehow, though, he didn't think that Joan would go there to worship except under compulsion from her master and mistress. That big old church had to have been standing for centuries already, and if it didn't have a bishop of its own, it surely had considerable prestige. No lowborn Presbyterian would preach the word of God, as he saw it, at that altar.

Turning around, he spotted what he presumed was the master's safe cupboard, built into the bulk of the huge chimneybreast. It was a good place to have it, Duncan thought, because short of taking part of the wall or the chimney down, its only weakness was the front, and the keyhole spoke of a substantial lock on it. However, what he really wanted to find was somewhere to hide his claymore. The huge sword had been strapped to his back when he came in, and Sorley had hidden it under the pallet bed, but Duncan was horribly aware that it, more than anything, marked him out as a Highlander. If someone came into the house, in his borrowed clothes, and without the claymore or his dirk, as long as he kept his mouth shut and his eyes cast down, he might just pass for any old servant. With them he was the enemy.

Feeling a terrible sadness at this sense of being an outsider in a way more intense than anything he'd experienced before, even on his one and only visit to Edinburgh, he limped away, softly singing,

"Farewell to Lochaber, farewell to my Jean,
Where heartsome wi' thee, I ha' many days been,
For Lochaber no more, Lochaber no more."

Chapter 10

When she couldn't stand sitting in the flat any longer, Holly went down to *The Renegade* and found a corner seat on one of the long bench seats, intending to stay out of the way. However, the pub was somewhat quieter tonight, probably because of people needing to go to work tomorrow, so Shea-Lea – who seemed to be on duty on her own tonight – came and sat at her table with her. Feeling that she ought to have something more like a normal conversation than just blurting out her troubles, Holly asked, "Who's the renegade the pub's named after?"

She wasn't expecting Shea-Lea's hoot of laughter. "Oh, that's Jesse's kid uncle!"

"Uncle?" Holly wasn't expecting that.

"Yeah, he's the one who actually owns the pub. He's been in England for decades. Used to be in a rock band that had a run of hits in the very late '90s and into the Noughties. Actually they did even better in the States than here – they didn't sit well with Brit pop – and made a ton of money, if not quite in the Bruce Springsteen league, but then the band folded and Ash went solo. Jesse's dad thinks he's a total waster, but actually Ash had his head screwed on and invested his money well while it was coming in. So now he runs a recording studio just over the border in Wales, but wanted to branch out. He knew he knew sod all about running a bar, whereas Jesse ran one for years back home in Oz, so when the chance came up for this place, he asked Jesse if he fancied coming over here and running it for him, and where Jesse goes, I go."

"Is that actually Ash on the pub sign?" Holly was thinking that there must have been something in the water where Jesse's family lived if so, because even facing away so you couldn't fully see his face, the guitarist on the sign had slim hips, broad shoulders, and the same tousled dark hair that Jesse had. He must be one hot guy. Looking closely at Shea-Lea now, Holly could see that she was probably only just around thirty, and Jesse was probably not far off the same, whereas she was grimly closer to forty these days, though she hadn't hit that milestone yet. If Jesse was even in his early thirties, that would put his dad at least in his mid fifties, but how much younger was Ash than Jesse's dad?

She hadn't realised that she'd said that last out loud until Shea-Lea answered, "Oh, there's nearly twenty years between them. Pops is the oldest of the family, with another brother and a sister close to his age, while Ash was their mum's menopause baby. Pops had already left home by the time Ash came along, so they had nothing in common, whereas he was a bit of a hero for Jesse back when he was in school. Well having your own rock star in the family gave him huge street cred' at that age." She gave another of her throaty chuckles. "I think Pops had kittens worrying that Jesse was going to end up being dragged around the world as Ash's roadie as soon as he was old enough, but Ash wouldn't have done that. He's a really nice guy. Too nice in a way. He'd never be able to throw people out of here when they get rowdy."

He sounds gorgeous, Holly thought wistfully, *but I bet he's got women hanging off his arm at every turn, if he's not already married with half a dozen kids*. Unfortunately, she didn't get chance to ask Shea-Lea any more about Ash, because a large group came in, and Shea-Lea had to go and help serve, but Holly could only hope that he might turn up one day, even if all she got to do was take in the view.

She was just getting her things together and bracing herself for a cold and lonely night up in the flat – because staying here in the pub and getting well and truly tipsy wasn't an option either – when a familiar figure came in through the door. Wesley DiPaoli! And he was looking about as if searching for someone.

Oh please, Lord. Not me. Please don't let him be looking for me, Holly prayed silently.

What on earth could she say to him?

Yet far from the antagonistic confrontation she was expecting, Wesley only looked relieved to spot her. "Holly! Thank, God I've caught you!"

He must have seen her stunned expression and realised that it sounded odd. Flopping onto the seat which Shea-Lea had used, it brought him down to more on Holly's level, and she could see that he looked worried sick. "I've been stuck in work, so I tried to ring you about an hour ago on the off-chance that you'd still be in the shop. Then when I didn't catch you, I wondered if you just didn't answer in case it was some customer pestering you when you were closing, so I came over. If I hadn't have found you, I was going to ask the guys in here if they knew what time you'd be in tomorrow, even if I had to be late into work myself."

"Oka*aay*," Holly said dubiously, vaguely recalling that Wesley worked in some kind of tech support, so presumably had to do his share of on-call late nights and weekends, which would explain why he hadn't come on Saturday or Sunday. "But what on earth do you want with me?"

He dragged a hand across his face and looked at her with worried eyes. "I wanted to know if you've heard from Angie and Chr…Topher?"

Holly shook her head. "No. In fact I was going to ask you the same."

His groan of despair wasn't what Holly was expecting.

"Why did you think I would know?" she asked him, trying not to sound antagonistic while accepting defeat on her chances of leaving without getting even deeper entangled. "You know Topher can't stand me. That's why he's pulled this bloody stunt of whisking Angie away to the Caribbean just as we opened, and leaving me well and truly in the lurch!"

"Eh?" Wesley's eyes shot up to meet hers in shock. "What do you mean, Topher's stunt?"

Resisting the impulse to be savage, because this wasn't Wesley's mess – or not as far as she knew as yet – Holly said bluntly, "Topher. He booked this big romantic holiday for him and Angie just as we were about to open the shop. I got told I was doing it all, and all on my own, less than a week before we opened. We'd got stock coming, and the opening announcement ads had gone into the local papers, so *somebody* had to be here to open the bloody doors! I knew Topher hated me, but I didn't know how much until I got that dumped on me with only five days' notice!"

"Topher didn't book it," Wesley said weakly in protest. "Angie did! And three months ago! I was there when they had a big row, because Topher was cross that she spent all that money on the shop fittings and stock, and then couldn't even be bothered to be around for the opening. He kept demanding to know if you knew, and whether you were still going to be here, because he was beginning to wonder if he was going to come back to an almighty mess of dumped deliveries and bills piling up! Chris didn't drop you in the shit, Holly. Angie did!"

Holly couldn't move or speak for a moment after that bombshell, and thought it was a good thing she'd already sat down, because her legs felt decidedly weak.

"Angie?" she managed to croak, and got Wesley's nod in response.

"Christ, Holly, you didn't know, did you?" he asked in a voice shaking almost as much as hers. "God! I'm so sorry. So very sorry. ...And for what it's worth, I don't think Chris hates you at all. He told me that he wished you'd wake up and see Angie for what she is. If he hates anyone, it's Angie."

"Then why did he marry her?" Holly demanded, thinking that maybe she might get her suspicions confirmed.

Sure enough, Wesley went red and embarrassed. He looked around and at the way that people were pressing ever closer to them as the pub got even busier. "Look, is there somewhere we can go and talk that's a bit more private?" he begged.

Holly didn't fancy taking him up into the deserted flat on her own, but thought that the shop was a safer place. At least she had the phone there.

As they walked out, she caught Shea-Lea looking enquiringly at her and heard her, "Everything okay?"

She nodded and nipped back enough to say, "I think I might finally be getting some answers," before getting her keys out and letting her and Wesley into the shop.

She didn't put the lights on beyond the one she always left on in the middle archway for security, and led Wesley down into the basement office. It was actually blessedly quiet down here, and she went and retrieved the kettle from the flat hall and put it on, thinking that she needed a coffee to help her be a bit sharper, but also that Wesley looked as rattled as she felt and probably needed one too. As she doled out the coffee into the mugs, she realised that Wesley was probably dreading telling her what she'd already worked out, and she felt sorry for him for that. It wasn't his mess, and in some ways he was picking up after Topher the way she was after Angie.

"I honestly don't know how to begin telling you this," he said when she brought him the mug over to where he was sitting in Angie's chair. "If you didn't think much of Chr...Topher before, you're going to think even less of him now."

Holly sighed. It was no good, she couldn't sit here and watch poor Wesley squirming his way through this confession. "If it helps, I think I've worked some of what you need to tell me," she said, and told him about finding the alternative video of the wedding, and the overheard conversations.

Yet far from looking relieved, Wesley only looked more and more worried. "And you say that Angie has this video?" he asked, clearly dreading her saying 'yes'.

"In that drawer there by your right knee," Holly replied. "Or it was. It's back in my flat at the moment, because I was starting to wonder if I'd need to hand it over to the police to prove a motive. I can't guarantee that she watched it with all of the care that I did, because that's not Angie. Did she hear Laura in the church? No, I don't think she will have. Not even on the Nth repeat. Because at that stage in the proceedings she was – for most people and for her – centre stage up at the altar, and that's what she'll have focused on every time. Will she have heard you and Topher talking at the reception? Yes, I'm afraid she probably has."

"Oh bloody hell! Bloody hell!" Wesley groaned. "Why weren't we more careful? This is all my fault!"

"No it isn't!" Holly said firmly. "I know I don't know you very well, Wesley, but it strikes me that all you're guilty of is trying to be a good friend to Topher the same as I have with Angie. And please, if you normally call him Chris, then you don't have to carry on the Topher thing with me. I presume the two names were in case he was out with Angie and heard someone calling Chris, which he could ignore?"

Wesley looked up at her gratefully from where he'd had his face in his hands. "Thank you. I didn't expect you to be this understanding."

Holly gave a wry smile. "Well up until a couple of weeks ago, I probably wouldn't have been. But the way I've had the wool pulled from my eyes, I'd have to be pretty thick not to have started changing my mind," and she told him about Meryl, too, thinking this seemed to be turning into a night of confessions.

Yet poor Wesley went even paler, if that was possible. "So even Angie's *mum* doesn't know where they are?"

"No. Wesley, why are you this upset? What's happened?"

He took a couple of gulps of coffee and a deep breath. "Okay. So you now know that Chris adores Laura and their two boys. They're childhood sweethearts, you know. There's *nothing* that Chris wouldn't do for her." That didn't do much to quell the rising fear in Holly. "When Laura got her MS diagnosis it ripped the bottom out of their world. You see Laura had thought she was just having a rough recovery after having little Callum, but then she got worse. She's had to go back to live at her mum's for some time now, because her mobility got rapidly worse, and some days her mum has to go and pick the kids up when Chris is …was …at work. It's a lot better, mind you, since he's been able to employ a proper nurse for her and he's bought a huge bungalow that's getting all kitted out. Laura's mum has moved in there with Laura and the kids while

Chris keeps Angie out of the way until he can split from her. He's even been able to bullshit Angie that he's out learning to play golf – all that crap about networking you must have heard – so that he can spend time with the boys and Laura."

He shook his head regretfully. "I don't know what would have happened if he hadn't met Angie, and if she hadn't taken one look at the lack of a wedding ring on his finger and launched herself at him. She really hunted him down, you know. She was determined to have him, whatever the cost. He tried to get rid of her in the early stages. But then – and well before the lottery win – she started splashing her dad's money around like water, and suddenly Chris was able to do that bit more for Laura and the boys. It was heartless and cruel, and he knew it was, but Angie didn't help matters. If she'd been a nice person like you, I honestly don't think Chris could have gone through with it, I really don't, because he's not a bad person."

"Just someone with all the odds against him," Holly sympathised, and got another shocked look from Wesley.

She leaned back in her chair and sighed. "And I can't hate him for having seen through Angie faster than I have. That's been pointed out to me by someone else already. I've known her since we were at junior school together, so all the little changes that have built up into her being such a bloody nightmare have crept in bit at a time. You just don't register what's going on when it happens over a couple of decades. He had it thrown at him fully formed! So why *wouldn't* he see her in a totally different way?"

They sat in miserable silence for a few moments before Wesley then asked, "When was the last time you heard from Angie?"

"Personally? The last time she walked out of the shop door, the day before they flew out. But since I've started to get worried, I've checked all of her social media, and there's nothing beyond them getting to Gatwick, and excited posts about how Topher was spoiling her with this unexpected holiday.

"That's what freaked me out – the total media silence! I'd not looked earlier, because to be frank, I was pissed off at her for leaving me stuck like this. The last thing I wanted to see was her topping up her tan on some white-sanded beach, sipping a cocktail. That would be really rubbing my nose in it! But then I saw that absolute silence, and some other people asking if she was okay, and that began to freak me out. It's just not her. Not at all."

Wesley looked at her thoughtfully. "And now that you know that it was Angie who made the booking and surprised Chris? What do you think now?"

Holly groaned. "I don't know what to think. I'm still struggling to process it all. How long is it since you heard from him?"

"Oh God, that's almost as bad! You see, he told me back when he knew that she'd booked the holiday that he'd had as much as he could take. He was happy enough to make her a decent divorce settlement, but he wanted out. He wanted to be back with Laura and his sons, not pandering to madam's tantrums all the time – not when he didn't desperately need to for the money anymore. And in truth, Holly, the way she was planning on using you made him see that she cares about nobody. 'If she'll do that to the friend who's stuck with her all these years, what *is* she capable of?' he said to me."

That made Holly feel even sadder, as Wesley carried on,

"He'd been planning to tell her he was divorcing her a few months ago, but then she was the one who got the sale rolling on this building on their behalf, and before he knew it, you two were opening the shop here – although I'm going to guess that you didn't know much about that in the planning stages?" Holly shook her head. "No…I thought not. So his thinking was that if he gave her this building, so that she had somewhere stunning to live, and with a going business of her own, then he'd be seen as having been decent towards her. He didn't think he'd wholly get off with that, but that it was at least a good start so that she wouldn't totally clean him out.

"Then she rolled up with the tickets for the holiday. Money paid out of what he was shoving into her account – money given not least so that he could say to a judge, 'look what I've given her so far, and this is all she's got left! She'll never be satisfied,' – and he was pretty shocked when he saw that the booking had been done in his name. But again, he told me it would look better for him than her in a divorce, if he was perceived as still trying to placate her this late in the game. So his intention was to serve her with the divorce papers he'd already got drawn up after a week in the sun, and him come home leaving her to enjoy the last three weeks…"

"...Last *three* weeks!" Holly's squeak cut across him with. "I thought it was a *fortnight*! That's why *I've* been getting worried that there's been no word of her coming home! I never thought she was abandoning me for a bloody *month*!"

Wesley winced again. "No, it was a month-long holiday, starting on Jamaica, but then going on to some of the smaller islands. I think they were due to fly back from Aruba. Or at least that's what I vaguely remember from when he showed me the tickets. He laughed and said he hoped she'd meet some rich toy-boy out there and he could leave her behind permanently.

"But I started to get worried when he messaged me from Montego Bay and said that she was starting to act really weird. They'd been there four days by then, and he said he'd never have thought – had someone told him beforehand – that a holiday in such an amazing country could be such a misery. He was wishing he'd never got on the plane, because he said she was really volatile, throwing things at him and stuff. He thought she might have been on the local marijuana."

Chapter 11

Holly was aghast, both about the drugs, but also that Topher, at least, had been in contact with his friends for longer, and then been cut off. "Oh, God! I've been worried *he's* done something to *her*. And so has her mum. But from the sound of it, you've got more to worry about that she's done something awful to *him*!"

Wesley nodded. "It struck me, a bit late in the day, that if she found out about Laura, and how she'd been used, she'd be apoplectic."

"That doesn't come even close," Holly admitted. "When her last fiancé broke off their engagement, she wasn't so much heart-broken as furious. How dare he do that to her, was her endless demand. And with Tom, she'd only herself to blame. She was so jealous. So controlling. The poor man simply had enough. There was nobody else involved. He just couldn't cope with Angie, and she found that almost impossible to come to terms with. What she'd be like if she found out that she'd been second-best all along…!"then a thought struck her. "Has Laura heard from Chris? Because from what you've said, I can't imagine he'd not contact her if he could."

Wesley grimaced. "Here's where it gets really tough. I don't know where Laura is." He saw Holly's horrified expression and quickly added, "I don't mean she's vanished, just that I haven't got their new address. I know where Laura's mum used to live, but I never had Laura's mobile number because I always met her when she was *with* Chris. And I can't go to the post office and ask for the address the post is being redirected to, can I? Nor the estate agent that sold her mum's place."

"No, I see what you mean," Holly sympathised. "Only the police can make those sorts of enquiries. We can't."

"I'm going to have to go to the police, aren't I?" Wesley said miserably. "They're going to have to get in touch with the police in Jamaica, or wherever, and see if they can track him down."

Holly didn't want to say what was going through her mind, which was that Topher might even be dead, because when Angie was in one of her tempers, she was a grand one for throwing things at people. One heavy paperweight or vase, and Topher might literally not have known what hit him. Instead, she said, "I think it's going to have to be you who makes the first missing persons report, if only because you've had more recent contact with him than I've had with Angie. And, of course, you at least saw the tickets, so you've got reason to be concerned. I never did – for good reason, I now know, because I'd have spotted those dates, and when the booking had been made! I will back you up, though, if they come and speak to me. I'm way past defending Angie now."

Wesley hauled himself to his feet like a man with the weight of the world on his shoulders. "Thanks, Holly. I'm so sorry this has happened to you. I'm worried sick about my friend, but at least I've still got my job and my home," and he looked despairingly around the shop as Holly walked him out. Clearly Wesley was thinking that Holly had really been dumped upon, and that at least made Holly like him even more for his consideration. He'd probably never want to see her after this was over – which would be a shame but understandable – because Holly was thinking that she could get used to having another decent human being around as a friend.

Once she'd waved him goodbye, Holly popped her head around the door of the pub and signalled to Shea-Lea that all was well, and that she was going upstairs, and got a thumbs up in response. It made a big difference to her that there was someone who knew where she was and was watching for her.

Either her brain was already programmed to be alert for the singing, or the singing was getting louder, because she still woke up in the early hours on hearing it. *Christ, it's not Wesley off his face, is it?* she thought, that bringing her into proper wakefulness. She could have sworn she'd seen him heading out of town to where he'd parked, but then maybe the realisation that his best mate might be dead had made him come back into town and buy a bottle or two? He certainly wouldn't be coming out of any of the town's pubs at this hour, so it would have to have been him getting something from the big Tesco up the road, and then sitting on one of the church benches getting totally steamed.

Oh bugger, she thought, grateful that at least she wasn't fully undressed, and therefore it wasn't too hard to just pull on jeans, a thick fleece, and her furry boots to pad through to the front room on this floor. If it was Wesley, then in all conscience, she couldn't leave him face-down in the gutter until the morning. Not when she knew what he'd been through tonight.

Yet when she went to the window and checked, there was nobody around on *The Renegade's* outside seating, nor was there any movement out at the front, and she was resolutely not going up to the second floor at night on her own. Not after what she'd heard the last time. *Go back to bed, Holly,* she told herself firmly. *After tonight you can lock this place up and never set foot in here again if you don't want to,* and out on the landing she gave a sniff and thought that the smell was definitely getting worse – another incentive not to linger.

She hurriedly nipped to the loo on the basis that she didn't want anything else to wake her tonight, and then switched the lights off and crept back into bed. Unfortunately that didn't work, because the singing woke her up again not long after she'd drifted off. Determined not to get out of her nice warm sleeping bag this time, she just snuggled deeper, but then found that she could hear more of what he was singing. It made no sense to her, because she finally realised that whatever the song was, he was singing it in Gaelic. The melody, though, was definitely in a minor key, and sounded very much as though it was some kind of lament. It certainly wasn't one of the famous Scottish songs, but then despite her limited knowledge, Holly knew that most of them came from much later. Even the *Banks of Loch Lomond* was potentially from the time after Culloden in 1746, and it dawned on Holly that the famous battle at Culloden was a full century in the future from whomever these Scottish soldiers were.

Drifting in and out of light sleep, Holly suddenly realised that the singer had moved on to another song. That was new! She hadn't heard him for this length of time before. And then as he moved on to another song, and just as she realised that this was the song she'd heard him singing before, there came the sound of running feet along the landing upstairs.

Only very light.

Only very faint. But she was sure it was the wisp of a ghost she'd seen the night before.

And then they came again – the heavy tread of other men's feet on the staircase coming up.

As Holly shrank beneath the sleeping bag until just her eyes were peeping out over the top, the boots turned and went up to that quarter turn before the second floor, and then came back down again. And this time Holly was sure she could hear one of those men speak, though it was so faint and muffled she hadn't a clue as to what he'd said.

That does it, she thought, as she tried to get back to sleep when it all went quiet. *I don't care how much that bloody car costs me, I'm going home to my own bed tomorrow night and every other night!*

Yet the morning brought trouble of a different kind. She was vaguely aware of the fair rides being loaded up onto the low-loaders before the morning traffic got going, and by the time she opened up, more regular traffic was flowing through the town.

Clearly the car parks were back to normal, because she had a steady flow of locals coming in, most of whom actually bought something. None of it was big sales, but it was enough to cheer Holly up that the week wasn't going to be a total washout.

So she was completely unprepared when the door opened and a couple of ladies of late middle age came in.

"Afternoon," she said cheerfully in greeting. "Please feel free to browse around."

"We've not come to browse. We've come to see *you*," said the one who Holly would have thought was the older.

Trying not to give in to the panic which immediately swelled up inside her, Holly managed to say with passable calm,

"Me? I don't know you, do I?"

The older woman snorted, and the other, who Holly now thought might be her sister, said sharply, "Bloody short memory you've got then! You saw us at the wedding!"

"Wedding?" Holly's mind frantically scrabbled for what weddings she'd been to, and then the penny dropped. Both women looked very different to when they'd been dressed up and made-up to the nines, but this was Topher's biological mother – not the foster mum who had also been at the wedding – and his aunt! "Oh! Yes, I remember you now."

"So where is he?" demanded the mother. "Where's my boy?"

"I have no idea," Holly said truthfully. "Please tell me you've heard from him, because I haven't from either him or Ange, and neither has Wesley."

"What do you mean?" the sister snapped. "*You* don't know where he is?"

Holly shook her head, carefully reaching under the counter for the phone handset, and positioning a finger over the nine button. The way the two were looking, they were set for a fight, and since both of them were big ladies who were several inches taller, and many pounds heavier than Holly, she wasn't keen on her chances of defending herself if they decided to slap her around. She'd heard Angie often saying that Topher's mum was pretty rough, but until now she hadn't realised quite how rough that might be. It wasn't just that she looked like she hadn't taken much care of herself down the years – Holly wouldn't judge someone like that, because not everyone was going to be able to afford a full range of skin care. It was the fact that her nose looked like it had been broken, possibly more than once, and her jaw seemed like it had taken a thump somewhere along the line as well. And whatever else Angie had said about Topher's family, his dad being physically abusive hadn't cropped up.

"I'm really sorry. You must be worried sick," Holly began, trying to placate them.

"Bloody right we are!" the sister threw back at her before she'd had chance to say more. "So what's Miss Hoity-toity done with him, eh? You're her bloody pal. Her best sodding buddy! *You* must know!"

"But I don't!" Holly managed to shout over the top of her. "The last I saw of Angie was weeks ago when she walked out of here and said they were going on holiday the following morning! And I'd only found out about *that* two days before. Since then I've been stuck here trying to hold things together on my own. Nobody's answering my calls or called me. I've not even had as much as a postcard."

"But you know where they've gone," was a statement, not a question from Topher's mother.

"The Caribbean," Holly scoffed. "Pretty big place! I was never told even which island, let alone a resort name. And *I* thought they were only going for two weeks, but when Wesley came here the other night looking for them, *he* told *me* that he'd briefly seen the tickets, and that they were for a *month's* holiday." She saw that disconcert the two women and took her chance to add, "And don't go throwing your weight around with him, either, because he only knows that they were *starting* in Jamaica. Apparently there were other stops after that, but he never got to find out what those were."

Then a thought occurred to her. "Anyway, if you're that worried, I presume that like Wesley, you've been in touch with the police already? So why are you here expecting me to know more than them?"

At the mention of police, both women began to look shifty and uncomfortable.

"Bloody hell! You haven't spoken to the police, have you?" Holly guessed.

"We don't get on with the filth," the aunt muttered darkly.

Then the door of the shop banged open and another older lady hurried in with a second at her heels.

"God's teeth, Gloria! We told you to wait for us," the more smartly dressed of the two said, clearly annoyed, and at the same time the pleasant lady alongside her triggered the memory that this was Topher's long-term foster mum – the woman who he thought of as his proper mum.

"I'm so sorry, dear," she panted, coming to stand right by Holly at the counter. "They haven't gone off on one at you have they?"

"Just a bit," Holly admitted, generating an annoyed growl from the smart lady, who introduced herself as,

"Susan Willoughby – used to be Christopher's social worker."

"His name is bloody *Indiana*!" the mother positively screeched. "That's the name I gived 'im, and that's the name yous should bloody well use!"

Christ! Poor Topher...Chris! Holly thought, as Susan and the foster mum, whose name Holly thought was Erica, exchanged exasperated glances. It certainly explained why Wesley had never mentioned calling Chris' parents, not even his father if he was still living with the dreadful Gloria.

Susan took a deep breath then said very firmly, "Well given that he never called himself by that name, we weren't going to get very far asking if anyone has seen Indiana Sykes, were we? Gloria, Greta, will you please go and wait outside if you're only going to make trouble."

"We'll go to the fucking pub, then," Greta snapped. "Come on, Glo, let's leave Miss Fancy-pants to mollycoddle the snowflake friend," and the two of them barged out, then seemed to get stuck in the doorway as they tried to navigate getting out of Holly's door and in through the pub's when they were so close together. As they virtually pitched themselves into *The Renegade*, Holly crossed her fingers that it would be Shea-Lea on duty, having seen Jesse heading out for the cash-and-carry earlier, and not the sweet Aimee. Shea-Lea could probably eat those two for breakfast if they got rowdy and she got riled.

"Are you okay?" Erica was asking worriedly. "God, those two! They're an absolute nightmare! We only got in touch with them to ask if they'd seen Chris recently, and somehow that pair of bloodhounds got the scent the something was amiss, and we haven't been able to move for tripping over them ever since. They turned up on my doorstep just as we were in the car and about to leave, otherwise we'd never have brought them here, but once they'd got into the car, we couldn't get them out."

"Good grief, that's a bit rough on you," Holly sympathised. She looked to Susan, "Couldn't you pull rank on them, or whatever social workers do?"

Susan winced. "Well in reality, I retired a few years ago. Erica and I have always stayed in touch, so it was obvious for her to contact me when she got worried. That manic pair who've just left don't know that, though, and it's only the pretence that I could go back and report them to whoever is looking after their cases now, that's keeping any sort of leash on them."

Holly made a silent 'oh' of understanding.

"So we can't rock the boat too hard," Erica said with a wink. "If they really went over the top, then yes, we both know people who could help, but there'd be a certain degree to which they – or at least Gloria – would be perceived as having a right to be worried about her son. The fact that that would be a first, and has only come about because of Chris' lottery win, wouldn't be enough of a reason to keep them out of the loop."

"Ouch, that's mercenary…I mean Gloria, not you," Holly hurriedly clarified.

"Oh, Gloria's a right piece of work," Erica said grimly. "That's why Chris worked on telling her as little as possible down the years."

"Does she know about Laura and the boys?"

Erica and Susan exchanged surprised glances before Susan asked warily,

"You know about them? We were given to understand that Angela didn't."

"Oh heck," Holly sighed, and explained about finding the video, and then talking to Wesley. "So you see I do know, but really only since the last few days. As for how much Angie has worked out, I honestly can't tell you, but I think she must know something for the tape to have been locked away here."

She took in how frazzled both Susan and Erica looked and offered them a coffee. "It's only instant, I'm afraid, but you're very welcome to one."

They gratefully accepted, and Holly waved them to the pair of bar seats that were behind the counter, originally intended for both her and Angie, though one had never been used. With it now being past the time when the local schools turned out, the High Street had gone quiet, and so Holly wasn't worried about a flood of customers while she went downstairs. She came back with the coffees, and the packet of hobnobs she'd treated herself to this morning, putting them on the counter before leaning on it and asking.

"So what made you come to me?"

"Desperation, to be honest," Erica said sadly. "Wesley's done what he told you he would, and went to the police this morning, but he also rang me and told me what he was doing and why. Luckily, they're taking it seriously, because in a cockeyed kind of way it's done us a favour with it being over forty-eight hours since Chris technically went missing. They can't do much before then."

Susan nodded. "Most folks turn up within a couple of days, you see, and the police simply don't have the manpower or resources to chase after every errant husband or grownup kid who goes off on a bender. Young kids and vulnerable adults get priority, of course, but Chris wasn't in that category. At the moment, they're tracking down his movements. We've got as far as Angie's car still being in the long-stay at Birmingham airport. That seems to have been easy because of number plate recognition and Wesley knowing which airport they left from. But after that it gets harder, because we don't know who Angela booked the holiday with or much of anything else."

"I thought if we came and talked to you," Erica continued, "something might trigger a memory for you. Something that might give us an extra clue. But now, hearing how much you talked over with Wesley, I don't think you can, can you?"

Holly shook her head. "No, I wish I could. When this first kicked off, and I hadn't heard from Angie, I was blaming Topher...sorry, Chris. But then the more

I've found out, the more I'm worried about him more than Ange. She can be a real madam when she's been crossed over something, and I can't imagine anything set her off more than finding out about Laura."

Then there was the sound of the pub door being flung open, and the next thing they saw was Jesse – who must have come back without Holly noticing – manhandling Gloria and Greta out, then giving them a push out onto the cobbled lane.

"Out!" they heard him order through the glass of the shop door. "You've got your ticket from here! Don't come back again or I'll call the police!"

At which point Holly realised that the two women weren't stumbling because of the cobbles – they were absolutely steamed, and having to hang on to one another just to stay upright!

"Oh no!" Erica groaned, clearly thinking of the drive back. But Holly went and turned the lock on the door and gestured to the back room.

"Come back here for a while. In that state, I doubt they'll even find the right car park, let alone your car. There are buses from here back to Worcester. They can sober up on a bench while they wait."

Then there was a tap on the door and Holly saw Jesse. Opening up for him, she asked,

"Were they causing trouble?"

He grinned. "Not exactly subtle, are they? The moment they started necking their first vodka and cokes, they started blathering on about coming back when these two ladies had left and having 'a word' with you. Couldn't have that. So while I'd normally stop serving someone who asked for a third vodka in such a short time, this time I served them, and to a fourth. It gave me reason to chuck them out and send them packing. I'll give the police station around the corner a call and warn them, so don't be surprised if you see blue lights in a minute, because I also told the coppers about them threatening to come to you."

"Jesse, you're my hero," Holly said gratefully, to which he gave a bow and a grin, then went back into the pub. Seeing that the two women with her had finished their drinks, she offered, "I'll lock up and walk you through the back ways to your car park. There are lots of cut-throughs, so you'll never need to encounter those two drunks."

Yet just as they were leaving, Erica got a phone call. Her worried, "Oh, I see," didn't do much to ease Holly's qualms, and she told her and Susan after she'd finished the call, "The police just called Wesley. They've confirmed that Chris and Angie's baggage was checked in, and that they boarded a flight to Jamaica. They're now contacting the Jamaican authorities."

"I guess all we can do is wait," Susan sighed, "but it doesn't stop me being worried sick," and Holly could only agree with her and Erica as she led them outside.

Chapter 12

After such an unsettling day, it wasn't surprising that Holly decided to go home for the night, convincing herself that now that the fair was over – Gloria and Greta excepting – there was less danger of damage being done to the shop overnight. Yet fate had other ideas. When she got to where she'd parked the car down a side street, nothing would induce it to start. She didn't know much about cars, but she was fairly sure that it ought to at least wheeze or cough a bit, whereas this did nothing.

"Oh you useless pile of junk!" she swore at it, and resigned herself to having to call one of the emergency organisations out – an expense she could have done without. The temptation was to just abandon it, but then that wasn't very fair to the people who lived on the road. So she spent an hour or so waiting for the truck to arrive, getting colder and hungrier as time went on.

When the RAC man did turn up, it wasn't good news.

"The battery is dead," he told her, "but looking under the bonnet, and underneath it, I'm not sure I'd want to put you a new battery in. This is one very dangerous car to drive, you know!"

"It's not mine," Holly said miserably, explaining about how she came to have it.

"Bloody hell, love, don't drive it!" the mechanic said with real concern, realising now that she wasn't just a negligent owner. "I'll tow you back to your flat, but then don't move it! Get a scrappy to come and take it away when that owner bloke shows up."

She didn't like to say that the chances of that were starting to get worryingly slim, but at least she got a ride home in the warm cab of the truck, and got there in one piece. Yet her flat was cold after being empty for a few days, and a bowl of soup with some pasta didn't do much to ease her feeling of emotional emptiness either. Looking out of her living room window onto the deserted street, she found herself longing to hear the happy comings and goings of the pub. She might not be fully part of that scene yet, but at least she didn't feel like the only person left alive when she was there. Whereas here, the entire population could have been turned into zombies and she wouldn't be able to tell.

Her biggest practical problem with regard to staying over at the shop was food – because although Angie had talked about getting them a microwave for the office, that had never appeared, and with the way things were now, Holly didn't want to spend more than she absolutely had to to put any equipment in. But a cheap microwave had suddenly become essential, so that she could at least have hot food, especially with the weather getting ever colder. Even a hot soup would be welcome. Long-term, salads and sandwiches weren't going to keep her going heading into winter.

The need to come back to do some washing would be inconvenient, because it would be silly to pay for a laundrette when she had a perfectly good washing machine here. And again, Holly didn't want to move more of her stuff than she could carry to the shop, simply because she might have to leave in a hurry. Court officials turning up to seal off the premises was not something she'd ever had to deal with before, so she had no idea how easy or hard it might be to retrieve her own belongings. No, she was going to have to close the shop on Sundays and Mondays, then lug a week's worth of clothes in on the train on Tuesdays, and come back on Saturday evenings. There was no other way around it.

The only hiccup going in the following morning, was realising that when she had a fuller rucksack next week, she really did need to catch the bus to the train station. Walking with that load wasn't an option, and she'd be slower getting from the station to the shop, indeed she might need to invest in something with wheels to save her back. Today, with only clean stuff for three days and her wash-bag, it was doable on foot, though. The train journey itself was pleasant, and the walk at the other end not too arduous. So it was a real shock when she turned off the lane with her keys in her hand, and saw the glass of the door all crazed.

"Christ!" she yelped. What on earth had happened? It looked like someone had tried to throw a rock through the door, then down on the floor she saw one that looked like it had come from next door's garden, and realised that was exactly what had happened.

"Holly," Shea-Lea's voice came from beside her, making her nearly jump out of her skin.

"What happened?" she gulped, looking up at Shea-Lea, who towered over her by a good six inches.

"Those two drunken women," Shea-Lea said with a roll of her eyes in disgust. "Happened about nine o'clock last night. Luckily we had one of the local darts teams in playing ours, so there were plenty of lads around to stop it from going any further. The cops came and took them away – don't think it hurt that Jesse had already warned them that the pair were likely to cause trouble."

"Oh God, what do I do about the door, though?" Holly panicked.

"Well we checked it last night, and it's still secure," Shea-Lea reassured her, "which is why we didn't bother calling you to come back. It looks ugly, but that's good toughened glass, and the daft pair were too drunk to hit it with any real force. Your insurance should cover that."

"Thanks," Holly said weakly, as Shea-Lea gave her arm a friendly squeeze and then went back inside.

It was all very well to talk of insurance, but where were the specific documents she'd need for a claim? Please God they were in Angie's desk, because if not, this was going to get difficult. Yes, she'd checked that they were insured for their contents and the monthly payments had been made, but now she realised that she'd been in a bit too much of a panic to check that she had all of what she needed to make an actual claim. Yet despite going through the desk thoroughly, Holly couldn't find all the insurance things – the proofs of payments which she'd found before, yes, but what she needed now, she realised was the specific policy. The only thing she had was the certificate of third-party liability, which they had to display in the shop. But that wasn't the same as the policy for the contents and building insurances.

Even so, she rang the insurance company, and having talked to a really helpful chap, sent him photos of the damage from her phone. Luckily, because she could at least quote the right policy references, they were going to play ball with her, and arranged to have someone come out to repair the glass as soon as possible. But the lack of certain bits of documentation relating to the building – rather than just the shop – really began to bother Holly. Where was the rest of this stuff? Because she was absolutely certain that there ought to be more paperwork here than this, and in an emergency she might need it. Where the heck could it be?

It was good in one way that she was too busy during the day to worry about it much, and by the time she closed she'd had almost wholly cash sales, and good ones at that, all of which helped her. She'd also been able to ring a local shop, give her bank card over the phone to pay, and have someone bring her a microwave around, so that was a bonus. All she needed to do now, was walk up to the big Tesco and get herself some food for the next couple of nights. There was a mini fridge down in the office – but only because of Angie's addiction to having actual cream in her coffee – so as long as she only bought small quantities, Holly wasn't going to have trouble storing food, especially if she left stuff like veg and fruit in one of the colder rooms upstairs.

Yet once she was back in the basement office, and with her lasagne and pot of veg taking turns in the microwave, she decided to call Wesley. They'd exchanged mobile numbers to be able to contact one another if something came up, and Holly thought she could tell him about Gloria without it sounding as if she was only contacting him to call for help. He answered after the third ring with,

"Hi, Holly. Everything okay?"

"Not exactly," she replied, and told him what had happened.

"You have got to be kidding," he groaned after she'd finished. "I hate that bloody woman, I really do. She never wanted to know Chris while he was growing up – when he might have cost her money – she was too busy going off having flings with random blokes and then fighting with his dad when she had to come back. It's no wonder his dad drank, living with her. Chris said it was a relief to be taken into care. Then the moment she finds out he's worth a fortune, she's all over him like a rash."

Holly gave a huff of agreement. "She seemed like that sort to me. The thing is, Wesley, the daft pair came back later and tried to heave a rock through the front door – the shop one, I mean, not the big oak one to the flat. I don't think they even twigged that that's what that one was. But now I'm realising that although I have all the paperwork relating to the shop as a business, I don't have important stuff relating to the building itself. Things like the actual building insurance. Can you help me? Do you have any idea where Chris would have put stuff like that?"

It was a measure of how much her perspective had changed that it came naturally to her now to call him Chris, and not Topher.

She heard Wesley groan but waited to give him chance to think.

"If I come over and pick you up," he began, "are you okay with me driving you over to Chris and Angie's flat? I have a key – not that Angie knew that, because she'd have gone schiz' over it if she had. You'll know more what you're looking for than me, but I do know that Chris told me where he hid things..." she heard Wesley gulp, "...just in case, he said. ...Bloody hell, I never for a second imagined the 'just in case' would be for something like this! I just thought he was thinking he'd hidden it in case Angie decided to have one of her famous clear-outs, and he wasn't around when he needed to be."

That really threw Holly. "Famous clear-outs? Wesley, Angie was a hoarder. She *never* threw anything away! It was her mum who used to insist on her having a sort out of things like clothes, because Angie's wardrobes used to be bursting at the seams!"

She heard Wesley's sharp intake of breath. "Really? God! The last few months, she was always clearing things out. Insisting that Chris threw this out, or that out. Amongst other things, I've got his prized Hornby railway stuff at my place, not that he had much of it when he was a kid, but he was desperate to hand on the collection he'd made once he was earning a wage to his lads. ...Oh God, he couldn't tell Angie that's why he wouldn't just sell them. I think I knew that at the time, but thought that there was some sentimental value there as well.

But it was because he really didn't trust her not to go full *Psycho* on him, wasn't it?"

"I'm sorry, Wesley, but yes, I think it was." She didn't want to depress Wesley any further by saying it sounded like Angie had been trying to remove any clues to help people track Chris down when he vanished. Maybe she even thought it would make it seem like he'd walked out of his own accord if there was nothing of his at the old flat, so deflecting suspicion from herself? "And yes, I'm happy for you to come and take me to the flat. I think we both need answers. Can you come to the shop tomorrow for about six o'clock? That'll give me time to close up and micro' a bite to eat."

He gave a weak laugh. "Let's make it just after five and I'll treat you to a meal. I may not be rolling in money like Chris was at the end, but I'm in a way better financial position than you. Please. As friends both wanting to find the truth, let me treat you to this."

What could Holly say to that but 'yes'? But before then she had to get through another night up in the flat alone.

As before, the start of the evening was easy enough, especially as she'd brought her elderly laptop with her this time so she could also dip into online programmes, though she wasn't normally a great TV watcher. Jesse had said he was happy for her to piggyback onto the pub's Wi-Fi, so catching up on the latest seasons of her few favourite series at least killed the long hours alone. A mug of soothing herb tea before bed meant that she drifted off quickly enough, or at least she had no memory of lying awake trying to get to sleep. So at first she drowsily thought she was still dreaming when she heard a woman's voice saying,

"Come out and stretch your legs, Master McAllister. There's nought but the kitchen cat abroad at this hour." She was faint, but definitely somewhere out on one of the landings.

"Thank ye kindly, Mistress Joan," a deep, Scottish voice replied, and Holly heard a footstep and a clunk, then a footstep and a clunk, as if coming down from high up in the house.

"I bless the day I found you and the lad in the vegetable patch," the woman called Joan carried on in her very local accent. "The knock at the door you heard around midday was my cousin Patience, come to town for the market. She tells me that other houses haven't fared as well as us, though she's safe enough out at the farm with a husband too old to fight, and her lads just a bit too young. The good Lord only knows what Mary and me would have been put through if ye hadn't been here when those Royalists came a knocking."

Holly heard her tutting, and the voices moving through to the room above – or so Holly thought by the sounds of movement.

"Here. Sit ye down by the fire," Holly heard her say from what she guessed was the room's doorway. The footsteps moved into the room and the voice went slightly fainter. "I'll poke it up a bit. …There. Is that better? I'll go and fetch ye another bowl of stew I've been keeping warm."

Her footsteps came clomping down the stairs, and past Holly's door, only for another and younger woman's voice to come from just outside asking,

"Joan, when are they leaving? We can't keep them here! It's dangerous!"

"Now you listen to me, young Mary," Joan said sternly from just the other side of Holly's door. "Did the mistress give a tinker's cuss about what might happen to us when she left? No, she didn't. All she cared about was getting out of the town afore the soldiers came through. And if ye ask me, she was every bit as worried about those Royalists she supports as she was about Parliament's men!

"Has she ever asked us what we think? Who we support? No. But it would've been a different kettle of fish if we'd not been seen in the big church when she went. Never ye mind that when she went off a'visiting, that we went to the chapel down the town instead, and that's where we'd rather have been praying. She's the mistress, we must pray as she does. But we don't get to run to the countryside and safety when she does, do we? No. Then it's, 'ye mind the house, Joan,' and 'don't let them take the best linen, Joan,' and 'don't ye cook them the best stored root vegetables, Mary'. No thought for what might happen to us if any soldiers forced upon us for the night found out ye was feeding them slops compared to what was in the pantry!"

"I never though o' that," Mary confessed.

"Well think on it now, lass. I thought on nothing more than it being my Christian duty to take in Master McAllister with his broken leg, and his young lad. Nor that I was doing anything but being kindly when I gave him my dear Thomas' shirt and breeches while I cleaned the stink off that wool of his. But when those clubmen who are supposed to be protecting us came knocking at the door, it saved us from all manner of disasters that he came hobbling out on his crutch and stared them down. He looks every bit the wounded seasoned fighter, and they weren't to know he weren't on their side while he stayed silent.

"It meant I could say as we were already housing soldiers, without him having to open his mouth, and that will save us from Mistress Julia's fate up the road. That poor maid of hers will never be the same again, and that's if her belly doesn't start to swell soon on top of her woes. No, girl, you count your blessings that Master McAllister landed at our door, because Scotsman or not, he's been the saving o' us. So as far as I'm concerned, he can stay here until he's well enough to make a run for it and rejoin his friends. Now out of my way. I'm getting them something to eat."

At that point Holly realised that softer footsteps had come down the upper stairs and come into the room above. So who was the lad? This McAllister's son? His personal servant? Was he truly a kid – some teenager following because he had to and half scared out of his wits? Or was he just a younger man? She didn't get her answer that night because the footsteps of the men hunting them came again, and after that she drifted back to sleep while they were all silent.

Duncan McAllister 5

Duncan hadn't intended to play the defending hero. He'd been hoping to stay out of the way and leave quietly. Fate had other ideas.

He wasn't convinced that the soldiers who came knocking on the door, calling for them to open in the name of the king were actually Royalist soldiers. To an experienced fighter like him, they looked more like the local clubmen. The clubmen were local men who had banded together to prevent the ransacking of goods and chattels by armies of either side. The young men all stood at the main door, puffed up like so many farmyard cockerels, and making as much noise.

Thankfully, his plaid and breeks were taking a time to dry out after the vigorous scrubbing Joan had given them, and he was still in her husband's breeches and hose, though the linen shirt was his own. That shirt had its fair share of patches and mends, though, and could have come from just about anywhere. So he'd unbuckled the straps that held his dirk to his leg and shoved it under a big oak trestle, and then limped his way with one crutch to stand behind Joan in the doorway.

"You have no reason to come inside," Joan was saying sternly, but Duncan could see how she was shaking. "As you can see, we already have wounded soldiers here."

"Ah, but whose?" a cocky young man, with rather too much belly to have ever seen a hard life, demanded.

"Well you asked us to open in the name of the king, so who else's would I admit to having here?" Joan riposted.

"Who do you serve?" Duncan growled, doing his very best to quench his Highland burr and adopt more of a local accent. He wouldn't attempt much more, and instead gave the lad his steeliest glare.

Little did he know that appearing out of the gloom of the hallway, like some icy-eyed giant, put the fear of God into the lad and his friends who in truth, had only been asked by their elders and betters to go around to the main houses, and make sure everyone was all right. None of them had seen a fight in earnest, but the way Duncan's shirt gaped at the neck showing the end of a ferocious chest scar, along with the one on the heavily muscled arm that appeared against the doorjamb, said he had. The fact that Duncan had thumped his arm against the jamb to stop himself from pitching on his nose as his balance went with only the one crutch, was something they completely missed. All they saw were the scarred knuckles, that nasty scar across a tensed forearm bigger than any local man had other than the blacksmith, and those eyes.

"Off you go," Joan said with satisfaction, as she saw the six all take a step back. "I know you boys. You're just using your fathers' authority to strut around."

"We'll be back with others," the leader threatened, and with black looks, the young men walked away back to the high street.

When Joan had closed the door, Duncan asked. "You said you know them? So who are they that they dare come hammering on the door like that?"

Joan pursed her lips and crossed her arms under her bosom. "Sons of the town burgesses," she said with a sniff of derision. "I'm told that four of them, including the one with the big mouth, went off to join the king. That didn't last long when they realised they were meant to march away and keep going. I don't know quite when they came back, but I *am* sure they deserted. Their fathers keep saying that they came back to help defend the town and its people, but if we're depending on them, Lord help us, we're lost already."

Duncan nodded and left it at that, but unlike Joan, he couldn't dismiss the idea that they would come back with others – and next time it might be real soldiers who wouldn't back down. Behind him he heard Sorley's running feet coming to him.

"Duncan? What was that?" Sorley skidded to a halt and handed him back the dirk.

"Local clubmen, lad, but it means trouble. We need to find a hiding place for the claymore. I hate the thought, but if we need to get out in a hurry, I'm scarce able to handle myself, let alone wi' the weight o' that thing on my back. It'll be weeks afore I can wield it in anger, and it marks us as Scots as much as my plaid."

Luckily, Sorley had only had a thick wool blanket to use as a plaid, which was so faded it was no different from any other well-used piece of wool. Duncan was damned if he'd leave his plaid behind as well, it was too warm and too useful to abandon, but it might have to go in a sack for the first few miles. Sorley didn't have a proper sword either, only what was known as a hanger – a roughly hammered out short sword. So if they had to make a run for it, the best thing Duncan could do was take Sorley's hanger, being the better swordsman, and his dirk and leave the claymore behind. Luckily it wasn't a family heirloom or anything, though it had been Duncan's for a long time.

"The main room fireplace!" Sorley declared. "It'll be a long time before any fire is lit in there. I saw a hook up the chimney when I was sweeping it out for Goodwife Joan. They must smoke hams and stuff up there when they have them. You'll be able to reach it no trouble, but few others will."

Duncan doubted that a family as rich as this would stoop to smoking ham up the main parlour chimney, but if they had something more luxurious that required smoking, or just keeping out of the way of rodents, then that might be what the hook was there for. He just prayed it would hold the claymore's weight. Together they made their way upstairs to the first floor, and then Sorley went and fetched the huge sword, which was nearly as tall as he was. Even carrying it the short distance down the stairs had him puffing and blowing, enough that he knew Duncan was right to hide it. There was no way that Sorley could carry it across his back, let alone help Duncan at the same time.

Joan came into the main parlour just as Duncan had hefted it into his hand to lift it. "What are you doing?"

"Hiding this. You don't want men searching the house and finding it. Without it, you can say we were just rogues who broke in. With it, we're enemy soldiers you've been harbouring. I don't want any trouble coming down on you or Mary, not when you've helped us."

The muscles on his arms flexed, doing that funny butterfly thing to Joan's stomach, and then he turned and hefted the thing up and onto the hook. Half in the chimney, with Sorley hanging on to him so that he didn't lose his balance, nonetheless Joan could see the way the shirt stretched to bursting point over Duncan's shoulders. No shirt had ever clung like that to her husband.

As he limped away on his crutches again, Joan asked Sorley, "Is the Jean he sings of in that song his wife?" She was hoping it wouldn't be, yet Sorley's innocent answer – being a young lad who knew nothing yet of unrequited love – if anything crushed her hopes even more.

"Jean? …Ah! *Farewell to Lochaber*, that's what the song is called. No, Jean is just the lassie in the song. Isobel was Duncan's love, but she died. He's never wanted another woman. He says they can't compare to Isobel." Sorley was already brushing the soot carefully off his shirt into the grate, so he didn't see Joan's downcast expression. "Jean is no more a special name to him than, say, *Barbara Allen*…which is another song if ye' didn'a ken it, mistress."

He didn't look back to see Joan cuffing a tear from her eyes, but when she went down to the kitchen, sharp little Mary noticed. "What's the matter, Joan?" she asked slyly.

"I'm a foolish old woman, that's all," Joan said with another sniff. "I dared to hope that when they go, that Master McAllister might want the company of a woman and take me with him. I'm so heart-sore of being alone. It's been twenty years since my Jeremiah left me to go to his God. And yes girl, I do say *his* God. Jeremiah was more married to God than he ever was to me.

"I'm tired, Mary. Tired of going to that chapel, where nobody asks me how *I* am. All they ever say is how sad it is that a fine member of the congregation like Jeremiah was taken from them – *them*, not me! Has God answered my prayers? No, he hasn't. I don't want to end up a shrivelled prune in my old age, still scrubbing this great big house for the mistress, with Master too tight to pay for more servants to help us. *You* only have to cook a few meals, not for a household full, because they haven't entertained in years. But *I* have to clean the whole place, top to bottom, even if hardly anybody lives in it. I want my own cottage, Mary, and a man to get old with."

She gave another sniff and went off with the feather duster in her hand to clean yet another room that wasn't lived in. Mary, on the other hand, was furious.

Leave?

Joan leave her here? Alone?

Oh no, Mary wasn't having that.

Who knew, if Joan turned on the tears, that big lump of a Scotsman might just relent and take her anyway. Then where would Mary be?

No, she wasn't standing for that. Not being abandoned to be the only servant until the family could hire more. Tonight she was going to walk down to Burgess Holmes' house and find his son. He'd be spoiling to get his own back, so once he knew there were Scots in the house, he'd round up proper soldiers and get them thrown out. That would sort Joan's ideas of abandoning her!

Chapter 13

All thoughts of the ghosts were obliterated again by more worldly problems when Holly got back down to the shop. She hadn't been open for long before she got another phone call off Wesley.

"I know I'm picking you up tonight," he said, his voice full of stress, "but I thought you should know, I've heard from the police. They tracked Chris and Angie on the flight to Jamaica, and they got lucky with the travel agent because it was only the second one they called that Angie had used. So they've been able to ring the hotel – some top of the range place at Montego Bay, apparently, but then that would be typical of Angie – and they've confirmed that both of them stayed there for the week they were booked in for."

Holly heard him swallowing hard and drawing in a ragged breath before continuing, "The thing is, the manager says he's sure they didn't leave together. Chris took one taxi and she took another, and he remembered them because they'd been fighting like cat and dog in the foyer the day before, and he was glad to see the back of them. ...Well the DC who I spoke to said it sounded more like it was Angie they were glad to be shot of, but certainly, they remembered the pair of them going."

"Oh, I don't like the sound of that," Holly groaned.

"It gets worse. They were booked onto a twenty-two day *cruise*. A bloody boat out on the ocean, Holly! God knows what might happen out there. ...So after Jamaica they were all over the place – or supposed to be. Well the police have confirmed that Angie got on the cruise ship at Bridgetown, because she made a right pain of herself with the onshore cruise representatives, but nobody remembers seeing Chris."

"But is that simply because he got on the boat without making a fuss?"

"That's the point the DC made to me. The thing is, the coppers over here have done as much as they can by phone. They're now going to have to wait for their Jamaican counterparts to get in touch with the ship, and right now it could be anywhere between Saint Barthélemy, Anguilla, and the British Virgin Islands, none of which are exactly over policed. God help us, but they might have to wait until the cruise ends at somewhere called Saint Martin, when everyone gets transferred to an airport for the trip home."

"Oh Jeez, that doesn't sound good," Holly agreed. "And I guess that if *someone* has been using the cabin, and the double or king-sized bed has been slept in and stuff, the people who go in to clean up and replenish things won't really have taken any notice whether there's been one person or two in there? You can't imagine the poor souls who do that job are overpaid, and with what that cruise must have cost, I bet they get more than their fair share of complainers and moaners. You know the sort, 'I've paid, so I'm going to moan if any tiny thing isn't just how I want it.' So if someone isn't causing them grief, they're barely going to be aware of them."

"I looked up the size of cruise ships," Wesley added mournfully. "Holy shit, Holly, they *start* with about a thousand people – that's the same size as my old school, and you wouldn't notice one kid wasn't there amongst that lot – and they can go up to nearly nine or *ten* times that number of passengers! Did you know, roughly ten people a year go missing off cruise ships, and on average only a couple of them get found? I'm praying that Chris doesn't end up as one of those statistics.

"It would be too easy, wouldn't it? Just spike his drink and tip him overboard and not say anything. Those figures I've looked at come from people who panic when their nearest and dearest don't turn up for dinner, not some ice queen who just swans off the boat without saying a word to anyone! I mean, do they look at passports when people get off? Especially if they're told they're carrying on to somewhere on the island they've docked at. Would it be more likely to happen at the airport when they're assumed to be leaving? So if Chris never gets to the airport, will anyone notice?"

Wesley's words plagued Holly long after they'd finished talking, with his reminder that he'd be around about five that afternoon, so she was grateful for another reasonably busy day to distract her. Yet the thought of Angie smugly strolling off the cruise ship, and collecting Chris' baggage with her own to distract people further, just wouldn't leave her. Her imagination was running riot, with her even wondering if maybe Angie had, at some point when the ship had been out at sea, thrown Chris' packed suitcase over the side? Or had she asked one of the porters to take his bags off at one of the more remote islands with the excuse that they were breaking up and he was going home from there? That would make tracking Chris even harder, especially if the porter was local to whichever island it was, not on the ship. Was that even possible? Since taking such a thing herself hadn't even been the stuff of her dreams, Holly had no idea how luxury holidays to exotic locations worked, and what could or couldn't be done.

What she did know was what Angie was like when crossed – when someone blocked her from doing exactly what she wanted. Holly knew that in the case of two previous jobs, Angie had walked off mere days before she was going to get fired for barely having turned up amongst other things. But had then made all sorts of claims of bullying and sexual harassment which had cost her bosses time and money to defend themselves against, even though in the end they had been cleared of any wrongdoing. Nor did Angie seem to care about that. For her, the big thing was the striking back in a spiteful way against someone who hadn't worshipped at the shrine of Angie, and Holly knew that the bitter taste these memories were now leaving had only arisen since she'd truly opened her eyes to who Angie was. She could no longer kid herself that there had been at least some level of fault on the part of those Angie whom had accused.

Why was I so stupid for so long? she berated herself in a lull just after lunchtime, when the shop went quiet for half an hour. *Is this partly my fault? Was I so wrapped up in my own problems that I didn't even look twice at Chris and see him for who he really was? How am I going to live with myself if he really has come to harm, because what's going to happen to Laura and those two kids in that case? Did he have chance to make a proper will so that they get taken care of, and Angie can't grab all the money?* And there was the additional thought of, *Did they have a joint account she could access, and if so, is it possible she could drain the money while sitting in luxury in Mexico or somewhere?*

Again, international banking laws were something far removed from Holly's experience, so when Shea-Lea popped around at lunchtime to ask her about the window replacement and if that was going to happen, she found herself being bombarded with questions about how things worked when in one country and needing to access money from another.

"Steady, Holly. Take some breaths, babe," Shea-Lea said soothingly. "I get that this is really worrying, but for pity's sake, don't start blaming yourself. There's only one person at fault here...well maybe two...but neither of them is you! If Angie has turned violent, that's on her conscience, not yours. And if Chris, or Topher, or whatever his name really is, hadn't spun Angie a pack of lies, she might not be going full psycho on him now. He might be the victim, but he's not exactly blameless. You, on the other hand, are...so stop beating yourself up."

On the other hand, when she got into *The Renegade* again, Shea-Lea was sufficiently worried about Holly to have a long chat with Jesse.

"Poor Holly," Jesse agreed. "What a bloody tough life she's had. You know, I think this blaming herself must come from years of everyone telling her that stuff is her fault. You don't get like that if you've had normal parents and support."

"I wish there was something we could do for her," Shea-Lea said, "but I'm damned if I can think what."

"I do," Jesse said with a sudden grin. "I'm going to ring Ash. He wanted to buy the whole building back when it was on the market. It was only because Topher – or as we now know, Angie – out-bid him, that he's not Holly's landlord, instead of Topher being ours. I bet if they have to sell, he'd be here like a shot, so I think I'll go and bring him up to date."

"Bloody good idea," Shea-Lea agreed. "At least if we can tell Holly that we know who'd want the building, and that she might not get evicted before she's got herself sorted out, that ought to help."

However, Jesse had more than that on his mind.

"Hi, Ash," he said as his uncle answered the phone, "I've got some news for you," and proceeded to bring him up to date with what had been going on. But he also knew that Ash was a terrible sucker for a sad story. God alone knew, enough women had tried to take Ash to the cleaners on the back of one, and now Jesse was thinking that Holly, who was genuinely in need of someone who would help, might restore Ash's faith in human nature a bit.

He also knew that Ash was terribly lonely since the break-up of his last relationship, which had ended badly. Ash would give every last penny he had to have a relationship like Jesse had with Shea-Lea, a partnership in the true sense of the world, not just having someone who mindlessly went along with what he wanted…until the day they didn't and left to start lawsuits. It didn't mean that there was never a cross word, or that they agreed upon everything. For a start, Shea-Lea had been a true Australian surfer girl, whereas Jesse wouldn't have cared if he never saw another big wave again, and there were plenty of other things they didn't share. But they could be vehemently arguing their case to each other one minute, and then falling about in fits of giggles the next, all disagreements dismissed, and that was what Jesse knew Ash craved.

"I feel so bloody sorry for her, Ash," he said, and heard Ash's sharp intake of breath. It was rare that Jesse openly said he felt sorry for people, mostly thinking that (ill health aside) most people would be in less of a pickle if they just tried to help themselves a bit more. Jesse wasn't uncaring, he just had a strong opinion that you did what you could for yourself first before you went crying for help from others, not least because the people who were usually the first to offer help had their own crap to work out, and sometimes had much worse to deal with.

"Do you think I should come over?" Ash asked, hurriedly adding, "in case there's a chance I need to move fast to buy the building?"

Jesse wasn't remotely fooled. It was his talk of Holly that was playing on Ash, because Ash had a sharp, on-the-ball accountant, who was more than capable of handling any purchase without Ash being on the spot. But what he said was, "It couldn't hurt to come and have a look at the place. You said you never got to see the upstairs properly, didn't you? Well I'm sure that Holly would be happy to show you around the place. She's got everything to gain by getting another landlord lined up in case something really has gone horribly wrong."

"Is your spare bedroom still free? Only Eric," his very capable sound engineer, "just needs to put the finishing touches to the album we're working on for a local group, and then I've got a break in bookings."

He would have been surprised, had he been on a video call, to see Jesse dancing around the room, punching triumphal fists into the air, but his voice was convincingly neutral as he said, "Yeah, no problem, Ash. We'll have the bed made up and the beers in the fridge waiting for you. When would you like to come over?"

As he rang off, he turned around and saw Shea-Lea waving an admonishing finger at him. "You old match-maker you," she said with mock severity.

"*Moi*?"

"Yes, you! Bloody hell, you blokes talk about women, but when you set your mind to it, you're ten times worse."

"And what if I am? You've said yourself that what Ash needs is a *good* woman, not just some tart who'll try to drain his bank account. Well Holly is *good* – we've both said that."

"We have," Shea-Lea sighed, giving in with good grace. "And God knows, she's a hundred times more deserving of a nice guy like Ash than bloody Shazzy," referring to Ash's nightmare of an ex. Then a thought occurred to her. "Hadn't we better make sure she hasn't got some not-quite-yet ex-husband lurking in the wings, though? We don't want to get Ash embroiled in that kind of stuff."

"Over to you," Jesse said with a wink. "She's more likely to open up to you over something like that than me."

"Oh gee, thanks mate," Shea-Lea said with a roll of her eyes, but knowing that he was right – a wounded lady like Holly wasn't going to open up to a man in the way she might to another woman.

It took a bit of thinking on her part, but she finally came up with a reason to nip around to the shop when it went quiet after about four o'clock, and before she knew that Wesley would be coming to pick Holly up.

"Hi babe!" she called cheerfully, strolling into the shop with a nonchalance she didn't quite feel. "Only me again."

"Something wrong?" Holly immediately asked worriedly.

"God no! We just had a thought, that's all. I don't know if we said, but Ashley – that's Jesse's uncle, though you wouldn't know it to look at them together – nearly bought this building. Well Jesse gave him a ring to let him know what's going on, because it affects Ash's investment in the pub."

Holly clapped a hand to her mouth. "Oh my God! Of course it does. I'm so sorry, Shea-Lea, I never stopped to think that you were as much caught up in this as me."

"Don't be daft," Shea-Lea said, brushing it off. "Ash has enough money to see Jesse and me right for a few months while things get sorted. We're never going to end up out on the streets," and took in the way Holly's expression changed, guessing that if she didn't have money coming in, that would be a very real worry for Holly herself. "However, we thought we'd get Ash over here so that you can show him around upstairs," Shea-Lea carried on as if not noticing. "He didn't get as far as a visit up there before Angie out-bid him on the sale, you see. But if Topher or Chris, or whoever he is, wants to sell, or his lawyers need to sell to get stuff through probate, then it would be really good for all of us to have a buyer ready and waiting."

Holly managed a stunned nod.

"So Jesse and I were thinking…if you find insurance documents for the whole building, rather than you locking them in the shop – because as you feared, you could get locked out of it – would it help if we stored them in *The Renegade's* safe? That way, they're right here if either of us needs them, but we're in far less danger of being locked out than you are, simply because we have no personal connection to Angie or Chris. Any lawyer would surely acknowledge that we have the right to carry on trading, even if the building is in the process of being sold?"

Holly wrung out another nod. "Yes. That actually makes perfect sense. Thank you."

Shea-Lea gave her her warmest smile, the one she reserved for their more fragile customers in need of some extra care. "But what about you personally? Is there someone you could go and stay with? An ex you're still on good terms with…?" She left the question hanging, only to be deeply saddened by the way Holly gave a bitter laugh.

"An ex? Chance would be a fine thing! No, Shea-Lea, I'm not the kind of woman men are interested in."

That shocked Shea-Lea so much the words, "Jeez, Hol'! Everybody has somebody!" were out of her mouth before she could stop them, hurriedly qualifying them with, "What in God's name has given you that idea?"

Yet Holly only shook her head. "Looking like you do, I bet you've never had any trouble getting boyfriends. Me? I'm bloody invisible. I could never hold a candle to the girls around me when I was a teenager, and it's never got any better as I've got older. Men look straight past me like I'm a bloody ghost who's hardly there."

"Christ, Hol', that's awful! What about Angie? Wasn't she supposed to be your mate? Did that apply to her too? Was that what made you friends?" Shea-Lea was thinking she might have a whisker more sympathy for the dreadful Angie if she too had been endlessly sidelined, only to find that even when she got married, that she was her husband's second choice by a long mile, too.

Yet Holly's answer was rather worse. "Oh Angie was the one I couldn't come near to competing with. ...Look at me, Shea-Lea. Short, not exactly slim because I can only afford to eat cheap carbs instead of properly healthy food, and about as average as you can get."

"Holly, you're lovely," Shea-Lea protested, getting more worried by the minute. "You have a lovely smile and you're one of the nicest people Jesse and I have met."

Holly sniffed. "That doesn't count for much when it comes to first impressions, though, does it? There was me – non-descript brownish hair, slightly dirty-grey eyes, in charity shop clothes – alongside Angie. She had hair that would take being curled, straightened, or coloured as many times as the fashion changed, and with the money to afford the top hairdressers to do it. Me? My hair goes brittle and starts falling out if I try to use so much as a home colour on it. And Angie could afford to be in the latest fashion whenever we went out. I couldn't, and I'm an average size, so in the charity shops there were tons of trendy clothes that people had put weight on and couldn't get into anymore, but not in my size."

"Was Angie very pretty?" Shea-Lea asked, fearing that Angie had been one of those girls who'd suddenly blossomed into their looks without realising the effect of dragging her friend who was less blessed along with her.

"Pretty?" Holly said with a shrug. "No, not particularly. ...I suppose Angie was no more nor less than any of my other friends, but the lads at school never seemed to have trouble noticing them, either. All of them seemed to find someone who thought they were worth marrying. Then as we got older and Ange was the one who was still single, at least she was able to make the most of what she'd got...could *afford* to make the most of her looks."

Shea-Lea felt sick. This was awful. She'd never met anyone who thought themselves so undeserving of even the smallest loving attention. No wonder the dreadful Angie had been able to take advantage of her so much, and suddenly she was fully with Jesse. If anyone deserved to have the kind of life a nice guy like Ash could give them, then it was Holly.

Mercifully, she was saved from having to field any awkward questions back at her by Wesley turning up, so she was able to make her excuses and leave. But back in the pub, she relayed everything to Jesse, and he was as appalled as her.

"That Angie must be one cold bitch," Shea-Lea fumed at him. "I don't think Holly sees it – or at least not yet she doesn't – but I reckon Angie kept her around because she knew she could out-shine her at every step, and that's just unkind! You don't use someone to make yourself look better. You don't do that to your friends, you just don't."

Duncan McAllister 6

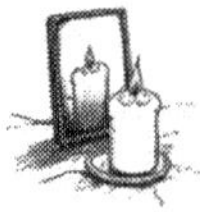

Duncan was right to be worried. It only took until the following evening for another thumping to come on the door, and this time he and Sorley knew from the deeper tone of the voices that there were older men with the young clubmen.

"Sorley! Out on the roof, now!" Duncan ordered, thanking his luck that they were up in the attic already.

"But Duncan..." the lad protested.

"No, lad, there's too many o' them to fight, and I'll no' have you dying to protect me."

"But I fight beside ye!"

"Aye, in battle, ye do, but this is no' a battle and it would be a senseless waste o' your life to be skewered by some fat local burgess." Duncan had the window open, and was hoisting Sorley up onto the sill even as he spoke.

Sorely scrambled out onto the tiles, but refused to let Duncan latch the window, just push it to. His worried little face was at the pane as he watched Duncan limp to the door and heave the chest across in front of it. Then Duncan positioned himself at the hinge end in front of the chest, dirk drawn, and listening intently.

It took a moment, but then both of them heard the tramp of heavy feet coming up the main staircase. Sorley saw Duncan lean a little harder to the door and then shake his head. Turning to the window, he held up seven fingers. Duncan had been right, there was no way he could fight seven men on his own and with only one good leg to stand on. They came right up to the landing below them and went into every room. Duncan even heard them opening and shutting the occasional cupboard.

To his and Sorley's great relief, though, for some reason they didn't come up the servants' stairs into the attic. Did they not realise that the door in the landing panelling on each floor led to another stair? All Duncan heard was the heavy footsteps going back down, and then a moment later the front door slamming shut. In a heartbeat, Sorley was back in through the window and past the door Duncan was holding open a crack to hear better. He ran lightly to the top of the main stairs and then ran back up the servants' stairs to Duncan making thumbs up signs.

Yet Duncan wasn't convinced. "*Shhh*, lad. Be still. They've no' gone yet," he said, and sure enough they then heard men coming back through from the direction of the kitchen, and wishing Joan goodnight. Only when the door had slammed a second time, and they'd waited longer did Duncan breathe a sigh of relief.

Shortly afterwards they heard Joan coming panting up the stairs to them. "Are you all right, Master McAllister?" she called softly.

"Aye, Goodwife Joan, we are," Duncan replied, sinking down on the chest, glad to get the weight off his ankle. He wasn't to know how lucky they were that Sorely was already back in the room with the window closed – therefore not showing his escape route – by the time Joan came in, and then Mary come stamping in after her.

"Look what you've brought down on us!" Mary said savagely, turning to Joan to say, "I told you this would bring trouble!" She turned and flounced out, leaving Joan rolling her eyes at her back.

"The good Lord knows what gets into that girl some times," she sighed, but Duncan was having a nasty feeling about Mary. She'd seemed almost angry that he and Sorley were here – or rather *still* here. Had she *expected* the men to come up here and drag them out? Did she simply speak unthinkingly in the market, or was there something more sinister in her behaviour? Would she have taken their hunters up into one of the other attic rooms, if she'd realised they wouldn't come up here, where they might see out onto the roof? If Mary had known of that escape route over the tiles, might it have been the end of Sorley as well as himself?

It meant that the following morning he made Sorley stay upstairs with him keeping watch, not going out and tending the garden.

"I'm sorry lad, and I'm sorry for Joan, but if that garden looks too well kept, that's going to raise questions. Better a few weeds and no soil obviously turned in the last few days when those men come back, and they will return."

When Sorley asked how he could be so sure, Duncan refrained from telling Sorley of his fears about Mary. One of Sorley's finest qualities was his unwavering loyalty, and Duncan knew that if the lad thought Mary had betrayed himself, Sorley would be down in the kitchen having it out with her in a heartbeat. Sorley might be philosophical about dangers to himself but not to his cousin.

"They'll search up here next time," Duncan told Sorley, "so we need a better place to hide."

With that in mind, the two of them began systematically probing and investigating every loose bit of panelling and hiding place. In what would in future years become a cupboard with shelves, Duncan found a space he could stand upright in, which was clearly only used to get to the back of the panels on the main staircase. A little work with his knife got the outside latch off, and then a piece of string attached to the inside for him to pull it shut with. A slim wedge of wood that he could shove into the opening side would help to make it stick if anyone tried it. For Sorley, they found a crawl space in the woodwork at right angles to Duncan's hideaway. It would mean that they could whisper to one another if they were careful, and Duncan wanted to be able to hear if anyone dragged Sorley out.

It was a good job they did find those places, because the men came back two days later. This time they did come up the servants' stairs, but each morning Duncan now made a point of hiding away everything that was theirs. His plaid had gone under a loose floorboard, and the blankets Joan had provided he made sure got folded neatly and put into the third servants' bedroom, where the dust was thick enough on the few meagre bits of furniture for it to be clear that nobody had been in there for a long time. They even turned the pallet mattresses, so that if someone came in the morning, the beds would not be warm to the touch.

Through a knothole in the wood, Duncan watched four men come into the room and search. Yet they weren't as thorough as Duncan would have been if the tables had been turned, and left after a cursory look around.

"We've been here too long, lad," Duncan said afterwards, as he sat on the bed, trying to rub the feeling back into his stiff legs from standing still for so long. "If I'm honest, when I planted my foot in that bluidy hole in July, I didn'a think we'd still be here wi' September only two days away."

"But Duncan, you couldn'a walk," Sorley protested. "Ye canna walk properly even now."

"Then I'll have to bluidy limp," Duncan said determinedly, "but we need to get out into the fields. It's too dangerous to stay here."

Yet as they made their plans, when Sorley went down to get their bowls of stew two days later, Mary was in an even fouler mood than normal. But her words brought a spark of hope for Sorley and Duncan.

"'Tis said that the army have given up on besieging Hereford," she said, splattering ladles of stew into the two bowls with even more venom than normal.

"But that's our army, on Parliament's side," Sorley gasped. "I thought you supported Cromwell?"

"I do!" Mary snapped. "But that doesn't mean I want more like *you* coming through here, raiding and taking everything we have!" she saw his blank look and added savagely, "'Tis said in the market that they've been ten days without bread. Ten days! Well you know what will happen when they get here – *we'll* be the ones without bread! And the bloody king has just taken Worcester, so *they* could come our way too," and she turned her back on him and began pounding away at a loaf of her own.

Sighing, Sorley left her to it, but already knowing that the bread they'd have tomorrow would be another loaf with all the life knocked out of it and as tough as a brick.

On the other hand, Duncan was much encouraged by the news. "I've been talking to Joan," he confided to Sorley, "and I've a better idea of where we are now. If the earl is leaving Hereford, he's got to get across that big river we crossed on the way here, the Severn. He can't go to Worcester if what Mary told you is right, because if he does, he's got to fight the king on his own with no backup. So I reckon he'll have to cross where we did on the way here, and that means he and our lads will come back through here – or at least close by. We have to watch for them, lad."

It meant that the two of them got ready each morning and went into the front parlour. If he could, Duncan wanted to get his claymore before leaving, and he knew they wouldn't get much warning. He sat in a chair by the big window, just into the shadows, from where he could observe the lane below for comings and goings. He guessed they'd have to be incredibly lucky to see a soldier, but people rushing to get to safety up at the church would be a sign that something was happening. Hopefully, Sorley would have time to dash upstairs and get the plaid, but

Duncan would stay cold and shiver all the way back to Scotland if he had to rather than miss this chance.

Suddenly there were sounds of a ruckus going on downstairs. Someone had come in by the back door!

"Go, lad!" Duncan ordered, but Sorley hesitated and it was too late. Those heavy footsteps were coming up both the main stairs and the servants'. At a snap of Duncan's fingers, Sorley handed him the hanger and then retreated out of the way. He knew Duncan's fighting style enough to know what was a safe distance once the blade started flying.

Three men came bundling in through the parlour's door, older clubmen by the looks of them, and totally unprepared for a raging Scotsman to come at them from out of the shadows, Duncan having positioned himself right by the door. Ignoring the excruciating pain in his ankle, Duncan's blood was up and he let out his war cry, taking a mighty swipe and severing the first man's sword arm even as that sword came up to challenge him. The hanger might not be a great sword, but Duncan made sure that it was kept clean and the blade razor sharp. Sword to sword, it might shatter, and so he went for body parts, not blades.

As the first man fell to the floor keening in pain, Duncan's blade was already coming back for the second strike. The man on the far side of the trio now fell, as Duncan's backhanded slash ripped his thigh open, and without hesitation, Duncan followed it up with a stab in the guts for the middle man. Tossing the hanger to Sorley, Duncan snatched up two of the fallen blades from the clubmen, not that they were anything like as good as the claymore, but at least they'd withstand a clash of blades.

From the landing there was a shout of outrage and horror, and then running feet announced more men coming. Duncan didn't hesitate. He ran to them, not away, and barrelling into the first one, heaved him up over the banister to plummet down the stairs. He tried it with a second but with no room to move retreated back into the parlour where he could wield the swords. Another man came hurtling in, tripped on his fallen friends and stumbled into Duncan, coming in so low that he was below Duncan's guard. Had Duncan been uninjured, the man would have bounced off his muscle and fallen at his feet. As it was, he took Duncan down in a tangle of limbs.

Wrestling on the floor, even so, it took Duncan no time to get on top of the other man. He was just hauling his dirk out to finish his attacker off when there was a shout, a scream, and he felt a burning pain in his middle even as someone else careened into him and drove him down. In his agony, he heard a man shout, "What have you done?" as if from far away, but also his nose was filled with the scent of lavender, a mop cap fell forwards over his face, and he felt a lock of hair brush his cheek. Then all went dark.

Back in the shadows behind the heavy curtain, where he'd moved to so as not to hamper Duncan, Sorley saw his beloved cousin fall over. But as Duncan was getting the better of the man who'd tripped him, Sorley saw Joan and another man come running in. As Joan saw the man raise his sword up to stab

Duncan in the back, she flung herself in between them.

The sword had so much force behind it that it went through Joan up to the hilt, driving her onwards even as the sword continued on into Duncan. Without Joan's weight, Duncan might still have survived, but Joan – already limp and lifeless – began to topple, dragging the blade sideways through Duncan and compounding the wound. As Joan's cap dropped off, and her hair fell over Duncan, Sorley was about to run out when he heard a scream from the door. Two other clubmen had come in but the scream was Mary's.

As the one man yelled to the man who'd stabbed Duncan, "What have you done?" as he saw Joan, Mary screamed again then shouted,

"You weren't supposed to kill *her*! She's supposed to stay here and help me! Now what am I going to do?"

"Shut up, wench," said the second of the men, and clearly someone of much higher status, cuffing her across the face. "You got paid for your treachery. This is as much on you as my men. Alfred, take her out. She can entertain the men as her punishment for our friends getting wounded by that savage."

As Mary was dragged away screaming, Sorley hid himself deeper into the folds of the heavy curtain, still as a mouse and barely daring to breathe. There was another scream and the sound of someone falling, and Sorley could only hope that treacherous Mary had tried to fight the men and been thrown down the stairs. Even at his tender age he knew she'd been beyond stupid to think that men so far above her in station would treat her kindly. *Ever serve her right*, he thought, but was focused on the men still in the room with him.

"What do we do, Master Holmes?" asked the man who'd been saved from being throttled by Duncan, as the other two hauled him to his feet.

"Get our men out and to a healer first. We lock the door, then tonight we come back and hide the bodies. If anyone asks about the Goodwife, we say she fell for a soldier and ran away."

"*Her*?" one of the men said incredulously. "An old baggage like her?"

Burgess Holmes looked down his nose at him coldly. "Well she clearly cared about him enough to throw herself in the way of the sword that ended him. That's not the act of a woman who hated his guts, is it? So remember her doing that when you're asked and make it convincing."

The men went away, the big door downstairs was shut with a thump, and young Sorley was left in the old house with Duncan and Joan's cooling bodies. For the first few hours, he could do nothing but sit and sob, holding Duncan's head in his lap as best he could, and saying every prayer he could remember for Duncan's soul. As darkness came, for a while he thought about maybe taking Duncan's dirk for himself as a remembrance, and trying to move him and Joan into something like a more reverent position. A twelve-year-old like himself couldn't hope to move a big man like Duncan, but he thought he might be able to tip Joan off if he could pull the sword out. Then at least he could roll Duncan onto his back and cross his arms over his chest, as he'd seen done when laying people out at home.

Yet even as he tugged at the sword, which stubbornly refused to move, it was like Duncan's voice came in his head. *If you move me*, it said, *they'll know someone else was here and they'll hunt you. This wasn't an act of war, this was murder. They'll want to cover it up. They can't afford for you to be telling the truth.*

With a sob, Sorley sat back on his heels. Duncan was right, it had to seem as though nobody had been here when the men came back. But a little of Duncan's steely spirit seemed to have crept into him, and Sorley stood up and summoned every ounce of his Celtic heritage. Standing over Duncan, Sorley uttered every curse he'd ever heard the old men and women of his home speak in wrath, and he directed them at the families of those who'd done this, and the family who lived here. If they hadn't employed such a nasty wee besom as Mary, none of this would have happened, and if they'd cared enough for Joan to treat her better, then maybe…then maybe…

At that point, Sorley ran out of blame to cast about, and he wasn't short on blaming himself either. He should have done something. Anything was better than standing here like this. Dying alongside Duncan would have been more honourable than lurking in the curtains, he scolded himself, even though his other side was saying, *yes, and Duncan would have lopped your head off before it got that far with the way he was swinging that blade*.

He got up and stepped back from the bodies, carefully checking the soles of his boots to make sure they weren't wet with blood. The last thing he should do was leave a trail of footprints going away from them. Feeling as if his heart would break in two, Sorley picked up the two packs that had been under a chair, out of the way, and made his way down to the kitchen. There, he risked lighting a candle from the embers of the fire, and rearranged the packs. One was filled with the things he didn't actually need or couldn't hope to carry far. The other was his pack that he'd take with him.

He took as much food as he could manage, then with his pack on his shoulders, and Duncan's in his hands, he slipped out of the back door. Duncan's pack would soon have to go into a ditch somewhere, but that was better than having those graveyard crows scavenging over it. Having cried himself out, he could look up and see the stars. Hereford was west and south of here, he believed. Well if he walked that way, hopefully he'd walk into the army heading back north, because someone had to tell the family of the treacherous stab in the back that had brought the great Duncan Alexander Sorley McAllister down.

Chapter 14

Wesley drove them into Worcester and parked near the cathedral, which was also close to Chris and Angie's rented flat overlooking one of the canals. Before tackling that, however, he led her into the Italian restaurant next to the car park and said, "Pick what you want from the menu. Chris was really generous with me when he had that big win. I don't fling it around randomly, but you of all people deserve to have something out of it."

For a moment, Holly feared Wesley would start splashing out on expensive bottles of wine, meaning he wouldn't be able to drive her back to the shop. That would mean a long walk to her flat, since there were no buses doing that cross-city run, and then her trailing into Ledbury by train again come the morning. So it was with great relief that he only ordered a small glass of red wine for himself and a glass of prosecco for her. As the meal went on, while he got a top up for her and then a third, he moved onto sparkling water, easing Holly's qualms considerably.

When they'd finished and he'd settled the bill, they walked out and around the corner to head for the flat. Holly had been there before, but only a couple of times. This was, after all, very much Chris' place too, not Angie's old flat which she knew as well as her own. She was surprised to see a keypad entry system, and noticing it, Wesley explained, "Chris didn't want to have to tell Angie just who had a key to the flat. Giving me and a couple of other friends the numbers was something he could do when Angie wasn't there, and we all knew to double-check that she wasn't here before we let ourselves in. In fact Angie was such a pain, I don't think any of us actually ever did that. We didn't want to risk walking in on her and the ructions that would follow, but it was Chris' emergency back-up."

"I can understand that," Holly sympathised, visualising the massive tantrum that would have ensued.

Wesley wandered into the living room and waved a hand at the ultra-modern decor. "This isn't Chris. It's not him at all. Until Laura got sick, he was happy in a little old Victorian cottage. He loved its quirkiness."

Holly had a sudden thought. "Do you think it helped him live his double life? You know, having this place, which was nothing like his real home? Did it stop him getting the two confused when he was half asleep, and saying something he shouldn't?"

Wesley's jaw dropped. "Bloody hell, Holly, I never thought of it like that...but yes! Yes, it could be you've hit the nail on the head, because I know he gave Angie a complete free rein with furnishing this place." He gave a bitter laugh. "Even though this was before the win, he told her to keep it cheap because this wasn't where they were going to end up. That they'd have something very different to this soon, implying much more expensive, of course." He shook his head. "Looking back, I wonder if he always knew that he'd end up divorcing her?"

Holly sighed. "Possibly. And Angie would have made that so much easier for him if at every turn she was showing how unreasonable her behaviour was. If Topher…Chris was thinking that far ahead – and given that he was trying to set his real family up for life, I suspect he might – then he could have been quietly keeping track of every time she went off on one of her rants or her binges. It's not nice, but with the situation he was in, you can see why he did it."

Wesley by now had moved to the spare bedroom, one which had a single bed in as the lone guest bed and which had never been used. Even Holly had never been invited to stay overnight, indeed she'd never seen the spare room, and she wondered if the reason why Angie had put a single in, not even a twin bed, was to discourage anyone from putting on her, as she no doubt saw it. Wesley now pulled that bed out of the corner of the room and lifted the end of the carpet. Holly was rather surprised because in this newish development, as with so many others, all the floors were concrete, so there was no chance of a hiding place under any floorboards. Yet what Wesley revealed was a very small area chipped out of the concrete, just enough to put a tiny thin tin in without causing a telltale lump in the carpet.

As he stood up with the tin in his hand, Holly heard a faint rattle, and when he opened it, it turned out to be keys.

"Come on," he said, leading the way back out of the flat and back downstairs, for this was a modest flat up on the second floor, but not a penthouse flat. Downstairs he turned and walked her to where some of the older houses in the Bath Road area were, and around to where half a dozen old garages were. Most of the flats' residents had allocated parking spaces behind locked gates in the modern blocks, so Holly knew instantly that whatever Chris had kept here, it wasn't a car. Wesley opened the creaking metal up-and-over door and flipped on a light switch. To the incurious, it looked like someone's dumping ground. An old parasol and plastic garden seats blocked the way, and behind them was an assortment of garden stuff, including an old lawn mower, and then the parts of a flat-pack wardrobe propped up against the wall.

"Chris raided the landfill for most of this," Wesley explained. "He wanted it to look like it wasn't worth breaking into if some kids ever forced the door." He led the way carefully around to the back, ducking under bits of wood and stepping over other stuff. There at the back he pulled a heavy tarpaulin off to expose a large and very impressive safe, which looked like it might be cemented into the floor. The other stuff under the tarpaulin appeared to be things that Chris hadn't wanted Angie to throw out, all packed carefully into plastic boxes to keep the damp out.

"If he doesn't come back, I suppose I'd better get Ed to come around and help me clear this out," he said with a sigh. "I'm pretty sure this is only rented, so if the payments stop, whoever does own it would be within their rights to just dump the lot." He gave her a wan smile. "You've met Ed. He was the one who drove the car around to yours. I told Chris I couldn't keep a straight face while he played Mr Nasty, and even Ed said he found it awful. It was only Chris saying he wanted you to be clear of any fallout when Angie found out the truth that persuaded either of us to go along with that."

"It's a dangerous heap of junk, and I've been told never to drive it again by the RAC man who came and towed it back to mine," Holly said darkly. "That's something I will be having words with Chris about if he ever turns up again. I don't think the damned thing even has an MOT anymore."

Wesley blushed. "Ouch. I didn't realise it was that bad." He was by now crouched down at the safe and turning the lock with one of the keys as well as putting some numbers in on its keypad. "Here you go. Take anything that's about the building or the shop. It's not fair that you're left in the lurch if anything happens."

It took them a draining couple of hours to go through everything, not helped by the need to lift things out to where the old and flickering strip light could shine enough for them to be able to read by. Yet finally Holly felt that she had everything pertaining to the building and the business, and had told Wesley of Shea-Lea and Jesse's offer to store them in *The Renegade's* safe.

"That's good, that's really good," Wesley agreed. "If Angie turns up trying to find stuff, she might come to me or Ed. She might just about think you'd have stuck stuff up in that flat if you'd come across it – because let's face it, Angie took next to no notice over the details of having that place – so I can't imagine she ever bothered to ask 'Topher' where things like the deeds were."

Holly gave a sniff of disgust. "She probably thought that, as with her dad, all of that was with an accountant or solicitor. So all she'd have to do would be come home and play the grieving widow and it would all be sorted out for her. Plus if Chris had got wrangled into using her dad's people for his legal dealings, then I can totally understand why he kept all of this stuff away from them. He might have done some of that to seem compliant to Angie, but had the sense not to let them too deep into his real life. I've long thought that both her dad's accountant and his solicitor sail a bit too close to the wind legally, and I can well imagine that her dad subsequently asking for things like deeds he had no legal right to, would be done with a nudge and a wink and a 'say no more'. That's what they're like."

"Then I'm glad we came here and got them. If Chris turns up alive and unharmed, it's easy enough to give them back to him, but I feel a lot better knowing they're safe. I'll keep things like the copy of his will at work, not at my flat. That way, if Angie turns up screaming on my door and forces her way in, there's nothing for her to find."

Holly could understand why Wesley would fear Angie getting past him into his flat. He was a small, slightly built man who spent so much time at his computers he didn't have much muscle on him. On the other hand, Angie was always working out at the gym keeping fit, if only to make sure she looked her absolute best in whatever she wore, so Holly could imagine how strong she would be if her temper lent her strength. As they walked back to Wesley's car in the gloom of an early winter night, Holly could only pray that both Angie and Chris would turn up alive, if not together.

Sheer exhaustion meant that Holly slept through the ghosts if they walked that night, which bizarrely meant that she got up feeling better than she had in several days for having had an uninterrupted night. There was also the added blessing that with today being Saturday, tonight she could go home for two nights and sleep in her own bed and deal with the simple domestic routine of her own life. The shop was pleasantly busy, with quite a few customers saying that they were doing early Christmas shopping to try and spread the cost. It made Holly optimistic that if she didn't have an actual Christmas rush in December, then she would have had rather better in the form of a steady month or two of sales which she could cope with by herself.

So she was just locking up the shop, about to go up to the flat and collect her rucksack for the walk to the station, when Jesse stuck his head out of *The Renegade's* door and said, "Come on in for a sec', there's someone I want you to meet." Then as she got into the pub, said, "My Uncle Ash is here. I thought you'd like to meet him."

Holly had been expecting Jesse's double, someone well over six-foot tall and muscled up, so at first glance her eyes passed a slimmer built man with his back to her, leaning on the bar. Probably only just scraping six-foot, with longer dark hair tied up in a loose man-bun, it was only when he turned around that Holly realised this was Ash by the obvious similarities in his face.

"Holly, pleased to meet you," he said, stepping forward with his hand held out. Holly just about recovered her manners enough to take it, because Ash was every bit as good-looking as Jesse in a finer featured way. Also, however long Ash had been over here, it had been long enough that all you could have said by his accent was that he wasn't native to the UK, because he lacked Jesse and Shea-Lea's distinctive Australian twang. Indeed there was almost a hint of the Welsh lilt in there as well. He had the same warm brown eyes as Jesse, but whereas Jesse radiated bounding energy and cheerfulness, there was something a lot softer and calmer about Ash. It meant she found herself mumbling something about Jesse having told her about him wanting to buy the building, before Angie had blown in like a storm and snatched it from under his nose, trying not to look too smitten at the same time.

"Yes, I did and do want it," Ash said with a quiet smile. "And I'm glad that you got all of that paperwork out and safely tucked away down in the office. God forbid, but you want things like your fire insurance to hand, just in case. Jesse and Shea-Lea have been telling me about the complicated set-up with the owners, so I get why he wouldn't have wanted his wife near the paperwork, but he was taking one heck of a risk not letting *you* know once he realised her holiday plans."

"Thanks," Holly said weakly. "*Erm.* I'm sorry guys, but I'm going to have to run because otherwise I'm going to miss my train. There aren't as many at the weekend, and if I miss this one I'm going to be stuck upstairs until Monday."

"Oh God," Shea-Lea groaned, "the bloody car, of course. So it's totally un-drivable?"

Holly sniffed in disgust. "Dead as a dodo and dangerous to boot. Wesley told me that Chris actually *wanted* me to say 'I'm not driving that!' and back out of being here with Angie, because by then he didn't trust her to stick it out, but that's not much consolation right now."

However, Jesse was quick to say, "Look, if you show Ash around the flat now, one of us will drive you back. It's cold, and dark, and it's soaking wet out there. You can't walk all the way to the station, you'll be soaked to the skin if you do."

"I can't put you out like that," Holly protested. "It's Saturday night. You're already busy and it'll be heaving by the time we get back downstairs."

She didn't see Jesse's less than subtle kick to Ash's ankle, but Ash took the hint, saying, "I don't work in here – not unless Jesse intends to make me sing for my supper tonight, anyway. I've got my car parked out around the back, I'll take you. You're doing me a favour, so it's the least I can do."

Feeling outmanoeuvred, but equally dreading squelching all the way to the station, and then making the long walk back to her flat at the other end, Holly had to agree. She'd been dreading these next couple of hours even if she did want to go home, because on Saturday nights the buses in Worcester were non-existent out to her area, something she'd forgotten about in her plans because she so rarely went out at the weekends in the evenings. So taking her keys back out, she and Ash made the quick dash out and around to the flat door, even so getting rather wet in that short distance.

"So here you have it," Holly said, switching on the hall light, and shutting and locking the door behind them. As she turned to him, she could see the way Ash's eyes had lit up at the sight of the old place.

"It's beautiful," he gasped. "That wood panelling is just glorious. I remembered it was lovely when I got a peek in at it, but not *this* good."

His reaction was so much closer to her own than Angie's had been that Holly found herself instantly warming to Ash. "If you think the panelling is good, wait 'til you see the staircase in all its glory. It's a piece of art. Totally wasted on Angie. She'd probably want to paint it white or some other dreadful idea."

Ash looked at her slightly askance. "Jesse said that she was your best friend, but I'm guessing that when he said that things had gone wrong, it was a bit of an understatement?"

Holly sighed, knowing that she had to explain. "I've been such a fool," she said wearily, and began telling Ash all that had gone on as she led him upstairs. By the time she switched the light on above the stairs she'd given him the edited highlights, not wanting to blurt all the grubby details out to someone who was effectively a stranger. She'd done that to Jesse, she knew, when she'd been at her wits' end, but it wasn't something she wanted to make a habit of. Luckily, Ash's gasps of delight as he turned around and around, taking in the hanging staircase, meant that she was saved from having to go deeper.

"Let me show you the rooms," she said, leading him through to the big front room.

"What a shame those strip lights are in," he said. "They do nothing for this place." Then he gave a shiver. "There's a weird atmosphere in here, though, don't you think?"

"Good grief, I thought it was just me."

"No, there's definitely something...hostile, almost, about this room." He laughed sheepishly. "I did some digging into our family, and it turns out we've got all Scottish Highlanders on the one side, and a couple of First Nation Australians in with some more Scots on the other, so it's no wonder I'm a bit tuned in to things."

"You'd better tell me what you think of the room next door, then," and she took him to the smaller of the front reception rooms where again he shivered. Yet like her, he agreed that the strange double room behind there where she'd spent her nights had a totally different feel to it. What she didn't see, because he covered it well, was his horrified reaction at seeing the old camp bed and the sleeping bag.

"So you're having to sleep *here*?" he asked, hoping he'd masked his dismay enough so that he didn't sound judgemental. "I thought when Jesse said about you stopping, that there was at least furniture in the place."

"Oh no," Holly answered blithely, walking on ahead of him to put the light in the other half on. "This was all going to be done out when Angie got back. Knowing her, there would have been brand new carpets fitted, and new – or at least top of the range antique – furniture going in." She sighed. "Or there would be if she didn't flit off onto some other 'project', having got tired of this one before she'd gotten anywhere near finishing it."

She showed him the back room and they were climbing up to the second floor when Ash observed, "God, there's a nasty smell up here."

"I know, and it's been getting worse. I think there must be a leak up in the roof somewhere, or in the pipes on the top floor, but I can't get to it to put buckets down. So I'm assuming that that floor has got something getting wet and mouldy up there. Mind you, it's weird that the dripping sound has stopped given how much it's rained over the last couple of days. I'd have thought it would get worse."

"Holly, that's not a leak."

She turned and saw that Ash had gone very pale. "What's wrong?"

"I know that smell. I wish I didn't, but I do. Holly, we have to call the police."

"The police? Why?"

Ash took a ragged breath. "Because I think there's a dead body up there."

Duncan McAllister 7

Immediately after he'd passed over, Duncan was frantic. He couldn't console Sorley and he couldn't seem to talk to him, let alone touch him. Yet when Sorley got up and began cursing the men who'd done this, Duncan joined in from the Other Side, but cursing them for what they were putting young Sorley through.

But then Sorley left the room and seemed to vanish. What had happened to Sorley? His spirit searched the house from top to bottom, but when he tried to go outside, he found he couldn't. For good or ill, he was trapped in this place, and had he known it, that belief that he was caught like a fox in a snare hindered his soul from moving on.

For days he prowled up and down, worrying himself sick over the lad. Then suddenly he heard a ruckus down in the street. Looking down out of the big parlour window, he saw men in tartan breeks and some with plaids, all looking thin and bedraggled, but angry too. They were trying to get in through the big door, but the stout oak and its lock defeated them. If they'd been in their full strength it might have been different, but Duncan had seen enough people near starving in his time to know that curse-her Mary must have been right – these men hadn't seen decent food, not even bread, in a while.

Then his heart lifted.

A familiar high young voice, and then there was Sorley. He was tugging at the men and pointing around to the back.

Duncan's ghost tore through the house and down to the kitchen, his broken ankle being no inhibition to moving anymore. To his horror, he could see nails sticking through the kitchen door on the inside, and guessed that someone had come and nailed planks across it. He heard men tugging at it, but also voices saying that they didn't have time to attack the door or they'd be left behind. Through the flawed glass of the kitchen window – for good glass only went in the main rooms – he saw Sorley leading men to where he'd hidden the produce from the garden. Like the biblical locusts, they stripped everything, some men gnawing on carrots, too famished to even brush the soil off properly.

Well if it helped Sorley get back home, Duncan thought it only right that this family suffer a little too. And in truth, what could Sorley and the men really have done for him? He'd become very disorientated when the clubmen had come back and moved his body. He knew he was somewhere removed from where he'd died, but in those first days he sometimes felt as if the world would suddenly start swirling and he didn't know down from up.

At this point he began to drift. He couldn't find a way to leave, but he didn't want to stay, either. For a while he felt Joan's spirit lingering, but not enough that he could connect to her, and oddly, also Mary's.

The night he and Joan died, their murderers had come back, and at that point Duncan was furious. He watched as they lifted Joan's body and took her up into the attic, drifting behind them, but unable to do anything.

"The wench said there's a hiding place up here," the one said, and as he followed them into the attic, Duncan saw that the board to Sorley's hiding place was lying on the floor, exposing it.

"Shove her in there," the second man said, with not a shred of compassion. "Silly old besom. What did she want to do a thing like that for? If Jeremiah was alive to see this he'd turn in his grave."

His two friends turned to look at him.

"That's a bloody daft statement to make," the one said with a roll of his eyes. "He *is* dead, so he *can* turn in his grave, but he can't *see* it as well, can he? You really are a daft sod sometimes, Wilfred."

"Don't let the burgess or the minister hear you swearing," the third one warned. "You know there's fines for foul language."

"Oh give over, Martin," the first one said. "You're not so pious yourself when you've been at the cider. And don't try and kid us that you don't. Even that fire and brimstone preacher with the army didn't stop you sneaking out to the barn for a few pints after his sermon."

"*Shhh*! Don't tell everyone," the one called Martin said, looking around them furtively. "You don't know who's telling who what these days."

Disgusted at the lot of them, Duncan allowed their words to drift over him, just about managing to watch how they bundled poor Joan into the hiding place with such little respect. He might not have loved her, but she'd deserved far better than this. As for Mary, he could guess that she must have died on the same day, but her body had been dragged away as soon as the men left. Clearly a lowly serving wench's death could be more easily explained then Joan's. But then he realised that if Mary had died from the fall, that at least looked natural, whereas a bloody great sword wound in Joan would make it obvious to anyone that she'd been killed. It angered him that Mary would get a Christian burial and Joan not. For himself, he hadn't a clue what would happen.

For Duncan the years passed slowly, oh so slowly. When the war ended, the family returned and were told some cobbled together story about what had gone on. They certainly hadn't come back poorer, that was for certain, because work began with the arrival of an adult son on the house, sealing up Duncan's bones in the process.

He heard men arguing about that. The current master of the house was worried how they would explain why two people had not received a Christian burial, for even in the war normal burials of civilians had taken place. Joan, at least, should have been given that scrap of kindness, although it was already years too late to find a way to make that convincing without questions being asked. Yet Duncan also heard the burgess who'd been part of it all whispering lies and threats, and like Joan, his bones never made it to the graveyard.

Moreover, this new master of the house was another nasty piece of work, frequently beating his wife in the smaller of the two front parlours, until one day he beat her while she was heavily pregnant and she began miscarrying. Duncan watched her being carried to the main bedroom, but from his side of the veil it was clear that the child was already dead and she wasn't long in following. Thereafter there was always a lingering sense of sadness in that room, and Duncan avoided going in there, not knowing that centuries later Holly and Ash would pick up on that lingering misery too.

People came and went in the house, but Sorley never returned. It was after some time that Duncan was forced to recognise that while he himself never seemed to change, that Sorley must be long dead by now. Even if he'd lived through the war, and returned home to raise a family of his own, looking at the way time was passing with those in the physical world around here, Sorley couldn't have lived this long. It made Duncan sad and very lonely.

After that, he drifted on the tides of time until suddenly, after so many years he'd lost count, he felt something.

No, not something. Some*one*.

Kin!

Someone whose blood was of his blood, albeit far distant. It woke him up in a way he'd not been in centuries, and he began taking notice of what was happening in the house again.

The one who was of his blood spoke strangely, an odd accent Duncan had never heard before, but as he watched, Duncan got the feeling that he and the woman who spoke like him were good people. Down in what had been the kitchen and the master's place of business, there was now an alehouse. That made Duncan smile. People came here to be happy, to meet friends, and the man and woman made sure that there was never any trouble. It meant that these days, Duncan liked to drift down and soak in the welcoming atmosphere.

Unfortunately, the two who ran the alehouse weren't the only ones around. There were two men who came and went, and Duncan could tell there was something off about them. Unless he'd really lost his touch after all these centuries, both were hiding something, but one's secrets were darker than the other's. There was also a woman, and Duncan really didn't like her. She reminded him of Mary, always saying one thing to one person and something very different to another.

There was also something strange going on with her and the two men. Sometimes she was up here with the one man on her own, and all loving and playful, then another time she'd be here with him and shouting like a fishwife at him. With the other man she was never quite as volatile, though Duncan had the feeling that she was someone who'd never learned to think first and act after. He couldn't work out that relationship at all, especially as the two men gave the appearance of being friends, though Duncan was certain that the friendship only ran one way in reality.

Yet there was another woman who at first he only saw briefly. Like the two down in the alehouse, he felt something wholly *right* about her. What on earth she was doing being friends with the screaming harridan, he couldn't fathom, but he was sure that the harridan was planning on using her friend in some way, and possibly taking the blame for something very bad. He'd heard only snippets of conversations, not helped by people talking to one another with those strange things they clamped to their ears, meaning he often only got one side of a conversation. But Duncan was sure something bad was going to happen, and he began watching very carefully. He might only be a ghost, but that didn't mean he was completely powerless.

Chapter 15

Holly reeled back from Ash. "A dead body? No, surely not! How do you know?"

He took her arm and gently but firmly guided her back down the stairs to the ground floor. "I'll explain in a bit, but first we're making that phone call."

He opened the door and headed to *The Renegade*, leaving Holly little choice but to lock up and follow him. By the time she got there, he had ducked into the bar area and was using the landline, with Jesse looking at him wide-eyed as he heard him start to speak. When there was a pause, and Ash was holding on the line, Jesse hissed to Holly, "A *body*? Did he just say a dead body?"

Holly shrugged. "To me it was just a nasty smell, but he said he knew what it was."

"Oh Christ." Jesse put his hands over his eyes. "Oh no, poor Ash." He looked up at Holly and drew her to the side. "It was one of the reasons why Ash never came back home to Oz. My dad and my granddad, his dad…well let's just say they're very much men's men. Not much time for the touchy feely stuff. You grit your teeth and get on with life. My gran – Ash's mum – she wasn't like that. She's where Ash gets all his artistic talent from. But life out on a sheep station was a dreadful life for her. Far too isolated with next to no female company. She's the one with the connection to First Nation people, but she had little contact with them, or at least far less than she wanted, because they might have helped her with her being a sensitive when it came to spirits and stuff.

"And having Ash late on, she suffered with what I now know was post-natal depression made worse by the menopause. She didn't get much sympathy from anyone over that, and even much later on, whenever it came up in conversation, even my mum was a bit unsympathetic, but then she's a very different personality. I don't really remember Gran except as this quiet, rather distant lady, because I was only five when she died. What they didn't tell me until I was much older was that she went out to one of the remote barns and hanged herself."

"Oh no." Holly could suddenly guess where this was going.

Jesse nodded. "At first the men were…well, a bit bloody indifferent, to be truthful, over the fact that she didn't come home one night. I've since heard from Ash that he was worried sick, but that nobody would listen to a teenage lad who was thought to be a bit of a mommy's boy."

"That's cruel."

"It was. And by the time they went looking for her, nobody had a clue where she might have gone. Ash was at school as normal – which meant him boarding in the nearest town during the week, because it was too far to come home every night. So that's why it was so easy to dismiss his worries, he wasn't there. She vanished at the start of the week, and it wasn't until the end of the week when he came home that he could go looking for her himself."

"And he was the one who found her?"

Jesse nodded. "And it wasn't pleasant after several days in that heat. So yes, Ash knows what…well, the smell…"

By now Ash had come off the phone. "They've said to wait downstairs and they're sending someone over. Bloody awful luck it's a Saturday night and they're busy anyway. I don't think they call out the detectives until an ordinary copper has come and confirmed that there is a body. They don't just take it on someone's say so."

"You and Holly go down to the office," Jesse said kindly. "Go and make yourselves a hot drink. We'll call you when they turn up."

The wait was longer than Holly could have dreamed. Clearly someone who'd been dead for days, and was behind a locked door, came second to the living causing disruption. Understandable, but it frayed her nerves something shocking. Sitting in the office, at first she and Ash sat in silence, both of them too rattled by their discovery to talk. But as the wait went on they began to chat, at which point Holly discovered a bit more about Ash. Having travelled all around the globe he'd been glad to come and settle down.

"Originally we'd all been at school together in the band," he told her. "Then we started doing the clubs and bars in Sydney. We made an album, got it played on the local radio stations, and then we got lucky – a big record company signed us, and that's when life went crazy. The next two years we did nothing but tour, or at least it felt like it. Tours back home were one thing, but a tour of America was something else. I got so that I didn't even know which state I was in, let alone which city, and the record company wanted us to be writing our next big hit while we did it."

First the lead singer had burned out and left, at which point the record company had found them a new, American lead singer, but he never quite gelled with the rest of the band. After six albums and ten years of touring, Ash and the only other remaining original member called it a day, both frayed wrecks and artistically burned out. "We made a pile of money," Ash admitted, "but the cost to us ourselves was too high. It took me years to get back on my feet. I'm doing other stuff now. I'll never go back to that."

It was two in the morning, with the pub long closed and just the four of them sitting in the bar waiting, when a weary pair of constables turned up, having left their car at the bottom of the lane.

"You say there's a body?" the older one asked, clearly doubting there was.

"You'd better come upstairs and see what you think," Ash said with more calm than Holly was feeling. Dog tired and emotionally worn out, she had been about to snap that they weren't the only ones who wanted to go home and go to bed. But she got the keys out and went through the whole repeat of opening the bottom door and taking them upstairs. There was a part of her that wanted the police to laugh it off, however hard that would have been for Ash. Knowing his history now, she felt he could be forgiven for overreacting, but she was praying that it really was just some grotty old carpet gone wet and rotten with a dead pigeon on it.

The police, however, started sniffing when they got to the second floor and suddenly started taking it more seriously.

"Go and get the cutters," the older one said to his colleague morosely, and when he returned, proceeded to make short work of getting through the padlock on the door. The moment they opened the heavy old oak door the smell hit them like a ton of bricks.

"Oh Jeez," Shea-Lea gagged, turning and running back down the stairs, and Holly found herself covering her nose and mouth with her sleeves, but trying to take deep breaths to stop herself from throwing up there and then. The younger constable dived across into the bathroom and was heard being very ill, while Jesse, Ash and the older police officer all went pale but managed to control their stomachs. When the younger man reappeared, he was told, "Go and get the tape to secure the scene and call it in. We're going to need the full team after all."

Then taking a deep breath, and with a "You all stay back," he began to go upstairs. They heard his footsteps reach the top and then turn towards the front of the building, but then very quickly come back.

Holly whispered to the others, "Weirdly, the biggest room up there is over the smaller of the two rooms at the front on the other floors," who of course had never seen up there, though why she was whispering she couldn't have said. The footsteps then seemed to make a strange pattern, with Holly explaining, "Over the big room on this floor, there's a bedroom at the front but also the little kitchen and the bathroom. Why on earth they did it that way I don't know, because all the pipe-work on the other

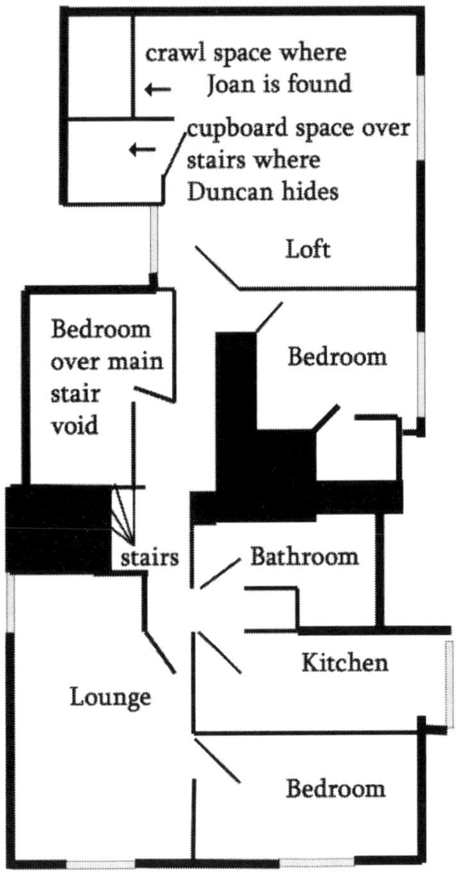

Top floor plan

floors is on the other side of the building at the back – that's partly why I was so convinced it was a leak in a pipe if not the roof."

They heard the constable come back to the head of the stairs and head towards the rear of the building.

"Where the bloody hell's he going? Where is it?" Jesse wondered aloud. "I'd have thought he'd have found something by now."

But the footsteps came back out of what Holly told them was a back bedroom and go across the landing.

"Oh no," she whimpered. "Not there. Not right above where I've been. Please not there," but the footsteps halted right by the huge chimney breast, which they could hear because the door to the room below it was open to the landing, and they'd all drifted towards it.

Both Ash and Jesse reached out and wrapped a protective arm around Holly from either side of her, and could feel her shaking. A moment later and the footsteps were coming back towards and then down the stairs. When he emerged, the policeman looked shaken. "I haven't seen whoever it is yet, but they're locked in a big walk-in wardrobe or cupboard in the chimney alcove," he said gruffly. "They're definitely in there, because something's leaked out under the door. I'm not touching it, though, that's for the SOCOs to deal with." He took in the way the three civilians were dreadfully pale, and in Holly's case, visibly shaking. "Go back downstairs to the pub," he said kindly. "Someone will come and speak to you down there."

That should have been the end of it.

But it wasn't.

Only Holly could have told them what the hour signified.

It began as a faint sound, then built to what was for her the familiar voice singing.

"Who the fuck is that?" the constable exclaimed, spinning around to look. "Who else is up here?"

"It's the ghost," Holly said wearily. "He's a noisy bugger. Every damned night he does it, waking me up with his laments."

"Ghost? Don't be ridiculous," he snorted.

Rather fed up by now, Holly snapped, "Well if you can find him, throw him out, will you? Because he's defied me to find him," and went and sat down on the stairs at the first quarter turn, her head in her hands. Before anyone could go to her, the tune changed and suddenly came from the room on their floor that was under where the body was. Jesse, with one foot already on the top step as he'd moved towards Holly, gave a high-pitched yelp and bolted down the stairs. They heard his feet pounding down the turns and then running out of the door, and the startled cry of the other PC of, "Oye! Watch where you're going!"

Ash, on the other hand, was standing perfectly still, listening intently. "I think that first one was *The Parting Glass*, though the tune's a bit different to the version I know, and this one he's just started is...oh, what's its name? ...Yes, *Lady Anne Bothwell's Lament*, though it has another name that eludes me right now."

"You know these, sir?" The suspicion in the constable's voice was plain, and Ash realised that he'd created the question as to whether he'd somehow planted a recording somewhere.

"Yes, I'm working on a degree in early music, albeit rather slowly, I'm afraid. We've got some Scottish ancestry, you see, and…well…long story short, I got interested in early Scottish popular songs. Ones like *The Parting Glass* are sung even now, but it's been around since the 1600s. Others are really obscure. …*Huh* …I think he's moved on to *The Trooper and the Maid*. I think that's what it is, though it's not easy to tell."

Looking up at Ash, Holly caught sight of the constable's expression and could tell he was one step short of clapping the cuffs on Ash.

Then came the lighter sound of running feet, coming from the front and going straight past both men without anyone being seen.

"Oh no, not again," Holly wept, because she knew what was coming next. It made her stand up and flatten herself against the wall, because she had no idea how either Ash or the policeman would take it.

Sure enough there came the tramping of heavy feet, sending the constable tearing past her to shout down, "Keep everybody out, you idiot!" only to see that there was nobody on the stairs. By the time the white face of the other constable appeared down at the second turn, the boots had come as high as Holly knew they got, paused, and began stamping back down.

"Pete?" the younger man called up, voice shaking, and then like Jesse before him, gave a squeak of pure terror and flattened himself against the wall as the ghostly sound of feet went straight past him.

The eerie Scottish voice up on their floor once again said, "*Shhh*, lad. Be still. They've no' gone yet," and fell silent.

For a moment everyone was frozen where they were. Then Ash looked at Holly and said with astonishment, "You've stayed here on your own every night with *that*?"

She gave a weak laugh. "Didn't really have much choice."

"Both of you, out," the PC said, though it was obvious that he wanted them out so that he could also get out, his colleague having already vanished out of the front door. "Does it come back?" he asked when they were outside, grateful for the fact that at least it had stopped raining for now.

"No, not normally," Holly answered with a weary sigh, and with that they had to be content as Ash ushered her back into *The Renegade*, where Jess and Shea-Lea had got pots of coffee going and were making sandwiches, anticipating both their own needs and the team who were about to descend to start investigating.

When somebody did come into the pub to speak to them, it was an older detective who looked as if he'd seen pretty much everything in his time, and who gratefully accepted a mug of coffee and a ham sandwich.

"I'm DI Tim Chesterton," he began. "You've got a right mess up there, so I'm afraid that the building is going to have to be secured for a while." He saw the worry on Jesse and Shea-Lea's faces and quickly added, "That only applies to access through that main door. I presume there's no way into the house part from either here or the shop next door?"

"No, we've no way into the upper floors," Jesse confirmed, with Holly adding,

"No, not from our shop's side, either."

Ash took a deep breath and then asked, "I'm sure I'm going to regret asking you this, but what do you mean by a mess?"

Chesterton grimaced. "To save you from nightmares, I won't go into the process of decomposition, so let's just say you can't see who he is right now."

"And it's definitely a 'he'?" Jesse asked. "You can tell that much?"

Chesterton sighed. "Only by the size of the boots which were up against the door, and fell out on us the moment we got the door ajar, as if he'd tried to kick his way out, poor sod. I don't think there are many ladies walking around in a size eleven."

Shea-Lea and Holly immediately shook their heads, even if the men weren't too sure about women's footwear.

"They were relatively new, you see," Chesterton continued, "so we could see the size on the rubber sole quite clearly. But beyond that, no, we can't tell much. I suspect it's going to be down to things like dental records to confirm who he is, and with what we can see, at least he does look as if he's been to a dentist in recent years. You don't want to know how complicated it can get with people who've come in from Eastern Europe, or further afield, with poor dental health."

"Chris…topher," Holly stumbled over giving his full name. "I know Angie said he'd had a lot of dental work done now that he could afford it. I think his dentist is in Worcester somewhere."

Chesterton nodded and made a note. "Thanks for that. We'd have started our search locally, but it helps if we know stuff like that. Anything that gets us an identity fast can be a great help. Now does anyone know anything about someone sleeping rough on the first floor? Only we've found a camp bed and a sleeping bag."

Scarlet with embarrassment, Holly found herself having to explain why she had been up there, finally asking, "Can I please go and get my stuff? Only I don't even have my toothbrush with me if I don't."

Regarding her with considerable sympathy, Chesterton said that the police would bring all of her things down to her. That didn't help Holly that much, however, because she was fretting about how she was going to cope next week if she had to catch the train in and out every day. Realising that they were already into Sunday, and so she didn't need to open up today or on Monday, if she stuck to her new plan and the opening hours which she'd already put on the shop door, she had time to draw breath. But from Tuesday onwards it was going to get both more complicated and a lot more expensive if she was going to buy return tickets every day. Even a weekly ticket was going to force her to buy it from the cash in the shop's safe, because she simply didn't have that much going spare in her own bank account.

"Don't look so worried," Ash' voice came softly in her ear. "You can have the spare bed at Jesse's and I'll sleep on the couch – it's a huge thing and insanely comfortable, so you aren't depriving me. Come on, let's take your stuff down to the shop's basement, and then you can take just what you need with us across to Jesse's."

Chapter 16

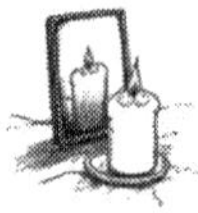

When she woke up, Holly experienced a moment of complete disorientation. For a start off, she could have sworn that what woke her was somebody knocking on the room's door, but why would anyone be knocking on her bedroom door when there was nobody else in her flat? Then as she opened bleary eyes, it dawned on her that this wasn't her bedroom. In fact it was somewhere a lot nicer than hers, with a tall ceiling and a lovely big window.

"Holly? Are you awake yet?" Shea-Lea's voice came through the door, finally bringing Holly back to reality.

"*Gnmff*...err, yeah," Holly managed to splutter, heaving herself up into a sitting position, and realising that Shea-Lea must have loaned her a t-shirt to sleep in.

Her hostess came in preceded by a wonderful smell of fresh coffee.

"Oh my God, that smells good," Holly said, already feeling her eyelids peel back a bit more as the caffeine scent hit her. "Oh heavens, I'm so sorry, whatever is the time?" as she took in that it was definitely fully daytime by now, which at this time of the year meant well into the morning.

"Aah, don't worry," Shea-Lea brushed her protests aside as she handed her a mug. "Jesse just got up to let the cleaners in, then came back to bed. We only got up in time to open the pub at eleven, and when I came back up, Ash was barely inhaling his first coffee. You're not that far behind us, and of all of us, you've had the roughest couple of days. You needed a decent sleep."

"I think I did," Holly reluctantly agreed. "I went out like someone whacked me over the head with a hammer."

Shea-Lea just grinned and pointed to her left. "Shower-room is the next door along. I've put you a clean towel out. Come on through when you've had chance to freshen up. There're bacon butties on the go in the kitchen. I don't do lunch on Sundays, just hearty breakfasts and a meal later on because we shut at seven."

While she was getting what felt like the psychological if not physical detritus of ages off her in the shower, Holly thought she heard someone come and ring the flat's doorbell, but since she was hardly decent enough to go out, she waited until she was properly dressed before heading into the kitchen. The sombre expression on Shea-Lea and Ash's face warned her that something wasn't right.

"Oh dear, what's happened now?" she asked, dreading the response.

"That was a DS giving us an update," Ash said with a sigh. "You know you gave that guy Chesterton the contact for Chris' foster mum and the social worker?"

"Yes."

"Well they contacted them first thing this morning. The thing is, Holly, those two ladies were able to give a really detailed description of Chris, and the police are now saying it can't be him. The body, I mean."

"Oh Lord, no! Not some other poor soul caught up in this too?"

Ash pulled a face. "I know, leaves a nasty taste in your mouth, doesn't it. But Chris' foster mum was telling them that it really bugged Chris when he stuck at five-feet-eleven as he got into his twenties, and couldn't quite make six feet. Well the pathologist says the guy upstairs was at least six-four, so whoever he was, it's not Chris."

Shea-Lea was nodding. "We were just wondering as you came in who on earth could have got into the building in that case. They're saying that whoever it was, the forensic guys are saying that going on the bugs and stuff they've examined so far, he must have died easily the week before you opened the shop, and more likely the week before that, although obviously they'll qualify that when they've had time to do tests. So that means that you wouldn't have been around all of the time, doesn't it."

Yet Holly shook her head. "No, I'm afraid it doesn't. Those two weeks before we opened, I was working like a maniac in the shop even before I left my old job. I was here in the evenings with Angie. Oh, Angie drifted in and out, but I was the one painting the walls, and sorting deliveries, and then working out what fittings were going to go where, because Angie's plans were all over the place and didn't make sense." Then a thought hit her. "Oh no!"

"Holly?" Ash moved to catch her eye. "What is it?"

Holly shook her head, feeling as if she was shaking cobwebs out. "The last week, especially after Angie had already buggered off, yes, I was run ragged on my own. I never had chance to even think about the flat. But the week before that, part of the reason Angie kept disappearing off on me was because she kept going up to the flat. She muttered something about deliveries when I was there on my day off, which has to be nonsense I see now, doesn't it, because there's nothing up there? But I know that several times I definitely heard someone else going up those stairs with her.

"Now I always assumed it must be Topher…err, Chris, if it wasn't delivery men, but it might not have been. And when I poked my head around the shop door a couple of times, the bottom door to the flat was open. Again, I didn't question it because I thought it must be for someone delivering something since Angie was there, and I wasn't invited up to the flat during that week. And of course, until immediately before then I was at work at my old job, so I didn't see much at all."

Ash sighed. "So if the door was open, anyone could have walked in. It could have been Chris or Angie who did the deed if someone came in behind them, and they thought they were defending themselves. If this guy was bigger than Chris, he might have felt more threatened than you might expect."

Holly flopped down onto the seat at the kitchen table and looked glumly at the others. "I've learned in the last few days just what a sad life Chris led. His mum is a violent old bag and his dad was a drunk. Wesley told me that Chris had had enough violence to last him a lifetime, that's what he couldn't stand the most about Angie – the way she'd hand out slaps and shouting without any thought for what it did to people." She squeezed some ketchup onto the bacon sandwich Shea-Lea presented her with, but wasn't sure she could face eating it right now. "I don't think Chris would have been violent, I just don't."

What she wasn't expecting was for Ash and Shea-Lea to block her attempts to go back to her own flat.

"What are you going to do there?" Shea-Lea asked bluntly. "Sit there all alone worrying yourself to death over this? If you can tell me who can come and sit with you, and I hear you talking to them and arranging that over the phone, then we'll let you go. But we care about you Holly. We're not going to let you make yourself ill."

Ash looked at her with a sad smile. "I know how delayed shock can knock you about. I admit it seems like we're being bossy, but truly Holly, you sitting alone for the rest of today and tomorrow isn't a good idea."

"But I've got to sort out how I'm going to cope with the shop," Holly protested. "I need to go and buy things like a weekly rail pass."

Shea-Lea looked pleadingly at Ash, willing him to take control of this situation, and was relieved when he moved his chair a bit closer to hers so that he could cover her hand with his.

"Holly," he said gently, "this has gone far beyond you simply caretaking the business until Angie or

Chris turns up. Can't you see that? ...Think about it. Do you really imagine that Angie could have been going in and out to the flat, and possibly Chris as well, and them not hear that poor bloke trying to make someone hear his cries for help?"

Holly went white and pushed the bacon sandwich away, feeling sick. "Oh God! I forgot he said that...that detective last night. The boots up against the door. Oh no. Oh, that's horrible."

Ash squeezed her hand a little tighter. "I'm not deliberately trying to upset you. I just want you to realise that after last night everything has changed. How and why that man was lured up to the second floor we may never know, but you don't have to be a super sleuth to realise that he was probably semi-conscious, or out of it altogether, when he got shoved into the space and the door locked behind him. But at some point he came around and tried to get out. That's not an accidental death, Holly, that's at the very least manslaughter, and more likely murder. They say he was a big bloke, so if it was just a fight, a disagreement, it defies belief that it took place in the one and only room – and on the top floor at that – where there's a convenient place to lock him into."

Holly gave a sob, making Shea-Lea give Ash a black look and hurry around the table to come and wrap a comforting arm around her shoulders from the other side.

"I'm just being silly," Holly hiccupped with a sniff. "It's just that I remembered that I very nearly moved my stuff up to the room that's on the floor in between where I was and where he was found. I didn't because the smell was stronger," and she had to stop and resort to tissues for a moment, "and because I convinced myself that I wouldn't hear someone breaking into the shop from up there."

She had to blow her nose, wishing that she was one of those women who could weep prettily, instead of being a red-eyed snotty mess. "But the thing is, in that second floor room, there's another cupboard directly under the one he was found in. *That's* why I never found the drips! I didn't look in the damned cupboard there. If I had, I might have realised that it wasn't water but…but…"

"*Shhh*," Shea-Lea said gently, rubbing her back soothingly. "Don't dwell on that. You couldn't have known, Holly. Really, you couldn't."

"That's part of what I'm trying – probably very badly – to help you to see," Ash said. "There are a lot of rooms up there, so how did that poor sod end up in the one place where he could be hidden? An intruder coming in through the door might have been disturbed on the first floor, and with a stretch of imagination, up on the second. But that third floor? The stairs to that aren't even in line with the main ones."

"Oh!" Holly sat up straight as she caught on to what Ash was saying. "A stranger wouldn't know you have to go almost into the front bedroom to get to those stairs, would they? In fact, unless they'd stood in the street staring up at this place, they might not even realise that there *is* a third floor." Then she connected the dots. "Oh God. So only someone who'd actually been inside the building would know how to get someone up to the third floor, and that has to be Angie, Chris or me."

"Not you," Ash said firmly. "You'd be wasting your talents as an Oscar-winning actress if you could fake your level of shock last night. No, I don't think for a moment you are in the picture. Besides, when did you get the key to the bottom door."

"The day Angie left."

"Precisely, and at that stage I suspect our victim had been dead a fair while. Plus, you never had the key to the third floor, did you? No, I think DI Chesterton is sharp enough to have done the reckoning on that. But what it does mean, Holly, is that Chris and Angie's assets are likely to be frozen until it can be sorted out if one or both of them are innocent."

"Really?"

"I get it," Shea-Lea said with a sigh. "The police won't want them skipping off to some place that doesn't have extradition to the UK. It's bad enough already that they're abroad. They won't risk them getting away even further."

Ash nodded. "Now, that won't affect us at *The Renegade*, because that's trading as a totally separate concern. But your shop? The card payments are still going into an account that presumably either of our missing pair could access. I'm sorry, Holly, but I think they'll be saying you can't carry on trading for now...or at least, I'd be very surprised if they don't."

"But what about my wages? What about me paying *my* rent?" Holly gasped, really worried now.

"I think you can reasonably take what cash you have and bank it in your account," Shea-Lea said. "If it's your living expenses you'd normally pay out of your wages, I think it would hard to argue you shouldn't do that."

"Well I'm not going to wait to ask," Holly said firmly. "I'm not being made homeless on Angie's account." She didn't want to say that she was more and more of the mind that Angie was behind the death upstairs, even if potentially Chris had then done for her out on the open sea. And if Angie was the guilty party, then she herself was really in trouble, because Ash was right, the shop would be closed since Angie wouldn't be able to profit by her crime, so she needed to have enough in her bank to tide her over until she could get another job, and that might take months.

She was brought back to reality by Shea-Lea saying, "Please eat something," and nudging the bacon sandwich back in front of her.

The first few bites had to be forced down, but after that she realised she was actually hungry. Shea-Lea went down to help Jesse with the Sunday afternoon rush, and Ash came with her into the shop for her to get everything she needed from the office. Even so, she'd had to explain to the PCSO now guarding both doors why she needed to go in, and she recognised that Ash had been right to try and warn her.

"Why don't you let me book you into the hotel over the road?" Ash offered. "I'm heading over there now to get a room myself, because lovely though it is being with Jesse and Shea-Lea, that flat isn't big enough for them to have me around for days." He gave her a mischievous wink. "They also have a very 'active' love life."

Holly blushed. "Oh heck. I wouldn't have presumed to stay anyway, but that's really made up my mind."

"Then please, let me do this. The police are bound to want to talk to us again, so it looks better if we've stayed close by, and an extra room for you won't put even a dent in my bank balance," which meant Holly felt it would be churlish to refuse.

Chapter 17

The day had turned bright and crisp, and so although she was glad to have her heavy jacket on, Holly really fancied a nice walk, and when she said so, Ash said he'd come with her. They walked back to the old Market House, but this time Holly led Ash up the left-hand fork in the road, up the slight hill, and around to the community garden near the church. Out of the wind, they found a bench and sat to enjoy what was left of the autumn sunshine. At this late stage in the year, there weren't many flowering plants still out, but the leaves on the trees were turning into the last of their autumn colours, carpeting the grass. There was a soothing scent of greenery, and as she watched a squirrel running up a tree with his mouth full – clearly hoarding something against the winter – she felt her shoulders start to loosen and come down from where she felt they must be up around her ears.

Noticing this, in an attempt to find a less stressful topic of conversation, Ash said, "I have to say I'm much intrigued by your Scottish ghost. I wouldn't have expected that down here."

For Holly, the ghosts suddenly seemed a far less worrying prospect, and she found herself telling Ash what Sally had told her about the Scottish army coming through during the Civil War.

"How fascinating," he said. "That certainly fits with the songs he was singing."

"So what's this with the music degree?" Holly wondered. "I'd have thought that would be as far from your interests as you could get?"

Yet Ash smiled and shook his head. "Me and the rock scene are done with. Oh, I still enjoy listening to it, and while I've had the studio, I've sat in as a session guitarist when needed. But thing is, Holly, standing there in a studio – even if it's nothing like the ones we got shoved into – with an electric guitar in my hands, brings back all kinds of bad memories. It's taken all of the joy out of it for me. Then about four years ago, we had a folk group come to record an album, and they had all sorts of instruments that I'd never seen before."

He laughed. "They were very patient with me, but then they had immense enthusiasm for their instruments too. So I got to have a go playing a Renaissance-style lute first of all, and all of a sudden, having this *acoustic* instrument in my hands, whose balance and feel was so totally different, was like coming home. I felt all the old happiness again over making music. A very different kind of music, but it was back. By the time they'd left, I'd put in orders for a lute of my own, plus a Elblag gittern, a cittern – which is a different beast again – and a baroque guitar, which is smaller than any acoustic guitar I'd played until then."

He gave another laugh. "I think Eric, my engineer, thought I'd totally lost the plot with the amount of money I spent on them all in one go, but honestly, the bug had bitten me, and it hasn't let go. So at first I was just experimenting, getting to grips with what sounds I could make and stuff. Then it dawned on me that there must have been music written for these instruments, given that they've been around for centuries. I bought tutorial books and sheet music, and by that time an old-style mandolin had joined the collection, too. I really wanted to learn how to get the best out of these wonderful instruments, so I did some digging and found a distance-learning course I could get onto."

"It sounds fascinating," Holly said wistfully. "I wish I'd got the time to even *find* something that grabs me like that." Then mentally kicked herself for sounding so pathetic, but Ash was already asking,

"Is there nothing that you've thought, 'Ooh, I'd love to do that'?"

Slightly embarrassed, Holly answered, "I kind of hoped that at some point I might be able to start making my own candles for the shop." She grimaced. "That went down the pan, though, when Angie bought this building. Hot wax and flames in a timber building wouldn't go down well with fire inspectors."

Ash laughed. "You probably have a point there. But no hobbies?"

Holly gave him a mock-severe stare. "Like you do anything else apart from music?"

That shocked Ash. "Blimey! I love music, but it's not the only thing in my life. Well not these days, anyway. I've had great fun tracking down our family over here. The whole ancestry thing. That's where the Scottish interest with the music came in, you see."

"So I'll be seeing you wandering around in a kilt, will I?" teased Holly.

"With my knees? I don't think so!" Ash chuckled. "But it's funny how it gives you a sense of belonging once you find out where you hail from. A sort of extra layer of identity. I know it's the standard grim joke that Australia got colonised by convicts, but actually, many of the people on both my mum's and my dad's sides of the family went out there because of successive Highland Clearances. So we've got one branch from right up in Sutherland, who arrived after the First World War, when extra mechanisation finished off them working on a farm up there, but they also go all the way back in various generations to the infamous clearances that started in the 1750s and went on well into Victorian times.

"The ones I really loved digging into, though, were the ones who were Jacobites. Several of those came to Australia via other places like America or the West Indies, because of course, the ships that started transporting to Australia didn't appear until much later in the eighteenth century than Culloden in 1746. So it's been a real detective job tracking them across the oceans."

Holly could feel herself getting a tingle of excitement about that. "How wonderful to have such exciting stories in your family."

Then he asked the dreaded question. "What about your family, Holly?"

With a sinking heart, she told him about her parents' on-off relationship. "Looking back, I don't think my mum had the healthiest attitude towards Dad. It was him and absolutely nobody else. Even after he left the last time, all she obsessed about was how to get him back. She just couldn't accept that he was happier with someone else. But then after she'd gone, it came out that her family blamed *me* for them ever getting married in the first place. How ridiculous is that? I didn't have any say in the matter. But it guaranteed that I wasn't taken in by them."

"Yet your sister was? That doesn't make sense either."

"Who said families have to make sense?"

"Point taken."

Holly leaned back to look at the sunset colours starting to bathe the sky. "You know that's why Angie's betrayal hurts so much. It didn't come to me until I was in the shower this morning, but all the way through my life I believed that the one person I could trust, the one person I could be *sure* would come to help me, was Angie, all based on that single moment when I thought she offered me a lifeline in my teens. To then find out that that was a lie has just ripped the carpet out from under me. It's totally thrown me off balance. I don't trust people easily, Ash. I'm always waiting for them to drop me in the shit in some way and walk away without a backwards glance. If you can't even trust your parents, it leaves you very wary of others. And now my one compass point, my one true North Star, has gone out."

"Have you ever heard from your family?"

She shook her head. "No, and I've been easy enough to find if they'd wanted. I'm still living in the same area, all of half a mile from where Mum's house was."

"Could you contact them? Let's face it, even your little sister is an adult by now. She should be capable of making up her own mind about you."

Yet Holly wrinkled her nose in disgust. "I did try once when I was in my twenties. Even by then, my grandparents had moved house, and so had my aunt. They never bothered to leave an address even with my social worker. To be frank, my sister was so young, I doubt she has any real memories of me, and what she had have probably been warped all out of shape. Our cousins on that side were more her age, so she'd have had more in common with them anyway, so I guess they're all the family she needs. As for my dad, he turned his back on us and never looked back – I think Mum polluted whatever relationship he might once have wanted with me. You can't make your family love you."

Ash sighed heavily. "No, I'm with you on that one. I think my trust in mine took a beating the day I found my mum in that barn. I was heartbroken, yet everybody else seemed to be relieved that the 'mad one' was out of the way. There was precious little understanding of mental health problems amongst our lot. And they couldn't understand why I was so upset either. My dad and my brothers – including Jesse's dad – kept telling me to grow up and 'be a man' when I had nightmares about the state I'd found Mum in, and they seemed baffled that I'd actually *miss* her.

"They wanted to be out on the farm with Dad before they even reached senior school age, and thought themselves past needing Mum, so they'd already sort of detached emotionally from her – much encouraged by Dad. I never did. I get what you're saying about not being bothered about doing all the hard work of finding your family, Holly, because I feel that way about mine. Jesse's the only one I have any feelings for. I think it's why I'm so much more engaged with my ancestors – they never told me to sod off and stop crying."

They continued their walk across to the old church, and had a wander around inside, Ash fascinated by the age of it. Feeling much more relaxed, they took the main lane back down to *The Renegade* and went and found a quiet table in the farthest corner. So it was only as Holly was thanking Ash for a second G&T that the thought hit her.

"They said the man was six-foot-four?" she asked him in a choked voice.

"Yes."

"Oh no. Oh no please don't let it be him."

"Holly, what's the matter? What is it?"

She took a gulp of the gin, barely having put any tonic in yet, which made her splutter but she was glad of it burning its way down. "Before Chris, Angie was engaged to a man called Tom. He was a lovely man, Ash, far too good *to* her and *for* her. He was the one who broke off their engagement because she made his life an utter misery with her jealousy." She had to take another swig of the gin. "Angie never forgave him. Even at the time, I was appalled that she wasn't so much heartbroken as enraged that he would dare to reject her. Oh what a fool I've been."

Ash reached over and took her hand. “You’re doing it again, Holly. Stop it. This is not your fault.” He dug into the inside pocket of his heavy waxed jacket and pulled out a card. “This is Chesterton’s number. I’ll call him now and you can tell him your suspicions.”

Holly nodded mutely, and was relieved to see Ash signalling the barmaid for another gin even as he waited for his call to be answered. Holly felt she was going to need all the help she could get for this conversation. When Ash had done the initial introduction, he handed his phone to Holly and went to pick up the gin from the bar.

“I’m so sorry I didn’t make the connection before,” Holly apologised, “but I honestly thought that Tom had avoided Angie like the plague after the way they broke up. He was such a nice man, so kind and caring, but even he couldn’t live with Angie’s mood swings. Then when Ash said how tall the man was, the penny suddenly dropped as to who I knew who fitted that. Christopher had dark hair, but Tom’s was a light brown.”

She took a ragged breath. “It might help you that Tom had an accident while doing a charity triathlon several years ago, and had to have his one leg pinned and plated. Of…of course Chris’ foster mum wouldn’t have thought to tell you, because she never met him, but I’m surprised Angie’s parents haven’t.” Then she winced as she realised that she was dropping Meryl in the shit even if she didn’t like Angie’s dad, Norris, very much.

Chesterton’s sigh was audible even to Ash, who had come back and sat close to her. “My colleagues in

Worcester who went to interview them said that Mrs Wright wasn't in a state to say much. She was more worried about what might have happened to her daughter, and let's just say that Mr Wright was rather aggressive in making sure no blame was attached to her."

"That sounds like him," Holly agreed, feeling even worse for knowing that Meryl would be sobbing her heart out and getting little consolation from Norris. She had already fished her own phone out. "Look, I've got a phone number for Tom and an address. I know that's not much use if it is him up there, but if you go 'round and he's there and hale and hearty, at least you've eliminated him from your list."

She passed the information on to Chesterton, who then said, "I'm very much afraid that it does sound as if Tom Cavanaugh is the victim. If it helps you rest a bit easier, the body isn't upstairs from you anymore. We took him away early this morning. Obviously, forensics are still working up there, so you can't go in, but please don't distress yourself thinking that he's still up there. He's in a proper mortuary now and being treated with a bit more dignity."

It did help Holly, but she was now feeling even worse, if that was possible, because if the truth be told, she'd had more than a bit of a crush on Tom, despite the fact that he'd never been able to see past Angie to her. Luckily, Ash was being kindness itself, and sat with her without bombarding her with questions until she herself broke the silence saying, "I don't think there's much doubt that it's Angie who did the killing. Not now. Chris would have had no reason to harm Tom. He'd be more likely to put the flags out if Tom said he'd take her back – though that would never have happened."

Ash agreed. "Angie's the only one who had a motive, but you have to wonder what possessed him to go upstairs with Angie in that case."

"I can't imagine." Then an awful thought came to her. "I could believe that Angie thought she'd got some hold over him, though. Maybe threatening to tell his boss something, even if it wasn't true, if she thought it would make trouble for him. She has form for doing that sort of thing."

Ash shook his head, baffled. "What on earth was a lovely person like you doing being best friends with a bitch like that?" Then tutted. "I get it. It's back to her rescuing you again, isn't it? You always felt you had to pay her back for that, or if not actively 'pay back', that she'd earned your unwavering support. ...Holly, you don't need to tie yourself in knots like that just to make people like you. True friends would never ask that of you, and I suspect that the worst thing that Angie has done to you is chase off the people who would be real friends. She sounds like the kind of person who doesn't like competition."

Holly pulled a face. "Angie won't allow that. You either put her first or she moves on. I'm such a..." which was stopped by Ash leaning in and planting a kiss full on her lips.

"No, don't you dare," he said when he leaned back. "You're not a fool, or an idiot, or any of the other negative things you keep calling yourself. What I see is someone who has been incredibly brave coping with a whole raft of situations you should never have had to deal with on your own. The very fact that you aren't curled up in a ball in the corner, rocking and weeping, says everything for your courage."

"Kinda feel like doing that at the moment," Holly admitted with a watery smile.

"Well if you want to weep, there's a shoulder here for you, and Jesse, Shea-Lea and I are not about to let you get through this unsupported, okay?"

"Talking about me?" Jesse said, coming and sitting down across the table from them, clutching a pint of beer. "I'm on a break, so come on, tell what the drama was about, because something's happened, going by the way Holly was hunched over your phone."

When they finished telling him, Jesse said, "*Aagh*, that's horrible," wrinkling his nose in disgust. "Jeez, this Angie sounds like a piece of work. And I'm with Ash all the way. You deserved better than her, Holly. In fact, I'm going to make a leap and suggest that part of why you find it hard to trust people and feel you can't – or mustn't – lean on them is probably down to her too. Think back and ask yourself how many times she's drip fed you doubts over someone. I bet it's far more than you've realised."

Holly's jaw dropped, and the two men gave her time, realising that she was mentally playing back an awful lot of conversations in her head. By the way she gradually flushed red, they guessed that Jesse had hit uncannily close to the truth. "Oh the cow," was all she said softly, then tried to take another swig of the gin, only to find it was empty.

"'Nother one coming up," Jesse said, taking the glass and heading to the bar.

"Don't worry, Jesse and I will carry you to your room if you get legless," Ash joked, and was glad to see his words break her tension.

"I don't think getting carried roaring drunk into the poshest hotel in town will make me very popular," Holly laughed, "but thanks for the offer."

After that she stuck plenty of tonic into this gin and the one after, and made them last, after which, she and Ash joined Jesse and Shea-Lea up in their flat for a late Sunday meal. It was only as she and Ash were walking out and across to the hotel that it dawned on her that she had no idea how she was going to fill the coming days. Never in her adult life had she not had something to do. Either she was at work, or she was on a day off and kept busy doing things like washing and shopping. Her few weeks' holiday a year were spent doing the jobs she simply lacked the energy to do in a normal week, with the occasional day out. But now she was facing weeks with nothing to do but apply for jobs, and how on earth could she explain why she was job hunting when she was part of a murder enquiry?

Duncan McAllister 8

Duncan watched as one of the men came back. What was he doing? There'd been other people in holding strange things in their hands and seeming to be taking some kind of measurements with them, but the workings of twenty-first-century surveyors was beyond Duncan's comprehension. All he knew was that they came and they went, but it was after that that the one man came back and began rummaging around. All Duncan could think was that he'd been told that there were spaces in the house that weren't rooms but gaps in between.

It struck Duncan that since this man didn't seem exactly the law-abiding type, it wouldn't matter if he was the one who found Joan's body – or bones as they were now. So Duncan did his best to waft air and make noises in the appropriate spot, though the man was a bit thick on the uptake to Duncan's mind. It seemed to take an awful lot of effort to get him to go in the right direction.

Nevertheless, eventually the hints worked and the man began thumping and bumping around in the right places. Unfortunately, he turned out to be a wimp. One look at Joan's skull and he'd nearly passed out. What Duncan liked less was the way the man's face lit up when he spotted the claymore. What was he planning?

The man took the claymore out and nearly fell over with the weight of it.

'Ach ye puny wee thing,' Duncan said with derision. *'Sorley could lift it as well as ye can, wi' him a wee lad and ye a grown man. Tsk!'* He'd noticed that these days people seemed to be taller than they had in his day, but the two who came in here were shorter than he'd been, and neither overly well-muscled. God alone knew what the pair did for a living, but it couldn't involve much in the way of honest labour.

The man made an attempt to lift and swing the claymore, damned near stabbing himself in the foot in the process, making Duncan laugh out loud.

"Who's there?" the man called worriedly.

'Aah, ye heard me then, did ye? Then let's see what else ye can hear. GO AWAY.'

What Duncan wanted was for the man to drop the claymore and run from the building. That didn't quite happen, but the man hoisted the claymore into his arms and hurried out of the attic.

Duncan followed him as he went out onto what was now a proper top floor, not the servants' space Duncan had shared with Sorley. *'Now where are ye going, wee man*?' The man turned into a room with a big cupboard in it and began laughing. Duncan didn't like that. It was a nasty laugh and it had the touch of madness about it. For now, though, the man put the claymore into the cupboard and left.

The man came back another time and had a row with the woman. He seemed to be threatening her, and for all that Duncan didn't like her, he was now getting worried that the man meant her real harm. There was something unhinged about the man's behaviour depending on who he was with. The other man hadn't come around as much, and Duncan even wondered whether this one had done away with him. Were they fighting over the woman's affections? They must be daft if they were. Duncan wouldn't have touched her with a pike staff.

Then came the day when the man came back and brought a ladder with him.

'*What in God's name are ye doing, laddie?*' Duncan wondered, as he watched him climb up after putting a wedge in the door at the hinge end to hold it ajar. To his horror, he watched the man struggle up the ladder with the claymore, and then position it on top of the door. '*In Christ's name, ye mad man, Get it down from there! Ye'll kill someone if they walk under there!*'

Before he could even summon what strength he had to try to scare the man, Duncan heard another man come in the door downstairs and call up, "Angie? Are you here?"

Scurrying down the ladder and hiding it in the shadows on the landing, the wicked one shot to the stairs and called down, "She's up here. I'm keeping her company until you get here." Then he went downstairs and there was some kind of whispered conversation that Duncan didn't have chance to catch before both men came back upstairs. "In here," the wicked one said, and stood back, as if to open the door for the other one.

This new man was Duncan's height if not the same burly build and the doorway had been built for the servant's of Duncan's day who had been altogether shorter. Consequently, there was no chance for the claymore to fall away from him. Instead, it came straight down on his head, knocking him to the floor.

Instantly the wicked one was in the room, grabbing the claymore up by the time-blunted blade, and bringing the weighty pommel down on the other man's head, this time knocking him out cold.

"I'm not splitting the money with *you*!" the mad man screamed. "If she gets the money, I'm having *my* share! Not you! You don't deserve it. You've done nothing. You haven't put up with the whining and the 'poor me's'. After what I've put up with, I'm having my reward."

'Jesu, you're as mad as a sea-swimming cat,' Duncan intoned, watching as the wicked one dragged the fallen man across the floor to the cupboard. *'No, no! Ye canna do that!'* he shouted, as he watched the unconscious man being bundled into the cupboard and then it being wedged shut. *'He's no' dead ye murdering bastard!'*

Yet the murderer must have been in such a grip of his insanity that Duncan's words this time didn't reach him. Instead, he went and grabbed what looked like an old curtain and wrapped the claymore in it.

'Where are ye going wi' that?' Duncan wondered, as he followed him back through into the remaining attic space.

He saw the man shudder as he looked at where Joan was, and then wrestle the hatch to another hiding space open and slide the claymore in. Duncan followed him down the stairs and watched with increasing horror as a new lock was fitted onto the stair door to this floor, effectively sealing in his victim.

It meant all Duncan could do was go and try to comfort the fallen man when he came around hours later. The poor soul was never quite with it, fading in and out of sleep, and Duncan couldn't get him to see that he needed to kick the door harder. '*There's only a wee wedge under it,*' Duncan kept trying to tell him. '*The stupid bastard put it in at the wrong place, so it'll shift if ye only kick a bit harder.*' But the man sank deeper and deeper until he stopped breathing. For one awful moment Duncan feared there might be another soul trapped here with him, but to his relief, this time the man's spirit passed on to the Other Side without hesitation.

Duncan said prayers for him, and swore vengeance for him, but the mad one didn't come back after that for a long time, and when he did it was only briefly. What worried Duncan more was that the woman came back. She even came upstairs into the house, not just down in what even he could see was going to be a shop. He hadn't got a clue what the things were that the nice woman was putting one shelves, but she seemed to be working her socks off at it, while her 'friend' swanned in and out.

Why did the woman come upstairs and never even try the new lock? She looked at it and turned away as if it bothered her, so why didn't she do anything about it? Surely there was someone she could report it to? Or had she set the man up to do the job for her? Was she the mastermind behind the murder? Duncan had known of a few women who could tie men in knots and get them to do dirty work they had no desire to do themselves. So was she one of those? If she'd set the mad man to do the task, maybe even knowing that he wasn't wholly sane, then it was hard to know who was the worse of the two.

Then there was the day when she came back and there was a kerfuffle down in the shop. The nice woman was asking why she was doing this. It sounded as if the unpleasant one was going away somewhere. Then a grim thought came to Duncan. Was she planning on letting the nice woman be blamed for the body? If so, Duncan needed to do something about it, but what that was defeated him. Could he make the nice woman hear him? He didn't know, but he was going to try.

Chapter 18

Holly also realised that she wasn't sure about that kiss with Ash. She felt faintly ridiculous having to confess to herself that she'd got to her age with so little experience of dating and men, but it just hadn't happened. Lacking the self-confidence to push herself forward in social situations, she now found herself reflecting on the number of times she might have got somewhere if Angie hadn't intervened. Lying in the comfortable hotel bed, utterly exhausted and yet unable to sleep, once again she was kicking herself for not seeing the truth earlier. Then she'd replay Ash's words about not blaming herself and trying to be more positive, only to fall into her mental loop of wondering why he'd be interested in her, and whether he really was, or was just being polite, with her too dumb to know the difference.

As a result, she crawled down to breakfast, having had what little sleep she'd got disturb by weird dreams that at least once had turned into a full-blown nightmare. She should have been thrilled to have spent the night in this wonderful place which she'd previously gazed at and wished she could afford to go inside, but somehow, what had gone on had sucked all the joy out of it for her. Ash was already in the dining room and waved her over to his table.

"Oh dear, it looks like you didn't get much of a restful night," he said sympathetically, and poured her a coffee.

It impressed Holly that already he'd remembered how she liked it as he moved the milk over to her but left the sugar where it was on the far side.

"Cooked or continental?" he asked her, spotting a waitress already moving towards them.

"Oh, continental," Holly said with feeling. "After all the meat I've had at the pub, I'm a bit meat-ed-out. I'm not used to it."

She gladly tucked in to a yoghurt, fruit, and some croissants, but then sat back feeling totally lost.

"You really don't know what to do, do you?" Ash said sympathetically. "Would it help if we went to a library, or up to Jesse's flat and used my laptop, and tried to track down your ghosts?"

"I don't know how far we'd get," Holly admitted. "I don't think we're overflowing with sources going back that far, but it's better than sitting here doing nothing. All I know is that I heard someone who sounded local talking to the man and calling him Master McAllister."

It shook her almost as much as him when Ash physically started when she said the name.

"McAllister? Really?"

Holly looked at him, wondering why that would matter.

"Jesse and I are McAllisters in several strands of our family. It's a bit more diluted on my mum's side, because it's her maternal grandfather who was a

Scottish missionary to the Aborigines, as they would have called them. So arrogant. To think that a culture that had been around for millennia needed to be converted, but that's the way things were. Her grandmother was his housekeeper." Ash's face wrinkled in disgust. "Bed-warmer too, given that the old goat fathered Mum's mum onto her, and two more kids, without ever marrying her. But after he died, his sister was a lot kinder to mum's gran and let her live on in the house with her, making sure that the kids got an education and stuff. She was a McAllister too, so they weren't all bad in that strand.

"But on Dad's side, I found that while he was born in Australia in thirty-nine, his father came over as a young man in the early Thirties. You might think it odd that I had to research that, but honestly, my dad and I never talked much – he never thought much of me, and I didn't like him, and I came along when he was in his forties and thought they'd got past having squalling brats about the place, so most of the time he ignored me. He might have mentioned it to my oldest brother, Jesse's dad, but he isn't the sort who'd care about stuff like that, so never thought to tell me, either.

"The whole reason our grandfather came was because he was coming to relatives. He didn't think there was much in the way of opportunities for him back in Scotland during the Depression, and there were cousins of his parents already over here who were willing to put him up until he found his feet. My grandmother who connects to him was born in Adelaide, and her folks had been over for generations, but she had Scots on both sides of her family too, and some of them are the ones who ended up in Australia having gone the long way around via the West Indies."

"And the Jacobites?"

"Dad's dad's lot. They were rather easier to trace because the main line I'm connected to stayed in Scotland, but they weren't the senior strand. We go back through a female line who managed to keep their heads down after Culloden, but the senior men back then got deported. There's a lot of links to Argyll with that lot. It made me go and take a good look around up there, and I would've settled up there except that I knew I couldn't just sit back and hope the money I'd got by then would keep me for the rest of my life.

"I knew I'd have work or invest in some form or other – I'd already had the idea for the studio, but I knew it would have to be a bit more accessible than western Scotland for less well-known bands to reach, in order for me to make a go of it. The days of Led Zeppelin turning up to a remote location, and spending a year making an album while being funded by their record company, were already long gone, and young bands don't have a fortune to spend on hotels. My studio isn't far from Monmouth, so folk either come south down the M50 and the A40, or they cross the Severn on the M4 or M48, and come north. It's not a hard journey by either route, and it makes it reachable from London, Bristol and other cities." He gave a shrug. "Purely a business decision that I've been there for so long."

"You sound like you've had enough of it, though?"

Ash gave another shrug. "I've drifted away from the current rock and pop music scene, and Eric – the engineer I told you about – wants to buy me out. To be frank, he does most of the work with the younger bands now, and it's only fair that he gets the credit. The days of my name bringing bands in have gone, and they come more because word has got out about him. I'll be happy to let it go, I just need to find a new place to live and a new project to get involved with. That was part of what prompted me to set up the pub." He gave her a smile. "A bit like you, I'm rather in limbo at the moment, so I know how you feel."

Further conversation was halted by Holly's phone ringing.

"Oh dear, it's Wesley, I'd better take this," she said and got up to hurry out to the lobby where it was quieter. "Hi, Wesley, is everything all right? Oh, that's a stupid thing to say. I mean, I know nothing's 'right' at the moment, but you know what I mean. Are *you* okay?"

"Not really, Holly. Apart from the police at your end getting in touch with me, I've heard back from the ones I reported Chris missing to. Oh Holly, what a mess!"

Holly felt her heart sink into her boots, and she flopped down on an old oak settle, glad that Ash had followed her out and came to sit beside her. "What do you mean, a mess? What sort of mess?"

"Well it seems that the hotel manager in Jamaica was right – Chris and Angie did leave separately. They haven't got any further with regard to Angie on the boat, but they've now found that Chris never got on it. Instead he took a separate taxi back to the airport. He flew home, Holly! He's been in England for something like ten days."

"Well if he's only been back that long, he can't be responsible for the body we found," Holly said soothingly, thinking that was the source of Wesley's distress. "I'm afraid we think we know who that is, you see. It's Angie's previous fiancé, Tom. But he died…oh shit! Damn, he still died before they left. But Chris had no motive to hurt Tom, Wesley, he just didn't. I'm not even sure he ever met him."

"I'm really sorry about that," Wesley said, "but my worry is where's Chris? Nobody's seen him, Holly. I've asked everyone I can think of, and nobody's seen him or Laura and the kids. It's like they've vanished off the face of the earth."

Holly's mind was racing. "Surely, with Laura's MS she must have to be in contact with specialists? If she needs meds, she'll need prescriptions."

"She does. But she's also not long had her prescriptions renewed. As far as the police and I've been able to work out, she's got at least a month's worth left, so until she tries to get more, there's no way to trace her by that. And of course her mum's her main other contact point for the hospital, and presumably she's with them, wherever that is, because nobody can reach her either."

Ash tapped her on the arm, making Holly say, "Hold on a moment, Wesley," and turn to him.

"If Angie is still on the cruise, and Chris is back here, why is he so worried?" Ash asked softly. "If Angie had come back with him, I could understand it, but not when she's thousands of miles away."

Holly relayed that to Wesley, and since she was by now holding her phone so that Ash could hear too, they both heard Wesley's sigh of relief before he said, "Point taken. I'd be more worried if she was here. But I really don't like that he's not spoken to Erica," and Holly mouthed 'foster mum' to Ash to explain who that was. "It's totally out of character for him to not speak to her in so long."

"Maybe he's just trying to make sure Laura and the kids are in a safe place before he gets divorce proceedings started?" Holly suggested soothingly. "It might be that he's got a lot on with that and just hasn't had chance. Plus he knows that Angie knows Erica, and what Angie can be like for emotional blackmail. Perhaps he simply doesn't want Erica accidentally letting something slip if Angie goes around to her house and starts with the sob story?"

Ash was giving Holly a thumbs-up in encouragement, but Wesley's 'huh' didn't sound convinced.

"Wesley, is there something you're not telling me?"

There was another of those sighs before, "I opened the envelope with the copy of his will in. I know I shouldn't, but I had to know. Chris left *everything* to Laura and the kids in a handwritten will that's got the most recent date on it – and I reckon it's legit because it's been witnessed – but there was a preceding one by a solicitor. They must have told him that Angie could contest a will like that handwritten one, given that she was still his wife at the time. I talked to a pal of mine who works in a law firm, and he said that it was likely that they said that since

Laura has no legal status with Chris, that if Angie got a smart lawyer, she might be able to overturn it so that she got everything, not even split equally like that other will has it. I'm worried that Angie knows it, Holly. What if she did something to Laura before they left? Because she's capable. And if Chris got back and something has happened to Laura he'd be inconsolable. He'd never be right again. And if you add in the kids…"

Holly felt sick. Once upon a time, by now she would have been vehemently protesting that Angie was many things, but she'd never hurt a child. But that was before they'd found Tom. Tom, who she now had to face might have died a terrible lingering death over several days. If he'd been alert enough at some point to try and kick at the cupboard door, he hadn't been so out of it at first that he'd have just slipped away. How long might he have lingered in pain and with no food or water? "I think you'd better tell Detective Chesterton," she managed to choke out.

"I already have," was Wesley's reply, "but I thought I'd better let you know as well, because they might mention it to you."

Holly managed to thank him and ring off, but was very glad to have Ash wrap her in a hug. As muscular as Jesse he might not be, but there was a gentle warmth to his hug that was even better, so that she leaned into it and didn't pull away.

Later that afternoon, with Shea-Lea having bundled Holly into her car to go and get changes of clothes from the flat, Ash sat at the bar while Jesse manned it, but on a chilly October Monday lunchtime they had the place to themselves. It meant that they could talk openly and Ash asked, "Have you ever seen that Victorian workman ghost Holly told you about? Has she said anything about her seeing him again?"

Jesse was cleaning the brass fittings on the hand-pumps and paused to think. "No, I don't believe she has, and we certainly never did. I thought he must be fixed to a point on her side of the cellar. ...But what made you think of him?"

"Okay, don't think I've lost the plot, but I've realised that I've inherited my mum's talent with the spirit world."

"Seriously?"

"*Mm-hmm*," Ash nodded. "I got a bit creeped out if I'm honest, when I kept seeing this ghostly old guy hanging around the farm where the studio is. Then I found out he was someone who'd lived there over a hundred years ago, so I went to talk to someone who got recommended to me as the local psychic. I felt a bit of a tit at that stage, but she was really nice and down to earth, and she told me that I could probably help him myself." He gave a roll of his eyes. "I was with *Her*, at the time," meaning his ex, "so I didn't go any further than following the instructions Ruth – the psychic – gave me. But then once I was on my own, I started going to the odd psychic fair, and gradually I realised I was really interested in this stuff."

"So...what? You went on some kinda training course for ghosts?"

Ash laughed. "Not quite. I did read up a lot on things like past lives, and I did a few short courses, but the big thing that prodded at me was being settled over here, where the past lies a bit thicker than Down Under – at least for folk like us – and I realised that I was seeing more than I'd been willing to admit."

He waved a dismissive hand. "But I didn't bring this up to talk about me. What I was going to say was that the Victorian gent sounds like the run of the mill ghost, if there is such a thing. He rocks up around a certain anniversary, because whatever it was, it meant a lot to him. Quite often these aren't so much trapped spirits as echoes that resurface. There's a deep imprint in time in one particular place that people get to see if they're tuned in. I think that's what Holly saw in the cellar, because there was no question of her interacting with him, and now his anniversary has passed, we might not see him again for years or at least not until next year."

Now he sat back with a serious frown. "But the Scottish ghost or ghosts? Now they're a different ball game altogether. I reckon something has triggered him. Something quite specific, not just an anniversary." He paused and looked Jesse straight in the eye. "I think it's you coming here."

Jesse's jaw dropped. "*Me*? Why the heck would it be me?"

"Because you're a McAllister in blood, if not in name anymore. Honestly, Jesse, I couldn't believe it – how many times our family kept coming back to that one clan. And of course when it's through the female line, you don't see it at first because the surnames keep changing, but several times 'McAllisters' married 'McAllisters' even if genetically they were far apart.

"Now there's nothing creepy or incestuous in that," he hurriedly reassured Jesse, who was starting to look appalled, "it's a big clan of thousands of people, and they were beyond distant to one another. But you can imagine my shock when Holly told me she'd heard someone in that past time calling the Scotsman, Master McAllister. That's when I began wondering if we were the trigger for him suddenly showing up. Blood calling to blood down the years."

Jesse grimaced. "Jeez, Ash! That's not creepy…much!"

Yet Ash shook his head. "Not actual blood, like you opening a vein, you daft bugger. I mean simply that calling of family to family. And it can't be me, because this was going on long before I turned up, so it has to be you. Now I know that this building had been empty for almost six months even when I bought the lease for this half of the downstairs and got the license for it, but up above it's been vacant for a lot longer."

Jesse put his polishing rag down and leaned on the bar looking thoughtful. "I see where you're going with this now. Even with the fast sale that Angie and Topher got, once you couldn't buy the whole building, you got the agreement from the previous owner to trade down here, with Topher agreeing that it would continue when he took over. So the fact that we've been here since Easter, but with nobody else in the building, it would mean that there's been nobody upstairs to hear the ghost if it 'woke up' not long after."

"That's exactly it," Ash said. "But I'm also

thinking that of anyone, I'm probably the one who can get this poor soul to his rest."

"Oh heck, mate, you're not going to start doing séances and exorcisms are you?" Jesse looked freaked out at that prospect. "Only I have to say that my one and only experience of that was at uni when some mates started fooling around, and it got very dark and very ugly fast."

Ash was already shaking his head. "No, no, I wouldn't do that, and I don't like people fooling around with what they don't know, either. What I was thinking of doing was trying to talk to the ghost once we have access to the building again. Let's be frank, at this distance, the chances of there being any remaining record of someone dying in this place nearly four hundred years ago are zilch. We're never going to place him that way, so we're going to have to go a bit alternative if we want to settle things down."

"Surely you're not thinking of living up there?" Jesse was appalled and concerned. Ash rattling around in that big old place all by himself wasn't a good idea, because Jesse knew how long it had taken Ash to get over his breakdown, and a haunted house didn't sound the healthiest option for him. So he was much relieved when Ash replied without hesitation,

"Live there? No. But if I buy the building as an investment, I can't be paying Council Tax on all those floors and not have someone making use of them because they're getting scared stiff all the time."

That sounded much more sensible to Jesse and let his stress levels come down a bit. "Okay, that's definitely a practical concern," he agreed. "So that's the 'why', but what about the 'how'? You're going to try and have a chat with our ghost, but to achieve what? How will talking help?"

This was the point when Jesse suddenly understood why Ash had brought this up when Holly wasn't here, as he said, "What if he didn't get a proper burial, Jesse? In fact, how could he have had a proper burial if he was in hiding? They couldn't have gone out and dug a trench in the garden, could they? Not least because common sense would have told them that once the fighting stopped, the owners would come back, and at that point the kitchen garden would be put back into full production. So the last thing they'd want would be the gardener digging a load of muck in and suddenly turning up a skull. 'What were you doing while we weren't here?' would have been a question servants who'd stayed behind would be dreading."

The realisation sank in with Jesse. "Oh bloody hell, you don't think he's buried *in* the house, do you?"

Ash grimaced. "I don't think we can afford to ignore it and assume he wasn't. And if the police are here already, I'd much rather they dealt with an old skeleton along with the modern body, because that would seem a lot less questionable that us ringing them up twelve months on and saying, 'we've got another one'. For Holly's sake more than anyone, I want all the questions and doubts got rid of once and for all."

That made Jesse smile, because it hinted that his plan was working and Ash was more than a bit interested in Holly. He wouldn't have been quite so relieved if he'd been able to read Ash's thoughts, which were running along the lines of, *And was it Tom being murdered up there that was the final call to the ghosts to wake up? Because that murder links too closely to Holly, even if she was never a part of it. I really don't want her to be personally haunted by any of this.*

Chapter 19

Meanwhile, Holly was having her own heart to heart with Shea-Lea while they packed thing into bags at her flat.

"Angie sounds such a nasty piece of work, why on earth did you stick with her for so long?" Shea-Lea asked, carefully folding a pair of jeans.

"She wasn't all bad," Holly protested. "When she wants to be, she can be charming and charismatic – she wouldn't have had as many boyfriends as she did if she was some pantomime villain. She's had me in fits of laughter, and at times when I desperately needed cheering up, and when she wants to be, she can be really generous," though in her heart of hearts, Holly was starting to think that maybe those times had been when it served Angie to hand out favours.

"What about her other friends, then?" Shea-Lea asked, wanting to hear who these people were and what they were like. "If she's a real charmer, she must have had plenty of other people around her – charismatic people are like that, they draw others like moths to a candle, who want a bit of their shining light and warmth."

Holly paused, embarrassed. "Erm...long-term friends, I'm about it. She's had loads of friends down the years, but they last a year or two and then seem to vanish off the scene."

Shea-Lea sat down on the bed and gave Holly a firm stare. "Listen to me, Holly. If it wasn't for Jesse coming to help Ash, and me wanting to be with him, I'd be working in mental health back home, and I did enough of that to recognise Narcissistic Personality Disorder when I hear of it."

"That's a bit much. I don't think Angie's ready for a psychiatric wards just yet." Then even before Shea-Lea could speak, Holly cringed, because if Angie had killed Tom, then a secure hospital really might be where she belonged.

Realising that she was going to have to explain a bit better, Shea-Lea softened her tone and began, "They can be incredibly charming when they want, you know. Narcissists. It's the way they worm their way into your life. And if it gets them their own way, they can be extremely persuasive, twisting things around until it seems like they're doing you a favour by including them in whatever it is. We're talking about a very functional mental illness here, not someone sitting in a corner rocking, or chatting to the fairies. That's one of the reasons it can be so hard to get them into somewhere to even get a diagnosis, let alone treatment. Sad to say, you work out what they've got more by the damage they do to the people around them then you ever do sitting across from them in a consultation or therapy.

"I bet nights out with Angie could be great fun, not least because it would be a 'stage' for her to perform on and draw others in. But the reason those other friends didn't hang around will be because the longer they spent with Angie, the more control she will have assumed to have over them, and try to exert over them."

She leaned over and sympathetically took Holly's hand. "The thing is, you knew her from when you were kids together, so she wouldn't have been anything like as bad back then. It takes time for them to learn what works and what doesn't, and of course there's also the control parents have over a child's behaviour to modify it – or at least if they're decent there is. But for people who met her as an adult, with her condition fully formed, it would be very different. The first time they pushed back and said they didn't want to do something, or go somewhere with her, they'd have got her flip side, the one that *demands* that everything goes their way."

Holly was looking increasingly miserable, but not saying anything.

"You've been massively gas-lighted," Shea-Lea said gently. "Most of the cases I've come across, it's usually a wife getting gas-lighted by her husband, who has affairs and god-knows-what going on that he doesn't want to come to light. Less often it's the other way around, although women do manage to gaslight their husbands and often very successfully. But you don't hear as much of people being gas-lighted by a friend simply because it's easier to get out of that situation before it gets really dangerous.

"What I'm trying to say, Holly, is that you're not alone. This isn't you just being whatever negative name you want to call yourself. Other people have this happen to them too, and like you, when something happens and they suddenly break free –

maybe even finally releasing them from questioning their sanity, should they dare to doubt that other person – they feel like they've been so stupid for not seeing it for what it was. Well they're not, and neither are you, and you won't feel like this forever. As you start to heal, you'll probably begin to feel really angry about Angie and the way she's used you, and that's okay too."

Holly gave a huff of disgust. "I think I'm there already. I'm so bloody angry with Angie. ...And disgusted. What on earth possessed her to do what she did to Tom?"

Shea-Lea grimaced. "He challenged her world view of herself, babe. Of Angie as the lovely, Princess Charming who everybody loves. One of the reasons I've pushed you so hard to come and stay down by us, even in our flat if necessary, is because if Angie turns up out of the blue and finds out that you no longer buy into her fiction, you too might be in real danger. Not every Narcissist turns violent by any means, but we've got sad proof that Angie does."

That truly shook Holly. She'd never remotely imagined that Angie might turn on her in that way, but it said everything for the way that her eyes had been opened that now Shea-Lea had said the words, Holly's imagination was filling in how it might actually happen. Yes, Angie could well get back to the UK, read that Tom's body had been found – because the police had confirmed it was him this morning – and work out that it could only be if Holly had let people in, or had called the police herself.

Moreover, Shea-Lea was right, Angie could be the best of company, but Holly couldn't avoid facing that

that only happened when they were doing the things that Angie wanted. When was the last time they – together – had done something she herself wanted? It was so long back she couldn't even remember.

It also made sense that she hadn't realised it before because of how long she'd known Angie. Back when they were kids, it wasn't just Angie who'd been over-indulged, all the kids in that family were. So a lot of Angie's behaviour she'd put down to Angie's parents not putting their foot down with any of them – something that was emphasised when she realised that the label of 'spoilt kid' was what people like Louise and Sam still thought of Angie as. They'd had little to do with Angie in the last decade or so, and since they'd never met the other people Angie had had brief friendships with, it was no wonder that they hadn't noticed what Shea-Lea had. It also explained why they hadn't tried to make her see what was happening beyond Angie being selfish.

"Is there anything here that you'd be heartbroken if it got destroyed if she broke in and trashed the place?" Shea-Lea was asking.

Holly immediately picked up Gladly, her threadbare old teddy bear who had gone everywhere with her since childhood. "Only him," she said, hugging Gladly's slightly sagging form to her, his stuffing having suffered from many years of cuddles.

"Then let's get this lot into the car and go back," Shea-Lea said, feeling that Holly had had about as much of a reality check as she could cope with in one go. Shea-Lea was grimly convinced that worse might yet come out, but they'd face that when they came to it. For now she was simply glad that Holly hadn't protested Angie's innocence harder. That was a good thing, because it hopefully meant that Holly wouldn't be hurt quite so deeply if something else as bad as Tom's death came out.

Shea-Lea was feeling very protective of Holly right now, and eternally grateful for her own wonderful and normal parents who she'd chatted to on the phone last night, and who she wished right now she could give a big hug, and tell them how much she was appreciating them on a whole new level having met Holly. Her older sister had gone through a stage of struggling with depression, and Shea-Lea knew how much time and effort their parents had put into supporting her. How on earth Holly had navigated the world growing up without anyone to guide her baffled Shea-Lea, who was coming more and more to the conclusion that it was a miracle that Holly was still standing and sane.

They managed to get through the rest of Monday and then Tuesday without any further disasters. The police presence at the building was sufficient that the locals didn't expect the shop to be open, while *The Renegade* got extra trade from the morbidly curious. On Wednesday, though, Holly got a call from DI Chesterton asking her if she could meet him later on, and that he'd already asked Wesley if he would be willing to come over and join them. Jesse promptly offered the office downstairs as a place where they could talk in private, wanting to make sure that he and Shea-Lea were on hand for Holly, and so that Ash could also be present as *The Renegade's* owner.

"Thank you for coming," DI Chesterton said when Jesse had plied them all with hot drinks and then left. He looked at Ash. "I doubt you can help with any of this, but I understand why you want to be here." He turned to Wesley. "Thank you for bringing the copies of the wills and the other things down to us, Mr DiPaoli. It's helping us to paint a picture of Mr and Mrs Sykes' movements." Looking to Holly he asked, "Is there anything at all in the paperwork you have in the shop, or up in the flat, that would give you any idea of where Angela would go? Either under her married name or as Miss Wright?"

"Ange?" Holly was baffled. "No."

Ash leaned in to look hard at Chesterton. "Why are you asking about Angela. Surely she's in the Caribbean somewhere?"

Chesterton gave a snort. "Not anymore she isn't. Oh, it was right when the police over there said that Christopher, or should I say Indiana, Sykes flew home from Jamaica. But we've now had confirmation that *Mrs* Sykes disembarked from the ship later at Antigua. She told everyone that the break up with her husband upset her so much she couldn't face carrying on on the cruise on her own. She showed them a booking for a hotel on Antigua, and as far as they were aware, that's where she went to. The rep' on the cruise ship says that as far as she was concerned, Angela was going to rejoin them for the flight back home. It's only been since the police in Antigua visited the hotel that they discovered she never checked in. So they promptly checked the airport and found that she flew back to Heathrow on Saturday."

That really gave Holly the shivers. What if Angie had come here on the Sunday and seen all the police around? She wasn't stupid. She wouldn't have tried to get access to the house the moment someone's back was turned in case the police came back. Plus the discovery of the body had been the talk of the town, so she'd soon have known that the game was up concerning keeping Tom's death quiet and that she'd be the chief suspect.

"Holly? Are you okay?" she heard Ash asking, as if from miles away.

She hauled herself mentally into the present but shook her head. "I just don't know what to think anymore." She turned to Chesterton. "I'm guessing that if you're asking me where she is, then have Angie's mum and dad not heard from her? Normally they'd be her first port of call, if only to get money off them to let her hide from you…or does she still have access to Chris' money?"

The thought that Angie might have literally millions to enable her to hide away somewhere didn't make Holly feel any better.

"Mr Sykes' bank is cooperating fully with us," was what Chesterton said. He looked at Wesley. "Can you think of any reason why he would make a large transfer of money and a large withdrawal of cash at a bank in the Falmouth area?"

Wesley was taken aback, but then after thinking for a moment said, "Mevagissey. That's a place Chris always said he loved. His foster mum and dad used to take them there on holiday as kids – him and a couple of other kids they fostered. He's got really happy memories of there. He never said so, but I think he might have dreamed of getting a place for him and Laura and the kids down there. Somewhere quiet, by the sea, where he could have a granny flat for her mum. Somewhere nice for Laura to enjoy while she still can."

Chesterton nodded, making notes. "The amount he transferred into another bank would be appropriate for the purchase of a large property, so I think we can guess that the cash is to rent or board somewhere until they can move in. Undoubtedly he didn't want to start using a cash point or his card regularly if Mrs Sykes has access to his e-banking account."

That gave Holly the shivers all over again. She could just imagine Angie sitting going through payments to shops and a hotel and quickly working out where Chris might be. She herself didn't know Cornwall well, but she guessed that Falmouth was far enough away from Mevagissey that Angie wouldn't be able to easily track him down from there without much more information. Of course, being Angie, she might rent a car and go driving around the lanes of Cornwall hoping to find him, but that was still a lot of places for one woman to cover, especially if she just missed him in one place and crossed it off her list, never going back.

The same thought had obviously come to Wesley, because he said, "I went down there once with Chris and Laura and the boys, so that I could help with things like her wheelchair on days out, you see – because back then, while Laura could mostly manage on level paths, any distance on slope was already more than she could cope with. But we stopped in St

Austell because Mevagissey is very hilly and we needed a bigger hotel with a lift than the ones down in the lovely old town there. So I know Chris could have done whatever he's doing in St Austell, because there are branches of some of the main banks there. I guess that means that he feared Angie doing exactly what you've said and going through all his transactions. He probably didn't have chance to change the passwords or anything."

Chesterton seemed to waver over whether to say something, but then said, "If it sets your mind at rest, the bank tell me that the password and access were changed as soon as Mr Sykes got back to England. There was never a joint account, you understand, but he clearly feared that his wife had got her hands on his passwords for his accounts. The bank will only tell us so much even at this stage, but they did say that there was evidence that someone had made several significant purchases without the card holder being present – including that flight back from Antigua, which was purchased before they even left this country.

"That certainly threw us at first, because we suspected Mr Sykes was trying to throw us off the scent of his wife, if he'd attempted to get rid of her while in the Caribbean. It was once we knew that he was already home, and then that Mrs Sykes had subsequently used the ticket, that we concluded that it had been her buying the ticket without him knowing, and that she had had some plan of her own going on, even if we didn't know what."

"Poor Chris," Wesley intoned miserably. "He must feel he's going to be looking over his shoulder for the rest of his life, waiting for bloody Angie to show up and trash things again. He's not going to know that she'll be done for murder, is he? He'll be thinking he's going to be her first."

It was a sombre thought which followed them through to the shop's office, where Holly once again got Angie's desk open, and let Chesterton go through the contents, as well as the contents of the safe. It made her very glad that she'd already come down and taken the cash she needed, because it was clear that Chesterton was in half a mind to take everything that was there to the station for further investigation. He had every reason to, but that wouldn't have helped her with her rent at the rapidly approaching end of the month.

Wesley left, excusing himself on the grounds of having a night shift at work, and eventually Chesterton left. However he did tell her and Ash that they would soon be done with the building.

Therefore it was a surprise, come the morning, to have a forensic pathologist turn up and asking to be let into the house again. "We found a curious piece of fabric in the...erm, fluids...when we lifted the floor boards underneath the body," he explained. "So I just need to make sure that it's just something that fell through and not attached to anything significant. Why your man or his killer would have had something that old, I don't know, but we need to rule out antique weapons."

Holly could only gasp, but Ash was quicker to put two and two together. "Does that mean that poor Tom was whacked with something old? Have you no idea what the murder weapon was – or at least what knocked him out enough to allow him to be dragged into where he was found? I'm saying dragged, because I can't imagine your chief suspect in the form of Angie being able to carry a man of his size."

The young pathologist, whose name turned out to be Callum, said, "It's a weird one, all right, and yes, you are correct – it does look as if he was dragged to the cupboard, going by the rubber residue from the heels of his boots along the floorboards. I'm hardly breaking protocol telling you that when you'll be able see the drag marks for yourself if you look closely. What's foxed us, though, is the wound to the back of his head. The flakes of rust I got given to analyse didn't make sense at first. No modern metal looks like that under a microscope. Too many impurities. Then the clinical pathologist got talking to her partner, who deals with historical deaths and stuff, and she immediately identified it."

"Oh no, please don't tell me it's Civil War era," Holly begged, making him looked at her askance and ask,

"How the hell would you know that?"

So yet again Holly found herself explaining about the ghosts and what Sally had told her about Scots being in Ledbury during the Civil War.

Callum was initially sceptical, but by the time Holly, with the backing of Ash, had told him that the two constables had also witnessed the ghosts on the night Tom's body had been found, he had to concede that they might have a point. "I'll get Sylvia – that's our pathologist Carol's partner – to see if we can narrow it down to Scotland," he said. "But what I really want to do now is find the actual weapon. Obviously, it wasn't left lying around, and since we initially presumed it would be something modern, we also assumed it had been dumped elsewhere, and I was being asked to try and match it to a modern blade of some description. But once I could say that whatever it was, it was almost certainly an antique and not a prized one either, that had been cleaned and polished with modern stuff, it occurred to us and DI Chesterton that the weapon might have been shoved under a floorboard, or behind a panel here in the house."

Chapter 20

Holly and Ash took Callum around to the flat and let him in, taking in his appalled expression when he realised just how much of a building he'd got to go through.

"We dismissed – or rather my boss did – searching all of this in detail the first time, because it's so empty of furniture or anything else. And of course we found the blood splatter in the same room as his body, meaning we could pretty certainly say that he'd been killed there. It wasn't as if we had to hunt for the crime scene to process it, all the evidence was there in the one room." He looked around him and at the staircase heading upwards. "I'm going to be here all bloody day."

Feeling sorry for him, Ash asked, "Can we help? I know we mustn't get in your way, but if to start off with you're looking for loose floorboards and stuff, surely there can't be anything wrong in Holly and me helping you? We've got nothing to hide and everything to gain by helping you get to the bottom of this. It's not doing my business any favours if the locals think I've got a murderer lurking upstairs."

That wasn't entirely true, since *The Renegade* had been doing a roaring trade on the back of the scandal, but Ash genuinely wanted to help. He gave a covert wink to Holly, and realising what he was doing, she chipped in with, "Why don't you start up on the top floor. That's where poor Tom was found, and that floor was behind the locked door, so logic says that if the murderer," she still couldn't quite say Angie's name to a stranger, "wanted to hide the weapon, it should be up there. But Ash and I can start down on this first floor and work our way up to you. There are four huge rooms on this floor alone, and as many on the next floor before you even get to the top one. You can't cover all of them on your own."

She saw him wavering and added, "Down here the exposed boards are all polished, so it'll be easy enough even for amateurs like Ash and me to spot if one is out of place and then call you. It'll be harder for you upstairs, because the old boards up there were covered in a skanky old carpet when Angie first showed me around, and from what I saw the only other time I went up there, some of those boards have been lifted umpteen times – they don't half creak when you walk over them."

Callum gave a grim smile. "Okay. I won't tell if you don't." He reached into his bag and pulled out latex gloves. "Put these on. Then if you do open a cupboard door and find something, your prints won't be all over it." The way he said it made them think that given what Holly had said, he believed they weren't going to find anything, only creaky boards.

Ash gave him a reassuring smile back. "We'll do this floor and then go and make us all a coffee. I'm sure you'll be ready for one by then."

Looking slightly less harassed, Callum vanished up to the top floor, and Holly and Ash wandered in to the smaller of the two reception room at the front on this first floor. “There’s still an odd atmosphere in here,” he said with a shiver. “What’s more, I don’t think it’s got anything to do with Tom, either. This feels older and more sad than angry. Not like the room next door. That definitely feels as if something violent went down in there.”

“Please don’t say things like that,” Holly pleaded. “I’m having a hard enough time being back in here as it is.”

“Sorry,” he apologised and wrapped his arm around her shoulders to give her a hug. “I forget that not everyone has my fascination with the spirit world.”

Holly managed a watery smile. “It’s not spirits that give me the shivers, it’s the murdered that bother me.”

Luckily she didn’t notice the quizzical look Ash gave her for saying that. What had made Holly make that distinction? Because it made him wonder whether she too was a sensitive, and having spent more time here than him, had picked up on something he’d missed. Who was that ghost, and had he died a violent death here rather than dying from sickness or pre-existing wounds?

In deference to Holly’s nerves, though, Ash said nothing, and they began by walking the floor, searching for loose boards. However, as Holly had said, down here the boards had clearly been waxed over and over, to the extent that there was visible clogging in the gaps between the planks, and it was clear that none of them had been moved in years if not centuries. Feeling that they had to be thorough, they then started to work their way around the wood panelling.

"They didn't have banks back in those days," Ash explained, "so there'd be nothing unusual in them having a concealed cupboard in the wall where the old merchant who had this place built would have kept his valuables."

They walked around to the other front room, which to Ash now felt considerably worse than the other room. Careful tapping on the wood, they nonetheless got all of the way around the huge room without finding anything. With great care, Ash lifted the gas fire out a short way and peered up the chimney, shining a torch up there but shaking his head. "Nah, nothing up there but soot."

Holly gave a shaky laugh. "No murder weapons stuffed up there, then?"

Ash kept his response of "Nah," light-hearted, but once again wondered why that should have occurred to Holly. Something had definitely happened in here, and before he did anything with this building, he resolved to give it a good spiritual cleansing. Yet once again they found nothing in the room itself, and what he said to Holly was, "Whatever happens with this place, these chimneys need a damned good clean. I'd not be happy about anyone using even the gas fires until they have. I doubt anyone's hidden anything up there, not even a murder weapon."

"I can't see Angie doing that," Holly said. "She's far too worried about her appearance. Anyway, she's scared stiff of spiders, and she'd have screamed the place down if she'd gone in there and found even a tiny one."

"Oh there're cobwebs aplenty up there," Ash laughed. "Right, we can discount that as a hiding place then."

To Holly's huge relief there was nothing in the room she'd been using, either, and so they moved on to the back room. This had been the one that Holly had been quietly dreading. It had a whole wall of cupboards, and she'd wondered whether at some time this might have been some kind of kitchen area for the family, because the cupboards looked old but not as much as the building itself. Yet to her relief, there was nothing in any of those, and since the separate loo only had room for the toilet and a washbasin, it meant that this floor was done.

Recognising that Holly needed a break, Ash took her around to *The Renegade* and they made coffee and sandwiches, which they took back into the flat and called Callum down for a break. He, too, had found nothing in the way of a weapon so far. But he did tell them that he'd found the rest of a substantial piece of ancient material, which he agreed with Ash could well be a Highlander's plaid – the great swathe of material which most ordinary men would have wrapped around them as a coat, but also used as their blanket.

"I've had to lift two big old floorboards to get it out without tugging it," he said, clearly enjoying the discovery of this antiquity more than some gruesome remains. "Sylvia will be in raptures over this," referring to the osteo-archaeologist and team leader who Chesterton had mentioned.

Holly even expressed the hope to Ash that the removal of the plaid might quieten down the ghosts, though he didn't like to dampen her mood by saying that he didn't think it would be that simple. In an attempt to keep her spirits up, Ash suggested that this time they tackle the back of the second floor first. In some ways, this was the part of the building

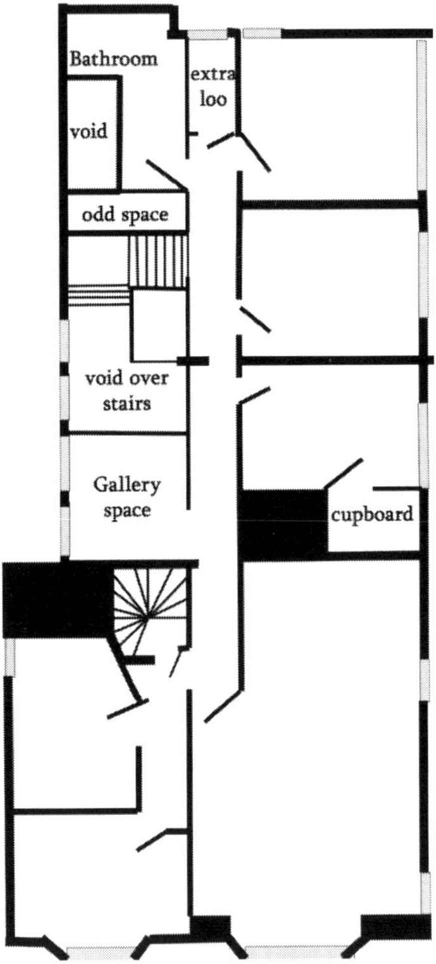

Second floor plan

that had seen the most alterations. Long before Grade listings for buildings had even been thought of, someone had messed around with the subdivision of this rear part of the floor. The floorboards weren't of the same quality, and the dividing walls were more recent, if not actually modern. There was no wood panelling here to hide anything and even in its heyday, this had not been the prestigious end of the house.

"What's up above here?" Ash wondered, as they came out onto the top floor of the main staircase. He was looking up and had noticed that the ceiling seemed higher than the rest of the floor, but without any higher landing, or the like, looking down the stairs. The well of the stairs had a higher ceiling to accommodate the tall windows, but clearly, above this floor the light-well's walls must be backing onto something. With both the first and second floors being jetted out beyond the floors below, in typical Tudor fashion – and therefore ever so slightly longer than the space below in each case – sometimes it was hard to tell where they were in relation to what was below or above.

"Oh, it's a loft space," Holly answered. "Quite a big one actually, because when Angie was trying to con me into coming and living up there, she said that it would be easy to convert it into more living space if I needed it. Why on earth she should have thought that, I don't know, because I'd have had a sitting room and three bedrooms already. Angie reckoned there was even a walk-in cupboard up there, but I never saw that. Just opening the door onto the loft space gave me the shivers. I never went in."

Yet Ash was starting to put more faith in Holly's instincts than she did herself. "I think we'd better tell Callum about that," he said, and instead of going into the room above where Holly had stayed, led the way up the smaller, twisting stairs to the third floor. They found Callum, head and shoulders in the void between the floor and the ceiling below. Not wanting to startle him, Ash called his name, and told him about the loft when he emerged and shoved back the dust-encrusted protective hood of his white coverall.

Given that the door to the loft was just outside the room Callum was working in, they agreed that the team who'd removed the body must have checked in there. Callum himself had been on leave at the time, so he hadn't been involved, but when Holly told him that there was a cupboard which may not have been spotted, he agreed with Ash that it needed checking. Holly was bracing herself to have to go in and show him, so she was surprised but very grateful when Ash quietly said to her while Callum was getting his luminal spray and a torch, "Tell me where it is and I'll go in with him. You don't need to go, Holly," and he gave her hand a reassuring squeeze.

Even opening the loft door, and the waft of chill air that came with it was enough to have the hair on the back of Holly's neck standing on end. There was no way she could have forced herself in there, and knowing that Ash was tuned in to atmospheres, she appreciated him going in her place all the more. Even as he stepped inside following Callum, she saw him give a shudder. Yes, Ash was being a real hero going in there.

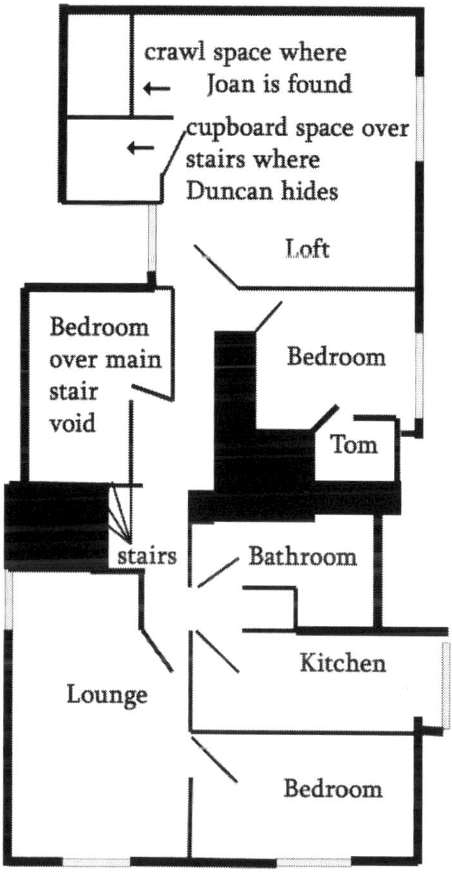

Top floor plan

Inside the room, Ash was glad when at first Callum said to put the light on. The modern strip light blazed through the gloom, proving that there wasn't a thing in here. However, it instantly struck Ash how thoroughly Angie must have gone through the place, because even so, he wouldn't have spotted the cupboard had Holly not told him where to start looking.

"It's in that far corner, or so Angie told Holly," he said to Callum, leading the way across the bare boards and with dread building up all the way.

"It's well hidden," Callum said with a gasp as they got to the recessed part of the wall and he poked and prodded around, trying to find it. The cupboard door could easily have been mistaken for just another tatty wood panel, such as covered the rest of the loft wall at that end. Undoubtedly some of the backs of the uppermost panels on the great staircase, this side had never been finished to the same standard, and their rough surface was covered with generations of spiders' webs. Only close up and with the aid of a torch could you see that there was a simple wooden handle inset into the side of one panel.

Callum sprayed the area around the handle with the luminal and then got Ash to go back and turn the main light off. Shining his torch over the area, he quickly decided that no recent blood has been in contact with it. "Of course, if she used clean gloves to come and hide something, then it won't show," he said to Ash, who'd put the light back on and come to join him. "Oh well, since I'm here, I might as well investigate."

Expecting the door to be stiff, Callum hauled on it hard and was then shot backwards into Ash's arms as the door opened far easier than he expected. The pair of them staggered backwards, Ash just about stopping Callum from going flying.

"Oh crap," Callum gulped, because sat down at floor level he found himself looking in deep under a shelf attached to the sloping roof of the cupboard that followed the line of the eaves.

Recovering himself once Callum had got to his feet again, Ash bent down and saw what he'd seen. A piece of timber, which must have until relatively recently provided a backing to this lowest part of the cupboard had fallen away, and behind it he could see greyish-white, which could only be bones. "Well I fear we've found our lost Highlander, even if we haven't found the murder weapon," he sighed.

"I'd better call it in," Callum said morosely. "The boss is going to kill me for this. We're already up to our eyes in work. We didn't need this."

"Never mind," Ash consoled him. "If this is who I think it is, it's one for the archaeologists, not you." On the other hand, once he'd gone back out to Holly and told her why Callum had gone hurriedly past, fumbling for his phone, he looked around again. "Do you know of any other cupboards?" he asked her. "Only we still seem to have an unaccounted for space in there. I think it might be a bit over the staircase and that odd space down here behind the staircase wall, which doesn't seem to be useful for anything besides storage."

"I honestly don't know," Holly confessed. "Angie was a whirlwind when she was all enthused about something. I was towed around at such a speed I barely had time to register anything. The only reason this attic bit stuck with me was because I was so repelled by it, yet Angie seemed to be pushing me towards it for some reason."

Ash didn't like the sound of that. Had Angie tried to make it so that wherever the murder weapon was, it was somewhere where she could stand back and point the finger of blame at Holly as the only one who would know where it was? He had a horrible feeling she might, and so when Callum came plodding back through, having got a signal at the front of the building, Ash suggested that they continue their search of the attic. By the time he'd taken Callum out onto the landing, and pointed out that there was unaccounted for space, Callum reluctantly agreed.

They started on the far side of the loft space, because with the eaves sloping down to the floor there, they could see that something which looked very like an extra-deep skirting board had been put in. Yet that proved to be sound and immovable. They found a dingy old curtain across a dust-encrusted window and pulled that back, letting a little more feeble light into the room. However, it was the peculiar shadows it threw, in combination with the modern fluorescent strip, that made Ash spot something on the far wall. It wasn't as deeply recessed as the cupboard the skeleton was in, but instead made an odd corner projection into the room.

This time, the door turned out to be more of a hatch, made out of a single panel of wood such as was on the staircase walls. When tugged, this also came free more easily than expected, but this time Callum was braced for it. What it exposed was a strange shaped area with some thin strands of light coming through holes in the staircase side wall, almost like peepholes.

"I wonder if someone hid in here?" Ash wondered. "If the house is sixteenth century it's of an age to have priests' holes, but the details I got of the building said that this floor was added in the seventeenth."

Callum looked at him blankly, forcing Ash to explain, "Priests' holes are a thing of Edward the Sixth and Bloody Mary's reigns which come in the middle of the sixteenth century. After that, there was no need for people to hide Catholic priests, or for Protestant families to hide, and I'm talking by a good half century at the very least. You'd have to have been one very paranoid family to build one into your nice new house in the time of the Civil War. On the other hand, a family with something, or someone, to hide come the end of that war, might well grab such a chance if they'd also come into the kind of money they'd have needed in order to build this extra floor up here." Then something caught his eye, even though he was looking over Callum's shoulder. "On the other hand, I don't think Laura Ashley is contemporary with that period. What's that on the shelf?"

Handing Ash the torch, Callum reached in and carefully lifted out something which, going by his grunt of effort as he held its full weight, was very heavy. Heavy and long.

Staggering back with it, he put it down as soon as he could, Ash backing up out of the way to give him room. The wrapping was an old curtain, but definitely late twentieth century, no older. With great care, Callum lifted the cloth away, and although he couldn't immediately unwrap it all, the curtain fell away exposing a large hilt.

"Bloody hell! It's a claymore!" Ash gasped. "I never thought I'd see one of those outside of a museum."

"It's a monster of a thing, I tell you that," Callum said with feeling. "The man who used that must have been one hell of a fighter."

"Ah, but they were used two-handed," Ash explained. "This isn't your nice neat fencing sword. This was the kind of sword you got swinging and let its momentum carry it forwards. Think of some really big guy, like Liam Nesson when he played Rob Roy, and him charging into battle swinging it two-handed and ploughing through everyone in his way. You didn't worry about accuracy with this thing, you were taking heads and arms off and keeping going." Then a thought came to him. "Holly?" he called. "How much would you say Angie could lift?"

Holly leaned in through the door and said, "Probably more than you'd think. In the last six months she'd got into doing weights at the gym. Her trainer there could tell you more than me."

"Well that's definitely recent blood," Callum said, sitting back on his heels, and showing where he'd sprayed a tiny amount of luminal onto a patch on the sword, and how it was fluorescing brightly under the light of his torch. "Whoever did it, I'd say we've found the murder weapon."

Chapter 21

Ash and Holly vacated the flat immediately on Callum's pronouncement, and went and waited for the inevitable questioning. DI Chesterton turned up again and eventually made his way down to them in *The Renegade's* office.

"Callum tells me you helped him find the sword," he said rather disapprovingly, and Holly was glad that Ash immediately explained that they'd only been there in the first place because Callum had been left to cover so much space on his own. "We were only going to see if we could spot something that didn't look right and tell him," he explained, "and with the main rooms having been gone over by your own people already, as far as we were concerned it was more on the wild off-chance that they'd missed something. It was only when we were at the back of the second floor that I realised that the space just didn't add up – not that I'd even seen the top floor before then. It was Holly saying that there was a gloomy old attic up above, which made us go to tell Callum. Even then, he said that his colleagues had been through it once already."

Chesterton turned to Holly. "And you say that you recalled Mrs Sykes pushing you to use the attic?"

Holly sighed. "It was odd back then, but to be honest I was more worried about getting everything ready to open the shop than whether Angie was going to bully me into using the top floor flat. And I'd dismissed the attic space anyway, because there was more than enough room for just me in the flat as it was. It was only when Ash asked me what was up above us that I remembered it."

Before Chesterton could say anything, Ash interrupted him to ask, "Do you think Angie was priming Holly so that she'd look like the guilty one when Tom's body came to light? After all, Angie would be hoping that she could use the alibi of being far away on an exotic holiday. If she made Holly the only one who would know of the hiding place for the weapon, was she planning on coming back and giving the Oscar-winning performance of being horrified and shocked?"

Chesterton nodded. "That's very much the conclusion I've been coming to. However, I have to ask you, Holly: have you ever been in to the attic or near the place where both the old body and the sword have been found?" Holly vigorously shook her head. "So there's no way we'll find your DNA in there?"

"God, no!" she exclaimed.

"Have you ever seen that curtain before?"

"I didn't even see it this time."

Chesterton gestured her to come with him, and took them back up to where the forensic team were just putting the sword and its wrapping into a sterile container to transport it. "Could you just open a bit of the fabric out for me, Claire?" he asked the one team member, and as she did so, Holly felt her knees go.

As Ash caught her as she sank to the ground, she could only repeat, “No, it can’t be, it can’t be.”

Crouching down in front of her, Chesterton asked gently, “What can’t it be? Holly, what do you recognise?”

Even with Ash cradling her in his arms, it took Holly a moment before she could string her words together. “That curtain…it’s one of the ones that hung in the room I used at Angie’s parents’ house when I was a teenager. I haven’t seen them in years. How is that here?”

Chesterton looked grimly at Ash, seeing in Ash’s eyes the same realisation that Angie had deliberately set Holly up to take the fall for her.

“Don’t worry,” Ash said, “I’ll take care of her,” and virtually picked Holly up to get her back on her feet and into *The Renegade*.

The rest of the day passed in a haze for Holly. As some point she knew that Jesse and Ash had got her up to the spare room in the flat, Jesse and Shea-Lea both insistent that there was no way that Holly was spending the night in a hotel room now, not even if Ash was in there with her. Jesse knew one of their regular customers was a local doctor, and rang him, persuading him to come out and give Holly a check over and a sedative. Getting a scheduled home visit was something that rarely happened these days, but as Jesse said to his doctor friend, the alternative was Ash taking Holly to the nearest A&E and her waiting hours to get seen – hardly the best solution for someone who had gone into shock.

It was a relief for her to slide into oblivion and miss the rest of that day. Ash never left her side unless Shea-Lea or Jesse came in to sit with her, worried stiff that she might slip into unconsciousness and stop breathing. She was muffled under a double layer of duvets and with a couple of hot-water bottles at her feet, and yet she still felt colder than she should be. The doctor, who'd previously been an army medic and had no qualms about treating shock, was going to come back in again later in the evening, but told Ash that if anything changed he was to call treble nine.

When Chesterton called in to see how Holly was, Ash demanded, "You aren't seriously going to treat her as a suspect, are you?" He had a good solicitor who had helped him with his own nightmare of a break up, and he was all ready to phone him to come to represent Holly.

However Chesterton immediately shook his head. "No, she's not a suspect. Firstly, you can't fake shock like that. And secondly, someone has already been over to speak to Meryl White, and she's confirmed that yes, curtains like that did hanging in their room over the garage which Holly used to use. But she's also said that Angie was the one who came and took them away the same day that she had the big row with her parents. I've no doubt she thought she was being very clever, but it takes a bit more than that to pull the wool over our eyes."

Ash felt a small amount of relief. "I've no doubt that Holly, being the nice person she is, will feel very sorry for Angie's mother having to face up to what a monster she's raised. I'm afraid I'm not quite so sympathetic."

Chesterton nodded. "I see it all too often. Parents who are totally blinkered to what their kids have become. I get it. I love my kids dearly too. But I'm not blind to the fact that they can be little sods at times, and that's when it's hard work being a mum or dad. You have to put them straight for their own good. Hoping it will just blow over or go away, because you don't want to play the bad guy, isn't doing them any favours at all."

He left them in peace after that, and when Jesse and Shea-Lea stuck their heads around the spare room door to wish Ash goodnight, they found him asleep on the bed beside Holly, his arms wrapped protectively around her. Shea-Lea went and got the thick throw off the sofa to cover him with, and they went to bed, praying for a peaceful night.

Holly was surprised to wake up and feel someone bedside her. That it was Ash, and he'd clearly been with her all night, was even more of a surprise – she wasn't used to people taking that level of care of her. But lying there, having thrown the second duvet off, since by now she was positively cooking under the two, she lay there plagued by her thoughts. *How will I ever trust anyone ever again?* she fretted. *How did I never see that coming? Does everyone see me as such an idiot that they think they can do anything to me, and I'll just lie down and let it happen?*

Shea-Lea must have been anticipating something like this, because when she came in and Ash woke up, Shea-Lea shooed him out to go and have a shower and sat on the end of the bed giving Holly a very stern look. "Before you say a thing, I don't want to hear a word about you blaming yourself," she said firmly. "Remember what I said about Angie gas-lighting you? Well this is all part and parcel of that. The shoving off of blame onto you for things that she did. In her head, Princess Angie doesn't do bad things, people *force* her to do bad things. And that she wouldn't be in that position if people just did what she told them to do."

"For someone who hasn't met her, you've got her taped," Holly said weakly. "She must have seen me coming."

Shea-Lea sighed. "Holly, it wasn't you she 'saw coming', it was the whole bloody world! If you could go back in time and be an observer on her life, I'm sure you'd see loads of instances where she tried it on with people, and her being outraged when it didn't work. The one and only difference between them and you was that she got her hooks into you while you were still children. If you met her as someone completely new right now, you wouldn't like her, much less be fooled by her, because you'd see the adult Angie for who she is.

"What's messed with your head is you seeing adult Angie always through the filter of schoolgirl Angie, and the thing is, teenage girls can be a bloody nightmare! It's part of growing up. But most people *do* grow up. You have, and so have your other friends, whereas Angie has taken that behaviour and tried to twist it to fit adult life. She's a monster of her own making, not yours."

When Ash came back in, he backed Shea-Lea's assessment, but mistook Holly's completely baffled expressions as being simply down to that. He didn't know that Holly's hormones had taken one look at Ash coming back in wearing just his jeans, long hair damp and gently curling, and reiki symbol tattoos snaking down his damp torso over well-defined muscles, had set off a veritable explosion of lust. Her problem was that she wasn't used to feeling lust – certainly not over a man standing in the same room as her, even if she was normal enough to admire men on TV who ticked the right boxes with her. Plus right now, Holly didn't trust a single thought or feeling of her own. Her body was screaming at her to throw the duvet off and pull him into bed; her head was screaming and telling her to run out of the room, down the stairs, and keep going. Quite what her heart was doing was beyond telling, but it felt as if it was about to leap out of her chest and go off and do its own thing without telling her.

She managed to get up, but still felt shaky, so Shea-Lea came and sat in the bathroom while she had a shower, just in case she passed out in it. However, the hot shower seemed to help, and by the time they got into the kitchen, Ash was pulling croissants and pain aux raisins out of the oven for her. "Only pre-frozen ones, I'm afraid," he apologised, "but I remembered you saying that you weren't used to meat at breakfast time."

Holly half expected Shea-Lea to protest that she needed a full cooked breakfast, but Ash must have said something to Shea-Lea about Holly not being used to a meat-heavy diet, because she didn't argue, instead going and making Holly a pot of green tea.

"Strong coffee probably isn't what you need right now," she said with a cheeky wink. "We might be clawing you down from the ceiling if I give you my normal brew."

Whatever the brand was, it was much nicer than what Holly usually bought, and she managed a second mug almost straightaway. Shea-Lea then vanished to help Jesse in the pub, reminding Holly that somehow they were already coming around to the weekend again. Then when she went and sat down on the sofa, Ash came and draped an arm around her shoulders and asked, "How do you fancy coming down to my cottage with me for the weekend? I think you need a bit of quiet and relaxation, and there's nowhere here where we can go for a proper quiet walk. The town is lovely, but when I was stressed, I found being around hordes of people in a busy place wasn't helpful. Chesterton's got my home address, and Jesse can tell him where we've gone. It won't be a problem."

So by midday, Holly was wrapped up in her warm coat in the passenger seat of Ash's Range Rover, a packed bag in the back, and heading out into the countryside with her hormones still doing a happy dance, much to her confusion. Too wiped out by all that had gone on, even her worries seemed to have given up out of exhaustion and left her alone, so she sat and watched the countryside go by, her mind a blank. Therefore, when Ash pulled up and switched the engine off, she was almost in a stupor, and she had to make a conscious effort to pull herself back into the here and now.

"What do you think?" she heard him ask, as if from far away, and turning her head she felt her jaw drop as she found herself looking at what once must have been a pair of cottages. Not some chocolate-box kind of cottage, just the red-brick kind built for farm workers in the first half of the twentieth century, but this was now something more. On the right-hand side, the broad window of the front room had been left as it was, aside from getting double-glazed, but on the left side, it had been changed into a full-length window with a patio door in it. Around the arched tops of both, trellis held roses and wisteria in place, and Holly knew that in the summer it would be beautiful.

"Oh Ash, it's lovely!" she gasped. Then on looking around, spotted the roofs of what had to be farm barns across a low rise in the fields. "Is that where the studio is?"

"God, no," Ash replied, helping her out and then grabbing both their bags off the back seat. "There was no way I was going back to living above the job, so to speak. I learned that lesson the hard way. These days I have a healthy twenty mile journey over the border to get to 'work'. We're still in Herefordshire here."

He didn't tell her that he'd bought this house after his ex had begun stalking him at the cottage he'd had in the nearest village to the studio. That kind of negativity Holly didn't need to hear right now. Instead he said, "I lived in rented places for quite a while, not least because I didn't know what on earth I *did* want. Then these two cottages came on the market when the farmer needed some capital in a hurry – or at least as much of a hurry as any property sale takes. I took one look at them and the view and knew this was where I wanted to be."

Holly looked around, slightly puzzled. Yes it was a nice view out across green fields, but not that spectacular.

Ash laughed. "The view's at the back. Come on in and you'll see."

He led the way in through the patio door and deposited the bags on one of a pair of large squashy sofas, then opened oak-panelled bi-fold doors which exposed what had once probably been the modest kitchen of the original cottage on this side. Now it formed part of a glorious cathedral-roofed extension across the whole of the back of the buildings. It made sense of the drain pipe Holly had seen at the other front window, because the kitchen must now be the other big room at the front, leaving this back space free for the view. Through the ceiling-to-floor windows, Holly suddenly saw that the land fell away on this side, giving a stunning view of the valley beyond.

As she stood open-mouthed looking at the clouds forming patterns across the landscape as they successively blocked the sun and then let it spotlight other areas, he said, "Those roofs you can just see down in the valley are Hay on Wye. The Welsh border is there too. That's where I nip down to for my shopping when needed, although I have to confess that I'm not the best of cooks. Please don't expect anything of Jesse's standard while you're here."

To his relief Holly laughed. "I've hardly led the kind of life where I expect *cordon bleu*," she joked, "although I could get used to Jesse's bacon sandwiches for lunch, even if they're a bit hefty for breakfast."

She had no idea how relieved Ash was to hear those words. Too many girlfriends in the past, even the ones who hadn't a clue who he was when it came to rock and-roll fame, assumed that a man with his money must be eternally eating out at Michelin-star restaurants. Ash had had his share of meals at places like that, and he wasn't averse to taking someone out to one for a special occasion. It was rather that he preferred the normal kind of food he'd been brought up on for everyday meals. So to know that Holly had no expectations of being daily wined and dined was a relief, plus he suspected that it might be a while before she was fully comfortable with paying those kinds of prices for a meal, even if he was footing the bill.

It also wasn't lost on him that Holly gave what sounded like a sigh of relief as she flopped into what was normally his favourite chair, looking like a puppet with her strings cut. That was very much what he had felt the first time he'd set foot in here – peace and restfulness – and it confirmed in his mind that Holly was far more sensitive to atmosphere and spirits than she'd allowed herself to admit. Here, there were no ghosts, no strange atmosphere in certain rooms, and nothing to trigger bad memories.

He left her soaking in the view and took her bag up to the spare bedroom next to his. Each of the former cottages had had two main bedrooms upstairs plus a tiny third, with their primitive bathrooms downstairs beyond the kitchens, constructed out of what had once been simply outside toilets and outhouses. Those toilets and outhouses were buried under the new extension, and Ash had made an en suite bathroom upstairs for his bedroom out of the third bedroom on his side, and a luxury bathroom out of the back bedroom in the other half. That had still left him with another generous double bedrooms at the front where he now put Holly's bags. On his side that left another bedroom larger than most modern houses possessed at the back, and a store room in what had been the third bedroom on the other, the two halves now connected by a short landing and a single staircase where there had been two.

For a man whose only guests to date had been Jesse and Shea-Lea, these had been more than enough. Was he fooling himself to hope that maybe one day he might now need to add on a guest house if his own children filled these other bedrooms? Did Holly even want children after her disastrous childhood? He hoped so, but was surprised to realise that if she didn't, he'd rather have a life without kids than a life without Holly.

Chapter 22

For the whole of the weekend, Holly allowed herself to decompress. Nobody called demanding answers to questions she didn't have. Nor did she have to face up to the way that Angie had totally wrapped her around her little finger, and made her party to her awful plots and schemes. Something about that would not let her be, and she kept having strange feelings that she'd missed something, but right now she was so drained, so very tired of feeling a fool. By nine p.m. that first night she was dead on her feet, and after a blissful shower under the luxurious rainfall shower, she fell into the comfortable king-sized bed, and didn't surface until after ten the following morning.

She was even more impressed when she discovered that once again Ash had cooked her croissants, albeit frozen and not from scratch, but then what normal person had time to make croissant dough fresh every morning? It was too cold to sit out on the patio, even though the sun was shining, but with the bi-fold doors open, the sun warmed it enough that they could sit at the small table by the window for breakfast. For Holly, this was better than the best five-star hotel, not least because in such a hotel she would have felt far out of her comfort zone, whereas she couldn't believe how at home she felt here.

When they finally stirred, Ash took her for a gentle stroll around the lanes, and then cooked her fish and chips for dinner. It made Holly smile to herself as she recognised the same brands coming out of Ash's freezer as she bought herself, or at least just the next quality up. The fact that he wasn't endlessly trying to impress her made a deeper impression on her than if he had. She'd watched numerous men flattering Angie, trying to get her to believe that they could keep her in a style even better than her father could, and every one of them had come across as false to Holly. Ash was down to earth and very real, and that was comforting.

They had a quiet evening in front of the TV, and again, Holly was wilting and off to bed early. It was as if getting away from the shop had finally allowed her brain to realise that she could let go for a while and recuperate. She was embarrassed to discover that after breakfast on Sunday, she nodded off again in the big comfortable armchair by the open-hearth fire in the back room, the day having turned out wet and gloomy and hardly fit for leisurely strolls. As she came to, she hurriedly looked around for Ash, half expecting him to have gone out to the tiny music studio she now knew he'd built himself in the garden, having given up on his somnambulant guest.

Instead, she spotted him kneeling on the extension's tiled floor by the window, busy doing something, and when she got to her feet and wandered over, to her surprise he was re-potting a large houseplant.

"I've been meaning to do this for ages," he said, looking up at her with a smile. "It really likes it by this big window and it's practically climbed out of its pot."

Holly didn't like to ask what the strappy leaved plant was, knowing that even if he told her she wouldn't know what it was. The best she'd ever managed was a spider plant that had been reduced at the supermarket, and although with some watering and feeding it was thriving, she didn't have money to waste on plants which wouldn't like the conditions in her gloomy and chilly flat. She loved the idea of a house full of plants, though, and for the first time realised that Ash clearly did too, because there were plants perched in pots all over the place in here. None of the men she'd had close contact with in her life had shown signs of enjoying nurturing anything in that way, and she felt it must be a good sign that Ash so obviously did.

It also surprised her that by the end of the evening, she found that she really didn't want to go back – not only to the shop and the flat with its secrets, but not to her own flat either. In truth, there wasn't much about her life that she did like, and it bothered her even more that she couldn't recall a time when she had.

Ash's voice saying, "Holly? Are you okay? You've gone awfully quiet," roused her from her reverie.

"I'm just waking up to the fact that I don't like my life very much," she explained with a watery attempt at a smile. "People are always saying that it's up to you to make the changes, but that never seems to take into account the need to earn a living, and the limited choices there are for jobs if you aren't qualified in anything particular. Yes, you can get *a* job, but that's not the same as one worth having, is it?"

He smiled sympathetically. "It's great advice, but you can't always take it, can you?"

Holly shook her head. "I've done nothing but retail ever since I left school, because I couldn't afford to stay on to get more qualifications, and shop work was what I could get back then. The trouble is, I've since applied for other kinds of jobs, and they either say I haven't got relevant experience, or as more than one HR person has said to me, 'You're on how much an hour? Well what reason can you give us to pay you more?' The fact that I've said that I couldn't afford to sit around at home waiting for my ideal job because I had bills to pay, and had to take the jobs I could *get*, whereas they had a job I would actually *want*, never seemed good enough. And swopping one store job for another was rarely worth it – the pay wasn't any better, I'd lose whatever extra holiday I'd accrued, and there was no knowing if I'd run into the same kind of awful bosses I'd had in the past. Better the devil I knew, and all that. But it's hardly made me happy."

Ash thought that this was probably the biggest factor in Holly taking the plunge to work with Angie, even more than Angie's ability to persuade. That chance to escape must have been powerful. "What would you like to do?"

"That's the worst of it, Ash, I don't bloody know anymore! I thought that running our own shop would at least give me some control back over my life, but it hasn't has it?"

He stood up, dusting the compost off himself onto the rubber mat he'd put down to work on. "I think you have to allow that what's gone on these last few weeks has been pretty extreme by anyone's measures, Holly. I don't think you can judge what working for yourself would be like by them. On the other hand, the fact that you aren't itching to get back to the shop and get it up and running again, tells me that maybe you were less invested in it than you want to believe? Regardless of what Angie has or hasn't done in terms of harming people, *you've* been the one putting the hard graft into the shop, so I was half expecting you to be champing at the bit to get back to it."

Holly gave a huff of dismay. "So was I, but I'm not! I think what I really need is a total change. Everything! Where I live. What I do. Who I class as my friends. Honestly Ash, it's frightening me how much I simply don't want the life I've got. The best thing to come out of all of this has been meeting you and Jesse and Shea-Lea." She gave a bitter laugh. "I'd say I was a prime candidate for one of those makeover shows, but I think even they would give up on me in disgust."

Ash came and wrapped her in a hug. "This is the shock and betrayal talking. Believe me, in time you will feel differently about all of this. I certainly did after my life fell apart. It took a while, don't get me wrong. I didn't bounce back up straightaway. It took time. But looking back now from the vantage point of several years down the line, that was the point when

I started resolving to do the things *I* wanted – not what everyone else told me I ought to want."

"I do hope so. I don't want to feel like this forever."

"You won't."

"Promise?"

"Promise. And the first thing we can do to help you start climbing up out of this dark place is to make sure that until the shop gets sorted, that we make sure you stay at the hotel, not trying to make that awful commute back and forth every day. Commuting is fine if you've got an easy route, whether it's in your own car or by decent public transport. But it's wretched if it starts consuming the start and finish of every day. You've got enough to cope with without that, so let's take that out of the equation right now."

Holly looked up at him mournfully. "I can't ask you to fund that for me, and I certainly can't afford it."

Yet Ash just smiled. "It would give me much more satisfaction spending my money on a hotel room for you than ever it did splashing out cash on the useless fashion stuff my ex used to drag me out shopping for every weekend. That became torture, this won't."

Therefore it was with some trepidation that Holly allowed Ash to ring the hotel and book them in for the next week, but she realised that on this, Ash was right – it did take a weight off her mind over how she was going to get to the shop. She hadn't even realised it was that much of a thing compared to everything else until it wasn't. What she was going to do about the shop was a whole other question, but then she woke up to the fact that if it needed to be wrapped up, that wasn't her decision to make.

Feeling considerably less wobbly, it wasn't as bad going back to Ledbury the following morning, and even more so when Jesse was able to confirm that nothing had gone on in their absence. The bones they'd found had been taken away, but nothing more had been said about them. Even better, that morning she got a phone call from Chesterton saying that because of the bank account situation, there was no way that the shop could reopen until that had been resolved. For Holly that was another stress taken away, because her brain had been gnawing away over what on earth she could say to customers when she as soon as she was able to open the shop. What would she say – what *could* she say – about Angie, the owner who had singularly failed to appear, and who now seemed to be as entangled as was possible in a major crime? And Holly knew that customers *would* ask. They always did, that she knew from years of experience, even if it was about nothing more than a scuffle outside, so what they'd say about all of this had her mentally cringing. Not answering wasn't a solution, either, which she also knew from past situations. She'd have to come up with something...but not this week, not today.

She did manage to get Chesterton's permission to go in and do a stock take, on the basis that it might become necessary to know exactly what assets Angie and Chris did have. So she and Ash went in and took their time counting bath-bombs, candles, and gifts sets, and putting a value on everything. In a small shop like this, even with them taking long breaks for coffees or lunch at *The Renegade*, it still didn't take them more than two days, so by midweek, Holly was again feeling rather lost.

She was therefore sitting in the pub on Wednesday morning while Ash helped Jesse with a beer delivery, when Callum came in looking distinctly glum.

"We didn't finish searching the place," he told Holly, "and I've been told in no uncertain terms that I shouldn't have let you and Ash help me, even if without you I'd never have found the sword. So can you let me in, because I'm going to have to start from scratch again."

Feeling rather guilty that they'd got Callum into trouble, Holly took him around to the main door and then followed him in. "Surely they can't complain if I keep you company?" she said. "I promise I won't touch, but if nothing else, I might be able to answer the odd question."

Therefore when Ash came to find her, they'd got through the first floor rooms because Callum agreed with what she and Ash had decided, which was that if anything was under those floorboards, it had been there an awfully long time and wasn't relevant to Tom's murder. Together they all went up to the second floor, and now Callum could see what had prompted Ash to wonder what was up above the room beyond the staircase, because it was obvious that spatially something didn't quite match up. However, it was also as clear to him as it had been to them that there was nothing else there, and so they made their way to the front of the building, leaving the room above where Holly had slept until last.

Going through to where the stairs began their climb to the third floor, Callum suddenly got interested in the floorboards in the space in front of the first treads, before they climbed on upwards.

"Do you know, I think that once upon a time these stairs went on down to the first floor," he said, suddenly more enthusiastic about his search. "Look at the way they seem to sink into the floor. I wonder if these were once upon a time the servants' stairs for the house?"

Ash peered upwards, nodding. "That would make sense, because there must have been an attic up there even before the extra floor got added. That makes a bit more sense of the attic where we found the sword and the bones, too."

"It does?" Holly couldn't see how.

Ash explained, "I was looking at the roofline of this place from Jesse's flat, and I think that at the back of the building the roof was always lower. They probably had an imposing roofline at the front for the prestige effect, so it was easy to just take it up a notch or two to create the extra rooms. An important family like this would have been bound to have servants, wouldn't they? So they must have slept somewhere, which was most likely the original attic.

"Well they didn't fly up there, did they? There has to have been a staircase. And because they wouldn't have needed access to the business part on the ground floor, it would only need to be from the first, coming up to here, and then on up to the attic. That's why it's so closed off. Servants were to be seen and heard as little as possible."

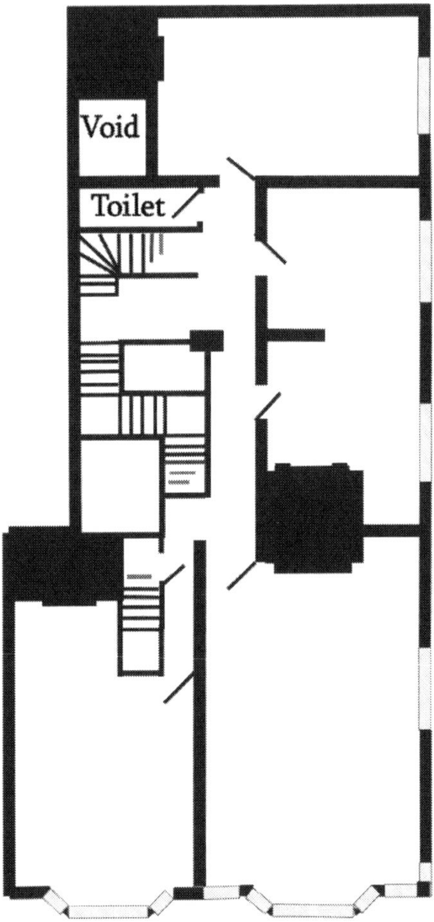

First floor plan

By now Callum was down on his knees, probing the floorboards. "I think Ash is right. Look at the panelling around this tiny inner hall, it's not fancy, but it does look as old as the stuff in the main rooms.

Go up to the top floor and you'll see what I mean. You get to the top of these stairs and then the panelling suddenly changes to match the walls of the third floor rooms beside the attic where we found the sword."

Ash led Holly up the stairs and straightaway saw that he was right. Not wishing to linger, they came back down, but then Ash wandered into the first of the two small second-floor rooms beyond the stairs. "Hey Callum," he called, "what do you think? Could these rooms have been divided more recently? Because taking what you said about the panelling, although more care has been taken to match the colour of the panelling in here, I reckon that the ones on these dividing walls don't match those on the outside walls."

Callum got up and walked through what had clearly been two smaller offices of late. "Yes, I think this was once one big room like the one below it. Interesting." He turned and ran down the main stairs to the first floor, and they heard him going through to the room below. "Hey, come and have a look at this," he called up to them, and when they'd joined him, he pointed to what they'd all initially thought was just an old cupboard under where the stairs were up above. "Look inside! It's like what you found, Ash. There's more space behind here than the cupboard accounts for, but I dismissed it earlier because I thought it was part of the big chimney breast."

"But it isn't," Ash agreed. "What I thought – the same as you – was that it was part of the shoulder of the chimney. Let's face it, there are enough old chimney breasts with a shoulder like that, so it's not abnormal. It's just that this isn't one of them."

"I think if I lift the floorboards at the foot of the stairs upstairs," Callum said, all eagerness, "then we should find the remains of the stairs coming down here."

Ash and Holly had donned gloves again when they first came in, so now Ash had no hesitation in helping Callum by using a second floorboard lifter. It took a bit of doing, because these boards had clearly not been moved in centuries, if ever since they'd been put in, but with a final heave, the first board came up.

"Ah-ha!" Callum exclaimed triumphantly, just as Ash gulped,

"Oh heck, no!"

Callum was immediately photographing the opening, which showed clearly a step going down, so Ash stepping backwards looking pale was lost on him. Not on Holly, though.

"Ash? What is it?" she whispered. "What did you see?"

"I didn't *see* anything," he answered equally as softly. "It's what I felt. He's down there, Holly. Our Highlander is down there."

"Then who did you find upstairs?" Holly asked worriedly, but Ash could only shrug.

There was a crack as Callum lifted the next board more easily on his own now that they'd got the first one out. He was so intent on exposing the full width of the staircase that he wasn't looking at what was actually down there until he'd put a fourth board to one side. His squeal of shock when he did look was enough to tell Holly that Ash's instincts had been spot on.

"Jesus!" Callum croaked. "How many more bloody bodies are there in this place?"

Ash leaned past him and looked down. "Well I don't know who the person was who we found upstairs, but this here looks to me like the chap who owned the sword."

"*Erm*, sorry, I should have told you. Sylvia says that one was middle-aged woman – the body upstairs, I mean. But she's old. Really old, possibly of the same era as the sword, so maybe this one is too?"

Curiosity overcoming her dread, Holly inched forwards and also looked down. A skeleton sat on the lower steps, leaning back on them, but with his head slumped forwards. He was wearing a Scotch bonnet, which was still at a jaunty angle. What looked like it might have been a linen shirt was around his shoulders, and what might have been tartan breeks remained draped on the bones of his legs. Stout leather shoes were just visible once Callum shone a torch down there, and what could once have been a bandolier of powder pouches for a musket lay diagonally across his chest. Of the musket itself, there was no sign, but in one bony hand was clasped a dirk.

"Hello Master McAllister," Holly breathed. "We finally meet."

Duncan McAllister 9

With all the digging around in the house, Duncan was praying that somebody would find him. *'Please let it be one of the good ones,'* he found himself pleading over and again. *'Please let it be someone who cares and will take me home.'* He felt foolish that it mattered so much to him now after all this time, but having been 'woken up', he was shocked at how deeply he felt the need to return to his roots. Yet the other side of him feared that it would be one of that lunatic trio who'd killed the young man, not least because Duncan had no way of knowing whether the man who did the deed had been coerced. *'Please God, I've had enough, can't you just let me go home?'* he prayed.

When they found Joan, he was much relieved. He wasn't too sure who the two men were, but he recognised the young woman standing outside the door, so he guessed from the way they were talking that they weren't anything to do with the murderer. Then he watched as people swathed in white came and took Joan away. Why was that? Did they think she had the plague or something?

However, nobody seemed overly worried, so he had to assume it was some new ritual he didn't understand. He was having trouble keeping track of people at this point, because the house would be filled with swarms of people one moment, and empty the next. There seemed to be a lot of taking samples of things, and scrapping tiny amounts off surfaces into glass tubes, but he hadn't a clue what they hoped to learn from such things.

One thing he did pick up, now that he was paying very careful attention to the people in the house, was that the two with the funny accents were called Jesse and Shea-Lea. He'd not heard such names before, so he could only assume they connected to where they had come from. Certainly, in his time on earth he'd not ever met anyone with those names. But strange names or not, they seemed to be keen to look after the nice lady, who he finally found out was called Holly. The man who was now with her a lot they called Ash, but Duncan wasn't sure if he was called after a tree, or if it was a shortening of a name he was unfamiliar with.

Whoever he was, Duncan approved of Ash. He treated Holly properly, and seemed very concerned that she was looked after. That made him a decent man in Duncan's books. But then the mad man kept turning up in the alehouse, and Duncan didn't know what to make of that. Were the decent ones unaware of how dangerous he was? That might mean that Duncan would have to push himself hard to manifest and be scary again, because he wasn't going to let that maniac kill anyone else.

Then the day came when he heard Holly with the young man in the strange white garb, and then Ash joined them. They were getting closer! Oh-so-much closer to his bones than anyone else had.

Duncan crossed his ghostly fingers and 'held' the breath he no longer had. Would they find him? *'I'm here,'* he tried to call, but that didn't seem to make much difference…or did it? The young man in white suddenly started paying more attention to where Duncan was trying to direct him, so maybe it was working.

By now the young man was on his knees examining the floorboards that were above Duncan's remains, and Duncan was so close to him he heard him say to the others, "Sylvia says that one was middle-aged woman – the body upstairs, I mean. But she's old. Really old, possibly of the same era as the sword, so maybe this one is too?"

A surge of relief ran through Duncan. He didn't know how they could possibly know that, but it gave him a whole new layer of hope if they could connect his and Joan's bones to the claymore. Yet what completely undid him was hearing Holly say, "Hello Master McAllister. We finally meet."

His name! She knew his name! To hear someone speak it after more than three hundred years, indeed coming up four, if Duncan had managed to keep any kind of count, had him sobbing in shock. He hadn't for a moment expected it to feel like that. For it to be such a jolt – such a surge of emotion. It felt as if he was on his way back to being human again. Oh, he knew he could never take physical form again. He wasn't that naive. But to simply be recognised as a person who had a name and a past after so long being just…nothing, was deeply affecting.

He heard Holly and Ash tell the young man who they called Callum that they'd better leave before his boss appeared, but Duncan followed them down to the alehouse, and listened in to their conversation with Jesse and Shea-Lea. And to his amazement, they actually seemed concerned about him. *I have to try to find a way to speak to them*, he thought, *I have to communicate to them somehow.*

Chapter 23

This time, Holly and Ash made a swift exit before Callum's colleagues arrived. As far as anyone else was concerned, Callum had found McAllister all by himself, because there was no way that either Callum or they wanted to explain why they'd been up there. Mercifully, this time, although Chesterton did arrive later, it was the osteo-archaeologist, Sylvia, and her colleagues who came out to do the inspecting and removal, and they were cheerfully enthusiastic about finding their ghostly Highlander, and far less probing in their questions.

"It sure explains why you heard ghostly footsteps running towards those stairs," Jesse said, when they told him and Shea-Lea. "That must have been their hiding place when those other men came hunting them."

"But why was his sword not with him?" Shea-Lea wondered.

However, Ash had a thought on that. "It's a monster of a thing to cart around, and as we said with Callum, those stairs must have been in regular use by the servants. Well you couldn't lug it around all the time, and leaving it on the stairs would be dangerous. Let's face it, accidentally nudging it and having it fall would have created one hell of a clatter.

So I'm wondering whether it was McAllister himself who hid it up under the eaves? With it, he'd be branded as a Scotsman. Without it, especially in borrowed clothes, he'd just be an unusually big guy – especially if he kept his mouth shut. And if he was sleeping up in the loft space, it would be to hand if he needed it, but out of the way of cursory searches. Heaven knows who the poor woman was, though. Some unfortunate servant caught up in the mayhem, no doubt."

"Could she be the one I hear running towards the stairs?" Holly wondered. "I hear what I now presume to be McAllister talking to a lad, and I assumed the runner to be that lad. But what if he wasn't? Maybe the lad was already with him? I'd have thought it would have been the lad whose bones you found, but now we know different, perhaps we need to try and find out who she was?"

"What religion would he have been? McAllister I mean," Shea-Lea asked curiously.

Jesse looked sideways at her. "It matters?"

"Well if we were considering getting someone in to say the funeral prayers for him in an attempt to quiet things down even further, it probably does," she told him. "It's odd that the woman doesn't haunt the place as much, but right now I'm just grateful we've only the one to sort out."

Ash agreed. "Just because he was in the Covenanter army, you can't take it for granted that that was his own faith. Don't forget, as so often in history, the ordinary men would have fought for the side their lord or laird fought for, regardless of their own persuasions. If our Master McAllister was a true

Highlander, he could even have been a Catholic. He would have had to keep that well hidden, of course, especially if there were many around him who did follow the Covenanting creeds devoutly, but then if he was used to keeping it quiet, it might have helped him when he found himself caught here. However, getting a local Presbyterian minister to say some prayers over where he died could actually make things worse if he's been craving a Catholic mass all these years, and vice versa."

Jesse grimaced. "And we definitely don't want to do *that*!"

Ash nodded, "And in the light of that, I think that when our guests are done upstairs, we need to use some of Holly's candles and some incense and see if I really am as connected to the spirit world as some folk think."

"Ash, is that wise?" Jesse fretted. "I don't want you falling apart on me because something nasty's got at you that I can't throw out with the drunks."

However, Ash remained firm, assuring Jesse that he'd spoken to enough spiritualists by now to know what was safe practice and what wasn't. Moreover, Holly now found out why he'd brought two cases with instruments inside to Jesse's flat for safe keeping. He must have packed them in the car when she wasn't looking when they left his place, but now he confessed that he'd been dying to play them in one of the big rooms to see what the original effect would have been like. "I've been longing to see how it felt to play a lute in a room that would have had music like that played in it," he said, his eyes shining with enthusiasm. "The acoustics from the wood panelling, you know? And yes, once I knew about the Highlander ghost, there was a part of me that was curious to see if playing a tune he'd have known would have any effect."

The forensic archaeologists finished, and Callum poked his head around the door to tell them they could lock up, adding, "I've been offered a place on their team because someone wants to do a job swop and they've the same qualifications as me. They want more of the blood and gore stuff. Me? I can't wait! This is far more me than being armpit deep in bodily fluids."

"I'm so glad," Holly said, pleased that Callum's passion for the past was going to be rewarded. "If you want to come and continue having a poke around the old place in your own time, let me know. I'll happily let you in."

With a cheerful thumbs up and thanks, Callum left, and now Holly was relieved that it was a Wednesday, meaning Shea-Lea would run the pub tonight as Jesse had his night off. Having someone as grounded as Jesse alongside Ash and herself made her feel so much better. She totally understood why Ash said that the sooner they made contact with McAllister the better, because there was always the possibility that something new would come to light that made Chesterton seal the house off altogether and demand the key to it.

On the other hand, she didn't want to be on her own up there with Ash if something did start to go peculiar. She had thought of contacting Sally, because of anyone she had more experience of doing things like this. Unfortunately, she'd belatedly remembered that this week it was Sally's daughter's birthday, and that Sally always went down to Exeter to stay with her for several days at that time. So Ash would have to manage without Sally's guidance, which Holly prayed wouldn't be a problem.

His initial preparations involved nothing more than putting some charcoal discs on the huge hearthstones in the various rooms and putting incense onto them. This wasn't like the packets of sticks that Holly had a stand of for impulse buys, especially by her younger customers. Ash had packed tiny bags of genuine resin, clearly having thought that they might be needed, and so now the old house began to fill with the scent of frankincense and myrrh, but also Greek rose and pine. Ash explained, "I don't want it to smell too 'Papist' – you know, too much like what he would have thought of as 'Roman' practices – just in case he *was* a dyed in the wool Covenanter."

"And frankincense is okay?" Jesse asked doubtfully. "Smells a bit churchy to me."

However Ash pointed out, "It was also used an awful lot in healing in the days before modern antibiotics. It genuinely does have medicinal properties – we now know it's an anti-inflammatory and anti-septic – though these days we don't expect it to cure diseases like leprosy. So if our Master McAllister was a soldier, he could well have come across it in that context. The rose is made from real rose petals, and even back then, the women of a household would probably have used dried rose petals alongside other plants like lavender as an air freshener. The pine I'm using will hopefully invoke some memory of his homeland. That's why the rose is in the big rooms, but the pine is out here towards the back where we know we've heard him."

Jesse raised his hands in surrender. "Okay, I'll shut up. You clearly know what you're doing."

However, Ash shook his head. "No, please question away. You might remind me of something I've forgotten. It's not like I've done this before. Not to this extent anyway."

Having been around Sally, Holly was far more relaxed about the incense, but what really had her sitting up on her cushion was when Ash got the cittern out of its case.

"Oh isn't that beautiful!" she exclaimed. "What lovely colours in the wood."

Ash grinned. "It is a beauty, isn't it?" He undid the other case and brought out the lute with its distinctive angled neck. "This one is a joy to play too. I'm probably best on the mandolin, but he probably never heard master musicians, just the local travelling ones, so I doubt he's going to be too critical of my playing."

She and Jesse watched as he carefully tuned the pair, then with a deep breath and crossed fingers waved at both of them, he began to play and sing. The first song, he told them, was called *The Two Sisters*, confessing that it was first written down a bit after when McAllister would have lived, but, "given that it's still doing the rounds at the folk clubs even now, sometimes known as *The Twa Sisters*, I bet it was already popular by the time it made it into print."

He moved on to a song called *The Four Marys*, about the four ladies-in-waiting called Mary who attended Mary Queen of Scots, because as he said, she was the grandmother of Charles the First who'd caused all the trouble resulting in the Civil War, so McAllister was bound to know that one. By the time he'd moved through *Sir Patrick Spence* and *The Battle of Otterburn*, Holly could have sat there all night listening to him. Ash had a lovely mellow baritone voice, not powerful but true, and to Holly this was the music he was meant to perform – she just couldn't imagine him belting out rock ballads, but then he hadn't been the vocalist of the band, she belatedly recalled.

However, nothing had happened ghost-wise. Ash paused, digging out some sheet music and propping it up on the cittern's case.

"I'm going to try this one," he said. "It's called *The Battle of Harlaw*, and it's about a battle that took place between the then Lord of the Isles and the Earl of Mar near to Aberdeen. The men from the Isles suffered a crushing defeat and this is something of a lament for them. It happened well before McAllister's time in the early fifteenth century, so hopefully he'll know it."

He checked the tuning of the lute and then launched into the song. Nothing obvious had happened by the end, but Holly felt a shift in the atmosphere of the landing where they were sitting and gestured Ash to keep going. Frantically wracking his brain for familiar songs, he launched into a song that Holly only knew by its chorus of, 'A roving, a roving, since roving's been my ru-i-n,/ I'll go no more a roving, with you fair maid.' Later Ash told her it was a shanty called the *Maid of Amsterdam*, but had probably been around in one form or another since Elizabethan times. Whether it was familiar to McAllister, or because Jesse knew it too and joined in making it feel more of a singsong, but suddenly there was something standing by the stairs. Not clear. Not fully formed. But definitely a presence.

Quickly making a professional segue into *The Parting Glass*, Ash was only at the end of the first verse before there was another voice joining his. By the second verse, Ash had gestured Jesse to continue with the main melody alongside McAllister, and he was singing a harmony. They got to the end and Ash immediately went back to the beginning again, because McAllister was getting more 'present' all the time.

As he struck the final chord, Ash left the lute sitting on his lap, but said in a friendly tone, "Hello Master McAllister. I'm glad you've joined us."

'*Ye ken ma name?*' McAllister said. '*Aye, but I'm glad that someone can finally hear me, too.*'

Ash waved a hand towards Holly. "You've been heard speaking to a person in this house. We know nothing more of you than that, but we'd like to hear more. What's your full name, and where are you from in Scotland?"

'*Ma name is Duncan McAllister o' Argyll,*' he replied, '*and I'm desperate to go home. I didn'a ever think I would spend so long away. I miss it sore.*'

"I'm sure you do," Ash sympathised. "Did you die in the fighting down here? We can ask for your bones to be taken back up north, but it would help if we could say why and where." He wasn't sure how the archaeologists would feel about that, but if necessary he was prepared to pay for the body to be transported himself.

'*I fought down here,*' McAllister confirmed. *''Twas na' that I was so verra keen to come and fight, ye understand, it was just unfortunate that the lad and I happened to be at Menstrie Castle by Glencarse when Lord Elcho took upon himself to round up men to go and fight wi' Earl Leven, as ye might ken him. Men like us dinna have much say in the matter.*'

"I did wonder if it was something like that," Ash sympathised. "Can I ask, although you were in an army commanded by the Covenanters, what were your own sympathies? Was that how *you* chose to worship, or did you just have to go along with it because it was dangerous to do otherwise?" Ash had thought long and hard about how he would phrase that question, and he'd deliberately left McAllister room to respond either way.

The ghost's sigh was audible. '*I wasn'a that bothered about the detail,*' he admitted. '*I simply didn'a like it that a king who'd scarce ever set foot in Scotland should take it upon himsel' to tell us how to worship. That he would bring in bishops from far afield who knew nothing o' how hard it was to scrape a living off the land in the Highlands. I had nought against the Catholics that I knew, all o' whom were decent, God-fearin' folk. 'Twas the fear o' having their practices rammed down our throats that I objected to.*'

Holly dared to ask, "You just mentioned the lad. Who was he? I thought I heard you talking to him, but we don't even have a name for him. Please tell us, did he die here too?"

'Ach, no,' McAllister said with what sounded like relief. *'That's ma wee cousin, Sorley McAllister, ye are talkin' about. A bonny lad and fleet o' foot, too. When the men came fer us, I made him run fer it. Canny lad that he was, the first time they came, instead o' runnin' across the garden and the streets – which would ha' guaranteed that he'd be caught – he went up onto the roof. He hid up in the angle o' the roofs behind the chimney.'*

For one awful moment, Holly thought he was going to say that this Sorley had become trapped in the chimney, then realised that the chimney breast in the smaller front room which had given her the shivers had been right by where they'd found McAllister himself. "So did he get fully away?" she asked, keeping her fingers crossed.

'Aye, he did. If he didna get all the way back home, then he died a long way from here, because I've never felt him on this side. I saw him wi' some o' our men when they made the retreat north, but they couldn'a get back into this building to find me. No' that they could ha' done anything beyond bury me, mind. Nay, only poor Goodwife Joan remained wi' me here. She doesn'a rest easy around the time she died, always tryin' to warn me o' what was comin' then. Twas n'a her fault. She knew naught o' any o' it until it was too late.'

"Was she local, then?" Jesse asked. "Not a Scot like you?"

'Goodwife Joan? Nay, she was the housekeeper o' this place. A kind and Christian soul, if a wee bit severe in her faith. I believe she used to worship at a chapel somewhere near here, though I never saw it.'

"We found Joan a few days ago," Holly said, and got an,

'I kenned ye did,' from McAllister.

"So where did you want to be buried, Mister McAllister?" Holly asked, relieved that the woman, at least, could and should be buried locally.

He turned to face her, and for the first time Holly realised that in his lifetime, he'd been a good-looking man. He had strong, slightly hawk-like features, but even now there was that hint of a twinkle in his ghostly eyes which she was sure must once have made him popular with the ladies. His slightly receding hair was neatly caught back at the nape of his neck with what looked like a leather thong, and he had a short, cropped beard that did nothing to hide his half-smile.

'Me?' he replied. *'I was hoping for a place perhaps at Inveraray, considering the amount o' legwork and riding time I put in fer the Campbell himself, but even better would ha' been to die working our family croft o'er near Tarbet and buried in the wee kirk there.'*

"And was that Presbyterian?" Ash wondered.

'Nay,' McAllister laughed. *'Episcopalian while there was such a thing, though no' o' any high degree. The good Lord only knows what it is now, mind. For a while the Covenanters in the government were good at forcing everyone down the same road.'*

"Happily, things changed back," Ash assured him. "In our time there's a mixture and its very much each man worshipping as he chooses. At the moment, thankfully, religion doesn't rule the country, though there are other places in the world where it does. So we should be able to find somewhere that's not too far from your old home."

Jesse waved his mobile at them. "I just had a look. Unfortunately, the church at Tarbet isn't a church anymore but a restaurant, but there is one at Arrochar. Would that be okay, Mister McAllister?" Like Holly, he called the ghost by his family name, not knowing if he would cause offence by being so familiar as to call him Duncan.

'Aye, Arrochar's a grand spot. That bonnie view to the mountains across the loch will do me fine. The Cobbler,' referring to the main mountain in the group, *'looks grand when its head is covered wi' snow and the sun shines on it.'*

That cheered everyone up, because at least they were in with a chance of getting him back where he wanted to be. However, Ash now had to tackle the trickier subject of why McAllister was still haunting the place.

"Is there a particular reason why you can't move on?" he asked cautiously. "Forgive us for asking, but not every soldier who died far from home still lingers there. Something has caused you to stay, so can you tell us what it is?"

''Twas the betrayal,' he answered with anger in his voice. *'Goodwife Joan took us in when I tripped in that thrice-be-damned rabbit hole and broke ma ankle.'* He gave a snort of disgust. *'Me, Duncan McAllister, who took cattle from under the noses o' many o' the Campbell's baliffs when times were hard. Me, who could sneak into enemy camps and steal plans from under their noses. To be laid low by a bluidy rabbit! The indignity o' it! If there had been e'en an old man tending*

the plot, I doubt the cheeky wee bastard would ha' made his home in the vegetable plot, so I wasn'a expecting it. Oh, I ken that rabbits will rob you blind o' anything they fancy, but they don't normal make their damned camp in your plot.'

Holly was struggling not to giggle at his indignation. For a fierce warrior like him, it had to be humiliating for that to have been his downfall, but it was funny.

'*Aye, lass ye might well smile,*' he said, causing Holly to clap a hand over her mouth, but he said it without rancour. '*At least wee Sorley caught the culprit and we had him in a stew along wi' his family. Mighty tasty he was too. That wee vixen Mary had a sure hand wi' the cook pot. It's a shame she wasn'a so clever wi' her loose tongue.*'

The three living exchanged worried glances. That sounded as though someone had betrayed them.

"You were betrayed?" Jesse asked tentatively.

McAllister gave a ghostly huff of disgust. '*Aye, we were.*' He was so present now that they saw him roll his eyes. '*Daft wee Mary. Ach, she dinna mean to cause the trouble she did – though she did mean to have Sorley and me out o' the hoose. There was some daft plan going on in her head, but 'thought' was somethin' she had trouble with, if ye ken ma meanin'.*'

Ash was the first to catch on to what he meant. "She said the wrong thing to the wrong person? Didn't realise the extent of trouble it was going to cause?"

McAllister nodded. '*No' a lassie over blessed wi' looks, she was easy prey fer any lad who gave her the eye. And o' course, every local lad o' her own age had long since disappeared into one army or the other. So she was already feelin' a bit left out. Other lassies were longing fer their sweethearts to come back – or so Goodwife Joan told me not long afore it all went to Hell in a handcart – but Mary hadn'a had one t' start wi'. She was explainin' to me why Mary had taken to goin' out o' an evening. I was concerned, ye see, that a lass on her own was easy prey should a new troop o' soldiers come through. But Joan said that all was quiet. Seems she didn'a know of Mary havin' designs on one o' the burgesses' sons, no' that a lad o' that degree wouldh'a looked twice at a servant.'*

He snorted in disgust. *'The worst o' it is, they weren'a even proper soldiers. They were clubmen,'* He saw their incomprehension and explained, *'Local men trying to chase soldiers o' both sides away from stealing the crops and fodder. Three o' them there were, and then more, and me wi' a game leg and no' able to get to ma claymore – no' that it would ha made any difference to the sword that ended up in ma belly.'* They saw him give a shudder. *'Animals, that's what they were, to do that to both women.'*

"What? Even to Mary who'd told them?" Ash asked, horrified.

McAllister grimaced. *'Like I said, Mary wasn'a the best judge o' men. I reckon that laddie had already had his way wi' her, but while she was dreamin' o' a fine wedding gown, he was just thinkin' that she was his way o' proving' what a grand man he was to have around to his betters. Or gi'en what a fool man he was, probably just his pa.*

'Listenin' to what was said after I passed on, he sent a man to the back door, makin' out that he was a callin'

wi' a message fer Mary, but he saw enough to guess that there were men in the place.' He gave a ghostly tut. *'Mind, Mary had already told them that, but it says how little they thought o' her that they had to check fer themselves. And he spotted that the garden had been tended. That someone had been doin' some deep diggin'. Well he didn'a need to be a seer to work out that Joan wi' her stiff back hadn'a done that, and Mary's hands didn'a look like they'd been grubbin' in the soil, either.'*

"Ouch," Jesse sympathised. "What rotten luck. So I'm guessing he came back with his pals and decided to search the place?"

'They did. Twice we got lucky and they didn'a find us. The third time I fought them off as best I could, but like I said, ma game leg hampered me and I didn'a do so well, so Joan and I died. Tsk, they wouldn'a bury her in order to cover up what was murder, no' because they saw her as a traitor to the cause. Idiots! The master burgess wasn'a happy about it when he came the next day. I was past speakin' to him, obviously, but I watched and I heard. Aye but he was furious, because the family o' the house had given money to the cause. He made them make it seem like ruffians had broken in to the house and wrecked it. 'Twas them who hid poor Joan's body. He didn'a want anyone to ask how come she'd been killed, see? Thieves would ha' taken stuff, might ha' beaten her, but no' killed her.'

"But what of Mary?" Holly asked. "Surely she could have told them later what had happened?"

Yet McAllister shook his head. *'I dinn'a ken why she never came back, but I can guess. Sorely stayed in the house after they'd all gone and wept o'er me. I heard him saying that he was glad the men dragged Mary off wi' them and then she went down the stairs in a tumble. He was a good lad, but that day he prayed she'd survived the fall and they passed her around the camp fer what she'd done. He was broken-hearted at losin' me, and 'twas the grief speakin'. He cursed their wretched souls too fer murdering me wi' a sword in ma back. 'Twas no death fer a fighter like me, see? I was too heavy fer him to move, and there was nobody he could call to help carry me outside fer even a simple grave in the garden.'*

"So when did you get sealed up in the stairs?" Jesse wondered.

'Ach, that was when the first o' the household's men came back.' He gave a ghostly chuckle. *'I may ha' scared the shite out o' them, cause back then I was aye angry. So rather than move me, they sealed up the stairs. They told the lady o' the hoose, when she eventually came back, that the stairs were too damaged by shot to be repaired. If there'd ha' been a man comin' back any time sooner, I ha' no doubt I'd ha' been found a shallow grave. Instead, it took until the next generation fer any work to be done, and that was more about makin' the attic into a proper extra floor. I dinn'a ken why they didn'a open up the servants' stairs to the first floor again, but they didn'a.'*

"You weren't haunting them by any chance?" Ash asked, rather amused by the thought of McAllister causing havoc with a new owner's pretentions to grandeur with the extra floor. The Highlander seemed possessed of a mischievous sense of humour that wouldn't take kindly to pomposity.

The ghostly bushy eyebrows went up and even they could see the twinkle in his ghostly eyes. *'Me?*

...Aye, well I might ha'. I was still seethin' over the betrayal. Joan didn'a deserve what Mary did, even if wasn'a fully intentional. Sorley told me she had some daft idea that I was taking Joan back to Scotland wi' us, and didn'a want to be left alone. Ach, I wish I had made the offer to Joan seeing as she took the first cut o' the sword meant fer me. I didn'a want anyone to die fer me, let alone a woman.'

Chapter 24

They wrapped their meeting with McAllister up fairly quickly after that, because Ash was starting to feel the strain, but they promised him that they would return. For the remainder of the evening, something was niggling away at the back of Holly's mind, but it stubbornly refused to come any further forward. It flitted like some ghost of its own around the fringes of her brain, plaguing her, and by the time she fell into bed she was thoroughly frustrated. So it was typical that a bit after three in the morning she woke and sat bolt upright in bed, suddenly realising what it was, and why she had been so completely wrong-footed time and again.

"This isn't Ange," she said aloud, then thinking the same words over and over.

Holly and Angie had been in one another's lives since they were little girls, so if anyone knew Angie – really, truly *knew* her – it was Holly, and that was why none of this had made sense to her. Nor could she have anticipated it because there were none of Angie's normal tell-tales to go by. Too fidgety to stay another moment in bed, Holly got up, and went and put the kettle on, fishing in her bag for one of her sachets of herb tea, and it was as she was sitting at the dressing table-come-desk that her thoughts became more rational.

Angie had always been an impulse girl. It didn't matter whether it was buying a new summer dress or the latest boyfriend, Angie went with her emotions. Moreover, yes, Angie was selfish. And yes, she was often downright thoughtless. But the one thing Holly could never have accused her of was being conniving. Again…yes, she had been what could only be described as a bloody nightmare for the employers who had crossed her, but who had been the one who had instigated the tribunals? Not Angie, but her dad! That's what all the chaos had driven out of Holly's head. *Norris* had been the one who had thrown the tantrum over someone mistreating his little girl – as he saw it. Which was pretty two-faced considering the way he treated those who worked for him, but then Norris always had thought he was the ruler of his own petty kingdom.

Angie had never *planned* anyone's downfall in her life. Indeed Angie couldn't plan her way out of a wet paper bag, let alone anything like this. So where had this sudden burst of restraint come from? Because the one thing that was really screaming at Holly right now was the discrepancy in the timing of who knew what and when about that bloody holiday. The way Angie had bounced in and told her about the surprise holiday had been so typically Angie. That was why Holly had never doubted that 'Topher' had dropped it on her out of the blue. But right now Holly was desperately trying to work out exactly how long before that Angie had told Meryl. Because if there was another thing that Holly knew beyond any doubt about Angie, it was that she could never curb her enthusiasm. Angie keeping that holiday secret for weeks and weeks went beyond everything that Holly had ever know Angie be capable of doing. So as she worked backwards, Holly realised that the gap between her knowing and Meryl knowing was far less than she'd assumed before.

Going back over those weeks just before the shop opened, Holly was now starting to get a very bad feeling. If Angie really *had* planned the holiday and booked it – let alone so far in advance – Holly could now see that there was no way that the Angie she knew could have kept quiet about it. There had been a point, just as Holly had been working the last week or so of her old job, where if she was honest, she hadn't been paying much attention to what Angie said beyond anything that affected the shop. But there were odd niggling memories of Angie saying that she thought that Topher was keeping a surprise from her, and that he was acting a bit strange. Angie being Angie, she was convinced it was something wonderful, but what was now borne in on Holly was that Angie's reaction, upon discovering that it was the holiday, had been absolutely her to the last squeak of excitement.

Angie couldn't fake enthusiasm. She either had it or she didn't. You were never in any doubt as to whether she wanted to do something or not.

Therefore sitting in the darkened room, sipping her hot peppermint tea, Holly was sure that whoever had booked that holiday, it hadn't and couldn't have been Angie. On the other hand, Wesley had said that Chris/Topher had known about it before then, and had thought Angie fickle for upping and leaving before the shop's opening. But now Holly was wondering who *did* tell Chris about the holiday? Had it actually been Angie in person? Or had it come by text or email? Something along the lines of, 'Surprise! I've booked us a holiday of a lifetime!' Which she now realised could have come from someone other than Angie?

Holly was no tech genius, but she did know that people who really knew their stuff could easily get into other people's emails and phones, especially when it was someone like Angie, whose pin numbers were always 1234, and her passwords were all 'Princess Angie'. Get one and you got them all, access to Angie's entire online life – and Angie did a lot online far beyond social media posting, including shopping, and messaging. How hard would it have been for someone to send messages to Chris about the holiday so that *he* thought they'd come from Angie? And similarly, when it came to Angie knowing, had Chris really told her to her face, or had that come through a message of some kind?

The more Holly thought about it, the more convinced she became that someone behind the scenes, a third person, was pulling the strings. And she knew why this had finally come to mind – what had dredged the right memories to the surface. It had been Duncan McAllister talking about betrayal. In his case, young Mary had been foolish, thinking a young man would think more of her if she informed on the men hiding in the house, but what that had dragged out of her subconscious was that what had gone on with Angie and Chris had been so much more planned. *Someone* – and she was increasingly certain that it hadn't been Angie – had been planning this with meticulous detail.

Who that was she hadn't the faintest idea right now, let alone whether or not they knew them in real life. But whoever it was had wormed their way into the deepest heart of Chris and Angie's online lives, and that was something Holly knew Angie wouldn't even know how to begin to do. Every single time Angie upgraded to the latest thing in mobile phones, it took her weeks to work out how to use it, as Holly had witnessed over and again. Therefore, the thought that Angie could have created even the simplest of online subterfuges was just ridiculous, and that meant that Angie was innocent. Maybe not innocent of being thoughtless in clearing off on holiday leaving Holly in the lurch, but certainly innocent of plotting a murder. Holly wasn't sure how she was ever going to prove this, but in her heart of hearts she was kicking herself for ever having thought so badly of her friend.

By the time she felt she could reasonably go and knock on Ash's door to tell him all of this, her thoughts had clarified some more. Somewhat bleary-eyed and still nursing his first coffee courtesy of the in-room supplies, nonetheless Ash listened carefully to what Holly was saying, only at the end wondering, "Are you sure you're not making excuses for someone who's been a lifetime friend? Please don't shout me down. It's just that I've realised you're someone who takes your loyalty to friends very seriously. You feeling bad about doubting your friend is nothing to be ashamed about. I just want you to be sure *why* you're suddenly saying this."

Yet Holly was already vigorously shaking her head. "No Ash, you don't get it. There was a reason why the teachers at school always used to say that Angie was better at coursework than exams – it was because *I* did her coursework for her. She couldn't stick at even that for long enough to complete a project. Oh, she had ideas, but half the time they weren't even relevant! I think our teachers knew that, and so did her mum and dad, but nobody ever said anything because it was hard to prove. Ange could never work out even how to tackle a project beyond the first burst of enthusiasm – if she ever got that far – whereas I'd have more than one idea. So I used to do the research, then I'd write it out and dictate it to Angie. It meant the teachers got all of Angie's shockingly bad punctuation and spelling, and any time she'd say, 'Well I'd never say that,' we'd agree that she'd put her version in.

"But do you see what I'm getting at? This is the girl who couldn't even decide whether she wanted to argue for Nero being a bad emperor or not. In what world has she suddenly become blessed with organisation skills, and for want of a better word – heaven help me – the brains, to pull off something like this? I feel almost as bad for saying this as I do for thinking the worst of her, but while Angie is wonderfully decorative, by God, at times she can be dim. We were doing something on the Falklands' War in school, and she honestly thought the Falkland Islands were where Orkney is. She hadn't a clue that they were on the other side of the world. Yet you expect me to believe that she could organise a surprise holiday to the Caribbean, of all places, including a complicated itinerary around several islands, *and* cover up a murder so that it seems like she was out of the country when it happened? No, I'm sorry. Just no!"

Ash was sitting back taking in her words. "Put like that, I'm beginning to see what you mean. It just doesn't fit, does it? And yet who had a motive for killing Tom if not her?"

Holly gave a huff. "I think that's something Chesterton needs to do to earn his keep, don't you? He needs to do a deep dive into Tom's life and find out if anyone else had it in for him. Because it seems to me that finding his body in Angie's new home has pushed the investigation all Angie's way, and maybe it shouldn't be."

They were still mulling it over when they went to join Jesse and Shea-Lea after breakfast, and of the two, it was Shea-Lea who was hardest to convince. "You know what I said about narcissists being clever and conniving?" she reminded Holly.

"Yes I do. But no mental health complaint can miraculously gift someone with the brains to organise something that they've never shown an inkling of having before," Holly riposted. "I'm sure you *are* right. Angie probably does have more than a bit of the narcissist in her. But the worst traits you were talking about all relate to what's gone on in the last month or two. Yes, Angie could throw massive tantrums, and yes, they did involve her actually throwing things. But there's a massive difference between lobbing a flower vase at someone when in a snit, and whacking them over the head with an ancient sword up in a place where you've *planned* that nobody will find them for ages."

They had to concede she had a point, however Jesse pressed her with, "But who else had a motive?"

Holly grimaced. "I know it looks bad, but honestly Jesse, I don't think Angie had given Tom a second thought once Chris, or Topher as she knew him, had put that wedding ring on her finger. That was something she always craved, you see. That respectability that went with being Mrs Somebody-or-other. Angie knew she'd never have the stellar career, not in her heart of hearts. Oh, she may have muttered stuff about it, but she never thought she'd get it – deep down she knew she didn't have the ability, even if she'd never have said so to anyone else, not even me. But having what her mum had, that being the wife of a respected businessman, or at least of someone of wealth, that was an *acquired* status she thought was within her grasp – and Topher gave it to her, Tom didn't. So there was nothing that Tom had to give her that she really wanted. He certainly couldn't match Chris financially once that lottery win kicked in."

That seemed to finally win them over, but as Ash said, "How on earth we prove it wasn't Angie is another matter altogether, because it's hardly as though we have someone else to put in her place."

As if that wasn't enough excitement for the day, the four of them were sitting down to an early evening meal while the bar staff were in, when Wesley rang Holly.

"Can I come and get you in about fifteen minutes?" were his first words.

Taken aback, Holly could only ask, "Why?"

"Because you're the one person who might be able to talk Angie down," was not the reply she was expecting.

"Angie? Down? Down from where? You're not making any sense Wesley."

"I'm in a police car with DI Chesterton, and we're on the way to Mevagissy, or near there, anyway."

Holly had put her phone down on the table and onto speaker for the others to hear, meaning Ash responded with, "Oh no, don't tell us that Angie tracked Chris down?"

"This is DI Chesterton speaking. I'm afraid it's a bit more complicated than that. Yes, Mrs Sykes is at the house Mr Sykes recently bought. Luckily, he and the others weren't there at the time, because he's having some building work done. But Mrs Sykes is up on the roof threatening to throw herself off. There's a local trained negotiator down there as we speak, but they feel it would be helpful to have someone she knows there. Mr DiPaoli is with me to go to help Mr Sykes, but it's *Mrs* Sykes we need you for, Holly."

"I'm not letting her go down there on her own," Ash said firmly, "and there won't be enough room for three of us in the back – at least not in comfort for a long drive like that. I presume there's another officer with you, DI Chesterton?"

"My DS."

"Then I'll meet you on the main road through Ledbury and we can go in convoy. I'm driving a Range Rover registration…"

It took a bit more convincing for Chesterton to agree to Ash driving Holly, but once he knew that Ash had taken an advanced driving course, he finally relented.

"Come on," Ash said, grabbing Holly's hand. "We've just got time to get to the car before they come screaming into town with the blues-and-twos going."

Luckily, most of their clothes were still at the flat, even if they were sleeping across at the hotel, so they managed to grab an overnight bag each, and get to the car in time.

For Holly, the next couple of hours passed in a terrifying flash. Unused to driving on motorways, let alone at the speed Chesterton's DS was driving at, she was both grateful and relieved that she was with Ash, who confidently kept up without ever seeming reckless. The worst were the last few miles down to Mevagissey, because by now it was dark, and they were on narrower roads.

By the time they shot into the gateway of a substantial house just on the outskirts of the tiny town, Holly thought she'd be lucky to have her knees hold her up when she stepped out of the car, they were shaking that badly.

"Take a moment," Ash said firmly as he switched off the engine. "Chesterton needs to find out what's going on first," for which Holly was very thankful.

It didn't take Chesterton long to come and fetch them, and they walked around the large white-rendered house to where a generous lawn swept off into the night. There were lights belonging to the house already illuminating the garden by the house, and there were portable spotlights set up by the police shining back up at the house. As she turned to look at it, Holly realised that on this side it rose to three floors because the ground fell away at the back, meaning that what they'd come in on was actually the first floor, and there, up on the flat roof of the circular tower-like protrusion of the top floor was Angie.

"Oh God," Holly involuntarily gasped, because it was a long way down from there. They had to be right by the sea, because she could hear the waves on the rocks, though they were invisible in the darkness, but even that couldn't blot out the sound of Angie's sobs.

"Angie," she could hear the lady negotiator saying gently. "We really need you to come down from there. It's not safe for you. Let us help you."

Yet Angie was shaking her head vigorously. "No. You can't help me. Nobody can. Not now. You'll never believe me. You'll never believe that he made me do it."

Chesterton leaned in to Holly and said, "Apparently she's been saying that over and over. The negotiator has even offered to get Mr Sykes here to speak to her, but that nearly ended in disaster. She became totally distraught, telling us that he mustn't come near here. Heaven knows what's going through her mind at the moment, but we need to get her down from there and soon or she's going to get hyperthermia, and if her attention drifts as she gets more exhausted, there's a real danger she could fall."

Holly noticed that they'd got a huge inflatable cushion underneath where Angie was, making it look like some sick version of a bouncy castle, but it would still be amazing if she avoided serious injury from falling.

"Come on," Chesterton said, gently taking her arm and guiding her inside. "We'll get you to the balcony right beneath her. There's another of my Cornish colleagues in there, but she's responded better to another woman and at a distance, so we haven't pushed any harder."

"What do I say to her?" Holly pleaded. "I don't want to tip her over the edge by saying the wrong thing."

"Just talk to her the way you used to, as friends," he advised. "My colleague in the room will prompt you if necessary, but you might get through to her in a way we're failing to."

Far from convinced, and glad that Ash was following, even if he wouldn't be out on the balcony with her, Holly climbed the beautiful polished wood staircase, and went in to what was undoubtedly the master bedroom suite. Even in the dark, she could see what had drawn Chris to this house. A slightly more than semi-circular room beyond the bedroom itself had windows all around, and must have fabulous views in the daytime. For Laura, with her limited mobility, it would be not only a place to connect with the outside world, but somewhere where she could watch her sons playing in the garden below.

Now, though, the patio sliding doors to both balconies of the bedroom were open. The main lights were off, but bedside lights were on allowing Holly to see the four police who were already in the room.

"I'm so glad you've come," a woman amongst them said softly. "Come on, I'll take you out there." She stepped out onto the balcony and said in reassuring tones, "Angie, Holly's here to see you. She just wants to talk, okay? She wants to make sure you're all right."

Holly took a wobbly step out onto the balcony and was immediately aware of how bloody cold it was. The wind coming in off the sea wasn't that icy for the time of the year, but in this elevated spot it felt downright Arctic. "Ange? Ange, it's me, Hol'. What's up? Why are you up there?"

"He made me do it," Angie wailed.

"Who did, mate? Who are you talking about?"

For a moment there were just more wracking sobs, and then Angie said, "*Him*! He's evil, Hol', pure bloody evil. He makes out he's everyone's friend, but he's not. He's played us all. …He gets into your head. …Gets into your life. Your bank accounts. …He makes you look so bad, so wicked. …And there he is, dripping the poison into other people's ears."

Holly was aghast. She couldn't imagine who she was talking about. The one thing she was sure of was that it wasn't Chris. Not because she thought Angie was beyond telling lies to save herself, but because by now Chris had been proven to be the victim.

Teeth chattering with the cold, Holly nonetheless moved out to the glass barrier of the balcony so that she could look up fully at Angie. Never having had much of a head for heights, Holly had to be resolute and not look out or down, only up.

"Ange, you know I hate heights. Won't you at least come down here to talk to me. I'm getting all sorts of wobbles being out here," she said, and got a thumbs up from the negotiator inside. "Come on, wriggle your way a bit more this way. God knows how you got up there, but if you hang on to the guttering, you should be able to get your feet onto the top of the balcony rail. I'll catch you, don't worry."

For a moment, it seemed as if Holly had got through to her. Angie had begun a bit of a shuffle in the right direction, and then she froze.

"Ange? Ange? What is it?" Holly called worriedly, bothered by the way Angie was staring down at the people below like a rabbit caught in the headlights.

"Too late," she heard Angie croak through her sob-wracked throat. "He's here! He's here! It's too late for me. Run, Holly, run!" and she jumped.

Chapter 25

Caught off guard, Holly heard her own scream alongside Angie's, but then she found herself looking out into the darkness. Just for an instant, among the running figures, she saw him. Saw him running away when everyone else was running towards where Angie had fallen. Saw him looking over his shoulder and up, and if that expression wasn't a laugh she really was losing the plot.

Ash dashed out onto the balcony, took her in his arms and pulled her inside, immediately wrapping a couple of thick blankets around her shaking shoulders. Yet Holly caught his hand as he made to usher her out in the wake of the police. "I know who it is," she whispered to him. "I know who did it…and I think I know how."

"What?" Ash looked at her in shock. "Who?"

"It's been staring me in the face," Holly told him, even as they ran for the stairs, desperate to get down to Angie and make sure she'd survived the fall. "It's Wesley!"

She expected Ash to protest and question her, so his simple "oh!" of understanding encouraged her. "He's a bloody software expert," she panted as they ran. "How did I not remember that? Of anyone, he must be able to get inside people's online lives –

especially when they're as computer illiterate as Angie. It would have been simple for him to manipulate her social media posts. I bet he even shut her out of her own accounts so that she *couldn't* post anything from the Caribbean."

They'd reached the ground floor and dashed out of the patio doors to find paramedics lifting a howling Angie off the inflatable, clearly in terrible pain but thankfully alive.

Chesterton saw them and came to them. "She's got a badly broken leg – gone in three places, apparently – and she's broken a wrist too, but considering how far she fell, she's been lucky."

"Where's Wesley?" Holly demanded.

"Mr DiPaoli? Why? He's..." Chesterton was starting to point behind him and then froze as he realised that Wesley wasn't there.

"You need to tell whoever is with Chris – Mr Sykes – and his family that they mustn't let Wesley anywhere near them," Holly said urgently.

"For God's sake please radio them," Ash insisted. "They're in danger. He's the real killer. DiPaoli is the murderer! We'll explain, but please make sure that family stays safe."

Looking askance at them, nonetheless Chesterton turned – possibly convinced as much by Wesley's sudden disappearance as Holly's words – and spoke to one of the Cornish officers, who was heard relaying the information on to his colleagues. As the ambulance took Angie away, Chesterton gestured them back into the house, and when they reached the dining room, switched on the lights and waved them to take a seat. "I think you'd better explain," he said, beckoning his sergeant over too, who began taking notes.

A WPC appeared from somewhere with mugs of hot coffee for them all as Holly worked her way through everything she'd already told Ash, Jesse, and Shea-Lea. At first she could see that the detectives were sceptical. However, the more she spoke, the more they began to take her seriously. When she got to the point of talking about who had told who about the holiday and how, explaining that Wesley could undoubtedly know all of Chris' online life, she saw that they were finally getting it.

"Even if Angie had done something daft like losing her phone down the loo," Holly said with a sad laugh, "– and it wouldn't be the first time she's done that – the first thing she'd do is go and buy another one. And she never went anywhere without her address book precisely because she had done things like that, or wiping her contacts off her phone by accident, so many times she knew she needed things written down. The only reason Angie wouldn't contact me or her mum and dad would be because she was so far off the grid that it wasn't possible – and Angie hates wild, remote places, so she'd have had to be dragged there kicking and screaming – or she was too bloody frightened to.

"As for what would do that, for a start, suddenly finding that she'd been cut off from everyone would seriously rattle her. But I don't think this all started when they flew out. I reckon Wesley had already got his claws into her well before then. He may not have made it obvious, because knowing Angie, she'd never have been so bouncy and happy about the holiday if she'd known someone was blackmailing her over it, but I'd bet he was already manipulating stuff behind her back."

The sergeant, whose surname was Morton, chipped in to ask, "But what was his motive for blackmailing her? She only has money by virtue of being married to…Oh!"

Ash sighed. "I think you're seeing it now, aren't you? Angie may have been the tool to bring him down, but Chris was the target all along."

Morton shook his head. "But what motive was there for killing Tom Cavanaugh?"

Holly could only shrug. "You'll have to get that out of Wesley yourselves, and especially how he lured Tom up to the flat and managed to kill him with that bloody great sword, but I think you'll find that the motive was money. Not any from Tom, because he almost certainly couldn't match Wesley in terms of wages, not with what software writers like Wesley get paid. No, I fear poor Tom was murdered just to throw the blame onto Angie or Chris, and I don't think Wesley was overly bothered which one of them it was as long as he benefitted from it in the end."

"You said it was a massive blow to the head that did the damage," Ash said, looking at the detectives, "so given he's not the biggest of men, I don't think you need to find a way for him to have plunged the sword into Tom. With the weight of that thing, if Wesley had hauled it up on some rope and dropped it on Tom, it might have done the job. Did anyone check the beams up there? I noticed that there were some big old crossbeams for the roof in that room. He wouldn't have got anything like a screw easily into old oak like that, so you're probably only looking for rope marks."

Chesterton grunted. "I'll send the team back in." He didn't look best pleased that they might have dropped the ball on that one.

"There's something else, too," Ash said. "You told us that Chris changed all his bank passwords and stuff in person at the main branch in London. To me that screams that he'd worked out that someone was manipulating him. I know Holly probably hasn't had the need to do anything like that, but I've got a decent amount of money in the bank, and the first thing I was advised to do when I had an acrimonious split with a toxic ex was to change things. But I just went on the phone to the bank to change passwords and stuff. I didn't need to go there in person and prove who I was.

"For Chris to go there, possibly clutching his passport in his hand to prove who he was, means he thought he'd *need* to. Don't you see? He must have thought he was going to be locked out of his own bank accounts. Well he might not know Angie as well as Holly does, but even so, I think that having lived with her for over a year, he'd be pretty certain that she didn't have what it took to do something like that to him.

"But if he'd become suspicious of his old mate Wesley, who he knew full well could make computers sit up and do tricks, then the last thing he'd want to happen would be the bank contacting Wesley by phone thinking *he* was Chris – because Wesley had undoubtedly got into the account online and changed the number to his own – and the real Chris was the imposter. Them mistakenly contacting Wesley to tell him that someone had been trying to change the access to what he might well have already made into *his* accounts in all but name – you know, changing address and stuff – would be the last thing Chris would want to happen, because that would tip Wesley off that Chris was on to him.

"Don't forget, at that stage Wesley didn't have to change the *name* on the accounts. To the outside world they could still appear to be Chris Sykes'. But in all other respects, he probably had got control over them. The point at which Wesley would have to change the name was if Chris died, and the bank got informed and automatically closed the accounts. And let's not fool ourselves, if Wesley could kill Tom in cold blood, Chris wouldn't have lived for long once Wesley got what he wanted. But by then, Wesley could have drained them to next to nothing, moving the money – seemingly legitimately – into an off-shore account, or wherever, where he and only he had access to them.

"I'm convinced *that's* why Chris had to do it in person, and I bet that's also why the bank was so wary of you when you asked for details of Chris' accounts and asking when passwords got changed. If Chris had already reported fraudulent activity to them, they'd want to be very sure they were talking to real policemen, and forgive me for saying this, but some of your colleagues haven't been exactly squeaky clean in the past, have they? Chris might not have told the bank exactly who Wesley was, and with good reason, because Wesley could no doubt create a new identity for himself in the blink of an eye. Giving the bank one specific name might only have triggered Wesley into creating a different identity for himself to get around it, if he hasn't done that already in anticipation of leaving the UK and starting a life of luxury elsewhere. So if Chris wanted to be extra careful, he'd have instructed the bank to warn anyone and everyone off, meaning they'd want to be doubly sure *you* were who you said you were."

"Bloody hell," Chesterton groaned. "Right. We'd better put out an alert for the detention of Mr DiPaoli, then."

"Can we go and see Angie?" Holly begged before they vanished. "She'll really want to see someone she knows."

Chesterton spoke to one of the other officers who confirmed that Angie would be on her way to Plymouth, as the nearest large hospital, but arranged for the officer who would be waiting to take Angie's statement to let Holly in.

It was another long drive in the dark, but now Ash was taking the country roads much more steadily to Holly's relief.

"They won't let us straight in to see her because they'll be stabilising her first," he reassured her, "so there's no point in risking life and limb trying to get there fast. I'm guessing we'll be sitting in the corridor for a fair while."

With that in mind, he pulled into an all-night garage and got sandwiches and muffins each, plus two large takeaway coffees, along with fuel.

"If it's anything like every other hospital I've come across, the coffee will be awful," he joked to

Holly, as he handed her the food and put the cups in the holders between their seats. "In the morning, we can go out and find somewhere decent to have breakfast, but we need something to keep us going until then."

As he'd predicted, they spent most of the rest of the night sitting waiting for Angie to come out of surgery. She was going to be spending a long time up to her hip in plaster, and when they did finally see her she was a pathetic sight. Two rapidly swelling and colouring black eyes were the least of her physical injuries, and her nose had had to be reset from when she'd landed face down. Her right arm was also encased in plaster up to the elbow, and all in all she looked a sorry state. But more than that, Holly was worried about her mental state. Nothing really permanently bad had ever been allowed to touch Angie, and so she had no experience of coping with something that her father's money couldn't whisk away.

The moment she saw Holly, Angie's good hand shot out towards her and she burst into tears. As Holly grasped it and began murmuring soothing words, Ash stood back, watching. It was another side of the two women's relationship he was seeing played out, and it struck him that for all of Angie's supposed confidence, what he was seeing was an almost childlike need on Angie's part for Holly's support. He left them to it after a bit, and went to call Jesse, who'd insisted that they be kept informed.

"It's made it a bit clearer to me why Angie insisted that Holly be involved with the shop," he told Jesse and Shea-Lea. "I didn't get it before, but I suspect that in her own way, Angie has no more confidence in herself than Holly does. From what Holly's told me while we were driving down, Angie's parents alternately smother her and then ignore her – or at least her dad does, and he rules the roost. I reckon Holly is as much Angie's anchor as the other way around, the one whom *she* knows will always be there."

"Hmm," Shea-Lea's murmur came down the phone at him. "That would explain why she never told Holly the truth about it being her mum who 'rescued' Holly all those years ago. If in her own strange way Angie is dependent on Holly, the last thing she'd want would be for Holly to storm off and leave her because she'd been lied to. Easier to just say nothing."

"I think Angie's dad does a lot of laying down the law," Ash carried on, "but it sounds as if he flies off in a temper, then the mum calms him down, at which point he opens up his wallet and hopes that if he throws enough cash at whatever the problem was, it'll just go away, along with whatever hurt he's caused in the process. The trouble is, life doesn't work like that. Harsh words can linger longer and causing deeper damage than any physical hurt."

Shea-Lea gave a snort of disgust. "That must've been horribly confusing for Angie when she hit her teens, though. There'd have been no stability. No sense of where the boundaries lay. I'd bet good money on her having acted up a lot to try and find out where her parents stood – you know, that stuff you do as a kid in the hope that mum or dad will actually say no, 'cause you don't really want to do it that much, you just want to test how far you can go."

Ash heard Jesse's laugh, and his response of, "I did that a few times. Got the rough end of my dad's temper for it, too, but I always knew where I stood. Poor Angie. Benign indifference most of the time isn't what you need from your parents. No wonder she's a mess."

"But poor Holly too," Shea-Lea said firmly. "Guys, we have to make sure that Holly doesn't get sucked back into Angie's life as her carer, because if she does, she might never get away again. She doesn't realise just how much she's been doing that or for how long, so it will be too easy to simply fall back into that pattern of behaviour – and Holly needs to start having her own life!"

"Don't you worry," Ash said fiercely, "I'm not going to let that happen. We'll make sure that Angie is taken care of, but Holly's new life starts now!"

He'd have been rather surprised, had he been able to see them when they rang off, because Jesse was twirling Shea-Lea around in their lounge doing a happy dance. His beloved uncle, who was more like a brother, being together with the new friend they'd found was the best outcome they could wish for.

For Holly, it was a wearing and anxious day. Angie was far from her normal self since she was in tears most of the time. Even the female constable who was trying to take her statement eventually gave up, saying she'd come back again later, because Angie was largely incoherent. So it was a blessed relief when another policeman appeared just after midday with Angie's mum and dad in tow, having been blue-lighted down to Cornwall. As they swarmed to the bedside and began fussing over Angie, Holly was able to breathe a sigh of relief and leave the room.

To her amazement, Ash was still there waiting for her. She'd half expected him to have disappeared and found a hotel room, which she wouldn't have blamed him for, having driven such a long way and then been up all of the night holding her hand. The fact that he hadn't left her to it was such a strange new experience that for a moment she didn't know what to say to him. Luckily there was no need for words. He came and wrapped her in a hug and said, "I've got a hotel room booked for us. Come on, it's not far away. Let's go and get a proper meal and then you can crash."

Too tired to talk much, they found a place doing all-day breakfasts and then retreated to the hotel where they fell asleep almost as soon as they'd showered and flopped into bed. The fact that Ash had booked a double room didn't even register with Holly, she was that exhausted. Only when she woke up to discover him snuggled up against her did reality sink in, and she was far from objecting. Rolling over and cuddling into him, she thought that maybe at last her luck had changed, and even if it hadn't, she was going to enjoy it while it lasted – these last few weeks had proven that you could plan to the Nth degree and still everything could go wrong. Maybe letting fate take its course would be worth trying for once?

Chapter 26

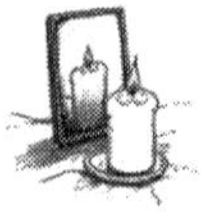

When they'd both woken up and discovered that it was already early evening, they made their way downstairs and availed themselves of the hotel's restaurant. Neither wanted to go far, so it was a bit of a shock to see Chris walking in through the restaurant door – Holly hadn't realised anyone knew where they were until Ash admitted that he'd kept Chesterton informed.

"I owe you such a debt," Chris said gratefully, coming to sink into a spare seat at their table. "They've arrested Wesley, meaning Laura and the kids are safe now, so I had to come and thank you. Honestly Holly, if you hate the sight of me, I wouldn't blame you, but DI Chesterton tells me it was you who worked out that it was Wesley who was gaslighting us."

Holding his hand out, Ash said, "Hi, I'm Ash. We haven't met before, but I've heard a lot about you."

"And probably none of it good," Chris admitted, looking a little shame-faced as he shook Ash's hand. "I'm not proud of the way I've acted towards Holly, but honestly, I was in between a rock and a hard place."

"We know about Laura and the boys, if that helps," Holly said sympathetically.

He looked at her in shock. "How?"

"The way Angie did – I found the video her friend made. I heard you and Wesley talking, just the way Angie must have done."

Yet Chris still looked at her blankly, forcing her to make a full explanation. Only when she'd finished did Chris sit back with a huff and say, "That explains so much."

Ash looked at him curiously. "In what way? Surely you'd realised that Angie knew what you done some time ago?"

However, Chris grimaced. "Not exactly. I knew that suddenly she began to behave oddly – well odd even by Angie's erratic standards. At that point I suspected that she'd found out and I was all braced for the wrath of the gods to head my way. That was when I made damned sure that I'd filtered enough money out into a totally separate account that nobody but Laura and I knew about, not even her mum. I was determined that even if I ended up in jail, that Laura and the kids would be looked after."

He paused as a waitress came across and he ordered another bottle of the wine that Holly and Ash had been sharing, getting a glass for himself, and putting it and their meal onto his card. "It's the least I can do," he said as Ash made to protest.

Taking a large swig, he set the glass down and looked at the two of them. "I realised something bad was going on when money started to go out of *that* account. I knew Laura wouldn't, and couldn't have anyway because it's a savings account that can't be used to buy online, and anyway her mobility in her hands isn't good enough to use something like a computer's mouse anymore. So I knew she couldn't have transferred money to another account, and I sure hadn't. What threw me was that at the same time, Angie was suddenly all lovey-dovey over me. I couldn't understand it."

"Wesley?" Holly guessed and got a nod.

"It took me a week or two to figure it out, but in the end it came down to who I knew who could possibly know that much about my life, and at the same time have the knowhow to be able to mess with things like bank accounts and emails."

"Did you never suspect a random hacker?" Ash wondered.

"Oh God, yes! In fact that was my first thought – never that one of my oldest friends would do that to me. I mean you get warned about stuff like hackers and scammers when you win big on the lottery. They don't just hand over the money and expect you to be able to cope with all the lowlifes that come out of the woodwork. You get support. What rang alarms bells with me, when I saw the extent of what was going on, was remembering Wesley saying to me that the precautions I got advised to put into place were over the top. Too much. That I didn't need them.

"Well he came from a pretty comfortable background compared to me, so I don't think he remotely grasped the relief it was to me to know that I could help the people who'd stood by me when my world was going down the pan at speed. When you've had nothing, you're much more wary of losing money." He looked sadly at Holly. "I bet you know what I'm talking about. The compulsion to save for a rainy day, however far off, when it might all fall apart. That's why I so desperately wanted you to wake up and see how much Angie was taking you for granted. At that stage I'd begun to wonder whether Angie was in cahoots with someone more tech savvy, because that was before I'd realised it had to be Wesley.

"I could foresee you losing everything, because if the shop went under, you had nothing backing you up. You don't have to believe me – God knows in your place I wouldn't – but I actually put some money aside in a separate fund in case I needed to make it up to you. You know, help get you a place of your own because Angie had talked you into giving up your flat, and stuff."

That really took the wind out of Holly's sails. She'd never for a moment believed that Chris had given her a second thought. However, what he said next truly shook her. "You said that Wesley took you to our flat, but I swear to you, there's no under-floor hidey-hole, and I know nothing about any lock-up garage. Are you sure it was our flat you went to?"

Holly was aghast. "I know I only visited you two a couple of times, and very briefly at that, and he was so confident I didn't even think of checking which number it was, but the decoration was exactly the same. Why?"

Chris gave a bitter laugh. "Can you seriously imagine Angie remembering an eight-digit door code if it was a keypad? It would have been more than my life was worth to put something like that in. But I know who has one on his flat – Wesley!"

"But it was the same block, the same floor and everything," Holly protested.

"Was it precisely the same number, though?" Chris' words made her sit up and think. "Only, as far as I knew, the flat next door was empty for ages, and that's an identical layout to ours – they all are on that stretch of our floor. I always assumed it was someone who worked away a lot, but now I'm wondering whether Wesley bought it, or at least rented it? He certainly could have done it out exactly the same as ours – Angie had so much modern stuff delivered he'd have seen the packaging out for the recycling, let alone after he'd been inside. It sometimes freaked me out how he could suddenly turn up on our doorstep seemingly out of nowhere. You have to walk past our kitchen window to get to our front door along the landing, you might remember, so I often saw people even before they rang the doorbell, but not him."

"But if he was next door on the other side, and just wanted to check he'd got something just so..." Ash suggested, leaving it hanging.

Chris nodded. "That's what I'm thinking now."

"What about all those treasured possessions of yours, though?" Holly objected, not expecting Chris to laugh.

"What treasured possessions? Holly, I was in and out of care my whole childhood. Kids like me don't have treasured possessions. Even if you go in with them, after the first time you don't come out with them. As for a Hornby railway set, God, I wish I *had* had one. They were my childhood dream. I was so envious of Wesley for having one."

Holly's soundless, "Oh," was all she could manage as the depth of Wesley's deception sank in. How easy it had been for Wesley to tap into her fears and manipulate her. Then something occurred to her. "He's one hell of an actor, then, because how did he fake the shock when you went missing?"

"Oh, I think I can answer that one," Ash said dryly. "That was genuine panic because he'd lost sight of you, Chris. I'm guessing that you went 'radio silent' when you left the Caribbean?"

Chris nodded. "You might as well hear the full tale. I realised it was serious when Angie came to me, bouncing all over me and saying I'd made her dream come true with a Caribbean holiday, and what a surprise it was. I tell you, that floored me. I'd got away from her on a supposed 'business trip', but in reality to spend some time with Laura and the kids to save my sanity, so *I'd* got a WhatsApp message from *her* with the surprise booking *she'd* supposedly made in it." He gave a shudder. "I honestly thought she'd finally flipped. I knew she was mentally all over the place, but I genuinely worried that she'd lost what little grip on reality she had."

He gave another shudder. "I was worried enough that when I got back home to her, and she'd bounced all over me, I waited until she'd gone to bed, and then got up and took her phone into the kitchen to start going through it. I was expecting all sorts of disjointed and weird texts and messages. But that's when I got really scared for a different reason.

"The phone she had in her bag didn't have WhatsApp on it. Now I might not know much about tech, but I do know that even those who run WhatsApp can't see what you post, and it came to me in a flash that if someone didn't want Angie to see her own posts, the only thing they could do would be to wipe it off *her* actual phone. So how had she sent me messages on it?"

He sat back with a huff and took another large gulp of wine. "To this day, I don't know why I didn't ask Wesley about this. Normally, anything to do with tech, he's been my go-to man. This time I went into the phone store in Worcester where I'd bought it and quizzed them, and by the time they'd finished, I'd grasped that if someone was *still* sending me WhatsApp messages supposedly from Ange, then they *had* to have her phone. There was no other way it could happen – aside from her being so paranoid that she had two phones, and you don't want to know how prescient that thought was to become!"

He took another gulp of wine. "Well, I went back to the flat and that night I grabbed her phone again, only this time I took it out of that bloody awful sparkly case it's in."

Holly gasped. "Oh my God! It wasn't the same phone, was it? I remember her having that awful snit when she scratched all of the one side of that new, top-of-the-range iPhone you'd bought her, and you refusing to buy her another one when it was working perfectly well. That's when she bought the case!"

Chris nodded. "I got the phone out and it was pristine. Not a scratch, not a mark. Somebody had swopped phones on her, and Angie being Angie, she was far more into posting publicly on things like Instagram than something private like WhatsApp. You don't get random likes and followers on that, she had no audience to play to, so I'm guessing that she didn't even realise it wasn't on there for ages."

Holly nodded. "And when she did, I bet she just

thought she'd wiped it by mistake. God knows, I've had to put half her apps back on her phone often enough when she's done that."

Ash leaned back in his seat and shook his head. "She was the perfect patsy, wasn't she? Someone who doesn't take notice of the important stuff, and who can't be bothered to learn how things work. I bet Wesley couldn't believe his luck when he discovered you'd won the lottery and with someone he could use like her."

"I love her like a sister – most of the time, anyway – but Angie really is her own worst enemy," Holly confessed.

"She played right into Wesley's hands," admitted Chris.

"But was that when you got suspicious of him?" Ash wondered.

Chris shook his head. "No, or at least not instantly. That night, I sat in the lounge half relieved that I wasn't dealing with some malevolent professional Russian hacker – because no distant hacker could have been there in person to swop Angie's phone – and half frantically trying to come to terms with the fact that the phone swopping meant it had to be someone we knew in person. It couldn't even be some internet friend of Angie's, you see."

Holly and Ash could both understand how horrifying that must have been; Holly especially as she recalled how empty the church had been on Chris' side at the wedding. Angie's side had been crammed with so many people that down at the back, they'd spilled over onto Chris' side. But close to the main family, no, Chris had had few friends and even less family. That betrayal must have cut really deep. Then she revised that to being even worse, because of Chris' family nobody of his parents' generation came close to being the sort to know how to do this, and he had to know that. Chris had never put any kind of rosy filter on any of them, and he'd only had his sister there that day because his mum had made such a fuss. In everyday life, Angie had told Holly back then, he saw them as little as possible, to the extent that they'd never even been to the flat.

But that must have meant that on that awful night, Chris must have known it was a supposed friend who'd done this, and that was a very short list indeed.

"Oh Chris, how horrible for you," she gasped as the thought came, and saw him blink, then nod as he realised just how fast she'd caught up with him.

"Yes it was. It took hours for me to believe what my own eyes were telling me – that it *had* to be a close friend." He grimaced. "Didn't take me too long the next day to whittle the list down to Wesley, though. Once I'd got that far, it came down to who knew how to do stuff, and while friends like Ed and Jules are bright lads, I just couldn't imagine them coming up with an idea like that."

"Was it just that?" Ash asked. "No other telltales?"

Chris sighed. "I'm not saying that I was completely certain it was him right away. He was the top suspect, yes, but I felt horribly disloyal for doubting him, so I made myself look hard at my other friends too. But the thing was, every other one of them – and I really mean *every* – said when I had the big win that they didn't expect any handouts from me because they knew I'd have to fund Laura's care. They got it, you see, being married themselves.

"Jules knows what it's like, because before his mum passed away, he was having to pay for live-in nurses for her. She'd been an elderly mum when she had him, so he'd known that because she was so old there was a limit to how long he'd have to keep paying when she kept on having strokes. But he said it was a relief to know that he wasn't going to have to find all that money for long. He was the first to say out loud when we got together to celebrate the win, that with Laura only being our age, I'd be needing all of that money." He gave a huff of disgust. "I remembered looking over to Wesley and seeing his look of disgust. I didn't work out why at the time, but thinking back, I realised that he must have been wishing the others would shut up, because he somehow thought he deserved a cut of the win."

Holly sighed. "Why does it always come down to money? Why can't people be grateful for what they've got? He must earn ten times anything I could even dream of earning."

"Oh, Wesley's not broke," Chris agreed. "But he does waste money. He's a shocking hoarder for a start. You can't call it collecting because it's so indiscriminate. He already has to pay for a large self-storage unit because otherwise he'd never get in through the door of his flat."

"Please tell me you've told the police about that," Ash prompted him, "because I'm guessing that any incriminating evidence will be in there, not his flat."

Chris' shocked expression said not, and he got up to go and make the call.

It gave Ash the chance to ask Holly, "Are you feeling a bit better about this now? You know, knowing that you weren't the only one being manipulated."

She nodded. "I feel bad for Angie – because we all thought so badly of her for a while, I mean. But Wesley? Wow, he really went to town on this, didn't he? He must truly hate Chris to do something like this to him."

"Jealousy is a powerful motivator," Ash sighed, "worse than simple hate in my book. You can hate someone and yet walk away from them. Jealousy is like a horrible chain, tying you to someone in the worst kind of way. If anything, it does more damage to you than the person you're jealous of."

Holly looked at him askance. "I think Chris is pretty damaged by all of this!"

"Oh, he is," Ash agreed. "But, think about it. Chris has still got Laura, who he loves, and his kids who he clearly adores. He'll still have them and that lovely house they're obviously going to make into a great family home for them all, long after this has faded. And even when Laura's gone, I can't imagine that Chris would throw her mum out – he'll want those two lads to have their granny close by as they continue to grow up, not least because he knows what it's like to have no family. He might have even more trust issues than he has already, but therapy will help calm them down, so in most respects, Chris can get on with his life, especially once he's divorced Angie.

"Now compare that to what's going to happen to Wesley. Because of Chris' win, there'll be a media storm over the trial, and can you imagine what a monster they'll paint Wesley as when they discover that Laura has MS? It's probably a good thing we no longer have capital punishment, because the red top papers would have him hanged in a heartbeat. And the other prisoners will take a dim view of a bloke who'd steal off a dying woman – his time inside won't be easy. But on top of that, who is going to go and visit him in prison? I don't know if he still has parents living, but they'll be hanging their heads in shame."

"I think they died in strange circumstances a few years ago," Holly said, then clapped a hand to her mouth. "Oh no! Could he? Could he have killed his own mum and dad? He's an only child, so he got everything!"

"How did they die?"

Holly went pale as she told him of how they had been found in their holiday lodge which had been flooded with carbon monoxide. "They said it was a faulty valve on the hot water boiler. A freak accident."

"Well don't be surprised if that investigation gets reopened once there's been a psych' evaluation of Wesley. I reckon he'd already totally lost the plot right back then. And if they do find he murdered them, then he won't be allowed to keep anything he bought out of that inheritance – you can't profit by your crimes. So even if he gets let out in twenty years or so, he won't have anywhere to come back to. ...See what I mean, Holly? Wesley's inflicted far more damage on himself than ever he has Chris in the long run."

Chapter 27

In the following days, Holly and Ash went back to Ledbury, and Angie got transferred to the hospital in Worcester so that her parents could visit her frequently. It took a while for Angie to be coherent enough to tell anyone the full tale, but when it came out, it shocked everyone. Like Chris, her first clue that something was going very wrong was realising that she'd had messages supposedly coming from Chris, which he'd then acted as though he had no knowledge of. Unlike Chris, Angie had thought it was just some random person hacking her social media, so she changed her passwords – foolishly all still to the same one – and assumed it was sorted.

She'd been shocked out of her complacency when Wesley began contacting her and telling her what to do, threatening not just her, but her mum and dad and siblings, and Holly too. He threatened to drain her dad's bank accounts and to put her sister's detail up on the dark web for modern slavers to see. This was all confirmed once the police's forensic tech team got to work on his phones and computers, of which there were several of each.

Bizarrely, she'd not realised that it hadn't been Chris who'd booked the holiday until they were on the plane on their way out there. Instead, her bounding enthusiasm had come not just from wanting the holiday itself, but the mistaken belief that if she was out of the country then Wesley couldn't reach her. She'd been shaken out of that the first time a phone she hadn't even realised had been in her luggage rang while she was in the hotel in Jamaica. It had been Wesley, taunting her by telling her to try and post something on her social media pages. To her horror, she'd found that she could only look at them as if she was an outsider, and that every post she'd made since they'd left the UK had been wiped.

In typical Angie fashion, instead of sitting down and talking to Chris, she allowed her emotions over knowing about Laura to override everything, alternating between ignoring him and shrieking at him. So after Wesley's call, she'd gone down to the hotel bar got through two bottles of prosecco on her own, and then had a blazing row with Chris. And being so drunk, she'd made weird, oblique references to him having shit friends who were hurting her, thinking that she'd been so clever not mentioning Wesley by name – something Wesley had threatened dire consequences for if she should dare to expose him. Had they had the row in the bar, she might have got away with it, but she did it in their room, and Wesley had bugged every bit of luggage, for which he'd broken into their flat when they weren't there, as they later discovered he'd done on several occasions – meaning he heard her.

That had been the start of the real nightmare for Angie, because Wesley rang her up as soon as she was sober enough to take in his words, and threatened her. Then when she threw that phone away, he simply rang the phone of wherever she was and asked to speak to her. By the time he'd tracked her through three bars and had a call put through to her room, Angie had been a terrified mess. It never occurred to her to leave her designer handbag behind, which was what Wesley was tracking. So for the rest of the holiday she did whatever Wesley told her to do, convinced that he had men watching her who would kidnap her and that she'd never see England again.

Yet finding her shouting at thin air in their room had been the final eye-opener Chris had needed, as Holly and Ash knew from what he'd told them after coming back from phoning Chesterton about Wesley's storage unit. He didn't need to know how Wesley was doing it to guess that somehow he'd put trackers on them. That same day, Chris had taken the sim card out of his phone and crushed it, throwing the phone away too. Then he'd packed one bag, after searching it even to the extent of cutting open the lining, and having found the tiny devices, dropped them into a glass of water in the bar, and headed for the airport. Thankfully he'd got plenty of cash on him, and one last large withdrawal close to the hotel got him enough money to head back to the UK. He left no credit card trail for Wesley to follow, and had first taken a one-way flight to Miami, then to Ireland, and home by ferry from there. Only the British police getting his passport details from immigration had allowed them to discover that he was back in the UK.

That discovery of Chris in England, it came out, had been the point when Wesley had really begun to panic. The person he really wanted to be able to manipulate was Chris, not a hysterical Angie, who was getting harder and harder to control. Yet at the crucial point, suddenly he had no idea where Chris was, let alone have access to his life. He'd set it up so carefully too, because by this time he'd already used Angie's phone to contact Tom and lure him to the house with a sob story of Chris beating Angie to within an inch of her life. The tragedy was that Tom was decent enough to have agreed to come and fetch Angie to take her to the police to report Chris, even if he had no desire to be with her anymore.

Wesley's motive for killing Tom turned out to be Angie herself. When she discovered the truth about Laura, she woke up to the fact that Tom was the one man who'd ever really loved her, and who she – in her own warped way – had loved back. On a drunken night when Angie had 'accidentally' met Wesley at a wine bar in Worcester – in truth, a meeting engineered by him – she'd confessed that she was planning on divorcing 'Topher' and getting back together with Tom. What had signed poor Tom's death warrant was Angie saying that when she took 'Topher' to the cleaners, she'd be able to rescue Tom from the dreadful job he hated. Apparently Wesley wasn't having any of that. Chris' money was coming to him, not being shared with anyone, not even Laura, let alone some ex of Angie's.

It was why Wesley had changed the subject so rapidly when Holly had brought Tom's name up in their phone conversation. The last thing he wanted to talk about was the man he'd just murdered! Wesley was confident, but not enough to be oblivious to the possibility that he might give something away about the circumstances of Tom's death, because at the time he'd been so rattled by Chris vanishing off his radar. Apparently he'd later thought he'd dropped himself in the shit when he opened the safe in front of Holly, despite trying to get her tipsy on prosecco. Yes, it was actually his safe, and he'd got into Chris and Angie's flat and taken the documents relating to the house and shop from there. But he belatedly realised that he shouldn't know the combination to a safe supposed to be Chris'. He could barely believe his luck when Holly was so distraught that she didn't notice.

Therefore, by the point Chris vanished, Wesley had a body in the attic, which was bound to be discovered sooner or later, but no Chris to blame it on. And it was harder to blacken Chris' name without using Angie as a means to spread the doubts, even though he was all set to try and plant evidence, because Chris was the opposite of Angie, with no online presence except a WhatsApp group with close friends, none of whom would believe what Wesley needed them to. Angie was the one he'd planned to use to plant evidence, but with Angie not having a clue where Chris was, either, everything was falling apart. That had been why Wesley's panic had been so convincing to Holly – he really *was* panicking, just not for the reasons he was telling her!

It also now dawned on Holly that Wesley had been careful to tell her about the cruise by phone.

She'd never had chance to see his expression when he did it. He'd been more confident about lying to her about Angie's supposed clear-outs, because that had thrown the blame more Angie's way than his. However, when it came to Holly's big question – the car – it now transpired that Chris had only said that he intended to buy Holly a bit of an old banger for a car. It hadn't been him who'd done the actual purchase. That had been Wesley, who'd told Chris that someone at work was selling their sister's old car for them. Believing that nobody would have their sister driving a car that was actually dangerous, Chris had handed the money over to Wesley, who'd gone to a demolition yard and paid for the car in cash, supposedly to strip for spare parts. That was unnerving for Holly, since it demonstrated Wesley's indifference to the harm that could come to anyone who stood in his way of getting his hands on Chris' money. It was also the final block removed from Holly having any doubts about Chris' innocence.

What really shook Holly was the fact that she herself had put the biggest spanner in the works regarding the shop and house. It turned out that Wesley had been watching her, expecting her to go home and forget the shop, especially over a weekend. He'd actually counted on having any Saturday night and all of Sunday to do whatever he wanted up there. That she would be conscientious enough to *sleep* on the premises just at the point when he desperately needed to change direction had truly messed with his plans. He'd planned to move Tom's body, though why and where to wasn't clear, because by the time he was telling the police everything, Wesley's mental state was crumbling. Neither Holly nor Ash felt like telling Chesterton that there was a reason Wesley had kept hearing a Scottish voice in his head, swearing divine retribution upon him for his sins.

Plus there was the problem of her burgeoning friendship with Jesse and Shea-Lea, which Wesley had watched with rising fury and anxiety, not least because tackling Jesse man to man was something he knew he couldn't do. Ash had been uncannily right that Wesley only need to thump Tom with the old sword, though it turned out that Wesley had put it up on top of the half open door, rather than a rope from any beam, and had nudged it down when Tom stepped through the door. But by then, another chat with Duncan had confirmed that when he told them what he'd seen – it was just that the testimony of a ghost could hardly be used in court to convict Wesley.

As for how he'd found it, it transpired that he'd been blatant enough to ask Chris if he could see the survey report on the old house, and of course, that had been before Chris had begun to suspect Wesley. The anomalies in the spaces had been carefully documented, so Wesley hadn't had to hunt too far to find them. And of course by the time Angie had been towing Holly around, talking to her about living up there, Wesley had already got his claws into Angie and told her where the cupboard, at least, was.

He'd then lurked around, watching the place, when he'd spotted the bottom door was open, just as Holly had described happening while Angie had been flitting in and out. It had taken no time for him to slip inside and hide on the top floor until she left, and unlike Holly, Angie had relied on the modern lock, never bothering with the old key, so it had been simplicity itself to slip out and close the door behind him. That night he'd gone through the place with a fine toothcomb, but the sword hadn't been where Ash had found it. It was probably him moving it which had loosened the board that had come away and exposed Goodwife Joan's remains to Ash and Callum. He had been aware of the ghosts, though, and they'd scared him even more than they did Holly. McAllister, it seemed, took a dim view of men murdering others in 'his' house!

Wesley then couldn't believe his bad luck the first time he watched Holly go to check on the post and then use the huge old iron key in the big lock. Wesley had had Angie get him one of the modern keys cut before she left the country, but even if he'd know about the old key in time, he'd never have found anyone to make him another like that. Why Holly would bother with the old clunky thing had baffled him, or at least until he'd come to try and pick it late one night. A professional burglar would probably have made short work of it, but Wesley's thieving expertise was all online, he couldn't pick a lock, and certainly not one as stiff and old as this one. When it had been the couple's modern flat, Angie had played into his hands by leaving her keys out on a worktop, which he'd taken, had a spare key cut, and then taken back, Angie being prone to forgetting where she put things and not suspecting what had happened.

There was one other thing, though, that still bothered Holly. Why had Angie taken the Laura Ashley curtains to frame her? Yet it turned out to be nothing to do with her at all. Wesley hadn't a clue that Holly had once used that room over the garage, indeed he hadn't remotely specified those particular ones. All he'd done was demand that Angie take a set of curtains from her mum's house when he was first twisting her life around his fingers. It was supposed to be Angie that got implicated, not Holly. It had been Angie who'd known that her mum would never let her have any of the decent curtains, and who had raided the garage as her only option.

"He got too clever for his own good," Jesse said as they sat in the pub talking about it after they'd shut for the night.

"What about Angie?" Shea-Lea asked. "Do we know what's happening about her?"

Jesse looked at her askance. "You don't think they're going to prosecute her, do you?"

Shea-Lea shook her head. "Not for what went on with Wesley. I think you'd have a hard time making a case for her helping him. What I was thinking, though, was about her and Chris divorcing. I mean technically Chris did nothing wrong. He wasn't married to Laura, so there's no question of bigamy, but it's going to be an accountant's nightmare trying to sort out which bits of her spending sprees with Chris' money were at Wesley's command, and which were her just being a fluff-head and blowing it all. How the heck do you work out a divorce settlement with all that to get through?"

Jesse nodded, saying grimly, "And in his shoes, I'd want that divorce as fast as possible."

"She wasn't exactly to blame for all that," Holly protested, but Jesse shook his head, saying,

"It's not blame for what Wesley did. For me the crippler would be that she never came and talked to me." He reached across and squeezed Shea-Lea's hand. "Never going to happen, babe, but if ever I was daft enough to get myself entangled like Chris did, I'd be braced for a kick in the balls for deceiving my wife over how I felt about someone else – someone I'd actually got kids with and who I had every intention of being around while they grew up, as well. Yes, I'd put my hand up to being guilty of that if accused.

"What I wouldn't like is the way she never came to me saying something along the lines of, 'do you know what your bloody mate is trying to do to me?' ...Do you see? The only connection she had to Wesley was Chris, so why did she never challenge him over his friend's behaviour towards her? Especially when he really started to threaten her and her family.

"At that point, however much of an arsehole you thought your husband was for 'cheating' on you emotionally...no, make that even more so *because* you'd think he was a shit of the first order...why *wouldn't* you challenge him? You'd have no loving relationship to ruin – not once Angie knew about Laura. In fact, some women would have seen it as a good opener for starting a stinging divorce. You know, 'you've been keeping another woman, and now your best mate is trying to blackmail me! I want shot of you!'"

The way the Ash was nodding along to Jesse's words made Holly realise that they had a point, and she agreed to raise the subject with Angie the next time she went to visit her. Ash had already made an offer for the building to Chris, who had all but bitten his hand off accepting it, saying that it would make it so much easier to simply pay Angie off if there was no lingering property sale involved. Because for all that Angie had been the one who'd found and pushed for the purchase, it had been Chris, and Chris alone, who'd paid for and signed for the purchase. For him, the sooner this was all over, the better.

What Holly wasn't expecting when she next saw Angie was how much her own feelings had shifted. When she asked, "Ange, why didn't you simply have it out with Topher?" – because Angie seemed incapable of calling him anything else, even though she now knew he was Chris to those closest to him – now she noticed how Angie's expression became shifty.

"Oh come on, Ange," she remonstrated, and more or less repeated Jesse's argument, concluding with, "What the heck did you have to lose? And didn't you *want* to know if Chris had put him up to it? If I thought someone had deliberately put me through the wringer like that, I'd be out for blood, and you'd have had every reason to take him to the cleaners in the divorce court."

Then she remembered Meryl's words. "Your mum told me that you had a massive row with them because they wouldn't fund a divorce for you, so you clearly wanted one at that time. Well you wouldn't have needed your dad to pay if you could prove Chris had been gaslighting you! You'd have had 'no-win, no-fee' lawyers queuing around the block to help you with the sums of money involved – and they *were* involved, because that was after Chris had the big win. What gives?"

Yet by now Angie was almost squirming under Holly's scrutiny, making her ever more suspicious. All she got, though, were a few nonsensical mumbles, and then Angie pleading fatigue and needing a nap.

"You're right," Holly said in disgust that night, as the four of them sat around the table to eat. "Angie's hiding something, and I bet it's something she's praying doesn't come to light."

It wasn't until Wesley's trial many months later that they found out what, and it was Wesley's barrister who mentioned it in Wesley's defence. There wasn't much that could be said to put what he'd tried to do to Chris in a better light, but when it came to Angie, it was a different story. Yes, initially Wesley had been manipulating her, but it was her response once she got to the Caribbean and realised what was going on that let her down. Far from being the innocent victim, once she'd realised he'd got her trapped, Angie had begun trying to negotiate with Wesley, demanding her share of the money once he got it off Chris. At this stage there were almost as bad as one another, for there was the evidence of many messages from Angie to Wesley threatening to expose what he was doing, her price for silence being a fifty percent cut of what he stole. That she'd thought he might kill her, and was trying to make sure he couldn't get the money without her, didn't excuse her actions, but also revealed that in her fear she was being completely illogical. One moment she was cowed and submissive, a message later – and the supposition was a few stiff vodkas later – she was threatening to expose him once they had the money, only to buckle again when he responded.

Holly had been closer to the truth than she wanted to be when it finally came out that when Chris had made his mad dash for safety, leaving most of what he'd taken with him behind, it had been Angie who had disposed of everything – suitcases and all. It had even been her who had suggested that Chris might get onto the cruise and then vanish, with Wesley then saying in his responses that he knew a way to make sure that Chris' remains were never found. Quite what that way was he refused to say, but Holly and her friends were sure that it involved the hiding places in the attic. By the time Wesley was convicted and sent down, Chris' offer to fund psychiatric treatment for Angie was about as generous a settlement as she was likely to get.

However, long before the trial, as soon as Ash had full control of the building even if the final paperwork was still being finished, there was something which needed the attention of the four friends – McAllister's ghost.

Chapter 28

This time, Holly made sure that Sally was definitely involved, because putting a ghost to rest was more than Ash had ever attempted before. So on the night of a beautiful full moon, which was shining in through the window of the main parlour, Ash, Holly, and Sally sat in the circle, with Jesse and Shea-Lea in the room but off to one side. Neither of those two wanted to actively participate, but they did want to say their farewells to McAllister.

With an experienced psychic leading them, Duncan was present far faster and more substantially than before, making Jesse and Shea-Lea gasp as they finally saw what an imposing figure he once must have been.

“Is there anything you want to ask us or tell us before we begin?” Sally asked, her instinct telling her that he would go more easily if all his ‘business’ here was concluded.

“We’ve spoken to all of the people concerned,” Ash said, “and there’s no problem with your bones going back up to Arrochar.” There was no need to tell him just how much this was costing and the negotiating they’d had to do to make it happen. “As we speak they are on the road heading north. They should have passed Carlisle by now.”

They all saw the relief on Duncan's face. '*That's awful kind o' ye,*' he said gratefully. '*It means a lot, and I'm verra grateful.*' He seemed to think something over and then said, '*I feel I ought to tell ye all, that other lass, Angie...she came back into this place after the man ye call Tom had died. She kenned about the lock on the stairs. She could have told ye, Holly. She could have confessed earlier.*'

Thinking fast, Ash asked him, "Did you see Wesley – the man who killed Tom – come back and put strange little things about the place? You wouldn't know what they were, but they'd have been the size of a small button, and he'd have put them in places where they wouldn't have been obvious. You see, those are a means of listening in on people, even when you aren't in the building. We know that Wesley used them to try and control Angie elsewhere, so if she knew they were here, she might have been scared he'd hear her telling Holly to call the police."

Yet McAllister shook his head. '*No, I never saw him do that. Nothing like it. And after he killed Tom, he didn'a come back up here. Oh, I saw him try, but ye foiled that Holly, by using the old key. He couldn'a get past that. And after that, the only times he went into the shop was when ye were wi' him, so he wasn'a alone.*'

Ash nodded. "And that would have been after Angie left the country, so even if he had tried to plant bugs in the shop when you left him to get the kettle, Holly, there wouldn't have been any point. He couldn't blackmail you, and if he'd tried it wouldn't have got him anywhere anyway. Well, well, so Angie knew that there was something wrong going on up on the top floor. I doubt she'll ever confess exactly *when* she found out Tom was dead, but Master McAllister is right, she could have told you, Holly. She might have been frightened to call the police herself, but there's far less reason for her not to have asked you to."

'Ye dinna have to be so formal,' McAllister said. *'I feel like we're friends by now. Ye can call me Duncan.'*

"Well thank you, Duncan," Holly said, "because knowing that has really settled something in my mind, and it's that Angie and I can never go back to being the friends we were." She wasn't going to burden him with telling him about a couple of long conversations she'd had with Ash about just what kind of friend Angie had turned out to be down the years, nor how much damage she'd inflicted on Holly in order to keep her close and with Angie as her only friend. Only now was Holly coming to recognise that Angie had twisted Holly's life so that she didn't trust many of the people she should have. Learning how to trust again was going to be the hardest part of moving on, but Holly knew that with Ash beside her, along with Jesse and Shea-Lea, she would get there.

However, tonight was all about Duncan, and Holly felt she had to give him her thanks. "If you'd not told us about Mary, and her betrayal of you, I might not have made the connection of what was wrong with Angie's story."

'Really?' he said surprised.

Holly nodded. "It was you saying that Mary hadn't given a moment's thought to the consequences of what she was doing, or how it might work out very differently, you see. That's what woke me up to Angie's behaviour, but also that she just isn't clever enough to have engineered that complicated web of lies. Like Mary, all she saw was what she wanted to see, or what she thought was going to affect her. So without you, I might not have realised that it had to be someone like Wesley."

Duncan regarded her thoughtfully. *'I think ye underestimate yourself, lass. You'd have worked it out.'*

"Maybe," Holly conceded, "but it might have been too late. Wesley was going after Chris and his children, you know. He was already down there in Cornwall with them. We were nearly too late to save Angie, because by then she'd finally woken up to the fact that Wesley couldn't let her live because she knew too much. So thank you, Duncan. You probably saved their lives."

'*Will he hang?*' Duncan asked.

"No," Jesse said, feeling confident enough now to move forward. "We don't do that nowadays, and anyway, there's some serious doubt about whether Wesley is sane enough to stand trial. *We* think he is, but even so, he's more likely to end up in a secure mental hospital, if you know what one of those is – an asylum, you might be more familiar with."

'Aye, well he needs locking up for everyone's safety,' Duncan said firmly and got no argument over that.

Sally gave them all a moment and then asked him if there was anything else he would like them to do.

For a moment he thought, then said, *'I ken ye willn'a be able to tell me what ye find, if anything, but would ye look for Sorley? I'd love to know if he made it back home, and hopefully he'll be there on the Other*

Side by now. But if I canna met him there, it would comfort me to know that ye might find him for me.'

"Sorley McAllister?" Jesse asked and got a nod. "And how do you spell that first name?"

Duncan told him, and Jesse made a note of it. "We'll give it our best shot," he promised Duncan, and got a ghostly smile in return.

"Anything else?" Sally asked gently, but Duncan thought for a moment and then shook his head. "Then if we're all ready, let's begin."

Ash picked up his lute and began playing *Farewell to Lochaber*, the song Holly had first heard Duncan singing. As he played, Sally encouraged Jesse to come and sit in the circle as the other person linked to Duncan by blood. As the music floated around the empty room, but lit by dozens of tiny candles, the temperature dropped a little and then a light began to form to the one side. Sally's scarcely heard words invoking the way to open were certainly working, and Duncan began drifting towards it.

As it fully opened to a circle of white light, Duncan gave a cry of joy, as if seeing someone or several someones whom he recognised, and then rushed to it. In a brief burst of light, he and it were suddenly gone, leaving only Ash to gently bring the song to a close.

"We never actually said goodbye," Holly said with a sniff, feeling strangely as though she'd lost someone like a favourite uncle.

"But it's never fully goodbye," Sally consoled her. "The only time they're really gone is if you forget about them."

By the time Christmas came around, Holly had moved in with Ash. It was quick –something she would never have rushed into before – and it might have been different if she'd had somewhere of her own that she valued and wanted to stay in under other circumstances, but letting the rented flat go was easy. On Yule – the winter solstice – they all assembled with Sally in the upstairs once more, but this time it was for Sally to do a full cleansing of the whole building. With the shop having been wrapped up as part of Chris sorting out his affairs, as soon as the documentation for the sale completed, Ash was intending to expand the pub into the whole of the ground floor. So early one morning, they had done a cleansing of that already, but as Sally said, that wasn't where the worst of anything had ever taken place.

Now, though, they went through every room. Incense was lit in each of the main rooms and the windows opened, despite the cold weather, to let any darkness be taken away by the wind. The worst two places were at least the ones they expected to be – the front parlour where Duncan and Joan had died, and the top room where Tom had passed more recently. The fact that they found no other 'black spots' was very reassuring, and Sally was confident that there were no other spirits lingering, not even Joan's.

"What are you intending to do with the upper floors?" Sally asked Ash, as they gratefully went and sat by the fire in *The Renegade* to drink hot mulled wine.

Ash cupped his hands around the warm mug and took a careful sip before answering. "Well first off,

I'm going to get the wiring and plumbing checked over. If I'm going to have people renting space off me, I need to be certain it's all safe – and that includes sweeping those chimneys. But then I thought I'd open it up to crafts people. That big front parlour could be somewhere where local artists could display paintings and other things for sale, but the room Holly stopped in would be ideal for someone to use as a small workshop space. It's the same with the rooms on the second floor.

"Even someone like a graphic artist might be glad of a decent sized room to work in that doesn't cost the earth to rent. And if there's a couple of communal kitchen areas and loos, it should be quite comfortable. Part of the rent will include a cleaner for the stairs and communal areas, so it'll stay clean and tidy. It's time this old house had people doing positive and creative things in it."

"I think that's an excellent idea," Sally said, but then looked at Holly questioningly. "And what are you going to do now? Did you not want to keep the shop going?"

Holly shook her head. "Too many bad memories. I need to draw a line. I need to move on. For the first time in my life I've got someone I truly trust to not let me down, and Ash is happy to keep me while I take the time to rethink my life. It's dawned on me that I've got a lot of healing to do, and rushing headlong into something else isn't allowing me to do that – in fact it'd be me trying to avoid doing that, using the excuse of work to keep burying my head in the sand. I've spent so much of my life with the need to keep a roof over my head that it's ruled my every waking hour, and while I had no choice at the time, it's not a way to live."

Jesse nodded. "You should work to live, to have a life worth living, not live to work and nothing more."

"There is one thing we've found," Ash said with a grin. "It turns out that when we dug into Holly's family history, she's also got a connection to Scotland, so in the New Year, I'm taking her on a holiday up there. I've already booked us in for Valentine's Day at a place called *Nun's Kirk Haugh Country House Hotel*, and then we're heading on up into Argyll. Who knows, we might even find out more about Sorley McAllister?"

FINIS

Thank you for taking the time to read this book. If you've enjoyed it, you personally (yes, *you*) can make a big difference to what happens next.

Reviews are one of the best ways to get other people to discover my books. I'm an independent author, so I don't have a publisher paying big bucks to spread the word or arrange huge promos in bookstore chains, there's just me and my computer. Honest reviews help bring books to the attention of other readers, so it would mean a great deal to me if you would spend a couple of minutes posting a review on the site where you purchased it. Just a star rating can make all the difference. Thank you.

Author's Notes

If you've read any of my books prior to this, you'll probably have guessed already that no house like this exists on the lane leading up to Ledbury minster church. That road does have some beautiful half-timbered building on it, but the only one that comes close to this one is a very handsome private house right up by the entrance to the churchyard. The rest of Ledbury is as described and is a lovely town well worth a visit. The model and floor plan for the house comes from a completely different building in another Midlands town. As described, the upper floors are jetted, meaning that each floor gets that little bit longer than the one below it as it projects out over it, so the floor plans are realistic.

Ledbury Mop is a real event and takes place every year. Mop fairs were originally hiring fairs, and there are many still held around the country, but are now more focused on rides and stalls than anything to do with employment. The re-enactment of the skirmish in Ledbury in 2019, the year before all the lockdowns, was a real event too, and one which I went to. I would definitely encourage you to attend any of the Sealed Knots events if you are interested in the English Civil Wars, because the society is meticulous in making sure the details are correct.

It is also true that members of Scottish armies got right down into the English Midlands during those wars. With it being over two hundred miles from Worcester, let alone Hereford, to the border, that was no mean march in a time when the roads were nothing like as good as today's. By the end of those wars, the only soldiers who were still fighting for the king – by then the would-be Charles II, his father having already been executed – were in fact almost wholly Scottish. There is a plaque commemorating those hundreds of Scots who died in the final battle at Powick, down by the River Teme, but they were the last, not the first, of their nation to die a long way from home. As pointed out in the book, sometimes it's hard to know who was exactly where during those turbulent years, not least because so many records simply haven't survived. So the exact route the Earl of Leven and his Scots took returning to the north of England is hard to work out, but I hope I've got it as close as possible.

Many thanks for taking the time to read this book. If you have enjoyed it, please help me out by leaving a review where you purchased it. For writers like me, the best way for others to discover my books is by getting reviews, so it's really appreciated when people do leave one.

Printed in Dunstable, United Kingdom

76261141R00251